DESTROYER OF WORLDS

GOD'S CHAIN

Book three
in
GOD'S CHAIN

Nikolaus Baker

DESTROYER OF WORLDS

Published by Mikey Books 24.02.2020

First Edition 24.02.2020

ISBN: 978-1-9162589-1-4

Dedicated to Scott, Suzanne & Christopher.

THE PROPHECY

They will come first and smite.
All will shake in terror.
Cold is the land.
Nowhere to hide.

The cursed will come and bite.
All will run in terror.
Pained is the land.
Nowhere to hide.

Devil's will come and spite.
All will fall in terror.
Dead is the land.
Nowhere to hide.

Darkness will come and blight.
All will bow in terror.
Black is the land.
Nowhere to hide.
Souless and suffering in the land of nowhere.
Nowhere to hide.

INDEX

PROLOGUE

⅂Ⲅ ⸱Ⲻ⌐ ⸱Ⲻ⅂＜☐

Man's reign is through.

Universal laws are breaking in the cosmos with the coming of the dark lords to the world of man. It is they who intend to complete God's Chain and become a God of gods, destroyer of worlds.

The Expedition is in tatters after it discovered a hidden valley in Amazonia known as the Vale of MalisIblis, where a mythical temple appears every five hundred years. Inside the temple an object of ultimate power exists that is a direct link to God.

Harjit Singh is team leader who is lost with her friend Biotechnologist Christopher Hrycuik and some others somewhere inside the upper temple. Her job is simple. Survival!

The killings have already begun with human sacrifice. Suddenly all communication is lost with civilisation sparking a black-op concocted by the Vatican to secure this fabled relic of power but the temple exerts an evil supernatural influence on anyone who enters it…

CHAPTER I

INSIDE THE UPPER TEMPLE

Harjit and the others continued walking up the long-abandoned slope. They were lost and lucky to be alive. Having already escaped death and being trapped with poisonous spiders, at this moment, everyone felt spent. The distance ahead was lit in a soft light and by an unnatural illumination emanating from the walls. She needed to press on, she had too.

Looking around at the solid walls, they stood impenetrable to any sound or external influences yet Harjit studied her digital watch for some comfort in accuracy but it had stopped working. Having departed Fabio's company, so much had happened to them since. Unknown to the group in real time, it had just gone past midnight. Harjit continued her arduous temple journey, wondering about the ranger and the others.

Mathieson, I can handle fine; it's that idiot Barbaro whose deceitful and scheming all the time. With his greed for money, power and publicity he's dangerous. Harjit knew the Vatican media man could do a lot of damage.

The group was far enough away from the danger, and eventually came to a wide-open rectangular entrance with large stone frame blocks, dry as bones. The blocks positioned to the left and right of the entrance had a huge horizontal lintel support high overhead. Harjit knew this was a good place as any to stop.

"We all need to rest and relax. Let's go through here and see if there is a place we can hold up and take it easy for a few hours."

She could tell they needed sleep if they were to go any further. It would also give her time to think. Harjit had no way of telling just how long they would be inside the temple. Her words met a mumbled sigh of agreement muted along through the tired men, and she badly needed to rest too.

Observing the entrance, it looked like this place may have had large wooden gates positioned here long ago, and on closer inspection, Harjit was right. Seeing fixtures into the walls and hinge mechanism, judging that it once allowed movement and might be swivelled opened or shut. The barriers were long gone millennia ago.

Harjit rationalised, *I think our immediate danger is over. Let me see what is inside this place. One wrong turn and my men will not be quick enough to react to danger. I feel so tired and I need to rest too. But I need to find out first where this goes.*

"Right guys let's go inside here to rest. If those little spiders are anything to be judged by, then the temple is not finished with us yet. Let's eat and then sleep."

Harjit instructed the others to follow her inside, unaware that her self-confidence was growing, and that Fabio knew that the men would listen to her.

"I would give my soul to be outside this place right now Harj!" Christopher laughed light-heartedly.

The other men nodded their silent agreements. Entering wearily into another substantial area, they could see stone slabs placed on the floor throughout, effectively raising the floor level. It showed to be troughs put into the stone floors extending from one end of the room to the other. It was to hold livestock at one time.

The ceiling reached up about thirty feet high, the walls and ceiling were colourful and completely covered, including paintings of domesticated animals and tall people tending them. Some surrounding walls had metal rings inserted that were likely used to secure strange-looking animals pictured there.

"Well the first domesticated livestock animals may have been those funny looking sheep around 9000 B.C. These guys that worked inside here were into animal husbandry as well, maybe even earlier than this. Ventilation must have been..." Cesaré made a sour face.

He heard a noise hissing somewhere inside the darkness of the large byre. That same compressed air sound coming from above, his eyes were drawn to the source. He could see the air vents near the ceiling.

"We must be somewhere inside the middle-tier of the temple." Christopher advised. Harjit and the others were already sitting down on a bench making their meals. The clanking of tinned cooking equipment and noise of stoves roaring gave them a familiarity and helped them come to terms with their incredible environment. Soon eating, their spirits began to lift.

"This place looks like an animal byre," said Harjit. "I can imagine it is used as stock for many sacrificial purposes and possibly also in a siege situation. This would be an important live food store." Harjit studied the area.

"Why worry?" Barbaro was disinterested.

"Look over there, another livestock area!" She pointed to the far wall and the darkness beyond. "I'm going over."

"I'll join you Harj." Christopher got up.

She and Christopher walked briskly towards it while the others were preoccupied with more food and rest and mute, indifferent faces.

Inside they saw that there was no evidence of any animal remains, only more pictures depicting functionality and a lifestyle that may have once existed at the height of this mysterious civilization. The surroundings were similar in dimension but different in style to the other. In their limited illumination, it showed paintings of a much different nature; of a struggle and warfare.

"My, God, they like their paintings don't they?" Christopher's astonished eyes roamed the

horror show before them, his mind interpreting all their awful stories.

Seeing horse-like creatures running and turning in battle, they appeared to be the battle tanks of their day, seen here all clad in sculptured armour, with spiked metal horns on foreheads to protect their faces. They were armed with peytrel for the front chest, flanchard for side protection and crupper for the rear.

They studied the painted images silently and with disturbed growing consternation. These hideous pictures of battles were finely detailed and graphically captured an outlandish-looking enemy. Nothing pictured here was human and everything engaged in mortal combat. It resembled a medieval battlefield and not somewhere in South America. How could this ever be?

Their eyes pictured a bitter battle against madness and inside this substantial hall, it seemed like a recording, showing armour-clad animals and tall people fighting while under the gaze of *DEATH*. The alarmed knights pointed skywards in the direction of a great winged beast.

Christopher's face drew closer to the beast as he gradually recognised it. It was the same creature; the same beast they saw at the top of the temple eating their dead comrade. It was a complete fluke of nature or something much worse, a monster. He twisted his face while remembering the disgusting stink.

"My Lord, *who are these people?*" Christopher's growing fear impaled his mind. He felt that the temple had an unspoken prophecy still to give him.

"Look Chris, the mural continues along the length of the full wall. "Harjit drew his attention to the many devilish apparitions all cruelly attacking the outnumbered knights on their frightened steeds.

The knights desperately smashed down onto the ghastly foes with bloodied battle axes and dripping broadswords, cleaving off many enemy helmed skulls. Horrible creatures only wore light leather tunics for protection and mobility. It looked like old enemies that already knew each other through many battles over centuries.

The grizzly apparitions relentlessly countered the knights using deadly spears and long tridents to stab and stick the besieged horsemen and fallen foot soldiers. The two explorers mumbled low recognition for these tall people that looked like Lords. The tragic images put flesh onto the dead remains discovered earlier inside the temple!

The devils fought ferociously and with an evil scaly face, told them of hatred and malice, vicious warriors with long legs, no noses and bony holed slits where their eyes should be. It was an evil army that fought in battle stances in outstretched gangly positions, with their unnaturally strong long arms and legs, making them deadly.

"Their mortal enemy." Harjit concluded sadly.

"Hope not Harj. It's a story, only a tale." The true ramifications were a reminder of what might have been.

Observing the broody mural with its heavy stormy skies, clouds tried to contain explosions of dark greys and blacks, all embroiling gasses pictured broken up with deep cracked magma reds mixed in pumice greys.

Harjit and Christopher kept staring at its stark violence, its menace laced in fire and brimstone. The scene set on a grand scale with too many hellish foes numbering in the tens of thousands, all swarming, all running and fighting over the surrounding hills as far as the eye could see. In the distance, the artist had drawn things with large heads and other malevolent apparitions on the field of battle. The host poured forth in conquest. This was an army bred and intent on murder.

For those noble stallions and kingly masters who kept fighting on, *DEATH on the wing* would tip the balance. The mural paid a final tribute to them and their fallen comrades against an overwhelming evil enemy, a host far greater than could ever be imagined. Everything was caught here in some lost conflict. They would fall gloriously.

"Whoever painted these historic scenes did so after the event," said Harjit. "Whether in memory of a distant war or one more recent to this artist, all so ghastly, almost as though that person was there. *It's so real.*" She whispered secretly. The air inside was as still as a held breath.

"It's unbelievable that this place has such paintings. It seems like it's from the fifteenth century and those knights are different. I don't think they are *human.* Their enemy is *wholly evil.*" Christopher's recursive dismay studied the flying beast seen commanding the army against the knights of old.

Doubting all his previous theories of the superstructure and its links to the known world, he conjectured; *how can that flying beast be there?*

Christopher felt a cold shiver and cringed. He feared the truth. He thought about those terrified knights pointing helplessly towards the fiery sky, the atmosphere lit in flames and dark clouds.

"My God, it's the same beast I saw above! *This is fucking crazy,*" Christopher said in an ominous tone. Intuitively, Harjit waited, watching him slowly shake his head and sensed he was holding back.

"You must be wrong Chris, surely that can't be possible?"

"*But this place Harj, the whole lot,* it's all fucking impossible, it really is. Don't you agree? I might have been *wrong* about the Masonic link, that idea fit," he explained, "The symbolism, their coded words all made complete sense to me. It still does. Now with this, I am not so sure. Everything

we see here is impossible. This place is priceless."
His mind fogged in misperception.

Christopher's hard-won theories all messed up and entangled into more riddles but Harjit knew there was something more recent he was withholding from her.

They continued following the drawings, and for now the others were forgotten. Both people were pulled along by their mutual inquisitiveness, coming to another large door. Walking into another dark area, the place lit only by their flash torches, Christopher saw its power weakening a little when looking inside. It opened to reveal what resembled a *Smithy* or *Honey-Pot*, both companions went inside fascinated with their new discovery. Near the corner was a large furnace all rusted, old tools of that trade hanging on hooks or resting on top of ancient shelves. The furnace blazed no more, it was a lost relic in another time.

"If this place was a type of containment for domesticated animals, it stands to reason that there must be entry and exit to the outside. I do not think it's possible for any cavalry to move through those corridors. It would not be rapid enough to counter any threat." Harjit surmised the technicalities of military response and manoeuvrability.

"Yes Harjit, you are as always, correct," said Christopher. "And that would explain the wide sloped path from the base level to the top of the first tier and then from there to the second on the north-face of the temple. I imagine that a place like this would hold maybe three hundred soldiers and cavalry."

"It is an outpost and made for conflict." She gazed up at him tenderly as he moved closer to her. "It is a self-contained fort or barracks, self-sufficient for a limited siege with impenetrable walls, living quarters, grand halls, livestock areas and whatever else. It seems to me that the temple is also more than that. It is also some kind of stronghold used for a place of worship and sacrifice as civilizations did back in those days." In the sullen light, her breathing became faster and more excited as they were almost touching each other.

"Then it's a bloody one stop shop to the fucking Gods." Christopher stated. Sensing her anxiety, he placed his arms around her waist, drawing her slim and soft body onto him. This, was exactly where he wanted her. He kissed Harjit's full lips.

"Harj, you have grown strong. I feel your strength." He touched her soft face. "I have missed being with you, *so much*," Christopher whispered, almost pleading in tone. "It is difficult to hide my true feelings towards you."

"*Oh Chris!*" She smiled. *He's so sweet,* she thought. Her heart ached for him. She kissed him passionately.

"I feel so happy when you are with me. I would do anything you ask of me. Even although I wish you had never come to this place with me. I will try to keep you safe. It has become dangerous my love."

"I can look after myself Christopher." Christopher knew he had touched a nerve.

"I know you can. Please, Harj. Given the first opportunity, you must leave." She saw his sincerity but Harjit had no intensions of leaving without him.

Christopher felt her soft curves as her body moved in his strong embrace. Her smooth warm skin aroused him as he gently enthused her up against the wall, and passionately kissed her lips. Both were in love.

The young leader pressed onto him while pushing his shoulders gently back, biting him tenderly on his bottom lip. Both were very aroused. Christopher held her tightly. He wanted her.

"No Christopher, please, *not here*. I really do not like this place," she said reluctantly. "I feel that we are being watched. Let's get back to the others." She felt an unnatural presence with them and one she could not explain. "It is not you, *sorry*," she whispered, noticing his awkwardness. "*In this place,* something evil remains."

Christopher looked around and was about to say something when she silenced him with a gesture.

"I cannot explain. Maybe there are ghosts of long-dead people and *they* do not want us here. Don't you see, don't you feel it? We are *intruders*."

Harjit compressed her voice, her vulnerability showing.

"*My love*," he comforted her. "Do not fear every shadow. I think it is not all bad. This civilization also tells us of greatness. By understanding these paintings, they were clearly a noble race."

"These paintings tell a tale of devil warriors and a people who have lived here. We have seen them already lying dead inside; they are the same soldiers as those knights on those horse creatures. These devils are their mortal enemy and they all come from a land we know nothing off. *And, that place is red with blood and pestilence.*"

"Steady on Harj." Chris squeezed her hand and spoke quietly. "Those paintings tell a story and are only an interpretation. They are not true representations of real conflict." *He lied.* "Who is the victor and who is the vanquished, we have yet to discover." He lied again. Christopher knew this was a conflict; the evidence was everywhere inside the temple. He shook his head and said, "Who knows what really happened here. Who knows how long ago this place came into being? Fabio thought twenty-five thousand years ago, mind you, the Freemasons fraternity does not go that far back. Maybe another type of Freemasons does, just not *European ones.*"

Christopher still attempted to link logic to his hypothesis, and this distracted her fears for the moment.

"No matter what you say Chris, this place is truly evil." Harjit trembled and stared into his eyes. Christopher felt her fear and vulnerability, and then wrapped his arms around her and into his muscular frame. Her delicate hands began sweeping through his hair, "Oh Chris, *I love you.*"

Harjit held his strong jaws in her soft-cupped hands, kissing him tenderly when she could not stop. Her passion took over. Kissing, each time harder and with obsession, they couldn't stop. Their minds rolled in numbed ecstasy.

In those private moments together, Harjit and Christopher made love. She lay on him as he yielded himself to her rhythmic warm loins, their free spirits joining physically. She was a conductor working hard in seductive symphony while he played violin in this sexual serenade of pure and ultimate pleasure.

An hour later they returned satisfied, joining the rest of the team. Everyone was asleep except for Barbaro. He watched them thoughtfully.

"Well Christopher, find anything of interest back there? You both were gone for some time." Barbaro smiled at him and turned his attention to her, slowly looking at her from top to bottom. His eyes hinted at some mischief that made Harjit's flesh crawl.

He knows, he knows! She thought recursively. She instantly freaked, her eyes dropped quickly with guilt. Harjit felt *dirty* while blushing in the dimness, *that swine is sneering at me, he knows. He was sneaking and watching. Oh God*

I hope he did not see us. Harjit's stony face said nothing, yet he managed to make her have low self-esteem.

"Remind me Christopher, because now I am not so sure," asked Barbaro in a self-righteous tone. "Did Fabio not say that you were a *newly ordained priest* or are you studying to become one? If so, I need to speak with you, well you know, privately, in… confessional." Barbaro's tone hinted of virtuous anger and yet his expression stared blankly, while gauging Christopher's response. "And what about *you* Harjit? Sorry, of course not! Hindu's cannot confess to a Catholic Priest unless it is a more, *personal* and non-religious matter?" He provoked them both.

Harjit felt a surge of anger and wanted to slap him. Barbaro began laughing.

"You are sly *Barbaro.*" Her words remained like a verdict. "I do not need to confess to anything and certainly not to *your God!* So just shut your twisted face." She fumed at the small man's insinuations. Barbaro's goal was to make her snap. It worked.

"Touchy." He smiled softly, catching her off guard. The media man intentionally schemed to make this awkward moment. Barbaro began considering his next move.

Christopher is nothing and I will use him to destroy her confidence. She should not be part of this expedition at all. The young priest I can destroy at any time; easy meat and he is still wet behind the ears. A sinner! A few paragraphs for the Pope's attention and he's finished, excommunicated and he knows it. I'm sure he will try to keep me sweet.

Nothing and nobody was going to get in his way, Barbaro was a master of manipulation. He used his influence in higher circles and was in a pinnacle position right now. That was the real reason he was on this mission. With accomplices in high places, he had orders to report on anything and everything that went on here.

"You know fine well Barbaro that I have not completed my priesthood. Why ask? It took me many years to get to this stage and along with my other studies and commitments as a bio-technologist, exploits and expeditions. Si, I will still hear your confession, tomorrow, *but…*" Christopher was *not a conventional priest,* drinking the wine of Holy Communion as a choir boy, while above all else, he held love for God, all and Harjit. He was a sinner. God knew this.

Barbaro's rabid eyes kept tracking Harjit. She went off enraged, soon reaching the far end of the room. Christopher watched them both and knew that fate had brought them there and had bound them all together. Only God knew why.

Chris felt perplexed and had the same unanswerable question burning in his mind; why did he and Harjit come together as one? He had known Harjit for a few years and she had persuaded him to introduce her to Fabio. He wished he had never done so because it put her in danger. The expedition was turning out to be nothing he ever imagined. Christopher had many achievements under his belt at a very young age and found himself at a cross roads in his life.

****

Lying down, she prepared to sleep alongside the others while Chris sat down only inches away from Barbaro, speaking face to face.

"Right get this man. Just, leave, off, Harjit!" came his stern warning. "I caution you, this might be your own fucking undoing, shithead." The younger man's tone as sharp as shards of glass.

"I really do not know what you mean Christopher." Barbaro winced in pain then smiled again, almost ignoring him. The Vatican official knew that nothing would come of an empty threat. He thought, *this would-be priest would not want a scandal. I'll sort him out.*

Harjit's mind worked overtime. She couldn't rest thinking about what happened.

Barbaro is wicked. He never warmed up to me. I am convinced he will use Christopher's impropriety with me for his own purposes. Her intuitiveness spot on, she questioned herself. *How can I protect him? I know what we did was wrong but it does not matter; Barbaro hates me, simple as that.*

A mounting resentment grew within her; Harjit knew that this was exactly what the Vatican Official wanted. Knowing this did not seem to matter, because she was playing right into his hands yet. Wrath was clouding her judgement and

Harjit's tolerance for him was minimal. She was on the brink of eruption and that was clear.

I am Indian and proud of my Hindu Religion. It is monotheistic worshipping one God and one ultimate reality, Brahman the supreme spirit. That is probably enough of a reason to be a Pagan in his eyes! Other Gods do serve us as a way in which a devotee can see and feel the unknowable God. What makes us so different? Her thoughts moved defensively, *I know he will do something soon to discredit me again. Somehow this must fit into his hidden agenda whatever that might be. I must be ready.*

Lying on the floor, Harjit was unable to sleep and turned around for comfort, her eyes wandering around when reflexively they jerked to a dead stop. Barbaro's eyes were staring right back. He silently began smiling. Christopher had already gone to sleep. Barbaro began twisting his lips again. He was born disfigured and it seemed to be an offset nerve, slightly paralyzed with little to no movement to the left.

Weirdo. She quickly turned away from his unpleasant grin, eventually drifting off into another disturbed dream. Images came to her of him laughing and mocking her. She kept on running away from his unnaturally large head. Stalked even inside her dreams, stuck in a place where Barbaro was no longer a man but a monster.

****

With a sudden wrench, Aléssandro awoke about seven-thirty next morning, staring into the surrounding darkness with little light left of the candle wick to burn.

"Trapped in this manure heap, shit," said the young archaeologist, resigned again to being here. He remembered his father's farm, his home and where he grew up. His mind tried to reject his current reality. *This place is awful,* he thought. Aléssandro wanted out right now.

I cannot believe we slept for such a long time. This place feels wrong and unforgiving. We entered yesterday and I never knew it would be like this. The darkness is so intense. My God, I just want to get out. He prayed silently when unexpectedly something touched him.

"Ahh!" Aléssandro screamed. His consciousness was broken from prayer when a firm hand grabbed his arm.

"Right on man!" Mathieson shouted while grabbing him and began shaking it more for a joke. "Hey man that woke you up eh?" Mathieson bent over in laughter.

"I was in prayer you fucker, not asleep! My eyes were closed and the last thing I want to see is your black ass in the fucking morning! Do it again and I will give you a fucking pasting. *I mean it!"* Aléssandro exploded, which only made Mathieson happier.

The commotion woke up everyone.

Mathieson was bored and looking for a distraction from his own stress and fear. His younger colleague's temperament frayed to a near breaking point. The others moaned, coming to grips with their dark reality once again. Mathieson happily moved away swinging his short sword, fighting imaginary shadows. It passed the time.

"What the hell are you up to Mathieson?" Christopher growled.

"Watch what you're doing with that thing Mathieson, I think we have had enough." Harjit was irritated.

"Ok Harjy," smiling at her scowl. "Sure anything you say Babe."

Mathieson is in some mood this morning. She thought, and began advising the others what they had discovered last evening while looking around and viewing their candlelit caricatures.

"I think we need to investigate the stable or that smithy, there might be a hidden entrance or a quick way out? The large furnace must have an air-vent, so we could climb through it and eventually get out. Christopher and I didn't have time to investigate but it seems like a reasonable assumption."

"A dead end Harjit." Barbaro immediately threw a fly in the ointment. "What were you really doing in there, you were away for ages?" He parried just to see her reaction. Harjit ignored him although her body temperature increased.

"Yo Barbaro mother fuck!" Mathieson called over to the official, "What are you all about man?" He broke up Barbaro's obvious bickering;

he didn't like him either but was secretly enjoying the overall awkwardness.

"There is little time left. Our torches will not last much longer," she stated. "We have to get out of here today. Right you guys, get packed and let's go."

"We should go back to where we all came in yesterday and investigate further along that corridor," Barbaro continued to speak. "At least inside there is a light source to follow, albeit quite dim and as you say, our batteries will not last more than another day. Mine is already out of juice. What do we do if your suggestion leads nowhere? The Holy Father does *not* want us to leave the temple empty handed or without something of rare importance to show him. Leaving here is like admitting defeat and demonstrates a lack of leadership, *Harjit*."

He articulated an authority not bestowed on him and brought the Pope into the conversation. Barbaro's mind festered on inflicting more damage.

She is a coward his eyes red with malice. Twisting his mental rack up another notch. This time pulling tighter at her mind, bit-by-bit, until he knew she would breakdown. Yet, this twisted his own mind too, building a pure hatred towards the woman, when Cesaré's torch flickered a warning.

Under stress, Harjit could see her own demise staring back at her. If they did not get going soon she knew by losing their light sources, it would be everyone's undoing. They were her responsibility.

"Things are going to get desperate if we lose our lights," Harjit's tone was earnest. "As I said, we need to ration the batteries and any candles we have left. It is critical that we escape these walls today." The young Indian girl made everyone check their torches and backup batteries.

"Escape! Escape, is that what we are doing? What are you afraid off? May I remind you that I contracted for this expedition, we have to find out more before leaving?" Barbaro's lips twisted obscenely, lifting his tone a few octaves to challenge her authority.

"Barbaro has a fair point." Cesaré agreed, as did Aléssandro and Mathieson.

"To go on, would be very dangerous and a great folly. We may only have one shot at this, then say *adieu* to our visit and our lives! I have seen and heard enough, and I would like to put off meeting God just yet." Chris paused while looking at the gang of would be crusaders. "*Do you* want to take permanent residence here? Stay here, and you are dead. Join the company of the dead soldiers we met yesterday. We will die here if we do not take Harjit's lead and follow the vent system. She is right." He waited for a response.

"Let's put it to a vote!" Barbaro prompted.

"You are not in charge of the expedition Barbaro." Harjit spoke calmly but her soft voice shouted volumes.

"Si let us vote!" Cesaré and Aléssandro agreed, Mathieson too.

"It is like this, Harjit. The group feel there is a better chance of getting out of this place alive by going, *on.* We can decide about our own safety. We are not children or in the army." Cesaré reasoned with her in his soft melodic Sicilian accent.

Sagging a little, Harjit looked disappointed while the other men were nodding their approval. Her authority had been undermined and she knew it. Then Aléssandro came in, speaking in a deep voice.

"We have come this far together Harjit and going on a wild goose chase next door is simply foolish." She winced at this view. He continued to speak, "Sorry Harj but that's the way it is." There were no guarantees either way.

"Our strength is in our unity. It always will be," she said. The girl resigned to have lost this battle. *They are making the wrong choice but I must see where this takes us.* Harjit was determined to win the war. She needed to lead again, "Ok we will go on together." She took back the high ground.

Mathieson was overjoyed. To them, she had made the correct choice. Nonetheless, Barbaro sneered at her and said nothing more.

"We will go on up the temple again and hope to find an exit." Even now after this disagreement, Harjit could not relinquish her responsibility and would not be to blame for any death by splitting up the company. Christopher reluctantly stuck with Harjit's decision. Barbaro had won, yet his lips swore cold curses under his breath as she regained her authority.

****

The corridor seemed no different from the previous day, dingy and dull with a diffused light emitting from the apparent solid walls. The group were walking without the aid of torchlight, Cesaré sauntering in front of the group. He was singing and whistling with indifference, his mind on a soundtrack to the tune of 'Giuseppe di Stefano', his hero. Both were born in Sicily. Cesaré Padovesi was an excellent singer, and hearing his voice echo was raising all their spirits from the brooding temple.

Harjit followed behind Cesaré, then Mathieson, Barbaro, Aléssandro and Christopher in the last position completing the column. Christopher perceptively looked around into the murkiness because with every uneasy step taken, it felt as though they were being watched. He continually looked around to see *nothing*. On edge like this was unnerving and the walk felt more like being out on patrol.

Time passed slowly, walking with tedium for company. Boredom took its toll and they started walking upwards on a long slope when eventually it ended. In front of them was a worn stone staircase. In a murky, phosphorescent atmosphere, everyone stared at its ancient ascent, steps saddled at the centre with cracks in many places. Bits of stone lay broken off everywhere.

This ragtag band of explorers were cursing warnings to each other while switching on their torches to begin their next challenge. They began climbing wearily upwards. Pushing on for another twenty-five metres, the group delved deeper into the mega-structure. Everyone had lost any notion of location and judgement as to how high or low they had climbed. Harjit instinctively knew the importance of keeping her men tight together. She did not want to lose anybody, *not even* Barbaro.

"What is this place?" Cesaré whispered while staring straight ahead. The corridor divided off left and right from his tunnel vision.

"Keep together," Harjit's tone cautious and certain. Moving along the top of the stairs, it led into a wide stretch of corridor with numerous exits leading off from the main pathway. It divided further up into two directions, each at obtuse angles from each other. On either side, a series of what used to be doors lay all broken and wrecked and there was little doubt this place had been completely plundered. These were once sleeping quarters and now an empty shell.

"Dormitories for the garrison," stated Mathieson. He quietly walked inside and went to the other end. The distant door partly hanging off its hinges, Mat pushed it further open when it fell with a clatter.

"Whoops…" He said smiling cheekily back at the others.

"Watch what you are doing Mathieson," Harjit scolded. And with considerable caution, Mathieson stared through to the other end.

Beyond him appeared to be a long-shaped armoury, linked to all other dormitories to allow quick access to weapons. Life had departed a long time ago leaving only broken mementoes, debris and the dead.

Death was everywhere. Mathieson looked around at the multitudes of hacked skeletons lying where they had fallen, ripped and pulled apart, their chainmail scattered around in pieces.

All the dormitories and sub-rooms built in an overall *hexahedron-shaped* structure with the ceiling twenty-foot high. Each dormitory was segmented and designed to be like a sun construction with a corridor coming off, synonymous to a ray of light. Each dorm led in towards the middle of the temple.

They followed Mathieson inside, placing their steps carefully all the way through, not wanting to disturb the bones. Evidence of violence was everywhere, with plenty of broken debris strewn around. They picked up small bits and pieces of interest. Working their way through the armoury, scattered around were battle ready swords, spiked flails, numerous crossbows and bronzed spearheads strewn across the large floor between the old broken weapon racks.

Numerous large square shields with curved bases hung on all the walls bearing a coat of arms, this being a green and blue quartered background and a powerful picture of a white wildcat leaping from its centre, wearing a golden crown. Disrespectfully, the coat of arms had been used as target practice because many long thin arrows or long wooden nails were deeply embedded.

Great dusty drapes were torn into shreds although some lay partly hanging on the wall. The rest had fallen onto the floor and all faded brown over time lying in heaped disarray. The garrison dormitories were arranged the same way. All assembled and constructed as an integral part of the spokes of a wheel, each housed about twenty beds. In its day of utopia, Harjit estimated there must have been about two hundred troops billeted; as others would be elsewhere, including cavalry and nobles. Unfortunately, this place had become a site of massacre!

"Presumably, the rest of the population would be living outside the temple, including any civilians and administrators. I would estimate the population inside may have supported up to three hundred personnel or more." Harjit tried to work it all out. "What do you think Chris?"

"Maybe the temple's existence was for its nobles as a holiday retreat. A place of rest and security, away from any mainstream areas and that the military force stationed were the Noble Guardsmen, their elite, and dedicated to the protection of their Deities." Christopher was piecing it together.

"Yeah! I got those brochures too Chrisy boy! The tropics, good food, good company, beautiful babes and excellent air conditioning to boot. Well what else could a Detroit boy ask for!" The ranger laughed heartily.

"And the next flight home *is for you mother fucker!*" Harjit stated, her face expressionless. He stopped laughing looking at her features staring coldly at him.

Team leader Harjit kept looking, gauging his awkwardness while suppressing her need to laugh. Mathieson's questioning face fixed on hers. Everybody went quiet too. Harjit had never said anything like this before.

Mathieson burst into copious laughter, slapping his hands together too. The others began rolling about joining him.

It was something they all needed to do, laugh, and once again Harjit's spirit had raised their morale. Well timed, her humour immediately boosted their resolve for the next phase. Barbaro was secretly seething at her newfound popularity.

Leaving the armoury and soldiers quarters, the small team headed inwards and into the temple's spine. It was a place where all similar exits from the numerous armouries opened onto. It was an assembly or rallying point of some sort.

Here they could see the many tall statues, stone warriors made of white marble, giving this place a presence. These were just like the ones outside the mines and like them they were all standing as if on guard. The statues were positioned left and right at each doorway. Several had been defaced but a few remained proud and sacrosanct even though most had noses chipped off or been mutilated in some other way.

Tall and noble, all were facing upwards towards the light, their shields and spears affront and ready for war. Modelled faces of stone, each sculptured handsomely and finely featured, their presence prevailing. None wore sculptured helmets as seen previously on the dead warriors; instead they were sculpted with wide headbands on what looked like feline carved insignias.

Stone-fashioned leather tunics and short skirts; each noble had thick shoulder length wavy hair tied behind their heads. They were a race of warriors with powerful Olympian-like bodies. In sandals or laced boots with rock hard legs of power standing spaced apart. Strong arms with amulets and massive hands held weaponry. Loyal effigies were known by their hallowed name, *The Eternal Guard*. Statues made in memory of what was once a noble race.

Outside the entrance, the group of explorers stood with the Eternal Guard at an assembly point and a huge stone column at its centre. The column contained a massive stone spiral staircase called the spine, which seemed to extend all the way to the top of the temple. There was no other way to go from here.

****

CHAPTER II

THIS IS NOT HUMAN

>⊓⌐∨ ⌐∨ ⊡⊏> ⊓<⊐⌐⊡

Entering the spine, it felt like a dark void, their surroundings brightened only in passing torchlight. Cautiously looking around at the walled vertical column and the stone stairs going up or down and curving around the outer wall like a Helter-skelter. Up was the only way for them. Everyone was amazed at the building's architecture and its sheer scale and grandeur. The confines were claustrophobic on a larger scale.

"Wow, look!" Mathieson got inside and focused his view upwards.

"Careful where you step, there's a huge hole at the centre." Harjit warned everyone after shining her torch downwards.

"No barriers. Don't go too close to the edge of the step."

Harjit's team began moving upwards very cautiously.

"Well this must be the way out, phew," Cesaré sighed with obvious relief.

"It looks like this may be the way soldiers moved quickly to defend any breach in defences, no matter at what level," Christopher rationalised.

Standing next to Christopher, Harjit looked downwards into a deep hole and distant core underneath them. The centre spine of the building was an empty space spanning near the temple's complete height with no barrier to prevent anyone falling over. Looking upwards, Harjit could see some sort of reddish glow, a light source coming from above!

"A light," said Harjit.

"Indeed." Christopher considered what it might be and gave up.

"A light, this must be good," guessed Cesaré.

"Si, but it still suggests to me that there must be more than one way out in a place this size," Aléssandro agreed. Both men were more positive now.

"Just as well you listened to me," Barbaro said, wanting recognition. "Coming this way my friend Alé. Whatever happened here, happened a long time ago and I believe it was then that the Temple was taken over by new management." Barbaro believed that the Temple had been invaded by another civilisation.

"Oh and less of that friend bit Barbaro. Someone might start talking about us!" Aléssandro began laughing, seeing the funny side but the Vatican official never saw it.

"We are not out of the woods yet you two. And everyone, keep your eyes and ears open, watch your steps," instructed Harjit, the leader reinforcing the seriousness of their situation.

Large colourful urns, blue, yellow, red and green, all decorated with rich golden and silver codices stood near the centre on every other step. It was likely these were for decoration. Some lay smashed, leaving piles of sand from inside strewed over the steps while others lay knocked over in some cruel game play.

"Why fill those bloody urns with sand? What a mess," said Mathieson.

"Not a lot makes sense in this place. Let's get going." Christopher started his climb close behind Harjit. "Once we have deciphered these codices, I am sure a grand story will unfold for us. You know, we have been instrumental to this new discovery, and an ancient and lost civilization, I have no doubt it is of immense importance to mankind."

"Ah! And spoken just like a true Fabio!" Cesaré exclaimed. He was right, the young man's enthusiasm seemed to give extra energy to the team by lifting his own spirit and those around him when Cesaré bellowed out more songs from *Giuseppe Di Stefano* and *Beniamino Gigli.* It seemed fitting to be sung inside this mega-structure and strangely enough, this area had very fine acoustic qualities at its centre.

"Barbaro come up here!" Harjit called for the media man.

"What do you want?" Barbaro replied from behind Chris.

"You go in front. Christopher, let him past you please." She instructed as Barbaro's glare accused her defiantly like a rabid rat. It was his turn to be in front.

Satisfying, she thought. Recognising his hesitation and yet for a split second he had been undecided. He quickly gauged an opportunity to find something of value first but saw it as an unnecessary risk refraining from the strong temptation.

"No," his reply plain enough. "I never go first." He bluntly refused her, batting the challenge back to Harjit. "The others do this, *not me.* They can take their own risks." Everyone looked at him with even more dislike while listening to his rant, "The Vatican has ordered me to observe and report. Nothing else! I am not a soldier or an explorer. You cannot order me around, so take care who you offend. Do we understand each other?" He defied her. His threat was crystal clear.

"I will show you exactly how it is done you little coward." She marched off with wild embers in her eyes, taking on the danger again.

Inferiority conjured up inside her. The man had so easily manipulated her last decision; Harjit took the risk for him. Barbaro's warped face grinned after her with daggers. *Maybe she will fall down that hole…* Barbaro's mind twisted more extremely while leering at her.

Showing firm conviction with renewed strength unleashed by her anger, the others found it hard to keep up. Behind her came young Aléssandro then Christopher, Mathieson and Barbaro. Cesaré brought up the rear holding a large candle. Harjit insisted they keep vigilant and continued climbing towards the glowing light.

Their rations depleted, they still carried equipment for the exploration to take samples and artefacts back to base, but any thoughts of further delay would prove too dangerous. Each resonating step into the gloom and gradually depression started trickling back in again. No one was talking. On those few occasions when they did utter something, their voices seemed different, almost alien. Half an hour later they were nearing the top.

"I think we are coming to the top guys!" Harjit lifted her voice in surprise.

"Thank motherfuck for that man. This place is awful." The American was truly pissed off.

The emerging light above was subdued and eerily blood red. The ambient source undetermined. In this red illumination they emerged standing on a wider floor where three additional similar entrances came together. It looked like a communal floor of some kind that measured about two hundred metres square.

"What is this bloody place?" Christopher's eyes strained in the crimson light seeing tall shapes inside.

"I would say we have entered another tier of the Temple," Aléssandro guessed.

Barbaro was always ready to take notes and draw little sketches in a pocket-sized notepad since his digital camera was broken, he was doing it right now. He wanted to record everything.

"My God," Mathieson shined his torch beam along the floor and slowly upwards, as his light struck off weird-looking objects ahead of him.

It took them seconds to realise that these were strangely designed pillars, *lots of them!* Stone pillars, all sculpted into shapes of massive strong arms and washed over in the colour of pestilence. With their floodlit torches beaming inside the great hall, it looked like a strange alien world.

They could not see too much further into the distance due to the density of the pillars and everything enclosed by unseen external walls. Muted faces were held in alarm as their fortitude foundered. The hall blared its warning. Their strong light beams struck off numerous large sun faces inside, reflecting them throughout. This place was as inviting as walking through a graveyard. Who would take the first tentative step inside, their feelings caught between shallow breaths and heavy hearts, everyone waiting and watching. *Somebody had to go first.*

"Bloody outlandish," Cesaré whispered, not wanting to disturb the peace.

Everyone was captivated by this place and with what looked like a forest of great stone arms. Each limb was slightly different in facet; individually quite unique in their direct light beams, showing in multi-shadowed tones of blood red ambience. It was like stepping into a dark room for developing photographs.

"What the hell is this place?" Christopher cautioned in a low voice, staring inside and imagining danger everywhere. The atmosphere threatened everyone. His eyes kept roving for danger but his main focus was looking for an exit.

"*Really*, do we have to?" Cesaré gulped. He did not want to walk through those menacing pillars and shadows.

"Come on guys, where are your balls? Sorry Harj." Mathieson was unnerved too but kept it secret. He wanted to get through here *pronto*. Waiting would only be worse.

"Don't apologise big boy." Harjit winked at him, *my God, that's the first time he has apologised about his swearing* she thought, *something is wrong.* She needed to bolster him. "Get them out then and show us what you've got." Harjit smiled. A pregnant pause followed when suddenly everyone exploded into fits of laughter.

The tension quickly changed again, uncontainable to the challenge ahead. Their nervous jitters levelled unsteadily between these and their fuel-injected adrenaline.

Ahead of them, a world of stone awaited. Huge stone arms stretched high up to the ceiling in worship to the heavens. Unseen only in parts, this central stone pillar carved into a mega-huge arm, held the ceiling in place with a massive stone claw, spanning the ceiling expanse giving it support. This and other lesser-sized arms for pillars all worked together to hold this part of the heavy structure in place. Each huge arm was splashed by artistic sun faces that must mean something. Time to go!

"This looks bad." Cesaré stared at the red arms inside.

Not again, thought Harjit fearing the worse. *We must go through, we are ready.* She preferred not to put off their fate, *ok let's get on with it, come on girl let the guys know.*

Taking a deep breath, she looked emotionlessly at them. "Ok Guys, this place looks dangerous. After we get through this bit, I guess that in a few hours, we'll be outside." She paused briefly, "Listen closely. *This is our path, our way out.*" Everyone remained silent while listening to her confident voice. "I, will go first. When I find a route through, I will shout for you to follow me. When I do, come quickly. *Clear?*" Authority articulated from her. She expected obedience. "And watch out for each other." Her tenacious eyes were ready.

"Harjit," Christopher called out to her but she cut him off.

"We will make it and I will show you how." She looked solemnly at the team.

Barbaro fixed his camera and took another photo, this time of Harjit.

"Just in case," Barbaro smiled at her when the flash went off.

"Shut up Barbaro!" Christopher shouted his rage, "You, cheeky shithead!" He moved quickly to smash his face.

"Christopher!" Harjit held his leash, "He is not worth it." She took a deep breath but inside she was far from her confident exterior. She had decided to lead her team to safety; that was her job. She pointed her torch ahead and began walking.

"Be careful," said Christopher anxiously.

"We go this way." She moved forward. Christopher's heart raced. He decided to stop her when suddenly Aléssandro came between them and stopped them both.

"Hang on you two! Sorry Harj I cannot let a girl do all the hard work," He grinned ear to ear. "You have already led by example many times. You don't need to prove anything to us. It's my turn. Ok with that Chris?"

Harjit smiled in admiration at the young student and Christopher nodded firmly with respect.

Aléssandro placed his hand on her shoulder, squeezed it affectionately and pushed her back long enough for him to take off at a jog.

The red stone floor felt rough underfoot while he quickly moved through the blood red gloominess. His powerful frame tramped on before the group and he was quickly out of sight behind numerous pillars. His torchlight bounced off the pillars in rapid succession. He set the light dancing like a discothèque on through the cloisters.

Barbaro watched silently conceited and twisting his face at the twenty-year old student who simply disappeared. *It should have been her.*

Harjit felt that the men were showing her a great deal of unfounded admiration, and for the first time she felt respected.

"Let's follow him. We cannot let him go alone." She immediately tracked him.

Mathieson and Cesaré went ahead and struggled to keep up with the student.

"Watch your step, it's hard to know where you are going!" He shouted back to the group someway behind. Surprised to see their torchlights, Aléssandro stopped. Turning to face the group, seeing their ghostly red silhouettes weaving through the claustrophobic cloisters, he began shouting more inspiration.

"Come on you lot! What's keeping you!" Humour resonated from his eager voice. Turning again, his pace instantly picked up before suddenly tripping on something. He was unexpectedly launched through the air.

"*Mama Mia watch-out!*" He twisted in mid-flight and suddenly hit the hard floor with a thud.

The impact knocked the air out of his lungs. He rolled over and propped himself onto his back. He was left staring up at a sun face while it stared right back down at him from the ceiling, as if mocking him.

Luckily the backpack took most of the brunt. He would live.

Bastardo, what caused me to trip? He stared in the direction he fell *and noticed a small mound.* He sensed something near to his face.

"Are you alright Alé?" Mathieson's concerned voice reached him, closing the gap with only fifteen metres to go.

"Ugh!" He desperately scrambled away from the offending object, as Aléssandro's rubber torch lay askew on the floor. Its light shot on him, dazzling his eyes annoyingly. He could not see what had tripped him. "Si!" He took a breath of stale air. "Si, I am fine, no problemo," his tone clearly relieved.

"I'll be with you in a sec!" shouted Mathieson.

"I fell over something on the floor over there," He moved on all fours, stretching for his torch while distancing himself further from the object.

In his blurry vision, he instinctively outstretched his arm and reached further in the darkness for the torch when his movement stopped dead with nervous uncertainty.

What was that noise? It was not the rushing footsteps from the others; more like a pack of playing cards being shuffled. His mind tried to understand what was going on.

Confused in the semi-darkness, Aléssandro could not remain like this forever.

His heart rate began beating faster, he regretted ever being there. Aléssandro had heard something and knew he was in serious trouble.

His instincts urged him to run yet survival told him to hold back.

He listened, prayed and didn't move one muscle.

Only stark silence. Aléssandro felt relief. He heard the others coming closer.

Instantly he heard shuffling sounds of cards again.

It increased, becoming more like angry Flamenco Castanets. His mind was numb with fear. Was it an animal?

Suddenly something sharp passed straight through his outstretched hand.

"Ahh!" Aléssandro could not believe it. He called out in agony, blood bursting from the topside of his hand and jetted directly onto his face. So fast it flew he could not avoid the dart.

"Aléssandro!" Mathieson shouted.

Aléssandro screamed in pain holding his hand. Feeling numerous other projectiles swishing past him, new horror came out of the light, smacking off the pillars.

Panic incised his ability to think. *I'm hit I'm hit! I don't want to die!*

He grimaced in agony when more arrows struck his rucksack, which quickly became a pincushion.

Each deadly dart thudded into his backpack, forcing him forward when one shot right through his body, bursting his lung. Warm red mist sprayed over his bloody face, Aléssandro dropped to the floor choking.

His mind swam in torment, writhing on the floor, he could no longer scream.

Shaking uncontrollably, he was drowning in blood. The others were approaching fast to his aid. Tears began dropping down his face.

Mathieson and Cesaré reached him first and only by pure chance, they had missed the same death trap.

"Aléssandro do not move! Do not move!" Mathieson gasped at the blood pouring out of him while holding him down so that he did not hurt himself anymore. There was nothing else he could do.

Aléssandro tried to say something.

"Stop!" Mat shouted a warning to the others.

Cesaré and Mathieson applied immediate pressure on Aléssandro's holes. There was too many to plug! Blood poured out.

"Hold on Alé!" Cesaré stared frantically at the boy's bloody face. "Hold on! You'll be ok!" Overwhelmed at all the puncture holes, Cesaré's shirt already sodden red. The men's bewildered torchlight beamed their alarm around like crazy.

They were not alone.

****

The torchlight unexpectedly fell onto two chainmail-clad soldiers lying nearby, one propped up sitting against a pillar, his head and metal helmet slumped forward with his sword still clenched in his gauntlet. The other lay like Aléssandro, dead.

A metal shield and long sharp tipped sword like the type used by a crusader or a knight templar lay by the other fallen warrior next to Aléssandro. Each warrior had an ancient bronzed helmet just like the other combatants seen earlier in the Temple. He was lying only a few inches from them.

"Aléssandro? Alé, Alé can you hear me?" Cesaré was almost crying and turned desperately to the American. "This is really bad Mathieson! Help him, help him!"

In a few minutes, Aléssandro lay there between the pillars motionless. Cesaré finished plugging the holes but no blood flowed from him any more.

"*Oh man,* come on!" Mathieson felt for a pulse on the side of Aléssandro's neck. His blood was spilled everywhere. "Aléssandro is dead."

Cesaré sunk. Mathieson held his shoulder as the group arrived fearing the worst.

"I'm sorry man," Mathieson hunkered next to him. Cesaré's eyes nipped as they welled up in tears of total disbelief.

"Nooo!" Cesaré moaned out in anguish, unconsolably cradling his dead friend.

"Look at those things in Aléssandro's hand!" Christopher arrived and stopped. Staring down at the evil-looking darts sticking about four inches out of his hand.

"Stop Harj, Barbaro, watch out!" Mathieson warned. "Aléssandro has been shot with darts!"

"Aléssandro is *dead?*" Barbaro was obviously confused. Harjit stared down in disbelief, and then back to Mathieson.

Distraught, Mat shook his head confirming the next victim. Harjit acknowledged him with a silent nod, as the poor boy's blood spread over the floor like an oil slick.

"I am *so sorry*, Cesaré," Harjit's soft voice tried to console him. His best friend's life gone, Cesaré cuddled him tenderly while feeling the man's warmth leaving. Cesaré's head lowered. He pulled out a dirt-stained handkerchief and began weeping.

"Natives!" Barbaro guessed, already looking wildly around in fear. "We are going to be picked off just like him!"

"Head hunters most likely." Mathieson tightened a better grip on his sword, "I don't have my rifle with me!" He sunk down and scanned the crimson cloisters.

"Hold on," cautioned Christopher. "I see what did it." Christopher's grim voice fixed their attention on an object five metres away. "That's what tripped Aléssandro." Christopher picked up a long sword from the floor and cautiously went to it.

"Take it easy Chris." Harjit warned him. Christopher used it to move some other body, his face drawn between miscomprehension and astonishment.

"This is not human," swallowing thickly. It had two long legs and long arms and that is where the similarity ended.

The spellbound explorers gathered to stare at the macabre spectacle. In the form of a skeleton, there it too had died. It had probably been dead thousands of years. Yet after all this time, lying dormant like an anti-personnel explosive, always ready with the potential to kill innocents even after war had long passed. Indiscriminate and deadly.

This skeleton was still vicious looking. It had once been wearing a deep green leather tunic covering its torso, the garment decomposed in parts. It had a wide belt to hold its sword. It looked more chimera than human; its legs seemed almost designed than purpose-born. Legs were grown in opposite direction to our own, and more akin to birds. It came completely kitted with a long metal shin guard that protected its legs, but the beast was no bird and clearly intelligent.

Bizarrely, its square head was big and flat on top. Three thin holes were where a nose might have been. The olfactory area was positioned between the large eye sockets and extended above the eye line.

Its flesh had long since rotted away exposed a nasty-looking multiple jaw structure. The gaping jaw lay wide open in four parts, exposing mandible mouthparts. With short black pointed teeth, all designed for tearing and cutting.

The creature wore a metal helmet and chainmail enclosed within its helm, its skull hard to observe properly but they could see it was not white bone, instead black, suggesting that it was made of different inorganic composition.

Evidence all around told of its demise with a large war axe stuck into it. A weapon capable of rending chainmail and piercing the heaviest of helms with its razor-sharp curved blade to front and metal piercing spike at the rear, the vicious weapon stuck squarely into its monstrous back. The axe's long tubular shaft had a wire-wrapped spiral bound grip used by one of the fallen knights before being mortally wounded. Cruel but effective.

"What the mother fuck *is that thing?*" Mathieson's grim face was aghast at the thought that this monster was even here.

Nobody could believe that such a creature could ever have existed, and this reality threatened to tip their sanity.

"Clearly intelligent," Barbaro stated. "How do you know this thing shot Aléssandro? Did it not cross your minds, that this might be another trap before shouting us over here?" His instincts burned.

"Fabio knows more about this place than he's letting on. Merda! *He has to be!*" Cesaré's voice felt bitterly let down with a picture of the professor in his mind, "Fabio has a lot to answer for." His tone held resentment.

"I think one of these soldiers must have taken that thing out before being killed themselves." Harjit guessed, her forensic mind working the rest out. "Notice the three clawed fingers and nasty curved talon for a thumb. It's good for gripping, cutting and digging." The girl scanned the area briefly, "Eyes decomposed long ago, leaving the brute's orbitals. Those are like large saucers which would suggest that this organism has good vision for darkness, and preferred habitat, *its home.*"

"Impossible," Cesaré blurted out through his tears. "I don't believe this is happening. This is not happening, that thing is not real. Someone put it here as a *sick joke!* This place is, *jinxed!*" Cesaré exploded. "We have all been *fools!*" He shook his head and mumbled obscenities in tears.

"It's bad shit, sorry man." Mathieson felt Cesaré's pain. He lost his partner Carmello in the mines.

"To answer your question Barbaro," Christopher cautiously moved the assailant's long arm with his sword. Its arm opened and inside something queer started rotating. Christopher was in shock staring at it. It had been born with a specialised organ that sounded like a mechanised revolver, turning with clicking sounds pointed right at him.

"Watch out Christopher!" Harjit shrilled a warning.

"Thank fuck, out of ammo!" He breathed out a sigh of relief.

Studying the organic mechanism a bit closer, internally it appeared like thin tubular pipes fused together and able to extend out from the main bone structure and rapidly rotate on a ball and socket joint. Watching it spinning fast, it mimicked a Gatling gun. This time it rotated around and sounded like hollow blow-pipes before finally stopping. It had killed its last victim. "Alé must have touched it, knocked it someway when he fell. The bastard had been fully loaded too."

"And right out of Hollywood." Barbaro admired its natural killing power.

"It is obvious that those darts did not come from any Head-hunter. They came from this thing born with a natural weapons system, reflexive in action and unquestionably deadly." Christopher hypnotically watched the tubes spin as they slowly came to a halt on the last click.

"Bred to kill." Harjit whispered while imagining it with flesh.

"Tripping over it made it shoot off those death darts, it's a biological firing squad rolled into one deadly fucker," said Mathieson.

"Grown inside this organism; it's a new species." Christopher looked at the others.

"A new species?" Barbaro stared at Christopher as if he was stupid. "No, it's been here for quite some time. A new discovery, like finding the remains of a dinosaur. Unquestionably an intelligent animal that is able to organize themselves for war," sneered Barbaro.

Christopher believed that the Vatican official was sick in the head.

The media man carefully watched to see if the body was completely inactive as Christopher prodded the mechanism again with his weapon. He could not believe that a fluke of nature like this could exist in the forgotten Temple.

"Watch what you are doing with that Christopher," Harjit's concerned eyes watched him moving its arm. "I agree. Those bones are not ones we know. They are black in substance, so they must be made of some other composition; not calcium and phosphorous like ours. Chris, this is getting more unreal by the minute." Harjit stammered as realisation struck her and the serious implications that these warriors were of another ancient civilization and obviously *not human*.

"You mothers!" Mathieson butted in angrily. "Aléssandro is *real*, this place is *real*, and that thing lying down there is *real too*. I don't want to shout too loudly but this place is more like fucking planet Mars than planet Earth! Let's get the hell outa here!"

The American's instincts on edge, his shifty eyes looked around to the darker places and for another attack. Mathieson no longer cared about wealth. A born survivor, he knew they had to get out of this place.

The ranger refocused and unconsciously fixed his eyes onto Christopher's. Christopher recognised that look. Both men saw it in Carmello before he committed suicide. Embarrassed, Mathieson's head turned away hiding his apparent weakness, ashamed by his own fear. Everyone wondered what else waited for them?

Christopher moved the warrior a little more exposing its open back. He gasped at what he saw.

"Shit."

"What is it Chris?" Harjit probed.

"Look."

"This expedition is bigger than anything we could ever have imagined. Chris it's a bi-vertebrate!"

"Yes, two backbones."

"What kind of animal has that? A new life form, a new intelligence, warlike. What a story!" Barbaro immediately snapped pictures, flashes lit up the chamber.

"Stop that you idiot! Stop it or I will break that damn camera of yours! *You do not understand do you!* There may be other things like that down here and *not dead* ones!" Mathieson near irate.

"Calm yourself, it is just a few photographs! Do you not think we have already lost that element of surprise, eh? That we would have already joined poor Aléssandro if anything were here?" Barbaro's sarcasm cut. "I am not an arse like you say signore and I believe that person, is you." Barbaro sneered more contempt at the

American's lack of intelligence. He expected immediate retaliation.

Mathieson's eyes burned instant hatred, springing at him. Mathieson's intent clear, he was going to break his bones.

Oddly, the smaller man was faster when the guide lunged, unexpectedly ducking down below and slipping away from under Mathieson's blow. Barbaro reverse punched, striking him mid-rift with a quick jab to his face.

Mathieson felt the surprising blows hitting him harder than he expected. The media man tripped him with his back leg as the ranger doubled forward, sending him sprawling along the floor.

Mathieson winded and down, turned and looked up. Taken by a weaker man. Glaring with rage, he sprung up to his feet. Both men breathed harder.

"That is enough Mathieson! Barbaro!" Harjit shouted at them, "Get a fucking grip, both of you! Mathieson no more. Please!" And as for you Barbaro, take no more God damn photographs unless I say so. *Got that!*" Harjit demanded immediate compliance and composure from everyone. "Now get both your shits together." Harjit instinctively took charge, "We have lost a valuable member of our expedition. Show some respect. We do not need fighting between ourselves so shape up or ship out. I mean it." Her voice was as certain as a verdict.

Something inside Harjit had changed, taking no more nonsense. All their lives depended on each other.

"This is like out of a bloody science fiction movie, totally fucking unbelievable! Finding ourselves in some lost Temple and getting fucking killed!" Cesaré shouted at everyone, the young man near his breaking point.

"None of us could know," Christopher agreed sympathetically.

"*Come on,* this is the find of the Millennium." Barbaro quickly irritated everyone. "It is very unfortunate about our friend Aléssandro. Sadly, we cannot help him now. We must leave him here and press on as Harjit has ordered." Barbaro paused judging their faces and twitched a smile from the corner of his mouth.

Harjit thought suspiciously, *what's he up to?*

"We can come back for him tomorrow or the next day," said Barbaro and urged them to leave. "What treasure, what discoveries there is to be made here is close by, I feel it." Barbaro attempted to appeal to their sense of discovery but their sense of discovery was lost, just like their innocence when the deaths began.

"Don't you understand it pal, Aléssandro has just been *killed* and *nobody* is going to just leave him behind. If anyone is going to remain here, it's going to be *you!*" Christopher bristled angrily. "It is not Christian to leave him," while glaring disdainfully at the pitiful official.

Slyly, Barbaro moved closer to the Indian girl who felt his stale breath whispering in her ear.

"It would be in *all* our interests to leave him. I would not like to mention those quieter indiscretions to the Vatican." Directing his eyes at Christopher. The small man's intimation was perfectly clear. "It could ruin his career and possible priesthood through lack of faith and impropriety," Barbaro pressing home his twisted advantage.

Harjit listened quietly – *he knows!* His threatening malcontent continued as he twisted a smile at her. She knew exactly what he meant, the girl pulling away from him and from his sickening bad breath. She was in a state of cold rage, feeling the same urge Mathieson had only a moment ago.

Harjit's brain jerked into judgment resisting her natural urge to bludgeon him. Instead, she displayed complete professional composure giving him a simple disregard to his odious words with a despondent wave. She would take the consequences, standing up to his intimidation.

"Aléssandro comes with us. Got that Barbaro," her cold steel tone shut him up. "Mathieson take that long plastic bag from your rucksack, the one you use for lying on with your sleeping bag. It has a zip and will hold Aléssandro. We can put him on a make shift stretcher using the rucksack frames clipped and bound together. Ok Mathieson be quick about it!"

Barbaro's face turned purple. He was livid. It made no difference to her. Her poker face hid her true feelings. Their situation had become more critical and they were soon ready to get going again.

"Barbaro, you and Christopher will be first to transport Aléssandro's body." Harjit was sure that he would already be scheming against her but felt confident she could handle him.

"No. I will carry him Harj." Cesaré spoke solemnly and in no mood for debate. The girl nodded her acceptance. She and Christopher set out off in front, Cesaré and Barbaro following, with Mathieson watching their rear and soon everyone was weaving in and out the stone cloisters again. Everyone was aware that anything could be lurking behind these mighty columns. All they needed was some luck to get out alive.

There could be any number of secret passages out of here and we might have missed all of them! Hopingly Mathieson may help us with that. She planned their escape, putting her hope in his hands.

"Keep alert everyone, I need you all to remain sharp." Her rhetorical tone required no answer from the escapees walking through this minefield of danger.

"Shit that's my battery outta juice. Only one spare and that will last about four or five hours max." Mathieson swapped it quickly to re-enable his torchlight.

Harjit followed her womanly intuition, her direction of travel seemed true enough, the group walking for about fifteen minutes more, but the strain was beginning to show when they spotted more bodies lying in the dark shadows.

"Watch out, take it slow and easy." Harjit warned sternly. "Mathieson come up here please." The ranger ran to the front.

"Yes?"

"What do you think?"

"Too dangerous." Mathieson immediately measured the risk, "We need a detour." He looked for an alternative way. "Look over there, it's a corridor with stairs. See it, over to our right?" Mathieson directed his beam of light to a large triangular shaped opening. "Let's miss those dudes out *shall we?*" He smiled at her.

"Ok, this is our way, follow me." Harjit started walking, the others followed.

But even this way was perilous too, the group stepped in between large amounts of broken masonry scattered around. Watching their foothold on the loose rocks, and carefully climbing through larger lumps of masonry, they moved on as best they could. Fallen soldiers lay broken in many places, their bodies unavoidable with bits of shield and smashed armour blown apart by some great explosion.

"Christ almighty these guys didn't do too well, did they? All killed. What could have caused this kind of destruction?" Mathieson was stunned and realised that the blast had to have been of great magnitude to break the doors.

"Just as well this happened a long time ago." Christopher tried to reassure the group passing through as they continued to weave a way through the rocky debris towards the entrance.

Once over this first part they stood before the broken gateway. Harjit stood in front with her hands on her hips surveying their route, she was passed caring about her dust ridden face and unkempt hair. Above and around this charred entrance, ancient runes had been chiselled into the cracked walls, blistered with intense heat, so the glyphs kept their secrets.

"Look Harjit, up on top of the stairs, a light." Christopher spoke quietly. Her sultry face had seen it too. The girl's fine bone structure was beautifully sculptured.

He smiled softly at her. If something should happen to Harjit, he would never forgive himself. In a daze the would-be priest could not believe his own thoughts, his manly desires. His pulse quickened and red blood began flowing with testosterone. Maybe Gods pure way was not his. *Keep focused. This is the way out, come on man get a grip of yourself. It could never work between us.* His emotions were interrupted by Harjit.

"Watch me carefully as you follow," the girl instructed. Harjit's eyes were keen to get on. *She is changing,* thought Christopher.

"Harjit, a few of those bloody steps are missing!" Even though she was leader,

Christopher felt wholly responsible. "We're not out of the woods yet."

"I see that." He shouted down. Harj gauged the dangers while climbing the stairs. "Take your time and take no unnecessary chances, I really mean it." She lead them into the next section at the missing steps. "It's going to be very dangerous."

Silver tinged light filtered downward reflecting off the acute shaped stonework and broken slabs. At this moment, the top of the triangular passageway above was beyond her view. The immediate challenge was to negate over the stone steps that were broken or missing.

The higher they climbed, the greater the illumination became. Christopher stopped. Breathing heavily, he needed to rest and take it all in.

"Well, it's getting brighter." He was more mystified than ever. "I cannot believe this place. It *must* lead to the top."

Harjit felt his false hope, "Let's get on with it. *Come on Christopher.*" They continued their joint efforts to reach the first larger gap.

"Watch now," she snapped. *"Be careful Chris."*

"Just total blackness down there," said Christopher looking into the scary void below. "And these steps must be built into the walls giving them extra support."

"Not here though." Harjit stared at a wide step that had fallen away.

"Ok I'll go first and you come after me." Christopher gave her no time to reply and immediately jumped the gap. "Ok Harjit!" He clapped his hands and laughed.

Unexpectedly, the stone step behind her simply *disappeared*. She was already in mid-flight as Chris's face was instantly mortified watching Harjit come at him.

Harjit shrieked, knowing there was no way back. And like a long jumper reaching the distance, she lunged forward and landed.

"Got you!" Christopher had her.

Her body knocked him onto the step. The others watched in horror at her unceremonious leap.

"That was too close Harj." Chris was relieved. "The step dropped behind you."

Looking back totally astonished she had made it, she shook with adrenaline and relief. Christopher looked at his secret companion for reassurance.

"I'm fine, thanks Christopher. No really, I am." She read his agonised eyes. "Come on, let's climb up a few more steps and get out of harm's way." A voice spoke out from the steps underneath.

"We will have less of that you two, a girl and a priest at that! Hey, Harj you watch out for his long candle stick now!" Mathieson began laughing and was really relieved to see them both across safely. Harjit did her best to ignore him although he meant it in good humour.

The crossing would be more perilous for the two men carrying Aléssandro's heavy weight. Steps were missing and it could easily happen again. Their laughter sobered because now it was their turn.

The overall gap was not too large and considered an acceptable risk. Undignified, Aléssandro's body bag was attached to the fastenings at each end using a rope. Christopher helped pull the body over onto a higher step. All the rucksacks and equipment were lifted and thrown across too, quickly redistributing their weights. Cesaré jumped last. This time there were no mishaps and once across safely, each person took extra. No doubt, survival had become a lottery.

"This place is becoming unstable. I sense it." Christopher feared their time on the steps might be running out.

"Come on guys let's pick up the pace!" Harjit feared the same thing. About five minutes later they could here distant crashes coming from behind them.

Not far from where they had been standing, a falling domino effect was occurring, step after step dropping away into the void. The clattering of more masonry striking the bottom somewhere could be heard. They moved faster, completely motivated in fear.

The group occasionally had to jump over other gaps where some of the steps were shaky. It was obvious in places that some steps teetered on the knife's edge of being there or not. Climbing inside the triangular stairway shell was nerve-racking.

The charred triangular walls inside had changed colour returning to a natural reddish salmon pink that transposed into a bleached-out whiteness further up above them. Harjit and Christopher watched the curious luminous transformation with a silent menace. What was going to happen next, was anybody's guess.

****

CHAPTER III

THE SENTINEL

"Watch carefully as you follow," Harjit advised him.

"A few more of those steps are missing!" Christopher felt responsible. "We are not out of the woods yet."

"I know." Harjit nodded. The others were not too far behind them, "Take your time and no unnecessary chances. *I mean it.*" The girl fixed her mind up ahead.

Many of the stone steps were broken or simply missing, leaving a gap that dropped down into dark oblivion. The unnatural light on top of the triangular passageway was out of their immediate view and the light source remained unknown. Christopher stopped to catch his breath.

"Well, it's certainly getting brighter," they were all mystified. "I cannot believe this place. Surely this will lead to the top somehow."

Petrified vines had gained entry long time ago from somewhere growing in from the forest; so there had to be an ingress point.

"*Those came from outside, follow them and we'll be out too,*" blurted Barbaro.

"I hope so," replied Harjit.

The vines tangled their way down the passage spanning some of the gaps. Luckily, the natural bridges assisted the team to cross some of the wider gaps making their passage easier.

The rooty vines were at first shaded dark black the closer they got to them and then began transforming the higher they climbed into a whiter more amorphous brittle structure. Their mangrove-like structures were covered with a floury white powder on its surface, like chalk.

Christopher took over the lead from Harjit and was first to step onto the whiter weave-work of dead vines, causing an unsettling crackling noise. It sounded like walking on thin ice and like tiny crystals were crunching below his weight. Each step was accompanied by a dust cloud. Bits of vine began to break apart turning into dust.

In the crisp, dry atmosphere something different came into view. Chris screwed his eyes tighter. He could see an obscure shape near the top. Unsure *he thought, it might be a person!* It was only a distant silhouette but it looked human. Everything else about it was featureless. The stationary figure seemed to be studying them.

"Company." Mathieson spoke suspiciously. "It looks like one of those big dudes."

"We'll have to take things as they present themselves," said Harjit with firm conviction. She would convince him to stick it out, without showing her own fear.

"Right on Harj!" Mathieson affirmed showing a degree of respect for the young girl's resolve while waving his sword in the air.

"Keep that down Mathieson." Christopher's tone was sharp. He hoped Mathieson's warring gestures went unseen. "Maybe we don't need to use that kind of persuasion but, whoever it is, it does not look as if he wants a fight."

Christopher knew quite well that his own sword skills were as good as *none* and he kept his sword concealed inside his rucksack but the handle stuck out of the top.

"You would be better jabbing that guy with one of my hypodermic syringes." Harjit beamed wickedly at him.

"How could there be one of these guys still alive?" Christopher was amazed, continuing the climb. Anticipation and dread crept in. "This is our path." Chris was determined to find a way out.

Christopher felt increasingly anxious. The large featureless person was bigger now but was still viewed as a dim silhouette surrounded in a great brightness. The intense illumination that shone down from behind the figure was creating a shimmering halo effect around it's edges. The opening started to widen at the landing entrance and the closer they got, the more anxious they became.

"Maybe he's the killer," Harjit whispered. "Maybe he murdered Dr. Castiglion."

"He's colossal." Christopher whispered.

"Yeah and I'm going to give him a taste of this blade first, so don't you worry Harj." The American spoke softly with controlled aggression, the tough man's adrenaline beginning to pump. Mathieson stepped up in front of Christopher while they all stared up at its massive frame.

The intense light made it hard for them to see clearly. The illumination flooded into their retinas causing blurry vision, trying to focus their eyes into narrow slits to make the pain go away.

At last there they were. They had reached the top. An intense bright circle of light emanated a short distance behind the tall figure. The light source some thirty yards form here was being projected through a clever set of complex large triangular shaped prisms. Here, the power of the sun had been harnessed. This seemed to be the source of the Temple's power, focused into a central ball of intense light about the size of a large truck wheel. Everyone guessed that it had to be the engine of the Temple.

This energy ball contained uncountable numbers of changing and darting veins of white electric energy, and all were held inside a thin spherical membrane. Uncannily, there was no heat or sound coming from the excitable object. Its intensity forced them to squint in more pain.

Prisms set midway around the large chamber with tapered walls extended from the dry vine convoluted floor base, and upward to meet a flat golden ceiling. An unseen energy crossed transparently through the airwaves. The large energy ball did not touch the prismatic arrangements while the orb appeared suspended by its own volition thirty feet overhead.

"Fan out and keep your weight light as you walk through," Christopher advised as he stepped his foot onto a crunchy white surface. The surface was not the floor but of a bleached white woody vine formation that had grown over it.

Observation articulated it to be once very much alive and thriving like an excited mangrove, now long lifeless and a mass of petrification. Before all this, a tall figure stood, the one that had watched them climb while staring downwards. The large humanoid figure was caught in a trap. Whatever grim story foretold the macabre scene, this one did not manage to escape a slow death. The petrified white figure stood alone and engulfed like everything else in this strange place. It was quite dead.

****

Before them, it appeared to be like a mad sculpture gone wild. A bone-dry formation of weird artistic shapes had been turned as if modelled into massive nightmarish architecture. It all stood here and was held in stasis. Numerous parts had once lifted into fierce high crests and sloped low troughs, all petrified and frozen in time. This bizarre structure presented a menacing obstacle course of what must have been once a writhing sea of living tissue of tentacles.

Of varying girths and lengths, there were many vines, which resembled a numerous tangle of thin worms or thick pythons tied in knots. There was an amorphous covering of fine, white powder over it, so light that wherever a person stepped, it puffed up into little clouds of white.

Cesaré and Barbaro arrived standing behind the others and placed the stretcher down onto the uneven floor. Looking around with dreaded misgivings at this bizarre scene, a large cloud of powder lifted around them for a moment then settled covering the dead body bag and their boots with a fine layer. The orb's brilliance quickly became sore on everyone's eyes. This place was indeed a white hell.

As if the orb was not bright enough, more surrounding supernatural light emanated uncannily, its energies pulsating from the walls and all added to the mystery. Changing in colour, all dependent on its internal crystalline particle's energy, one moment energising in red then turning gradually into various shades of pink and white but always remaining at the same intensity, and brighter than white.

It soon became self-evident that the tall figure's thick legs were bound and wrapped tightly in these suffocating vines. They twisted like a mummy's bandage, completely enclosing the large figure. His once powerful arms and legs were completely tied and immobilised. The desperate figure was trapped while the vines also gripped a sword that was outstretched a little to his side. It was as if he had no time to draw his blade and cut the dreaded things away.

It's as if the vines had intelligence, she thought to herself. "It knew what it was doing. It had consciousness," stated Harjit grimly.

"Impossible Harj, that's too far." Christopher tried to reassure her while considering what he was looking at.

The vines had engulfed the figure's head, body and legs. It died through suffocation or crushing. Witnesses to this macabre spectacle made them feel sad, the figure was petrified in that position forever.

"As God is my witness, this is the Devil's work." Barbaro's expression seemed to momentarily straighten his permanent sneer.

"Well, fuck ma… *fossili…zed black Ass man, phew!*" Mathieson humoured sarcastically and gasped as a nervous giggle came from Barbaro. "Looks like this big mother tried to escape, got caught and tried to fight all this shit away before being totally fucked over. Poor bastard. Whatever happened here happened a very long time ago." The ranger tried to reassure himself that they had missed the danger.

"Since when did your Jewish black backside become religious Mathieson?" Christopher jibed him a little.

"It is not just for *you Catholics* to believe in God almighty, *priest*," said Mathieson. "This is a God-forsaken place. We need all the help we can get in here mother and this big guy, well the dude just didn't pray hard enough, now did he?" He tapped at the effigy's white wrapped leg and laughed a little. If he didn't laugh he would crack.

Harjit spoke, "Strong as this warrior was, he got completely swamped by this stuff. He is *no ordinary man.*"

"Come again?" Barbaro's eyes about popped out.

"Maybe he is man but not *hu-*man, certainly not a modern man.

"Si, Si! I know that, *so what?*" Barbaro was almost irate with impatience.

"Within the *same genus* that includes *humans,* opposed to a different genus like Australopithecus. A genus is a low-level taxonomic unit. The genus Homo has been positively dated as 3.7 million years old, Homo floresiensis around 13,000 years and now here we stand, Homo sapiens, modern man. DNA evidence indicates that modern humans originated in Africa about 200,000 years ago."

"Yes, I see where you are coming from Harjit. These guys are real big, but I don't think that…" Christopher was a bio-technologist and understood taxonomic terminology and levels, as did Harjit. He stopped short as if stuck in thought. *She is hiding something, what has Harjit discovered?*

Harjit suddenly interrupted him. "I really, *don't think* that you do understand where I am coming from Christopher, look at his left hand! It is uncovered. I noticed this before in the others. Her body seemed animated with energy.

"What?"

"Si what are you keeping from us?" Barbaro seethed

"It's a new species! I've given this some thought too, and I would even be so bold as to give it the name of Homo iblisdeminstratus." I named it after the *Vale of Iblis* and the creature's elongated talon, which is like a retractable finger. Look again!" The talon and claw hand were the only parts not wrapped in vine.

"Awesome, Harjit!" Christopher acknowledged her unique discovery.

"As you can see, it is segmented like the digits of a finger and yet can also slash like a blade." Harjit was quite pleased with herself.

"A natural lethal weapon," Barbaro sneered.

"A talon for a finger. Can you observe between the thumb, and what should be the position of a forefinger? It's gone, replaced by this sharp digit. It has evolved into what we can now see." Harjit's face beamed with pleasure while watching their dumbfounded reactions, all except Barbaro.

"Go on," said the media man He was caught in the moment and writing notes.

"The others I observed earlier had something similar although not as obvious as this one. You can see the vines severed around it, then petrified. How or why? I don't know. Petrification takes time. However, I would bet that the DNA of

Homo iblisdemonstratus would be very interesting. What do you say, Christopher?"

"How brilliant! An excellent extrapolation on your part Dr. and your new species name *is well justified!*" Christopher was full of admiration for his girlfriend.

"Be silent both of you," The Vatican journalist hissed aggressively at them. "I don't believe any of it! This is total sacrilege of your faith. It can't be true. You are a disgrace for a priest!" Barbaro's face became red listening to their blasphemous, scientific hypotheses. "The Vatican will be told of this irreverent talk, make no mistake, you have gone too far this time!" Barbaro was delirious with rage.

The two scientists were taken by surprise.

"Shut up Barbaro, with that medieval crap. I am surprised you are not sending them both to the Inquisition or snapping this big guy up for yourself with that bloody camera of yours!"

"How dare you Jew!" Barbaro glared at the American's intrusion.

"Say that again to me and I'll kick your fucking ass man!" Mathieson sensed that their immediate predicament just got more dangerous and wanted to get going immediately. Barbaro would be wise not to offend him again.

White spaghetti-shaped masses laid before them, there for many millennia, long dead and bleached under the unending orb's rays. The orb hung suspended above the unearthly lattice, irradiating it in great brilliance. Yet no sound or heat came from the bizarre object, only light.

There was no time to find out about what the orb did or where it came from.; it existed and that would just have to do.

"Careful," Christopher warned Cesaré as he watched him walk around the figure. "We have no idea what we are dealing with." Christopher urged while shielding his eyes in the blurry light, unsure how long he could suffer it. Mathieson and Harjit put on sunglasses they had in their rucksacks.

"It's a light source more akin to a generator of energy, and I think the orb is channelling it into the walls and farming it out to the rest of the Temple. Maybe in the past it was able to produce for a whole city!" Cesaré tried to guess.

"You may be right. Strange that there is *absolutely no noise.*" Harjit was mystified.

"Energy is not allowed to escape, its directed and then re-focused. Using all the power with no energy loss, this could be the first ever fusion reactor!" Cesaré seemed surprised at himself. It was a *leap in his-own thought process.* The others turned to look at him with raised eyebrows; maybe he was right.

An undulating sea of whiteness lay still as if frozen in time underneath the orb's power, a complete place of amorphous white. Surfaces of white troughs and high crests twisted, spreading further inside this nightmarish place. Every façade was completely covered in light powder. Hard to distinguish, the vines had grown in endless curves; some bent and some jagged. Ragged ends stuck out or curved inwards, looking dangerously sharp and all easily able to slash any unwary victim. Disturbingly, there was no way out.

****

And that realisation was the moment something caught Harjit's eye; a glint not too far away, seen in the side of a trough.

Driven by instincts, Harjit began quickly crunching her way towards it, however getting there proved to be much more difficult that she had imagined. The vines were slippery and crunched underneath, each step sounded like broken glass.

"Watch Harjit!" Christopher shouted at her. Danger was everywhere.

Closer and well inside the petrified structure, it was more featureless and impossible to see any detail. It was almost like walking on pure white snow, very difficult to judge depth and gauge distance. Harjit's speedy eyes measured her footing. *Tricky* she thought, climbing over the top of a white creeper and sliding down into a shallow trough using her side. The group could see only above her waist.

Yes! There it is. Harjit was excited to find it. She could see a small, sharp metal object. *It is a polished disc or something, its underneath.* She attempted to remove it by wiping away the chalk surface, leaving a frosty glass surface.

Tenaciously, Harjit got down and kept on pulling and picking at it while applying more effort, moving her face closer to the thick, trellis surface to gain extra leverage and a better look at what it was.

"What *is that?*" She was unsure while almost kissing the surface, peering further inside at. *There is something else in there. Oh Shiva!* Her body jerked in total disbelief,

She released a high-pitched shrill of revulsion and stiffened like a plank. She could not tare herself away. A vague shape that had been waiting just below the surface shimmied a bit closer to her.

A strange peculiar looking head became much clearer at the surface. She knew that it was alive! Harjit's mind became split between clarity and madness.

Is it a big insect? Harjit watched it, uncertain of what it was or what to do. It too seemed unsure of her unexpected appearance, and with vile curiosity closed in on her face. Through thin frosted material; it could only be inches away. Harjit could tell that it harboured a deep sickness, and twisted malevolence.

The thing suddenly moved closer to touch the surface; its ugly presence intimidated her sanity. Harjit's heart began banging onto her chest, *it's looking at me.* Petrified just like her surroundings, Harjit could do nothing.

She screamed. She jolted instinctively and catapulted herself like a spring. Falling inside a dip between her and their line of sight, she was down! Hidden completely by this surrounding architecture, Harjit landed on her back.

"Harjit!" Christopher yelled. Running without any regard for himself, he headed to where large puffs of dust clouds rose. Everyone watched Christopher's white amorphous trail following him.

****

Panic ridden, Harjit kept scuttling backwards with no fixed route, her mind lacerated in cold fear. With crab-like ability, she was covered in white dust and propelled herself away as far as possible.

My God, it's a monster!

Worse than being on a polished dance floor, her feet and body slipped off the surfaces in frantic desperation, trying to get up as far away from there as possible. Harjit's chest was heaving, her skating feet attempted to scuff more traction while slipping in a dance for survival. She racked herself hard against the opposite trough with a hard-cracking sound. She slipped, scrambling helplessly down into the horrible trough.

Her fast breathing became shallow, having had come face to face with something she could not possibly understand. Her body rebounded *harder* off the next trough. With no grip to be had, everywhere felt like being on an ice rink.

Holding herself tightly with clouds of dust lifting around her, she was losing her battle for balance. The trough's curved side acted like a chute and teased her before her downward slide. She was caught in a balance between slipping and when the truth finally hit her. She was in utter terror. The crust cracked, its shape suddenly shattering into thousands of petrified bits with her body dropping hard.

Harjit stared outwardly knowing there was nothing else she could do.

She shrieked. She was in survival mode. Dropping fast and hitting the convoluted floor underneath, it broke her fall.

Damage minimal, Harjit stared numbly upward realising the distant ragged hole above was too high to get out. Debris was lying on top of her dust-covered body, while some larger bits kept on bouncing and rattling away across the powdery floor. She tried to make sense of what was going on. Harjit's lips quivered at finding herself stuck inside a hollow complex of white vines. Her worst nightmare had just begun.

I've got to get out, NOW!

The structure below was similar in density to above, light and brittle and in places where vines knitted together, making a complex wall of white sheets with dust covering what might be across large gaps. They appeared to be an effective barrier but were nothing more than dust filled webs easily wiped away.

Light projected down like a tunnel from where she had fallen. The orb's power filtered through the whole opaque waver roof, giving a lower luminescence below. She searched in every direction but all she could see were what looked like white mangrove-like structures making up an enormous labyrinth of tentacles. It went in every direction, creating a bizarre maize of hollow cavities throughout. She perceived that the warped creepers were alive a long time ago.

Harjit started hyperventilating in panic, trying to come to terms with everything. She stared wildly fighting off the feeling of unconsciousness as the sculptures went out of focus and blackness involuntarily enclosed around her.

No! She demanded not to succumb to unconsciousness and denial of the truth to where she had fallen. Unconsciousness would mean death. Harjit fought off the doom of darkness, her mind winning back the lucidity, her focus again on numerous shapes. Back from the brink, she could see they were everywhere. It was much easier to see inside this place than above, although her sunglasses lay in a dust pile. She was alone.

"Help me Christopher!" Any noise dampened like a cushioned radio room but above she could hear crackling noises getting closer. Help was on its way. "Hurry!"

"Harjit are you alright?" Christopher's head suddenly appeared above over the ragged edge. "God almighty." She was covered in what looked like white makeup.

"*Chris!* Thank God."

"Harjit, are you ok? My God, *what is this place?*"

Through the mist of her numbed mind, her eyes sharpened. She was fully conscious of what she had seen. Her whole body shrunk in disbelief; gulping hard Harjit had zoned onto something else, *an atrocity!*

****

Her mortified eyes beheld a tangle of dead bodies. People and soldiers all gathered together, all tied and tangled. Everyone had died in this twisted place, hanging here, forever.

Staring at the massacre, many bodies partially concealed and knotted, she could see that everyone had suffered a painful death. None escaped.

She began counting the dead, twenty maybe thirty, Harjit knew there were others. All were mutilated. Some strangled while others had been agonisingly pulled apart by incredible forces and left in extraordinary contorted positions.

Page 81

Harjit sobbed at their plight. *Those poor people. Lord, what is this hideous place?*

It made no sense trying to scream but she tried. Swallowing again, all she could conjure up was a silent shriek. Things only got worse when she realised those creature warriors that had killed Aléssandro were there too.

Even those big beasts had been caught inside the death tangle. A nasty animal race, yet they were not immune to this awful slaughter. Everyone had been caught inside the same trap. This was an indiscriminate and cruel end to any creature.

My God, we must get out of this place or this will be our end too.

"Harjit, let me pull you up! Take my hands!" He stretched down towards the girl. Cesaré anchored himself onto Christopher's legs and braced himself. Chris looked around the dead zone. *"Oh shit, look at this place."* Harjit shook her head rapidly as if stuck. *Oh God she does not want to leave!* Chris was shocked at her insanity. "Harj?"

"No, *no!*" She said firmly.

"Harj, *please.*" Christopher was desperate to get her.

"I can see another way out! It's at the far wall. Come down Chris, come down here and you will see it. This is the way to go! Hurry and bring the others!"

Christopher looked above the surface where the stony vines were amassed over at the far wall. *Surely, there is no exit over there?*

He stuck his head down the hole again trying to measure the distance but the mayhem below made him doubt it even more.

Harjit's patience was tested. *Does he not trust me?* Chris could see that she was becoming more anxious. To go her way meant travelling through slaughter!

"Are you out of your head young woman? To go down there?" Barbaro looked down too, his anger sharpened the lines in his sneering face. Harjit waited anxiously.

"Ok, make room," Christopher got ready to jump.

"Well, why worry?" He smiled at the mens' horror-struck faces.

Below, Chris gasped seeing the total carnage, breathing in a silent prayer. Unexpectedly, Barbaro landed right next to him.

"How can we take Aléssandro down there?" Cesaré asked.

He and Mathieson were the last people above.

"We cannot Alé, *we cannot*. He must remain here for now and we can return tomorrow, properly equipped and with a larger rescue team, Fabio will bring him back and you can count on that."

Harjit had admired Aléssandro, he had been larger than life, but their lives were held in the balance, and sentimentality right now would get them all killed.

"We must go." Harjit knew they had to get out fast.

"I cannot leave him." Cesaré was about to move away.

Harjit knew he would die up there. The creature's image had not left her. He had to come down immediately.

"Cesaré, *look at me.* You must leave. You really must, *please come down.*" Harjit pleaded with him. She knew that he was struggling in his own guilt. Cesaré had not been able to help his dead friend and right now his heart was grieving.

"No,"

"You must come with us," Mathieson cut in, "You will die in this place my friend. Aléssandro has sung his last song. I will come back here with you tomorrow. *I promise.*" He held his wrist in truth and comradeship.

By losing his own friend Carmello, Mathieson's pain was obvious, showing a different side to himself.

"Cesaré," Harjit urged.

"I will return or stay with you. Cesaré, you have my word." Mathieson vowed. Cesaré considered his words with Mathieson tugging him gently. Mat motioned them to leave with a kind nod. Cesaré looked back one last time at his friend, swallowing his tears. He did not want any more blood on his hands.

Dominating the mouth of the sun chamber where they had ascended from the stairs, the huge and solitary figure stood shrouded in its eternal bonds of death. Standing there bleached and mummified, here as a warning of what was ahead. The sentinel would be forever watch below for others to join him. No longer alone as at his foot lay the dust covered body bag of the unfortunate Aléssandro.

****

CHAPTER IV

BONES OF THE DEAD

Noises were continually floating throughout the creaky substructure, unmistakable sounds drifting minutely within its dead mass. All created from tiny unperceivable movements, it was like being under a shifting glacier.

Enough light penetrated down through the thinner parts of the translucent vine surface layer above, making visibility much easier in the wider and more spacious cavities. In other areas, the shadier parts where the mangrove-like rooftop that was more difficult.

"Follow me," Harjit said nothing more because every second counted.

Keeping up was difficult. Climbing over and squeezing through the dry pipework of dead vines, its tentacle like strands seemed to stretch down with ill intent throughout the confused area. Moving fast, this place was worse than hell. The group groaned at the bones of the dead. Nobody wanted to look too closely at the helpless mutilations hanging everywhere. It was best to keep going.

In some places they knocked *dead* bodies sending gruesome bits flying off in all directions.

The ancient vines had grown and stretched along the floor which were precarious to move over, sending them sprawling in a dust heap.

Harjit desperately tried to negate her way ahead looking for the exit.

The vines became much thicker the closer to where she judged would be their destination. But inside a place like this, disorientation was all too easy…

Below was a complete contrast to the silence above. Underneath sounded like the crackling of an ice glacier. They realised it was moving.

Christopher, Barbaro, Mathieson and finally Cesaré followed her. Their efforts extraordinary, but fatigue caused everyone to breathe heavily. Scurrying through the dry complex, they looked more like ghosts than explorers. Suddenly they heard what sounded like a pane of glass compressed and about to break, it was part of the upper crust!

The sounds were ultra-magnified down there and with the cataclysmic crash shattering acoustics its effects startled everyone. All were caught in the deafening development with numerous pieces of vines exploding. A fine powder dust storm produced a thick cloud and engulfed them and in seconds they could see, nothing!

The dust made them cough and become bleary eyed. Soon the white powder covered everything. Mental mayhem took over and terror was seen over their white faces.

Harjit turned her eyes petrified.

Barbaro squealed.

Cesaré fell.

Christopher dumfounded said, "Harj?"

"Mother F" Mathieson coughed to clear his throat.

Instantly covered in mess, they could not see each other.

Fraught panic gathered and strangled any rational thoughts. The area was submerged in a dust white out. Everyone started shouting! Harjit heard them.

She shrieked when Mathieson appeared in front of her powdered face.

He coughed heavily. She stared to where Christopher might be.

"Chris!" *Where is he? I see him!* The dust began settling.

"Is everyone alright?" Christopher shouted at the others.

Cesaré was unconscious on the floor, completely covered in broken fragments.

"Help us!" Harjit pleaded loudly. "*This is the home of Shiva the Destroyer, an awful and evil place.*" Harjit's crazy vision turned any doubt of getting away unscathed into grim reality. "He is alive!" Then she gasped in horror.

"*Chris, look! That's not him, there's something lying ON HIM!*" Harjit froze. Instinctively she did not want to get any closer to him. *"It must be that thing I saw!"*

"What is it?" Christopher begged, bleary eyed and not realising their danger.

"Look on top of Cesaré! *Shiva!* Some giant insect is on his back Christopher!"

Christopher stared wildly at the sickly-looking creature on top of him.

"In the name of God." Christopher stated and uncertain of what he was looking at, blinking hard to clear his eyes from dust.

Something silvery-white was on him, providing an excellent camouflage for the creature. They could see its six short scaly legs, each making a clicking noise. Everyone felt sick while gasping in dust. The thing began slowly crawling over Cesaré, fixing itself on top of him.

The creature had numerous tiny white albino eyes positioned all over its oval casing. Its hard exoskeleton showed a multitude of small sharp jaggy peaks used for protection. It seemed to be calculating their threat, studying them in fine detail.

Moving a little on the man, it stopped. Then its surface began changing colour from white into bright pink. It had stuck itself solidly onto the man's back. Cesaré shivered a little, moaning involuntarily and said nothing. Everyone looked desperately at each other then the man lay quiet and very still. All in a state of shock, watching as his body gradually became FOSSILISED.

The creature began feeding on his juices, rejuvenating itself with every slurp, its colour becoming healthier; more, fleshy. Inside its hard body they began to see internal organs working away, becoming more distinct. And incredibly, this translucence had only taken a few seconds.

"What the mother fuck is it?" Mathieson rasped while pointing his double-edged sword, steadily walking towards it. "Leave him alone you fucker!"

A sucking sound came from the beast squatting on top of Cesaré; the slobbering of unseen lips detached then re-attached onto him. Its large lips and small teeth began opening him up then cruelly forced his scapula and ribs apart.

Everyone groaned loudly at the sickening cracking sound. Yet the man was not quite dead when its long tongue began probing around inside him for his last heartbeat.

Mathieson kept cautiously closing in on the feasting monster, the brute watching his every step towards it. The closer Mathieson got, it began quivering like jelly and with Cesaré dead there seemed to be no reason for it to stay.

"Mathieson come back!" Christopher warned. "You can't help him. He's dead!"

"Fuck you man! And fuck this thing too! It's going to pay! Ok you white-faced piece of shit! Want a taste of this? Come on you ugly mother, come on!"

Mathieson's hot temper blinded his judgement as he ranted at the devilish creature. In a split-second, it launched straight up. It was gone. The creature's vertical take-off unbelievable, taking Mathieson and everyone else by surprise. The thing vanished and scurried on top of the fossilised upper crust. Matheson gasped as he looked at the gaping hole in Cesaré.

"Get back down here you dirty mother fuck!"

Unnervingly, everyone could hear it scurrying madly around the upper shell, it seemed crazy like a spinning top. Everyone's head twisted with it, following its shadow, nobody wanted to lose its wild antics.

Mathieson secured his sword, and like a spring jumped, catching onto the ragged edges of the hole. He pulled himself up slowly while snapping some of the brittle pipe-work. His position was unstable as he balanced precariously on a jagged rim. His forearms bulged while his head lifted guardedly a little above the white surface. His neck began shaking in fear, trepidation and great physical exertion. It was nowhere.

Mathieson instinctively felt it watching him. He suddenly heard the vile apparition moving in on him like a missile from behind. The hairs on his neck instantly bristled. Mathieson dropped back down when he saw its fleeting outline leap over the gap above him. The creature hit the wall with a loud crack. Such was the ferocity of the attack.

Mathieson knew that he was very lucky this time. He trailed its movements.

The others watched as Mathieson sprung back up and caught onto the rim of the hole. He pulled upwards and had to see the creature, it was not where he thought again.

"It's out here alright man, I can't see but it's here!" He warned the others.

"Get down Mathieson!" Harjit screamed up at him. "It could be anywhere!"

Looking in every direction, Mathieson felt extremely vulnerable. He dropped again and landed next to Cesaré.

"Let's get the hell out of here!" Mathieson urged everyone in a shaky tone.

The ranger grimaced as if something awful had just walked across his soul. He felt that the creature must be directly above him.

Hunching his shoulders while warily watching above, fear fuelling his fast footsteps towards the others. His navy seal instincts knew it was following him. It was catching up. The hunter closed in for the kill.

"Mathieson! We can see a way through, follow us!" Harjit screamed, "Run!"

The group had reached the exit and found that it was BLOCKED.

"No not again!" Christopher screamed. *"How many tests do we have to pass God? How many are going to die before you are satisfied!"*

Stuck and dismayed they could not get through. Approaching fast about twenty metres away, Mathieson came sprinting in their direction. He suddenly went sprawling when a long thin vine caught his foot.

Survival depended on getting up fast and getting away as he scrambled desperately to his feet. Death seemed to be closing in with certainty when he sprinted for his life.

****

Staring at a trellis of thick vines stretching across the way in, heavy vines barred their escape. How Harjit had been able to see this place was a miracle. Now, they needed another.

Frantic to get out, everyone jostled and peered helplessly through the mesh like prisoners behind bars. They could see a way out! On the other side, a darker and spacious antechamber about thirty feet in height was bare with complex cornices. It had wide stone steps near the far wall leading up to a shut gate that was an entry into a portcullis room. Everyone knew that if they did not escape they would soon be dead.

Meanwhile, Mathieson was coming at them full pelt. Nothing would stop him and nothing could catch him. The hunter closed in.

"I hear it! It's above you Mathieson! It's coming for you!" Barbaro warned him.

"He's right!" Christopher shouted. "Harjit, Barbaro, help me get through this shit!" Christopher started furiously whacking at the bone-like vines.

At first, his blade deflected harmlessly off the amorphous powdery surface then with shear will-power, he began chipping and splitting it, hacking away at its weaknesses until more pieces started flying past their faces.

Barbaro started levering off broken branches in blind terror. Harjit worked furiously too, pulling and kicking the blockages, breaking it in parts.

Sweat poured off them when they broke through. But, it had taken too long.

"That's it! Let's go!" Harjit shrilled. "Give me your sword Christopher!"

"No *way* Harj!" The Scotsman wielded the weapon like a revolving windmill, unleashing a fury he did not know he had. The ragged razor-sharp edges were dangerous but right now that did not matter because, there was a gap. At last!

"Si! Si!" Barbaro delighted, the barrier broke with shards flying away. There was just enough room to get through and with no time to lose Christopher unceremoniously pushed Harjit safely to the other side. Barbaro took full advantage squeezing past causing a piece of sharp vine to fly off cutting Chris's cheek.

"Oh! Watch what you are doing you fool!" Christopher cursed now with blood flowing down his face.

Breathing hard, Mathieson stopped running. The ranger stood among the debris; strewn bits of petrified vines scattered like dead bones, and while watching Harjit's scared face he began turning around slowly. It was right behind them.

Nobody knew how long it had been there observing them. Fierce and wholly terrifying, the vile creature defied nature.

The life form seemed to shudder realising it had their attention and suddenly it came scuttling fast towards them rabid for blood. Extra mobile for its size and shape, it jumped over vines and steered around obstacles at superfast speed, throwing itself between gaps with only one thing in mind. To kill and eat.

Christopher turned and saw the American's exposed position. *"Oh God!"*

The creature's great sense of spatial awareness enabled it to cover the distance within seconds. Horror struck the group as it launched itself to feast on Mathieson.

The creature landed on his rucksack and pushed him forward with a hard lunge.

Mathieson's eyes bulged on impact while stumbling forward.

Determined not to go down like Aléssandro, he let his rucksack slide off his shoulders, dropping it and the vile thing to the floor in one.

It started making guttural noises underneath his pack. Undaunted, the creature quickly flipped the rucksack, immediately attacking him again. Mathieson and Christopher knew that they would-not go unscathed. They stood their ground with swords and faced the short-legged predator.

The creature sat directly in front of them. Its legs quivered. Close-up, they could see its repugnant body heaving. Everyone poised, waiting for its attack.

It resembled a huge genetically malformed woodlouse. And that's where the similarity ended. It had a white armoured outer surface and scaled legs. Its body was semi-transparent with white bristles and barbs sticking out from all over its surface.

With jointed shaped legs, bristles and barbs, it was able to climb and stick onto vertical surfaces or hang from ceilings. Its legs were fixed onto its body underneath and its leathery mouthparts moved instinctively, equipped with black, pointed gnashing teeth already stained rusty red with the blood from Cesaré.

The men gasped, quickly drawing their weapons at its appearance when in that split-second it coiled, springing at them. Mathieson lunged forward with his short sword and thrusted at its open mouth and legs.

As it attacked, Mathieson's blade began to exude a sharp blue light along its edge. The creature's legs automatically retracted, drawing them in to protect its mouth. With lightning speed, they opened again and extended them widely at Mathieson.

One leg tipped Mathieson's sword away and landed square on top of his chest and toppled him over. The creature's hungry mouthparts immediately set to work slobbering all over his body on his way to strike the floor.

Mathieson shrieked. His eyes were paralysed in fear.

"Mat!" A sharp scream came from stunned Christopher.

"Help me!" Mathieson shouted, feeling cutting and tearing at his tunic. His shirt ripped easily apart by the jagged teeth, biting into his skin in a feasting frenzy.

His sword lay across his chest and protected him from a full bodily assault. The beast slobbered digestive fluids all over him. Mathieson began losing consciousness.

Christopher judged that a direct strike at the creature would kill Mathieson too, but ran and gave it one almighty kick with full power.

"Get off him! You, filth!" The creature flew off him like a football. Mathieson laid there semi-stunned; wounded but not dead.

Semi-conscious Mathieson tried to get up. His clothes in tatters, chest bare and with red teeth marks on his dark skin. Blood flew from the nasty gash below his left pectoral muscle. He had been lucky.

Undeterred, the vicious creature immediately attacked once more. The noise more guttural, and although the monster's shape was far from being aerodynamic, it somehow managed to compress its legs springing at them again with great ferocity.

Inside its wide mouth and thick fleshy lips, black reddish teeth snapped. The creature's jointed legs were strong enough to knock over both opponents at once.

Both men hit the ground with a hard knock. Christopher instinctively lifted his arm to protect his face.

In a powerful downward arc and deliberate motion, something fast and blurry passed his face, in a sickening crunching sound.

The crunching noise sounded like a huge waver being broken. A blurred object swept so close to his eyes. But he could see the creature.

He watched its body crumple easily. Its many layers suddenly broke apart. Its body split wide open splattering a pinkish white ooze everywhere, sliding its internal organs with a squelch onto the floor.

Its heinous eyes were still watching them and all the time the fetid organism made pig-like grunting noises, when suddenly its legs quivered and stopped. It died.

Harjit sighed. Her double-edged battle-axe was indeed a handy weapon, still sticking into the life form's hard outer casing.

"A woman's touch," she stated coldly. Watching her companions' astonished faces, twitching a smile at the dead thing with self-satisfaction. It was her kill.

"Harjit," Christopher's dry throat gasped. "You came back."

"Let's not hang around, boys," her energised voice sounded deranged.

Harjit and Christopher helped each other get Mathieson up, wounded but moving. Huddling him along between them, leaving their backpacks behind. No time to observe details but when they got there, it was no ordinary room. It was a huge portcullis room.

"How is he?" Barbaro asked.

"How do you think you arse!" Harjit swore at him.

"Bloody hell, *what is that thing!*" Chris tried to make sense of it. "It's dead." She stated coldly with a nod.

Not far away, the sounds of shattering glass, followed by hollow pipes bouncing onto the floor could be heard. It had to be part of the upper crust breaking.

Pallor draining from their fearful faces, their keen ears tuned to the threat not far away, pushing panic through their brains. No words between them, each person knew that the outer crust on the other side had been breached again, and that meant…RUN!

"God help us! Come on Mat, let's go!" Harjit told the American, and to his credit, the bloodied man's remarkable survival instincts kicked in.

Back inside, he grimaced to where he had been attacked. He looked for any sign of threat.

And there it was. White dust. *Right on queue,* thought Mathieson.

Somewhere inside those dusty shadows, a monster was moving in closer.

Harjit's eyes scanned anxiously; she had only their escape in mind. She stared inside this new area and checked it out. The place was a sizable portcullis room with a very high ceiling. It was about thirty feet high with no other distinguishing features except for its complex cornices bordering the room. She could also see wide stone steps over at its far wall leading to a smaller portcullis gate.

"I'll follow," Mathieson told her while gripping his strange sword with its edges glowing blue. He got set and straddled defensively at the entrance to the room. He was determined and fixed into a defensive position; this time he was ready.

"Go while you still can," his tone rasped hard at Harjit.

Harjit understood that valuable seconds would be bought to help them get out. Her mind impelled on a mad search of the room, nodding her approval.

And that was enough for Barbaro, who without waiting was already off and running quickly climbing the dusty steps to reach the second smaller portcullis gate. Harjit sighed, disappointed in the little man but resigned, *at least one was through.*

"Mat, soon as we're up top, follow us!" She demanded his attention knowing that he was determined to make a stand.

"I'll bring up the rear." Mathieson confirmed with a sharp nod.

With little or no time to lose, Harjit and Christopher made a mad dash to get away. The ranger stood alone and looking above while trying to work out the mechanics of the rock heavy portcullis gate he was standing below. It was a stone door framework with downward spikes like at the entrance to a castle. But this was no castle.

He did not have long and he knew it. His eyes were sharp with urgency. The whole doorway all part of a defensive frame constructed to make a portcullis; if he could only figure out *how to close it.*

Mathieson needed to use the ratchet and chain mechanism; he could do it. Weakened yet undeterred, Mathieson began pulling down hard onto the nearby chain. The gate started to move, and yet his pain did not matter seeing the barrier slowly coming down, this gave him more reason for hope. *Keep on going…* Soon the stone links were clinking and lowering the gate, bit by bit, the spikes by now reaching directly in front of his worried face, knowing that an attack was imminent.

Only a few more feet to go, come on! It's going to be close man, I feel that ugly mother is out there. Mathieson's eyes peeled in between the square spaces of the gate and frantically pulled more urgently with an attack imminent.

"Hey! Hey!" He called out. "Another one of those things is out here!" His nerves shouted a warning to the others, his thoughts squeezed into compressed panic. *Too Late! I'm too late to get this shit down man* There were numerous scuttling noises coming from different dust filled places and just out of view. "It's outside man!"

He did not want to die. Pulling harder, his tortured breathing was ignited by fear and survival while using both hands to pull faster. *Shit!*

"More than one's out here man! This place is infested!" He warned the others.

Standing in his blood-clotted and tattered clothes, Mathieson desperately tried to see any sign of the creatures. The gate descended agonizingly too slow for him. Breathing hot curses into the dusty air, knowing that the thick heavy red sand stone barricade would be down in another minute yet he knew *it was too late.*

A hideous creature suddenly came out of the dust, moving clumsily over.

At first it had been hard to distinguish by its stealth but now, unmistakably there it was. It looked like a large insect and strangely it had not seen him when it stopped.

"It's stopped," he whispered. Suddenly, the thing came bursting forward heading straight for him with snorting noises. It viciously focused its albino sight onto him, intent on a kill.

Mathieson was transfixed onto this apparition with only seconds to spare and he glanced behind him to see where the others were.

Harjit, Christopher and Barbaro all shouted from the top of the stairs. Fear held him like quicksand and swamped him with dread. Instinctively, he turned to face it, Mathieson's heart racing in split seconds between life and death. This was it. He called a war cry at the beast charging at him.

It's me again mother fucker.

Parts of the upper crust were crashing inwards like falling masonry. *Shit!* Breathing quicker, his throat rasped in the dry, dusty air, aware of the brittle top layer hitting the floor and smashing apart into lumps. Pieces of sharp bouncing debris went flying in all directions, the place again a complete white out. *More mothers.*

But now the thing was on him. His muscles shook with adrenaline.

Mathieson focused, his mind electrifying into action knowing that his final stand would be here. The futility of his fight was certain.

Acutely aware creatures were dropping in from everywhere, already crawling, already coming for him from somewhere in the dusty haze. Suddenly, he could see another creature charging in with the other. Both monsters had his full attention. All in seconds, he took quick shallow breaths; his last. He rose his sword's burning blue edge.

****

Barbaro stood shaking at the top of the inner steps, seconds before Matheson's last stand, which would place him at a height above the energy Orb inside the adjacent hall. The media man's lips were quivering, as he stood impatiently. He almost soiled himself as he watched Harjit and Chris run! He could also see that crazy American waiting.

The carved symbols on the stone entranceway above him read:

Translated:

THE SYMBOL OF DEEP WISDOM

He saw their laboured breathing, as Harjit and Christopher came belting up the steps, roughly pushing past him and giving him a taste of his own medicine — both with more to worry about than getting even. Inside this dark anti-chamber, the place curiously emitted a strange glow with just enough light to see.

Page 104

Harjit stood underneath a much smaller Portcullis Gate. It had a Pentagonal design. The girl, Christopher and Barbaro turned anxiously to look down at Mathieson's lone figure. The stone chain clanked quicker but not quick enough. Sweat was dripping off his bloodied face as he watched the crazy Ranger. They knew he had to get away right now, or be killed.

"Come on, Mathieson!" they said. "We're safe, make a run for it. Come on, man, RUN!" Christopher could see the American's plight as he tried to lower the heavy stone gate. Upon giving up, the man gripped his sword tighter and pointed. "For God's sake, man, get out of there!"

Mathieson knew his own limitations and abilities, especially when it came to how fast he could run. At six-feet, he could easily cover a hundred metres in just over ten seconds. And right now, two nasty creatures were running straight at him!

"Aaaaagh!" he yelled in complete frustration as he saw the others behind them! *Motherfucker. Enough of this shit, man, I'm outa here!*

He made a snap decision. The gate had stopped a little more than midway — about three feet from the floor. It was too late and he knew it.

However, despite all his injuries, pure adrenaline rushed through him and he overcame his fear. Mat reached the stairs in seconds, knowing they were right behind. After gauging their proximity by their slobbering noises, he launched himself up the stone steps, then looked up and saw his target!

Christopher and Harjit stood waving at him, trying to encourage him, but their horrified faces said it all.

"Quick, Mathieson! Quick! *Quicker!*" Harjit warned him as he watched the two awful life forms crawl after him on the steps, hot on his heels.

He was too far from safety. His legs were not fast enough. This nightmarish chase could only end one way. Agonisingly, Mathieson jumped and limped up the steps to reach them, but to reach them was like reaching for the Moon: impossible!

The impending snorting and slobbering was only inches from him. He was going crazy. *Close, too fucking close. I'm not going to make it.*

"Behind you, Mat!" Christopher yelled, staring at the creature as it jumped and went for the ranger's back!

"Turn, Mathieson!" Harjit screamed. Mathieson unexpectedly tripped over a step.

Turning instinctively, he swung his sword around, and with a severe and heavy blow, the edge struck the creature mid-flight.

His desperate eyes lit up as he watched its crisp body crunch and break in two, accompanied with a horrible sickening sound of the florescent edged blade cutting through its hard exoskeleton.

Suddenly, a thick and smelly white fluid spilled out, and the creature uttered an unearthly and deathly scream. The other creature, instead of continuing after him, unexpectedly stopped and squatted on top of the dead carcass. It started cannibalising the other creature's innards and slurping on the white ooze — its quench giving Mathieson a chance to escape.

Madness ensued when another vile apparition joined the other and they both slurped and sipped greedily on the horrible oasis of viscous fluid. The smelly juice now ran freely down the steps.

With only a split second to react, he regained his balance and shook his head questionably. The horrors before him were all too real, and now a multitude of them was pouring in under the half-closed gate.

Mathieson's eyes almost popped out of his head at the sudden arrival of a much bigger and wider creature. Its eyes immediately went to him. In seconds, it jumped on top of the others who were busily slurping on the carcass of the creature he had killed. It rabid for a new victim, him!

"No way, man," Mathieson gasped. "No fucking way!" He quickly retreated to the top of the platform and standing up, he turned and readied himself. "This is for you, bastard!" As he wielded his sword high above his head in a fury, something unexpectedly grabbed him around his waist. "Uugh!" he screamed in surprise.

He was caught by something but didn't know what. It pulled him off the floor, then threw him down against the ground, banging his head and sending his mind spinning.

He was done, like a boxer wobbling after being knocked-out, still trying to fight aimlessly. He couldn't understand what was going on and was slowly losing consciousness. *What mother's. got me. fuck.*

In a semi-conscious stupor, Mathieson stared upwards at the sound of numerous obscure and oblique warning calls coming at him.

Christ, I'm losing consciousness. No! He rejected death and defeat, which allowed him to stay cognisant. At first, everything seemed blurry, then quickly took shape and he became aware he was lying down somewhere else. *Where. am. I?* Mathieson found himself inside a smaller room. *I'm alive! Motherfucker.*

Then, he heard the rattle of stone chains, and looked in the direction the sound was coming from. He could see the chains moving and the heavy stone gate slowly dropped to the floor above him. Mat observed as Barbaro closed the gate, then noticed the chain snap and watched as the chain quickly rattled down from its pulley, coming towards him.

Mat managed to quickly roll over, just in time to avoid the impact, as the links broke into numerous pieces of rock.

"Phew!"

Moments later, a loud noise reverberated throughout the room.

Bang! Bang!

The noise seemed louder than thunder in the closed confines of the small room. Outside, a squat creature was repeatedly hitting the gate.

Bang!

The gate stayed in place but there was no respite or escape for the survivors from their new reality. Mathieson jolted up into a sitting position when another forceful impact battered the gate. His heart raced.

Barbaro jumped back in revulsion at the sudden attack.

Harjit and Christopher gasped at the sight of the monsters outside and stepped away.

Bang! Bang!

The smashing continued.

The room emanated a strange kind of luminosity through which they could see one another. Nobody could predict what would happen next. Everyone rallied around Mathieson, who was at a safe distance from whatever was screaming and pounding on the gate at the other side.

Zeeeeaachgggggrrrrr! Zeeeeaachgggggrrrrr! Zeeeeeeaarrrrrmm!

With each heavy blow on the door, the gate fortunately held up. Suddenly there was a loud noise.

Crack!

The creature's bone broke and a vile ooze dribbled out of it. The horrible fluid quickly seeped out of its fissured exoskeleton, and dripped over the stone gate and into the room. A putrid, decaying smell filled the air.

"Eeeagh, yuck!" Harjit jumped back when the thing began clamping its fetid self onto the gate. The gate was completely covered with its snarling foul mouth, which blocked most of the light that might have come in.

"Let's get back from here." Barbaro felt a cold shiver go through him. He wanted to get as far away as possible.

"Mathieson, we do not want you to be a hero just yet!" Christopher smiled at him. Mat had given them enough time to get to safety. Christopher said, "You're a mad, tough son of a bitch!"

"Speaking like a true mother, Chrisy!" said Mathieson, "Christ sakes man, what *are* those things outside?"

"I don't know." Chris replied bluntly, as he paused to look at it. "We are safe for the moment."

"You think." Mat grimaced a smile back to Chris.

"Bloody hell, Mathieson! Too many heroics from you. so, stop it! We need you alive. Got it? Harjit demanded. She admired what he had done and the sacrifices he made to save them. "You bought us the time we needed to reach safety. Thank you, Mathieson." The girl was grateful. She looked at his wounds, which were sore but only superficial. His shirt was ripped and bloodied.

"Exploration" had been a part of Mathieson Stuart's life for over twenty years. His physique—his torso, legs and arms were made of solid muscle, built over time from numerous travels all around the world and in the most inhospitable of terrains. Mathieson was a born survivor.

"How much time do you think we have?" Barbaro looked around the small dark chamber. "Where exactly are we? I'll tell you." Barbaro was annoyed. "We are nowhere, and there is nowhere to go. you have brought us to another dead end! Nowhere!" Barbaro yelled. "Harjit, this is your fault! We are all going to die and those devils outside are going to do it!" He swallowed hard and looked at her. He blamed her for everything that had gone wrong.

Unfortunately, he was right. Everyone was caught inside a deadly trap.

"You wanted to go ahead and not us, remember?" said Christopher as he tried to control his anger against the malicious Vatican official. He was defending Harj. He could have gone the route he and Harjit suggested, but chose not to.

Barbaro looked exhausted. He was battered and bruised, with his clothes torn in pieces. He looked like a castaway. They all did.

"Look, Barbaro. It's time you started dealing with this reality." Her hard tone hit the mark. "So, what about this place, then? Any ideas? How do we get out?"

She was not expecting an answer but wanted him to at least shift his mind towards a less destructive path because, right now, his condemnation and continual negativity would ultimately undermine them all.

The portcullis was shut and secured. The predicament was critical.

For once, Barbaro was not thinking of fame and power. He lay in tatters, like his shirt. The man seemed unable to comprehend what was happening, and acknowledged Harjit with a quick nod. The Vatican official started searching around his new surroundings. Keeping in mind what waited for them outside the room: terror.

****

CHAPTER V

THE FALL OF LUCIFER

They couldn't tell the size of the room, nor how high the ceilings were.

Looking upwards, they couldn't grasp what they were witnessing. The height of the ceilings was not important as they appeared to be quite literally, out of this world — in a place where the finite met the infinite; a place where this world met the next because wondrously and impossibly, they beheld the heavens!

It was hard to pull their eyes away from it. They watched a myriad of sparking stars, all enclosed inside a single room above them. It wasn't a painting. It appeared real and alive with excitement. The floor was mysteriously decorated, and the walls were carved with extraordinary codices and enigmatic symbols.

Curiously, the flickering of light appeared to represent the heavens, the Earth and the moon in orbit. The other planets were also present in their correct trajectories around the sun. Distant galaxies could also be seen, and whoever calculated or extrapolated them, did so with uncanny accuracy.

It was a miracle that this room ever existed. In truth, this "Star Chart" lay in the middle of a pentagonal room—a magical and mysterious place indeed! How could this be? Again, another amazing discovery. Here, inside the MalisIblis Vale, a place at the very end of the Earth!

Specks of different sizes and colours of light infused the heavens and reflected against the walls of the room in a beautiful dance. Luminous gaseous elements, vague shapes and beautiful clouds spread across the sky, creating a wonderful and unique optical illusion of the constellations beyond our own. A vision indeed!

At this moment, they could not tell fact from fiction; yet, here they were, standing on the other side of the door with that thing waiting for them outside. What could be crazier than that?

They were standing inside the very first planetarium on Earth. Not even the sharpest of eyes could distinguish one wall from the next. The best way to perceive this environmental structure was to reach out and softly touch it. This place was known by the ancients who created it as the "Chamber of Deep Wisdom".

To the naked eye, the room could be perceived in any way, shape or form. The codices which ran along the top edges of the room were the only feature that could delineate a linear plane. Yet, who was to say how big they truly were? They could be of any size, with no scale for guidance. Aside from the portcullis, very little was discernible.

All around the room, shone an illuminated typeface. These fonts changed in shape — from a curved design into a sharper more angular font, then into a familiar angular typeface. Christopher gasped at the transformations.

"What *is* this place?" Christopher asked, while looking around uncertainly. "Can we go back somehow? What do you think, Harjit?" he added.

"Don't even think about it! No way, man!" Mathieson interrupted before she even had a chance to speak. "With those things crawling outside? Get real, mother." Mat hastily got up and groaned in pain. His legs gave way, and he buckled into Harjit's arms.

"Let's get you sorted, Mat," she said firmly. "We are not going anywhere soon," she said, reassuring the injured American.

Harjit went straight into "Auto-pilot". With the help of her medical background, she cleaned and bandaged his wounds with the supplies they had left.

His skin appeared punctured around his chest and had been very lucky to have escaped only with superficial wounds. Taking care of him took her mind off their hopeless plight.

"We will surely perish if we stay here. We have no water, no food, and in a few hours, we will have no light. We really need to get out of here."

"We have two torches left, a candle, a partially-filled canteen of water, and a couple of

chocolate and cereal bars. It's not enough."
Christopher confirmed, as he rifled through the
only rucksack that was not jettisoned in their
escape.

Christopher lit the last candle and looked
towards the stone gate. He lifted his eyebrows
when he noticed something was different, then
turned and spoke softly to the others.

"It's gone." His statement was simple. He
walked a little closer, then stopped. He twisted his
face in disgust as he could still smell the creature's
vile scent. "It must be close. I can smell it," he
whispered to the others.

He was right. Whatever the thing was, it
was there and just out of their view. The creature
sat still as a rock, with its legs splayed outwards.
Its many white eyes blinked patiently, as it sat
watching and waiting.

Unknown to the survivors, the outside of
the Chamber of Deep Wisdom was being filled —
and quickly — with even more hideous beasts.
They were entering the lower chamber, and the
place was already packed. The beasts scuttled
around quietly in a disorganised mess, reeking
with their stench.

Christopher was drawn to the rough noises
and the slobbering sounds, and as awful as they
sounded, he couldn't help but get closer. The
closer he got, the shallower and quicker his breath
had become.

The outside repulsed him — almost to the
point of vomiting — but he needed to know. His

survival depended on knowing what was happening. Like a thief trying to escape, he tip toed right up to the barrier.

As he stood there, he sensed something was wrong. Beads of sweat dripped off him. *Oh, this must be bad. God, oh, God, why am I here?* As he looked through the gate he saw the chaos on the other side. He swallowed hard. The odious creatures were everywhere. His heart dropped, and all he could do was turn away. Escaping seemed impossible.

****

"You are a sweet angel, Harj." The girl finished attending to Mathieson's wounds and smiled a little awkwardly. Harj had never seen his gentler side. It was nice.

"What time is it now?" he asked.

"It is one in the morning," Harjit replied, looking uneasily at Barbaro.
He was gazing at the far away stars above them, indulged in thought. She did not want him to go into shock.

"What's up with him?" Mathieson probed.

"I don't know. Barbaro, Barbaro, what is it?" she politely asked.

"These are stellar systems. Look on this wall and observe the constellations. It looks like the night sky over Europe, specifically northern Europe, but not from where I'm looking. Hmm. look there." Barbaro pointed at them. "Near

Cygnus, and there is *Pegasus* also, leading onto *Andromeda* and over here. is *Triangulum,* although it looks a bit different. It has another triangle, a right-angle one above it! There is something inside, but I'm not sure what."

"Oh?" Harjit didn't understand but went with the flow.

"Si, compare this to the other wall. It is very similar and it looks like a continuation. There are more stars that I recognize! I have studied this so many times from the Vatican walls at the printing office of the 'L'Osservatore Romanano'. Here is. *Vulpecula, Equuleus, Delphinus* and *Sagitta* off *Cygnus* again and now *Aquila.* there is *Andromeda too."*

"Pardon my ignorance regarding these matters, Barbaro," Harjit said as the odd-looking man moved his finger along the textured wall. Barbaro was fondly remembering his studies at the Holy Vatican Observatory as a young student. Back then, he was a more innocent man. He was untainted and keen, very ambitious, and at the top of his form.

"Si, *Triangulum* near *Aires* is not far away, but this time, it has only the one triangle and that is what I would have expected in the first place! The other wall is different."

"Bullshit mumbo fucking jumbo," Mathieson grunted, as he stood up abruptly.

"How do you know this, Barbaro?" Harjit asked curiously.

"I have studied astronomy as part of my doctorate studies and still regularly look to the heavens. It is my passion." The man continued, "This wall is a little different to the other. Maybe it was drawn at a different time, and in a different year because when do stars suddenly appear and disappear? To a trained eye like mine there is a glaring difference and the display is too accurate to be a mistake. Look." Barbaro demonstrated again.

"Ok, show me."

"Here, is Triangulum as I know it. And over there, it is without these extra stars!" Barbaro was absolutely convinced as he ran over to the opposite wall. His calculating eyes double checked the difference in these unique 'Living Star Murals'. "I am right."

"It is obvious, man," Mathieson said brashly. "When this star chart was created, the astronomers simply forgot to draw it in, that's all! Those old guys made a mistake on the other wall, man! It's not complicated. It's quite simple. Don't you get it?" the ranger laughed dryly at Barbaro.

"No."

"Mother. The old fools omitted the triangular set of stars. It has to be that!" Mathieson smiled as he attempted to play Devil's advocate to discredit the man's theory. His eyes taunted Barbaro with satisfaction. *Why make it easy for the ass? We are all in this shit together!*

"No, I am sure," Barbaro stated clearly. "What bothers me more is. how these stars could possibly display light. Well. perhaps the light is shining from somewhere inside these walls. What do you think?" Barbaro put the question out for discussion.

"Yeah," Mathieson groaned, he had him there. He turned to Christopher and Harjit for the answers. Chris was trying to piece it all together.

"Could it be possible this is coming from the energy orb we passed earlier?" Chris paused, then added, "I have looked at the symbols above the door." The bio-technologist pointed to the symbols above the portcullis, which read:

⌐ ⋁⌐≪ ⅃ᒐⵈ⅃ᒐ ⅂ⵈ ∩ⵈ⅃⌐ⵈⵈ

⌐⋂ⵈ⋁⌐≪≪ ⵈⵈ≻⅃≺⅂ ∧≺ ⅂∩ⵈⵈⵈ⅃ⵈ ⅃ⵈⵈ⌐ⵈ
⅂∩ⵈ ℇ⅂⅃ⵈℇ ⵈℇ ⅂ⵈⵈ

⌐ ⋁⌐≪≪ ⅃ⵈ∧ⵈ ℇⵈⵈ∧ ⅃ⵈ⋁∩ⵈⵈⵈ
⅃⅃ⵈ⌐

⋁⌐≪≪ ℇ⌐⅂ ∩ⵈⵈ⅃ ⅂∩ⵈ ∧ⵈ∩⅃⅂ ⵈ⅃

⅃ℇℇⵈ∧ⵈ≺≺ ⌐⅃ ⅂∩ⵈ ∩⅂⅂ⵈⵈ∧ⵈℇ⅂
⅃ⵈⵈⵈ∩ ⵈ⅃ ⵈⵈⵈⵈ∩

"I dread these words indeed," said Christopher, as he shook his head. He already knew what the symbols meant. "You should know their meaning as they are important. The symbols say this." his voice became as heavy as an obituary for the dead. "I will ascend to heaven. I will exalt my throne above the stars of God." Chris paused, looking at their withdrawn faces. "I will come from nowhere, and I will sit upon the mount of assembly in the uttermost north on earth."

Christopher became silent for a moment and thought of the word, nowhere. *It means something. it must,* he thought.

"Isaiab 14:12:16, I think." He looked at them with hesitation. The receptive audience waited.

"Chris, are you alright?" Harjit was concerned for him.

"We were not meant to be here, in this place, the Temple," Christopher stated. "Don't you see? This message is a warning not to enter, to go no further. To not go down through this passageway and venture inside." He shook his head again. "It is a quote from the bible about, *the Fall of Lucifer.* Those monsters, they are of the Devil's own making!" He fell to his knees.

"Chris!" Harjit held him up and tried to console him.

"If we had come in this way at the beginning, if we had come in from the top. then, we would have read this message first and not have entered. We would have gone no further."

"No, Chris, no. You are wrong and it's not your fault! Fabio would still have gone through with it!" said Harjit, concerned for his pain, "He is an archaeologist, you are a scientist and this Temple is what he has come for! It's his job. It's what he lives for! Nothing could have stopped him." Harjit stated the simple truth.

"We should not have come here!" Christopher's voice sounded tense. In hind-sight, everything seemed set against them, right from the start!

"Well. in that case, there must be a way out. There must be!" Harjit felt more optimistic. However, underneath her positivity, she bore a simmering blame and an overwhelming sense of responsibility. Her decision to go on with the expedition was down to her. She placed her soft hand on Christopher's shoulder and squeezed it firmly for comfort. Her eyes watered as she looked down at him, shaking her head in sadness. How much more guilt could they all take? How much more punishment? God, just how much more would they have to endure?

****

"Look over here!" Barbaro shouted, pointing excitedly at the star map. "Look at this wall. It is exactly what you would expect to see in our own night sky. And there it is. Orion!" the media man broke their moment of silent despair. "Whoever built this place obviously worshiped the heavens. Everything we have come across in this Temple has something to do with the stars or the planets, the sun or the moon."

"Can't argue with you there, man," Mathieson stated bluntly, "Now, tell us something that will get us out!" Mathieson said sarcastically, but Barbaro seemed unbothered.

"The others represent the three stars in the Orion constellation as you would see through a modern-day telescope. Look at these, they are pointing to Sirius, which as Christopher knows, is the 'Star of Bethlehem'."

"Sure?" Christopher agreed, wondering. *What's he getting at?*

Barbaro went on, "It is incredible, and some would even say impossible, that these ancient peoples are showing us this kind of detail.

"What are you driving at?" Harjit asked.

"This kind of technology has not been readily available to us in the last twenty to thirty years until now."

"So, how?" Harjit narrowed her eyes, slowly piecing it together.

"Exactly, Harjit. That's right." Barbaro knew she had understood. "This place is ancient." Barbaro considered the magnitude of what he had said. *What is this place?* He appeared to be dumbfounded.

Christopher stared at the floor, then spoke, "Bethlehem and Orion play in the '*Son of Man*' in the Gospels. On December 25th, *Sirius* rises above the horizon in Jerusalem, the first such event in the age of *Pisces*." Chris said, feeling Harjit's warm hand. He lifted his head and looked into her warm eyes.

"Si," agreed Barbaro, "the date of Jesus Christ's birth as being professed by the ancients is probably December 25th, 7 BCE, the exact date not quite as noteworthy to its symbolism as the age of *Aires* passing through to the age of *Pisces*." Barbaro concurred.

"The only thing I know of *Orion* is in regard to the Egyptians," Harjit began. "It was their god, Osiris, and their most sacred star, with its brightness rising during the spring equinox, that marked off each new year." Harjit added. "You see, gentlemen, I did listen to Fabio's lectures."

"From where we are standing, it is directly over our heads in this South American night sky. This should be familiar to you — at least its patterns should be." Barbaro continued arrogantly. "Look, underneath is the *Equatoris Scorpius* at -35 degrees 17h near *Sagittarius,* and here is *Capriconus. Hercules, Aquilla,* and *Equuleus* are above the equator at +15 Degree and 21h. incredible."

"What do you know about these?" Christopher asked.

"I would presume they are some other heavens, made up by these misinformed natives and savages. Their primitive ideas are bordering on sacrilegious." Barbaro smirked with disdain and superiority. His pig-headed viewpoint blocked out any new truth or enlightenment. He could not see past his own limited doctrine. It clouded his judgement badly. But the ranger guide had something to say about that.

The Temple was built with great accuracy, and the ancient's attention to detail was evident everywhere. It could be assumed, then that everything else inside this place was there for a good reason.

"The math is simple. it is another stellar system. Remember, *Chariots of the Gods*? Everybody has read it! Except you. motherfucker." Mathieson said, laughing.

Barbaro sneered and this only made Mathieson smile even more.

"Look at this picture on the floor," Christopher added. "It's the Earth, with the sun in the centre. A statement of their advanced astronomical knowledge! The Earth moving around the sun! Even before us, Catholics decided to open for business, eh, Barbaro?" Christopher felt happy to help Mathieson knock the Vatican official off his pulpit.

However, these anomalies were challenging his own faith too. At the end of the world, what would become of his own emerging identity? He looked at the wall Barbaro had observed earlier once again — the wall with the extra stars where *Triangulum* appeared.

"Mmm." Christopher pulled out a notepad and quickly began to draw its shape, then stopped. "Bloody hell." As he wrote again, his hands began to shake uncontrollably with energetic excitement. He had made a new discovery.

"What is it, Chris?" Harjit anxiously probed, sensing a change in him. "What have you found?"

Chris began purposefully pushing his pencil through different parts of the drawing he had done, making holes through the paper. They represented the stars on the wall, which were already drawn using heavily joined lines to make them more visible. He then held it up against the star map so everyone could look at what he had done, but it made no sense to them. The reason the holes did not line up correctly was only part of his enlightenment and demonstration.

"What do you think?" he asked

"What is that rubbish, Chris? It makes no sense whatsoever." Barbaro stated bluntly.

"Yeah, what is it?" Mathieson asked, his energy waning. He couldn't stomach another puzzle.

"Ok, I'll show you. What if I invert it like this?" He turned the paper upside down. "*Now, what do you think?*" Christopher said, smiling. With the paper turned upside down, they could see that the starlight lined up perfectly and shone through the holes.

Only Barbaro understood. What he was showing them was the Freemasons symbol. It was a massive discovery and it was no mistake! Christopher's earlier doubts washed away. The evidence was clear. He had found a direct link between this ancient civilization and our own old fraternity, known as Freemasonry!

What a wonder!

****

At last! thought Christopher, nodding to them. Congratulating himself for proving that the impossible had become at least. plausible as well as undeniable. *I have been right all along!*

He felt overwhelmed at his discovery. There were too many coincidences pointing to the Masons. Here was a place of dark and light, and the Temple was a direct and conclusive link to something unmistakably big!

"It is the symbol of the Freemasons, and based on this evidence, God only knows how ancient this fraternity really is. Could it be that this is where it all began?" Christopher was energised. "Could it be that freemasonry started here, with these olden Stonemasons passing their own doctrine from word to mouth, from hand to stone, and teaching their secret scriptures through hidden codes, then gifting them to our own European counterparts in some esoteric pathway?" he postulated.

The biotechnologist tried to link this South American continent to Europe. *I can see that it is possible.*

"Unbelievable and pure speculation!" Barbaro spat. "A fantasy and a complete impossibility!" he added. "You are making it up, charlatan! Excommunication to you for speaking. this, th. is, blasphemy!" he stuttered from pure rage.

Harjit silenced Barbaro with a gesture and said, "Astonishing, Christopher." The Indian girl recognized that he had discovered something of major significance and of biblical proportions!

"Thanks, Harj, much appreciated," he said, giving her a firm nod and smile.

"Maybe we can calculate just how old this place is, and it might be possible to do so by comparing one star system to the other, without the extra stars. then and now!" her mind was alight with wonder.

"How does any of this help in getting us out of here?" Mathieson needed some answers. All this talk and no action was terrible. He was getting agitated. He then looked over at the gate and swallowed hard. He could see another creature had appeared without anybody noticing. I was sitting there motionless, watching and studying them through the stone barrier.

The hard-bodied beast unexpectedly moved closer as if on cue, but in defiance of the portcullis, patiently stepped back, sat down and continued to wait outside in silence. It seemed to be learning from them.

Meanwhile, other creatures were gathering below as though they had a plan, going unnoticed to those inside the room. Occasionally, a fight broke out among them, resulting in a beast being killed and quickly devoured. That was their way.

Earlier, the beasts had been reckless and were motivated by hatred and the urge to kill the humans. But now, they were learning.

These vile creatures were working together, and were trying to figure out a way into the room. They were continually looking for a weakness in the stone.

Time passed and nothing happened. They weren't going anywhere. They were out of ideas.

Paradoxically, the chamber was lit in calm dim candlelight, and they were exhausted. Some lay quietly, thinking in the glowing darkness. It was a massive room, and the numerous small twinkling spots of light looked to be floating in a galaxy of stars.

Mathieson was fast asleep, sedated by strong painkillers, which Harjit administered. His infected wounds were painful but they were healing.

The Indian girl turned unconsciously as she lay next to the American. She moved in a disturbed rest. She was mentally and physically worn out. The group had naturally positioned themselves away from the entrance of the room.

Christopher watched as one of the candles slowly burned. The smell of molten wax did little to abate the pungent reek of the animal life forms outside. Its hot liquid dribbled and slowly spread onto the stone floor. It was time to change shifts. He gently shook Barbaro's shoulder.

"Barbaro, wake up. It is your turn for lookout duty, pal. It's your turn." The Vatican official opened his bleary eyes.

"Oh. what time is it?" he asked, yawning loudly.

"After three o'clock in the morning. Wake us all up in three hours, but no more. I'm whacked. The door is secure, I checked it earlier.

Those things are still out there, but they aren't doing anything except watching."

"Watching who?"

"Us." he whispered as though in prayer. "Listen, Barb." Christopher's tone had a genuine sincerity to it. "None of us can afford to drop our guard inside here, *ever*. Any hint of movement, any suspicion that those things outside are wanting in, anything happening — anything at all — wake me immediately!"

"You can be sure of that." Barbaro nodded. "What are we going to do, Christopher?" his voice was quivering.

"Right now, I've no idea. We are in a real tight spot. Have some water." The young biotechnologist handed him the water canteen.

"Grazie mille." The man was still not quite awake, even after drinking three of four large gulps. "Is there any more water?" he asked, turning the canteen upside down.

"Nope," said Chris. "Want to know something?"

"What?"

"If you look at these stars long enough, they are almost hypnotic. It's fascinating. Who could have ever guessed this place existed?" He paused, then added, "I kept thinking they were moving a little, in my imagination. I think."

"Si, I'm ready."

Christopher settled onto the uncomfortable stone floor with his head on a misshapen rucksack, the same one Barbaro had been sleeping on.

"This bloody place is completely disorientating," he said, then fell asleep as calmness flooded over him, washing away his troubles from this awful place.

****

The first half hour of Barbaro's watch passed easily. It was deathly silent, and with only that horrible smell to contend with, everything was normal. He looked from one wall to the next with a keen fascination and renewed interest. Standing up, he began to closely examine the impressions on the walls, silently walking around the chamber without paying much attention to where he was going. Soon, he found himself in front of the thick stone portcullis. He stood there, staring at the strange symbols and codices above the inside of the doorway. Doubt began to enter his mind.

This is a prison; how can Christopher be right? he thought. He took out his digital camera. A quick few snaps would do no harm. For a split-second, the flash went off like lightening, followed by the sounds of artificial digital shuttering. Then, the room below lit up too!

Inside the room, everything seemed magnified somehow — the flash, the shutter and the quiet, yet no one noticed and remained asleep. However, something made his flesh crawl. What was it? Something *had* noticed his camera handiwork! Something behind the barrier began closing in.

He felt bile rising from the pit of his stomach, regretting that last shot. A dread spread over him and he began to shake nervously. Something outside the door was approaching him. He was scared shitless.

I must get closer. I must get one shot. He hesitated to get closer but like a bee to the honey pot, he was drawn closer to the portcullis. Then, he heard a noise.

"What is that?" he whispered.

The vicious creature remained unseen. It shivered with excitement. Its hard casing covered other engraved words on the wall outside. The creature began shifting again and this time, moved closer to the human prey. It smelled him and began to salivate.

Barbaro felt uncannily more attracted to the doorway, and in a trance-like state, he inched closer. *I need a better look,* he thought.

He held onto the stone chain with the intention of lifting the stone barrier. *I just need a peek. It can't be that bad,* he thought, wanting to open the gate.

What am I doing!

At the last moment, something happened and Barbaro jerked himself away. Was he coming back to his senses? Or was it his survival instinct, divine guidance or something else, something deeper. a greater plan perhaps? Whatever it was, it literally jolted him out of his trance. Beads of sweat dripped from the sides of his face. He could not believe the suicidal thoughts he had just had. *My God!* he thought. Meanwhile, everyone in the room lay on the floor sleeping, unaware of what had just unfolded. On the other side of the gate, he could hear increased activity. Barbaro's skin was wet with sweat and he felt deathly cold.

****

The strange symbols and codices on the floor were different from the Masonic symbols above the portcullis. The symbols on the floor were also more curved and appeared to be more fluid, almost more thoughtful and less brash than the esoteric sharper Masonic type they had seen so far inside the Temple. The coding stretched along the surrounding ceiling, making the room a paradox of mystery!

Barbaro could not help but take another photograph. It was imperative he had some evidence to take back with him, no matter how risky it might be. This was his job. If they got out alive, then these photographs would be like gold dust to him and would be very, very marketable. No one was awake. There was no harm in taking a few more pictures.

Nobody will be any the wiser, he thought as he looked at their shadowed forms. Above them, colourful, luminous, and gaseous clouds were fanned out in every direction, formed from the galaxies and supernova bursts in the heavens. *What a picture,* he thought.

Barbaro felt quite alone. *God this is a lonely place. Will anyone believe what we have found here?* He sat down and looked around as he sucked up the magical atmosphere.

Then, casually turning towards the portcullis, he felt as though he had walked into a wall or touched a red-hot poker when he suddenly came face to face with a hideous creature.

"Ah!" he shrieked loudly. Without him knowing, the thing had stealthily attached itself to the gate, holding on by its scaly legs. He was about an inch or two away from it.

A long, flexible proboscis came stretching and probing at length through the stone squares, trying to get at him.

"Aaaagh!" he screamed louder as he staggered backwards in despair. Losing his balance, Barbaro fell and hit the floor hard. Everything went black.

****

Out of nowhere, something big suddenly struck the stone portcullis hard.

A tremendous clatter sounded, and a sudden impact hit the gate with the power of a locomotive.

The whole room shuddered. Whatever was outside, began hammering relentlessly at the gate,

Page 134

causing everyone to lurch up with a start. They were under attack!

Crash! Crash! Crash!

Boom! Boom! Boom!

Their hearts raced to the beat of the banging. Unknown to them, something bigger than any of them had ever seen before was banging on the door.

The room was dark. The candle had gone out a while ago.

Incomprehension reigned supreme. Why was the floor shaking beneath them? Inside the reverberating room, the sudden and sustained attack had worked, sending them into total confusion and rising fears which caused their legs to tremble. Fuelled by fear and adrenaline, everyone started shouting.

"Barbaro, Barbaro, you bloody *idiot!*" Christopher was enraged.

"What?" Barbaro's voice was laced in terror.

"Why did you not wake me?!" the scientist protested, "The candle is out! You fell asleep, fool!" Christopher looking desperately around at the others and said, "Is everyone ok?"

"I am sorry! I am so sorry!" Barbaro kept squeaking while rubbing his sore head. The banging at the gate was so loud it hurt all their heads.

"Is it an earthquake?" shouted Harjit, struggling to think and be heard above the surrounding clamour.

"No, this is coming from inside the Temple, I think," Christopher stated.

"I have a torch!" Mathieson shouted, switching it on and scanning everyone's death-filled faces.

In the light, Christopher could hardly distinguish them. Everyone looked haggard and dirty with untidy hair, and the men had all grown a heavy stubble. This strange environment was influencing them as they had all become completely unkempt within a matter of hours. Even Harjit looked worn out and tousled.

Boom! Boom! Boom!

"Thunder?" The noise was relentless. Christopher hoped for a better reason than he suspected, but it was only a faint hope. Armageddon boomed its almighty presence. Nobody could deny that.

The impact was so loud they could not quite pin-point the original source echoing around them. It was drowning out their senses!

"No, in that case, we must be near the top of the Temple!" Harjit concluded.

"We might be." Barbaro agreed, his voice was urgent with alarm. He had messed up big time and knew it.

"No, it's not that!" Harjit knew the answer.

"What the hell is going on, then?" Mathieson wanted immediate answers.

"I did not fall asleep," Barbaro said defensively.

"That's not important," Christopher fumed, now turning to watch the portcullis. It had to be coming from there.

Harjit looked at it as well, then they all turned towards it. Unexpectedly, the thundering noises died.

Relief, followed by an unnatural quiet calm came over them. Yet, inside their eardrums, the echo's kept reverberating. They looked at one another with trepidation because they knew something else was about to happen. An unnatural tranquillity was building.

"What have you been doing then, Barbaro?" Christopher had not forgotten the media man. He stomped over to him and grabbed hold of his hand, which held the camera.

Christopher forcefully retrieved the camera from Barbaro's hand and upon seeing the images, Chris possessed all the hallmarks of a mad scientist.

"I was only taking some historical photographs. *sorry*. This place is unique, and we need to record as much evidence as possible. It is the find of this century!" he defended.

Christopher studied Barbaro's small digital photographs which showed the Earth and the symbols within the white pentagram that were drawn on the polished floor. He looked at the strange flowing text that ran along each edge, making him even more curious. He recognized the ancient shapes from his esoteric studies as a priest. He understood these were *symbols of good* and nothing remotely satanic. In fact, nothing could be further from the truth!

Christopher's analytical brain began deciphering the mysterious codices and symbols on the floor. He then compared them to the images from the camera. *Surely this cannot be right.* The young man was more confused than ever. *How can this be? They are different, they really are! And that's plain impossible,* he thought, shaking his head.

"This is incredible. The symbols on the floor have been transcribed from whatever they were, a different set of alien symbols seen here on the floor, and then translated into what I understand to be Masonic symbols inside this camera. Have a look at the digital image. Compare them if you don't believe me."

Christopher held out the camera for everyone to see.

"Trickery," Barbaro mumbled in denial.

"*And*, I can do better than that."

"Eh?" Harjit was confused.

"I can also interpret them, see!"

"See what?" Mathieson wondered.

"Impossible," said Barbaro.

They all moved towards the centre of the room to look at the images on the camera.

Subconsciously, they all grouped themselves inside the real pentagram on the floor, as if they were huddling around a campfire for protection. It was strange and unspoken, but it seemed like the right place to be.

"None of this makes any sense to me. We have been dreaming this, all of it!" Harjit was finding it all to be too much; a bad dream was the only logical and rational explanation.

"Look at these curved codes," Mathieson said. "They are transcribed into code in the camera. This mother's been right all along! Son of a bitch, *they are Masonic!*"

Christopher smiled and acknowledged their mutual understanding. But Barbaro would have none of it.

"Not Masonic!" Barbaro said, trying to ignore the evidence. "Impossible, they just look like Masonic, *but* they must be something else! I insist you accept Fabio's ideas. The professor is right, *not this. what you say is sacrilege!* This interpretation is only a coincidence and nothing else!" Barbaro's voice accelerated into a crescendo, and his mouth twitched.

"I think Barbaro might be correct, Chris," said Harjit, supporting her adversary. *How can this be true?* she thought, desperately trying to adjust her mind-set to these new mega implications. "Chris, you are wrong."

Christopher looked disappointed but still had an ace card to play.

"Fine, believe what you want, but I do not agree." Christopher shrugged their criticism off but persevered, "But explain to me how I can understand exactly what these symbols say." Christopher waited, scanning their confused expressions. He found it difficult enough to accept his ability for the truth himself, but there it was, staring right at him. He might not understand what the ancient words mean but he could interpret the text almost without thinking. *"I can read them!"*

Bang! Bang! Bang! Bang!

Thundering noises reverberated all around them once again. Renewed violence struck the gate and with such ferocity, they all jumped and shrieked loudly.

The clatter ramped up more than they could stand, and the room began to shake with each cataclysmic strike. Something out there wanted to get them.

Boom! Boom! Boom! Boom! Boom!

Something was coming for them, that was certain. The noise was constant, laborious and relentless, and like a machine, whatever it was, would not stop.

"Bloody hell. Torch! Torch! Quick! Quick!" Chris screamed nervously at Mathieson. "Point it over to the gate, man. At the Gate! Come on, come on!"

Mathieson moved quickly, knowing their lives depended on speed.

The sickening sounds of dry cracking stone reverberated in their ears.

Then, his torch light illuminated the portcullis and surrounding walls.

"Motherfucker," Mat cursed.

"Oh!" Harjit called out.

"God, it's breaking!" Christopher watched as visible long shards like black tendrils grew all over the walls.

Their eyes fell upon one long crack that wriggled along the floor, with offshoot branches expanding from it. The place looked as if it were going to collapse inwards.

Boom! Boom! Boom! Boom! Boom!

Their shaky torch beams followed the crack as it moved towards them, when suddenly the stone lattice began disintegrating. Lumps of irregular shapes and sizes were battered out in seconds. What once had been a solid stone lattice was now crumbling and breaking as easily as polystyrene, snapping before their eyes. *Earthquakes are nothing compared to this,* thought Mathieson.

"Whatever it is, that motherfucker is pissed off!" Mathieson scowled. "It's the same damn thing that exploded through those big gates below, *remember?* Where the dead soldiers in chainmail were lying in all that rock? It has to be, man, we just haven't seen it yet!" his voice was full of fear as he spoke.

Smaller bits of stone began flying, made twice as lethal because of the darkened room. The noise of large lumps of stone falling to the floor frightened them even more. Mathieson started shaking his weakening torch to keep it alive. Panic began to set in.

"And they were all killed!" Barbaro was reaching his breaking point too.

"It's collapsing!" Mathieson kept his eyes on the gate. He watched the solid stone collapse like a sandcastle against the tide. The portcullis had been their last hope.

"Not now, man, not now!" Mathieson was desperately trying to keep his torch alive. What would they do in the darkness? Terror gripped him. The light crackled and turned back on!

"Come on! Come on!" Christopher called in utter despair.

Something evil must be working against us. Christopher under severe pressure steadied his nerves. He knew clear thinking would be their only hope. *Stay cool, stay cool,* he said to himself. *Think, think!*

Chris was desperately trying to see what was really causing the destruction. His eyes fell on Barbaro's camera.

It must be that; the answer must be in the images. They must have some meaning. The answer must be here. I cannot believe that God has forsaken us. God, wills us to live. Otherwise, what else has all this been for? Unless it is our faith that is being tested in full, I will be with the Lord this hour!

Christopher felt unworthy and wondered whether this was their hour of judgement; yet, he firmly believed that none of them should die like this. They were meant to be in this place, and ill fate would not be their end.

Hold onto hope! Trust in God and have faith! He still believed.

"I don't think we were meant to be here," Chris stated bluntly.

Crasssshh!

The remnants of the portcullis blasted inwards, bouncing away the last of any resistance from its frame along with parts of the outer wall. Their bodies froze in horror as they watched the tectonic violence. Now, no barrier lay between them and the outside.

they knew that whatever was out there had to be something gruesome, something evil.

"Man, get ready. I don't know what the fuck did that, but those *"things"* are still out there!" Mat stared at the wreckage. Mathieson shouted and braced himself. This was it.

****

Armageddon condensed into one single room, but through the obliteration, Christopher

Page 143

ignored what was going on around him and instead, began narrating the ancient text he saw before him. He spoke the following words in a loud, clear and steady manner and with truth of conviction:

"LOOK TO YOUR OWN HEAVEN. STRETCH TO THE STARS AS THE CREATOR IS LISTENING. FOR LINKS THAT WERE ONCE HIDDEN ARE NOW BROKEN. THIS PLACE OF KNOWLEDGE IS KNOWN, AND DOOM COMES TO MEET THEE. THE CHAIN MUST BE REMADE IN SECRET AND NOT SPOKEN. HERE INSTITUTE THE LINKAGE TO GODS CHAIN."

Armageddon grew louder towards a grand finale.

Batter, Crash! Batter! Batter! Crassssh!!!

Everything was gone and nothing remained of the barrier, leaving everyone standing helpless and completely alone. No sooner had Christopher finished his forlorn narration that a sweeping supernatural gale blew clouds of dulled white and grey powder laced with darkness into the room. What had once been a rock-solid bastion against an enemy, disappeared into a heap and ruin.

Then, a new horror made itself known. A monster just out of view called from beyond the open entrance. Its uncanny howling froze their spines. Its threat was primordial and spellbinding, and melted their minds in terror. The gale kept blasting into the room with the force and power of a sandstorm.

They shielded their eyes and mouths against volumes of copious dust. They could hardly breathe. Everyone was coughing spasmodically, and the dust made it difficult to see anything. How much more could they take?

Christopher felt spiritless; they had no chance against such odds, and the words he had spoken did not help. He had failed.

"God, guide me!" he shouted against the storm. *What does it mean? What else do I have to do?* Chris's despairing thoughts transformed into a last defiance, "What else have I to do?" Then, he called for divine help. "GOD! GOD! What else have I to do?"

Christopher coughed harder than ever, his thoughts waning as hopelessness began to overpower his will to fight.

That was the way the Temple was. It was like an evil consciousness and he knew it too. With a burst of rebellion, he stared directly to where the threat would most likely appear.

His heart beat faster. He had done everything humanly possible, but there was one last thing left to do: fight. He thought of Harjit. Fight to live!

"Whatever is doing that is well pissed off, man," Mathieson repeated. He had one hand on his puny sword, with its deep unexplained luminous blue edges, glowing brilliantly. They all knew this spelled trouble. He held his torch up, trying to squeeze a little more energy out somehow.

They still could not see what had caused the destruction. Then, Mat's torch burst into life, shooting a beam at the blowing white cloud around the wrecked structure. Suddenly, the turbulence and howling stopped.

Everything settled uncannily and what remained of the portcullis doorway was gone, obliterated. They all stood covered in dust, and out of ideas. Everyone was numb with terror, but knew it was not over, not yet. They all waited. Christopher looked at the media man.

"Ok, Barbaro, which star is *Sirius*?" Christopher asked calmly. "Look, I will lift you up to touch it. I don't know why, it's a guess, and there is no time to explain, so just do it and put your faith in God." Barbaro looked dumbstruck. "*Come on! Think! Which star is Sirius?*" Chris abruptly grabbed Barbaro and launched him into the air and towards the sky above them! Time had run out.

Barbaro looked for the three stars in Orion's Belt and found the one star he was looking for.

While Barbaro was elevated, the others stared in horror at the demolished gate. A gigantic arm appeared slowly from outside and came down with a heavy thump. The limb resembled solid stone but the creature was made of living tissue.

Whatever it was, it had taken little time to destroy what was left of the barricade.

"My, God," said the media man when he touched the one star. Simultaneously, several of the other creatures ran inside and began scurrying around the room like excitable dogs. Two quickly became three, then four. Everyone watched in horror.

On seeing their prey, these vile predators came running at them without any thought or care, when something unexpected happened: they stopped short as if commanded by their master. Like bloodhounds, they sat waiting for further instructions.

"What are they waiting for?" asked Christopher.

"That," Harjit confirmed tonelessly.

"What?"

"Waiting for that. Phew!" Harjit repeated loudly.

****

They all watched as the hellish monster squeezed inside the sacred room, breaking everything around it.

Crassssh!!!

They tried to protect themselves as best they could from the rocks that flew around them. The creature entered through the rubble. Unexpectedly, it stopped and sat down onto its monstrous hind legs.

Mortified the horror-stricken, the group began moaning curses at it. They could not believe what it was. They stared at the heinous creature, dreading what it was going to do next. Strangely, the huge beast was staring straight ahead at the opposite wall. Either the thing was unaware of where they were located, or it was not too clever.

Nobody knew what to do, and not wanting to disturb the outlandish creature's thoughts, they said and did nothing. They could only guess that the creature came from one place: Hell. But they would soon find out they were wrong as it had come from a place much, much worse. It had come from *Nowhere*.

They jolted unexpectedly when its long beak echoed a few pulsating noises straight at the wall and through the darkened room. It sounded like short claps, a sort of sonar, causing their stationary profiles to be picked out in the room. Their hearts thumped against their lungs, knowing this was not going to end well.

It now knew exactly where they were, as it turned its huge beastly head to watch without seeing; its movement creating dry noises of grinding stone with sickening clarity.

Its hideous triangular shaped head was almost kite like—long and angular with a long-tapered snout that began protruding towards them. The monster had no eyes.

Barbaro perceived something in its demeanour.

"Curious, its head seems to exhibit a permanent smile!" They saw what he meant. The monster began slowly turning its colossal rock-like body in the same direction as its head. "Strange. It sits like a dog," Barbaro said.

The enormous creature's forearms had no hands or claws, only blunt and tapered limbs used as large cudgels to batter and pulverize anything into a pulp or rubble, including a solid stone wall. Its thick powerful hind legs somehow managed to fold underneath its large and hard exoskeleton. The monster was truly incredible.

The huge beast deceptively hid its greater agility than its evil subordinates in front, the smaller creatures still waiting in a formation as if on guard. The huge creature was obviously the 'daddy' of all monsters, superior to the smaller sub-forms in their evolutionary chain.

As the monster opened its awful mouth wide, it made them all flinch. The stench of rotten corpses immediately hit them, souring their faces. Chris was still holding Barbaro up.

The Vatican official touched the one star as he uttered strange words that made no sense to him. Magical words he could not stop himself from uttering.

Sensing a sudden change of equilibrium in the room, the monster rose, expanding its hard body, and lifted itself onto its two massive hind legs, its height nearly touching the ceiling.

Its many layers of outer exoskeleton grinded dryly while it moved, opening outwards to reveal a hideous and enormous orifice from its underbelly. Shocked, they watched this nightmare unfolding before them. It would be over soon, the thing prepared itself.

Eeeeeeeeeeeeeeeegr!

The monster bellowed a final high-pitched death call, while snapping madly with its long beak at the heavens above in utter defiance of order.

"Get ready!" Harjit screamed a short warning. Everyone cringed and listened to its bone-dry plates sliding under or over rasping layers, emitting smelly powder from its exoskeleton which caused it great pain. But it loved pain and thrived on suffering from the moment it existed.

When it opened its hideous beastly mouth, everyone could see a vicious set of malicious black teeth inside and an uncountable number of probing tongues wriggling about wildly like a bag of fetid worms. The malformed beast released copious sickening cracks as its body grew. The creature readied itself to leap.

Like a starting gun, the sibling creatures instantly moved in a pack, fanning out, to quickly stop any escape and mop up any juicy remains. Their jointed legs shook with excitement. There would be no escape for the humans, not a piece.

"Watch out, watch out! It's going to jump!" Christopher screamed a last warning.

He needed to protect Harjit. Everyone was standing inside the small pentangle in a protective huddle. Helpless against such might and just like Christians in the lion games of ancient Rome, they would die horribly. The monster sprung, with its mouth wide open.

Barbaro dropped down in a heap, and in a split second, swiftly lifted his blue-edged sword and pointed it straight up as the monstrosity of death launched its huge body through the air.

Chris was screaming out in fear and defiance. Harjit was closing her eyes. All they could hope was that it would be quick. Like an out-of-body experience, the sky suddenly rushed down towards them, pressing their horrified faces flat against the heavens above. It was a physical feeling, the mind-numbing pain of asphyxiation. Nobody could breathe and they were unable to scream. Their dying thoughts remained for a second too long.

I am suffocating, was Harjit's last thought.

The Lord is my Shepherd. Christopher's final prayer was cut short. Then, there was nothing.

****

CHAPTER VI

BASE CAMP

⊔⌐∨□ ∟⌐⊐·⌐·⌐

Christopher's encrusted eyes slowly moved in the blackness. His eyelids were joined by hardened matter. Tired, so tired. His heavy lids flickered open, snapping the tiny crystals to see! Cool smooth air wafted over his haggard face, massaging it gently, looking skywards and with no memory, his blank mind taking in the fullness of this great transition.

Harjit moaned quietly. Her shallow breathing no more than a fairy whisper. Gradually becoming aware, as she watched the night sky and its seamless transformation into morning and daylight. Uncaring, almost accepting everything for what it was, she lay at peace with no antagonism or fear. There was only simplicity and a calm settlement.

Fatigue and time seemed like nothing, yet their senses steadily became more aware of things. Sounds, smells, and the natural noises, such as birds chattering and animals screeching. All around everything seemed to be getting lighter and fresher and gradually stirring their spirits. This place was unrecognisable yet, it seemed so familiar and almost like a place they had been *forever.* Exhaling with a comfortable sigh, they all wondered: *Is this Heaven?*

The group was partially hidden in a thin layer of ethereal mist, which came and went and mixed with the elements. It had been swirling around cocooning and healing their bruised and batter bodies, and with the sun, the light clouds began dissipating and the precipitous gas quickly left their limp bodies exposed to the sun's early morning warm rays. Moisture rose and blew away by the clean air, leaving the rest of the rainforest unseen below, while up on the top, it felt as though they were floating on a bed of air. Soon, this too would evaporate all the way down to base camp.

Here, they lay resting below the stone where the sacrificial altar stood nearby, turning to see the sunrise just when it peaked above the Temple top. Harjit twitched and her eyes opened brightly, and she smiled. It felt good.

I live!

They were out! They were free! They were alive!

Groaning a little drowsily, Christopher struggled stiffly onto his feet. His cold muscles screamed in the pain. The priest immediately clasped his hands together in prayer, *Thank you, God, thank you. Amen.*

"Christopher, are we *safe?*" Harjit asked as she stood up wearily and began sobbing. Chris pulled her closer to him and kissed her tenderly on the lips.

"No tears. We are alive, thanks be to God. I love you, Harjit. I love you." Christopher looked at her watery brown eyes longing for him, with his own blinded by crazy mixed emotions. He felt an unbounded love for this beautiful girl.

"Was it all a bad dream?" Barbaro asked, coming to.

"No dream, man. It's a motherfucking nightmare," Mathieson said as he studied his chest wounds. They were real and bleeding. If there had been any doubt in anyone's mind, then this was proof enough. It all happened. Looking at the large stone observatory behind them, they all knew horrible things waited on the inside.

"Let's get out of here. I think a storm is coming," said Christopher, glaring southwards. They could see fast moving clouds coming their way and eating up the early morning sunshine.

"You look awful, Christopher. Your beard," Harjit said raising an eyebrow.

"Eh?" he muttered, staring at her awkwardly. *What does she mean?* He didn't know he had grown a beard.

"Well, it got really big," she said, caressing the side of his beard.

Christopher smiled, realising what she meant. He could not believe it either. His hair had grown so quickly. Something strange had happened inside the Temple, something that nobody could explain.

The friendly smell of burning wood came to them in the breeze, stimulating a pleasant memory. They could not see the smoke as it lazily drifted upwards through the low cloud formation. They all smiled. Thank God for base camp!

Their short-lived happiness evaporated like the mist below when suddenly a queer feeling came over Harjit, almost as if a shadow suddenly clouded her heart. Then, she smelled it—the rotten stink. They all smelled it.

"Chris, down, everyone, down!" Harjit yelled. They all crouched down and watched as a strange flying reptile-like thing flew lazily in between their view, gliding along in the smooth air eddies.

The creature with sad eyes absorbed all things moving above and below. The flying beast began shifting and lifting its body high above the green canopy hidden by the clouds. *It was 'DEATH'*. The forest noises quietened down while the unearthly creature passed.

It vanished just as quickly as it appeared. The war-wearied group descended through the newly grown vegetation on the Temple terraces, with the green and brown foliage hiding their grim discovery. One thing was very clear, they must leave this place.

****

Harjit's team knew nothing of Fabio's successful outcome. His incision into the depths of the Temple had been dangerous and very successful. Fatigued, the group dropped down the steep Temple steps, observing that algae and moss had reclaimed back their territory. Shrubs and vines competed over the lower tier and soon the tattered group passed the entrance into where their fateful exploration had begun.

On their way down, they could hear the natural sounds of irate screeching monkeys in the trees, looking across at the surrounding treetops. Everybody felt utterly spent. Distant thunder could be heard. It was closing in fast.

Their minds were on the awful days spent inside that place, the Temple. And with shredded nerves of miscomprehension, they tried to assimilate just what had happened to them. Losing two companions—each one a gut wrenching loss. It still seemed impossible. It was impossible. Yet, it had happened. *Everything had happened!*

Guilt preyed on their minds, and with battled wits close to insanity, everyone had witnessed too much and had seen the grim horrors inside those walls. At this point, insanity seemed like a good place to be—a comfort. With two team members dead they were shell-shocked and reluctant to talk to each other about what they saw, just in case. They had reached the jungle floor wondering if anyone would ever believe what happened as they approached base camp. Did it really matter? Maybe they really were mad?

"It looks like Fabio's giving another lecture, folks," Christopher normalised. "He will be surprised to see us!" He smiled at the others. Everyone could make out Fabio's distinct and polite voice, edifying the expedition inside the large communal tent as they quickly approached.

"Just wait till I get my hands on that mother. He just about got us all killed!" Mathieson's temper was teetering on a knife's edge. He wanted to give the expedition leader a good slapping.

"There is no doubt about it. That rat knows much more than he lets on. His 'Gracious' will hear of this trickery," said Barbaro. The press officer agreed with his disgruntled companions. Everyone was livid with Fabio. He should have informed them about the real risks.

Barbaro was doubly miffed because the Vatican press office had held back vital information from him and had to assume they must know more about the mission, leaving the expedition leader to spoon-feed them. They needed to know the risks and to prepare them properly and prevent unnecessary deaths. Barbaro's thoughts were only on retribution.

Fabio must know more. He must! God damn him. He is getting the blame for this, just like his predecessor and I. I will make sure of that!

The group moved through the foliage towards the mumble of voices coming from the large marquee tent. They could hear laughter getting louder, then it waned as Fabio continued talking.

"It's a motherfucking party, man. For fuck's sake." Mathieson was angry.

"I am only too glad that we are still alive," Christopher said. "What happened to us back there?" His voice fell to a whisper as he observed the Temple. "It seems so surreal sitting there. Shit, I can hardly believe it myself!" Christopher's eyes clouded for a moment. He felt disowned and forgotten.

"Aléssandro and Cesaré are gone, Chris! *THEY ARE GONE!!!*" Harjit blurted out at him. She was almost in tears, as she squeezed his arm for fortification.

Harjit inhaled and Christopher's eyes forged into steel. Chris abruptly opened the large marquee flap. With the light fading fast and the storm clouds moving in through the vale, they stood and watched them inside for a moment. It was time for the truth.

****

Endrissi sat inside, his solid frame relaxing with his hands comfortably behind his head, his chair at an odd angle with his feet outstretched on the edge of his table, rocking gently. The geologist seemed happy enough. The others sat around preoccupied with their own thoughts, after listening to another one of Fabio's not-so-riveting lectures. Everyone quite unaware of their arrival.

The professor sat facing Endrissi. Fabio looked curiously at the heavy man's face changing like the weather. The expedition leader was confused as to why Endrissi's expression had become openly shocked.

Endrissi was the only one to see them arrive. The geologist wobbled and jerked into a collapsing heap, and unceremoniously fell to the ground, screaming as if he had seen a ghost.

"Aagh!" Endrissi shouted and hit the dirt. He was scrambling and looked foolish. Everyone started laughing at him.

A strong gust of wind began to blow inside. The surprised group turned around to see Christopher stepping forward through the gaping flap. Fabio twisted around to see what was going on when the others stopped laughing. The hilarity was instantly killed, dead.

"Lord above!" exclaimed Fabio, while taking a deep breath in. "Christopher, you have returned at last! I am so very glad." Fabio's pallor flushing pink behind his beard. The man looked genuinely relieved. "Where have you been? And the others?" he asked, gauging the man's demeanour. This was the last thing he had expected to see.

Christopher said nothing and just held the flap protectively high. Harjit entered and stood for a short moment, spellbound. Thunder clattered heavily, followed by wild forked lightening. It ignited the brooding darkness. Their arrival brought by a storm. Harjit and Christopher were lit up in a flash, with their bodies silhouetted against the elements. They had returned.

Dirty and bedraggled, the group stood in their threadbare clothes — some with bits of material hanging off them completely, while others in tatters. Unkempt, each person was more akin to a vagabond than an explorer or scientist. All wearied, scratched, bruised and bloodied. The men inside the tent jumped to their feet in alarm. *What the hell had happened to them?*

What an entrance, Fabio thought, shaking his head. The surprised professor stood up from his chair and walked briskly to meet them. First, he hugged Harjit. Next, Christopher. Utter relief spread across his face. He welcomed them all inside like long lost friends. The others quickly gathered around, patting their backs, shaking hands and laughing. But the newcomers did not laugh.

"I cannot believe it! Welcome back, my friends, welcome back! A sight for sore eyes and my goodness, your clothes! What has happened to you?"

Fabio grinned with euphoria as though a great burden was lifted from his shoulders. The men who had been passing time with Professor Mancini were happy too.

"Nice tailor, Chrisy boy!" Endrissi laughed as he looked Chris up and down.

"Si! Look at you all!" Fabio called. "I am overjoyed at your return, but you are all such a mess! Oops, apologies my dear, Harjit. I am not trying to offend you. You have been gone for such a long time and you're all torn to pieces, and well, the men are rather... how shall I put it nicely? Hirsute!"

"No offence taken, Fabio, we are all very tired and need food and a proper night's rest." Christopher looked wearied. The others were ready to crumple from exhaustion.

"Si, I understand. What is wrong? And where is... ?" Fabio's face solidified. A few people were missing.

"Mathieson is hurt," Harjit interrupted, "he needs immediate medical attention. My equipment and my drugs are in the wooden crates. I will need these brought here right now." Fabio acknowledged the emergency at once.

The professor knew the girl was different somehow but could not put his finger on it.

She has changed. She's harder and more confident. Fabio wondered what had happened to them and respected his own good choice in a leader. *Harjit has matured in such a short time, overseeing her group and she commands with such ease, contrary to my initial summation. I made an excellent choice in her!* The professor admired his own decision-making process with satisfaction, and mentally patted himself on the back.

"Mykola and Sebastiano, go and bring Harjit her supplies." The men fetched them immediately.

"Thank you," she said, although she was still steely eyed and suspicious and held him responsible.

"Where is Aléssandro and Cesaré? Are they outside?" *Something is wrong,* he thought. Fabio's mind was wrestling between dread and panic and his bearded face dropped. What was coming wasn't going to be good, and judging by Harjit's expression, the professor guessed things were worse than that.

Endrissi and Barbaro helped Mathieson over to a hammock. He dropped inside, making it swing back and forth like an out of control pendulum. He let out a forlorn groan as they made him more comfortable.

Fabio guided Harjit to the side and sat down with her. Christopher quickly joined them. They both had bad news to tell and watched as Fabio's face changed colour.

****

Kees was on cook duty and was preoccupied with preparing ingredients for their meals. There were more mouths to feed now. Mykola spoke to him.

"I don't know if I can stomach this shit of yours much longer, Kees." Mykola shovelled another mouthful of jungle muesli into his mouth; washing it away with watered-down powdered milk.

"Stop whining, Myk. More coffee for anyone?" Kees joked, looking around at their mute smiles.

"Our own provisions may last another four weeks, then we start to hunt again, or better yet, a drop-by parachute would be nice, only if our Heavenly Father wills us to eat. They know where we are." Endrissi was hungry too, and likewise did not want any more of that rabbit mush Mykola was eating.

Nuts and berries were in plentiful supply in the rainforest, but now that Mathieson was back, and with his' hunting skills, he was a great source for fresh meat—he was a natural. Looking regretfully over at the still hammock, they would have to wait until his wounds healed. So, rabbit mush would have to do for now.

Waterproof clothing pegged near the door entrance was continually wafting in the strong breeze as the men sat debating what to have for lunch and dinner today. Sadly, life at base camp had come to this: monotony.

Fabio brought Harjit and the others up to speed by giving them a brief resume of what had happened and how they had returned to look inside other easier parts of the Temple. He also spoke about their achievement in discovering the inner Temple. Fabio began showing Christopher his new maps and where they had been working. There were two main areas: the bridge and certain rooms they had discovered.

His on-going construction of a temporary bridge continued to be a major test of their resolve but was essential. It had to be made safe if further investigations were to proceed inside.

"Say that again?" Harjit's head pulled back in disbelief at Fabio's latest revelation.

"Si, I said that you have been gone three weeks."

"Nonsense!"

"No. Really, you have been gone for quite some time, at least that. We waited for days to see if you would come out. You never did."

"And."

"Sorry, Harjit, we looked for you all, explored in a little further. I deemed it too risky to try and follow you all the way, so instead, I decided to wait and see what would happen while continuing our systematic collation of the Temple. That seemed the safest thing to do." Fabio was defending his inactions. However, he was still eager to hear more of what had happened to her group.

"That's a lame excuse, Fabio," said Harjit, keeping her face as blank as a mask.

"I can't believe this! What you say is untrue. We have only been away a day and a night!" Christopher was angry.

"We can joke about the timescale later," said Harjit. "I will tell you what happened to us inside," she stated firmly.

Fabio was totally serious. He was not smiling. Then, unexpectedly, Endrissi noisily tuned into a small radio station. Lively South American music started coming through, and he moved his head to the catchy beat.

"Ah, quite good, that one." He hummed along.

"Give it a rest, Endrissi." Fabio was overly agitated with the geologist. He should be up at the Temple getting on with his work.

The professor knew that two more deaths would need to be explained to his peers. The mission was finished for sure, but maybe they could make one more attempt before going home.

"When will you have the bridge completed?" Christopher asked Fabio.

"Well, my boy. I would say our expansion has been good considering the obvious hazards. Mmm, tomorrow, you shall see." The professor's relaxed tone disguised his real fears. He had decided, the sooner the better.

"There must be something really special inside there, Fabio. You are not letting on. Come on, spill the beans. We have come here, found this place in the middle of nowhere and, ah, surprise, surprise... that's a pile of bullshit you shovelled us!"

"I say." He was in denial.

"Too many people have died here you son of a bitch!" Christopher cursed him, livid at Mancini's flippancy. It was clear that he and the others wanted answers and the professor's relaxed disposition would not work this time.

"I do not know what you mean, Christopher." Fabio showed no sign of compromise.

"Si, Fabio, Christopher is right!" Endrissi said. "Before, we believed in you. Surely with these latest tragic events you should come clean. *Are you getting this?*" He knew the Professor was holding back. They all did.

"Ok, I do apologize," replied Fabio, stone-faced. The professor stared back at them in a non-committal way. "All I can say is that given the funding from ONCOL and the church, they wanted me to find out as much as possible about the lost Temple. We already knew of its existence, but where it was located was uncertain to us."

"I knew it, son of a..." Mathieson cursed the man, as he lay in his hammock. "You told us nothing! I should kick your sad ass, man, for sending us inside."

"When we came across its whereabouts, it was only a matter of time. It corroborated the old manuscripts that had been kept secret for centuries by the Vatican office." The professor paused to take a breath as everyone listened quietly. "These papers tell us of a terrible power which Christianity has inherited. It is a deep secret. Si, I do apologise."

They all looked like a lynching mob rather than a group of scientists, so Fabio spoke more openly about his purpose; he had to tell them something.

"You apologise?" Mathieson turned angrily towards him from his hammock. "People are dead, man, and you can only apologise? BULL!"

"I know, I know." Fabio could not look at his enraged face. Barbaro smiled, nodding in agreement with his retribution.

"*Inherited*, what do you mean? Mykola wanted to know what Fabio meant. "If so, why is it only Christendom and not any other religion, Fabio? What is so special about Christianity that *it* should inherit this *power?* Why us?" Christopher pressed him for an answer.

"Yeah, I'm Jewish, why not Judaism? We came first?" Mathieson seethed at the professor's closed mind.

"Sounds more like the "Ark of the Covenant." Look, Fabio. I can't go along with this charade." Endrissi waited for the professor to give them more details, leaving Fabio with little option.

"These manuscripts have certain symbols of the cross and the crucifix and therefore relate directly to Jesus Christ. There is no doubt in my mind. That is the truth of the matter. Ah, but the Temple has many secrets and the manuscripts are only indications as they do not clearly explain its purpose or existence. Reading this ancient literature is like reading text in a mirror. It's a reflection *back in time!*"

"More bullshit, man, bullshit!" Mathieson rasped. The American had had enough. Fabio was losing control over the group and knew it.

"Alas, Mat, something sacred and priceless is inside there and we must have it. *My church* must have it first, this is a Catholic expedition. His

Holiness has full authority here!" Fabio's possessed voice grew louder.

"Si, and just how do you propose to collect this, er, power?" demanded Christopher in a soft sarcastic tone, deflating Fabio's increasing ego.

"I, I don't know. I'll think of something." His confidence was under-siege again.

"Look, Fabio, we need to get help," Harjit stated. Fabio knew it too but resisted. "We need to leave here," the girl insisted.

"Can't."

"Why not?"

"For the same reason I could not call for help from outside and then come and find you when your team went missing. The same reason," he lied.

"Which is?" Harjit eyes were like acid.

"The communication link is down. There is a technical hitch, it's been like that for days," the professor lied again.

Everyone's eyes were fixed on him. If they weren't careful he would get them all killed.

The professor's position was becoming untenable, yet he would never give up his authority or ambition for being here. Someday, he would be known as one of the greatest explorers and archaeologists of all time. Even his tone smiled.

The atmosphere had become so tense that no one noticed the tent flap opening behind them. Quietly and skilfully, a group of four or five heavily-armed men wearing camouflaged outfits and skipped hats to match entered.

****

At lightning speed, the trained professionals fanned out strategically throughout the tent and positioned themselves behind the civilians. The first to see them was Endrissi. A few mechanical clicks and the cocking of weapons was enough—the geologist swallowed hard and raised his hands high. The others turned to see what was happening.

Stunned, nobody was quite sure what to do other than stand in silence. The confused scientists were overwhelmed by what looked like a raid by drug traffickers. Who else would be out here?

"Back! Back! Indietro! Indietro!" the armed men shouted orders at them in perfect English and Italian.

The raiders' scanned the room and each target for any unseen risks or threats. If there was going to be trouble, it would be now. They began herding and shoving everyone unceremoniously to the rear of the large tent and were only met with pitiful yells and meek protests—it was nothing. A smaller man in similar combat attire appeared from behind the burly men. He spoke in a clear and concise voice, so there was no misunderstanding.

"I am very glad to find you all together. Now, please raise your hands so that I can see them." The leader drilled sharply into their eyes. "At once!" he snapped louder! Their bodies jumped in sudden shock, their obedience complete.

As he surveyed the expedition members, he smiled thinking, *they follow instructions. That's wise of them. The threat is minimal.*

"What do you..." Fabio tried to ask.

"Silence!" he shouted in response. Fabio shook quietly. They weren't natives. "I am sarvan, meaning captain. captain Abdul-Haleem," he said. The soldier stared at them, their eyes avoiding his. He waved a hand backwards at his men. "These men are part of my expeditionary force." He paused to let the information sink in. "Everyone is now under my security." There was another pause as he selected his words carefully, then added, "and protection."

He scanned the docile group before him to select the person in charge of the expedition. The raider's authoritative voice commanded everyone's undivided attention.

"Sit down!"

They did.

Mercenaries or terrorists thought Fabio. *Strange that they all look Middle-Eastern. That's crazy.*

Without a word, the soldiers raised their weapons a little, instructing them to sit in the nearby chairs.

And they did.

AK-741 39mm Kalashnikov machine guns marked each of them as pointers. They wanted to make sure there was no misinterpretation of who was in ultimate control here. Kees stood up and came forward. He disagreed.

"You have no authority over my government." As he spoke, he was suddenly struck down mid-sentence by a soldier. Kees collapsed with a groan. They had to understand that these men demanded complete obedience.

What the mother? Mathieson thought. He had not been seen and secretly evaluated the potential threat from his hammock, a knife would do or his hands, but the others might be killed. *I must be quick.*

Kees was roughly picked up and dumped onto a chair, as he nursed his stomach.

The American instantly went into survival mode, an ex-seal his stealth like quicksilver and silently moved off his hammock, almost without moving. He dropped to the floor behind the scientists, completely unseen. With great stealth, the American passed to the blind side of one of the outer guards.

Without warning, another larger guard who was keeping watch over the soldier's flank, came out and struck the American with a straight front kick to the chest. The ranger was knocked right off his feet and landed heavily amidst the stunned crowd.

That powerful kick would have been enough to stop a much bigger man, and with his recent wounds, Mathieson weakened lay on the floor staring up at the guard. A sub-machine gun barrel was pointed directly at him. Resistant, he still tried to get up but couldn't. He struggled to fight but his body would not let him.

"Leave him alone!" Christopher called. He and Harjit were shocked at this sudden violence. The guards took a few paces back and aimed their guns directly at the whole group. Things were not going well.

"Brutes!" Harjit protested.

"Please, understand this," the captain's hard tone commanded. "I demand your full cooperation." The captain's eyes stared stonily at them. His intent was crystal clear and cold.

"Sarvan Haleem," Fabio spoke casually, "by whose authority do you have to treat this peaceful civilian excavation in such an atrocious way? We are an organised civilian project, with full approval of both the Vatican and Brazilian governments, and you have no military jurisdiction in this country." Fabio moved away slowly from his chair.

"And you are?" the captain's Italian was broken but good enough. He managed to seamlessly switch back to English.

"I am Professor Fabio Mancini, expedition leader."

"Professor, it is of utmost importance to avoid any more unpleasantness, so you and everyone else must follow my explicit orders, *exactly*. Now, please be quiet." The captain dismissed Fabio. Then with a snort, added, "Take these guests to the interview room," he said, pointing at Harjit's team. Narrowing his steely eyes at Christopher, he said, "You, pick up your comrade." Christopher listened intently. "Use that wooden board and put him on that. Quick! Do not underestimate my patience, it is very short. I expect your full cooperation or more unpleasantness will follow." He gestured to both Christopher and Barbaro to help Mathieson onto the long wooden board so they would use it as a make-shift stretcher." Then, looking at Harjit, said, "*And you* will come with us."

With a set of quick hand signals, he picked out three of his men to escort Harjit's team away for interrogation. No sooner had these intruders arrived that they were gone, leaving a few sharpshooters on guard duty.

"Do not say anything!" Fabio called out as a last warning to Harjit and the others being taken away.

As they struggled to make their way through the Jungle, Harjit's group had no idea where they were going. Not long after, the last thing they expected to see were a few small makeshift green plastic shelters, about a mile or so from base camp, which were built right under their noses.

The officer in his light green and dappled brown camouflaged uniform spoke in a friendlier voice with Christopher.

"I apologise for my soldier's *over-enthusiasm,* but alas, this is a *most serious business.* We were quite surprised watching your group descend from the IBLIS Temple. I did not think that you were going to come out of there after all this time. I am *most interested* to hear what you have discovered." Christopher looked blankly and said nothing.

In a minute, they were inside a new makeshift accommodation, an enclosed room with no windows. It had a plain spartan interior, and they were warned to remain inside *for their own safety.* There was not much to see, save for a few seats, a table and some uncomfortable looking beds.

Unwell and in pain, Mathieson was back on his feet again. His rib cage was bruised and badly marked. Luckily, nothing was broken. Meanwhile, their captors had allowed Harjit to apply another dressing to Mathieson's chest. Imprisoned for over an hour, they still had no idea what was going on, when suddenly, they could hear hurried footsteps coming closer. The door burst open and to their astonishment, the guards came rushing in, holding a smaller man between them. He was hooded and his legs were dragging on the floor. They threw him down before them. He fell face down and unconscious.

"Our colonel, our *"sarhang"*, you will be meeting him very soon. He will be interviewing you all personally, including *this trash* again. Ah, and he enjoys his work as you can see." The big six-foot five gorilla jeered, showing off his chiselled white teeth. He walked up to each of them and inspected their shocked faces.

The soldier then turned around and banged the door shut behind him. The door locked solidly. The other guards stood just outside the door and listened to him shout blasphemy at them, before he marched off down the corridor. Christopher immediately dropped to help the unconscious man and gently turned him around. Harjit carefully took off his hood to let him breather and gasped in astonishment and disbelief.

"Mashir! Mashir!" Christopher called at him, while squatting next to his bruised and unconscious friend.

Harjit automatically geared up and checked his pulse. She opened his shirt a little to check his vital signs.

"He is alright," she said. "Other than his black eye, no bones are broken. He is beginning to come around. Mashir, can you hear me? Take some water."

"Not broken *yet*," Mathieson added with a tough smile.

With Harjit's examination over, Christopher spoke softly to the sallow-skinned man.

"Are you ok? Mashir, where did you come from, buddy?" Christopher was openly concerned and yet, ecstatically happy to see his lost friend again, and alive.

"Chris, *my friend,*" he mumbled, "*it is good to see you.*" He observed the others, then smiled. "All of you." His voice gained strength and he stretched out his hand to take Christopher's, when the door opened. Two guards entered with blankets, fresh water and a paramedic.

"Make yourselves comfortable, this place will be your home for a while," the paramedic stated casually. "If there is anything else you need — medicines or whatever — let me know now."

"Yeah, man, refill my hip flask, mother!" the American pulled out his empty metal bottle and shook it from side to side a little.

"Hip flask? What is that for?" the small soldier asked.

"Jack Daniels?" Mat said grinning, knowing he had no chance, but anything to make these guys look foolish would do.

"Ah, alcohol, spirits?" the soldier stared at him quizzically.

"Ah, yes. Alcohol helps wounds, it is good medicine!" Mathieson grinned even more. For a passing second, he coolly measured the possibility of grabbing the man's sidearm. It could be done, *maybe* while he appeared preoccupied with this odd request. *But it would need to be unclipped from the holster.*

There was no chance of overpowering him either, considering another soldier with an AK was trained on them.

"No, I am not allowed. We are not allowed to drink alcohol or condone its use." The man looked cynically at the American's attempt at circumventing his charge, oblivious to Mathieson's opportunistic mal-intensions. The guard departed.

"Try not to antagonize the guards, Mathieson," Mashir said sternly. "*They mean business.* And you, my God, you are in bad shape, my friend. What has happened?" he asked, staring at Mathieson with considerable concern.

"They mean business, *what business is that?* Who are these stuck-up sons of bitches anyhow? What do they want from us?" Mathieson wanted to know more, and Mashir would tell them for sure.

"Why are we prisoners? I do not believe this "guests" crap. They have no right to treat us like animals!" Barbaro protested.

"They don't look like terrorists. I think they must be the Brazilian Army." Mashir guessed.

"We have permission to be here, we are a scientific exploration. We have our papers and our project is ratified at the highest level. Kees will vouch for us, of that I am sure," Christopher said, justifying their right to be here.

"Well, they seem to see your rights a bit differently," Mashir countered.

"No, they are Middle Eastern. It's easy to spot, come on," Barbaro stated the obvious.

****

For the next hour, both Christopher and Harjit relayed their unbelievable exploits inside the Temple to Mashir. He could only shake his head; incredulity seemed topmost listening to their tall tale. Their ragged attire did not convince him of their narrow escape from the Temple, but the dead men disturbed him deeply. Why would anybody make up such a sick story? Something had happened, of that he was sure, but their story was simply too impossible to believe.

"If this story was not being narrated by you, I would assume everyone was suffering from a *communal hallucination* or was a part of some cock and bull conspiracy. But I know you all too well for the latter. So, either you need professional help, or tell me what really happened."

"Come on, Mashir! Do we look crazy?" Christopher shouted.

"Mmm, it is a very hard sell to believe you, my friend. *Come on*, you expect me to believe that a large ball of light is located somewhere inside the Temple, that wild creatures and poisonous spiders roam loose and all the rest! Something has befallen your minds, all your minds! What you speak about is impossible, a figment of your exhausted imaginations. Hallucination of this kind is more common than you would know, especially if you've been stuck inside a place like that." The man was not convinced.

"I know, I would feel the same way in your shoes. So, what about you, Mashir, what's your story? You disappeared from camp, and where did these henchmen come from?" Chris needed to know.

"As you remember, you were handpicked by Fabio to enter the Temple. Having time to think, I wondered what would happen if some fate befell you inside, where would that leave us?"

"*Yes, and?*"

"So, I decided to see if I could find a way out of this vale, get away and look for help. Unfortunately, a mile down the trail, I discovered a freshly cut path and well, curiosity got the better of me. I followed it and stumbled across this place! And that, my friends, is all I can remember until I came to."

"You were mugged?" Harjit asked.

"Someone must have hit me from behind. I felt a hard object strike me and when I woke up, here I was."

"Bushwhacking motherfucker's," Mathieson cursed.

"I have not seen Fabio and the others since they went into the Temple. I have been kept here all this time and in complete isolation, beat up and quarantined for over four weeks, until now." Mashir's relief at seeing his friends was obvious.

"*What? Four weeks!* Have you got amnesia? Surely you are mistaken!" Harjit's surprise was obvious.

"More like sensory deprivation," Christopher added.

"We have only been away *two days!*" Harjit continued. "Remember, we entered the Temple on the morning we split from Fabio and spent one night inside, followed by the next day. It's difficult to recall another night. I am not exactly sure what happened. We were being attacked and we were overwhelmed by something." Harjit's furrowed forehead showed her conflict. "Oh, I cannot describe what really happened to us. Next thing I know, we woke up on top of the Temple." Harjit found their experience too difficult to articulate. Something big was missing and she knew it. Mashir kept shaking his head at her amnesia. "I'm telling you, it was only two days!" she blurted angrily.

"Harj is right," Chris backed her. "Everyone lost consciousness and fortunately, awoke the next morning, but we came to *outside the Temple!* Two days and nights, really that is all it was. *Not four weeks, Mashir, come on. Do you think we are stupid?*" Christopher said as he realized just how crazy their story sounded.

"That's not what I said. Yes, attacked, lost consciousness, but monsters? You are all suffering from amnesia. You are all wrong!" Mashir looked at them in disbelief. *They're hiding something, the amnesia must be a feint.* Mashir did not believe them.

"I know what happened, *that is enough.*" Christopher raised his eyebrows.

"Look at my watch." Mashir wanted to prove his case. "What day and time is it?" he asked, lifting Christopher's wrist. Wrist to wrist they compared each other's watches. "It says today, 11:30AM, on the *twenty ninth of October!* You entered on the first of October, remember?" Mashir's bold voice demanded their agreement. "Look again. Yours, is the same as mine. *Yes?*"

"It can't be true, it just can't," said Harjit, feeling lost. Mashir observed their faces as shock and disillusionment washed over them. He had made his point. Mashir saw their defeat, but did they agree?

"Really, my friends, you have been gone a very long time. Didn't Fabio tell you?"

"My watch reads right and keeps perfect time. Er, Fabio said something, but then we were interrupted by those goons with guns."

"Something is wrong with my watch too," Mathieson agreed. "It has stopped."

"Mine has not stopped but quickened up in some weird way," Christopher said, looking confused.

"It is obvious, Mashir. *It's you and your watch* that are mixed up," Harjit concluded. "All your watches are fast, yours too, Chris. They must be and Mashir, it is you who are suffering from amnesia. Not us!" She looked directly at the Iranian, considering another possibility. *If he has been assaulted, then who knows what other brain damage has been done to him.* "Here, let me look at your bruised face, Mashir. It is quite puffy." She regained most of her composure and confidence. But Mashir would not give up.

"Christopher, have a good look at your appearance, and you too Barbaro. Except for Mathieson who is clean-shaven, all your facial hair has grown long, really long, has it not?"

"*Si*," Barbaro agreed, feeling perplexed.

"When was the last time you cut your hair, Mathieson? When did you last shave, Barbaro? Christopher, *please*, for the sake of Allah, take a good look at yourself!" He turned to Harjit for corroboration. "What does he look like, Harjit?"

Harjit was speechless. The girl knew that his observation was correct. They had become so used to each other's company. She feared what the real truth might be. *What happened to us inside there?* How could the men have longer beards and long hair? Her hair had grown too. *Incredible, what could be the explanation?* The others were silent.

That was good enough for Mashir. Even Barbaro said nothing, as he scratched his long stubble.

"This is impossible! Check your watches everyone. Let me look!" Harjit was still in denial. The girl roughly grabbed all their wristwatches.

Staring at her own, she believed it to be true. Her watch's second hand was still ticking too, and normally, and the date was *exactly two days after entering the Temple.* Her date showed the *third of October.*

"My watch was given to me by my father. It is an original Omega, and a perfect mechanical timepiece. It keeps perfect time and has always run flawlessly, and still does." She swallowed. "It is self-winding and has not stopped."

No wonder Fabio looked so surprised to see us if what he says is true! We have lost over four weeks! My watch is analogue; theirs are all digital and affected differently by an electromagnetic influence like the compasses somehow in the Temple. But my timepiece will not suffer from the same interference, unless he is lying. But, why would he lie? Yet Chris' is the same? Something is not right. This is not right, she thought.

"Our watches have suffered from the same malfunction. Mathieson's and mine. The Temple must have done something to all the electronics, slowed them down until they stopped? Yours, Christopher, I've no idea," Barbaro postulated, staring at the time differences.

"What about mine then, Mashir? This is the third of October and it runs perfectly," Challenged Harjit.

"It's mechanical. It stopped and has just started working again. It must have! Your watch is unaffected by the environment." Mashir had no other plausible explanation.

"We slept one night only and escaped the following evening, and that makes it only two days ago! None of this makes sense!" Christopher said.

"As I said," Mashir persisted, his tone soft and quiet. He needed them to understand.

"That place is full of weird and dangerous happenings. It is completely alien and that energy ball, motherfucker. What was that about?" Mathieson exclaimed to the others, while holding his chest in pain.

"Sorry, I really do not believe any of it." Mashir stated coldly. He knew the truth. "You all have had a nasty accident or experience. It has made you all lose account of both memory and time."

Mashir's blunt expression studied their scrambling explanations. *They are hiding something else, masquerading a secret. Mathieson and Barbaro could, but not Harjit or Christopher. Surely, not them!* Mashir thought as he pulled at his short beard.

"Christopher is right!" Harjit was angry.

"Look, my friends forget it," he said, appeasing them. It doesn't seem worth it anymore. "I am just *so glad to see you all!*" Mashir's soft voice sounded earnest. He looked around and smiled warmly at them. He took Harjit's hand and said, "I am sorry."

At that moment, the door opened.

"You!" the soldier screamed, pointing his sub-machine gun at Mashir. "Come with us!" he ordered.

"What date is it?" Mashir quickly asked one guard.

"It is the twenty ninth of October. Now, come with us!" He prodded Mashir out the door with his gun. Mashir looked back. The date was confirmed.

"What do you want with him?" Christopher pleaded. He could not understand why his friend was being singled-out again.

Mashir cast a fraught look back with apprehension and shrugged meekly, he had no choice. He wanted his friends to know the correct date before he was taken. This was important.

"All is as God wills it!" Mashir shouted defiantly. The door closed. Mashir was gone.

****

After lunch, Mathieson's wounds required redressing again. With the help of the medical officer, Harjit tended to him. It looked like his injuries were getting worse. Even small cuts can end up quite serious in a jungle environment, but this wound was quite different. The cruel injury was more enflamed in parts and poisoned in others. The hardening of the skin was becoming more apparent with ragged white edges. Mathieson suppressed the pain as best as he could.

"There you go, Mathieson, finished. I have applied different compounds to the other antibiotics I gave you. It should take a little while to work. By this time tomorrow, we will see a marked improvement."

"Thanks, Harjit," Mat said weakly, nodding to both the girl and the medical officer who had applied a new field dressing onto his chest. Minutes later, his sleeping tablets kicked in.

Taking Christopher quietly to the side, Harjit whispered to him so that the others could not hear.

"It is really bad, Chris. There is light green pus forming under his skin. The wound keeps on weeping. Yet, his skin structure itself is becoming too dry and hard, desiccated on the surface as if it's mutating and changing into a more brittle texture. It is only a matter of time. Unless we get him to hospital," she swallowed, "Mat will be dead in a week."

"My, God." Christopher held back nausea.

"Look, we need to get him out of here. Can you get someone to help?" she was at the end of her tether.

"I will ask again, Harj, but that captain does not show much human compassion. I will try."

"No, no, you don't understand, Christopher. Demand it. *They must listen to you!* We do not want him to turn into," she gulped and paused, while lowering her tone, "one of those, *things.*"

"You don't think?" There was a tightness in his throat. "Harjit, I have an idea. I have stored my specimens and cultures safely away and some are completely new antibiotics, ones previously undiscovered. They are a remarkable new species of plants and herbs as I hoped to find here, some I have tested and some I have not. They all show incredible healing properties even without any synthesis and refinement inside lab conditions.

The jungle is so diverse, real discoveries are made here and they all have completely natural healing qualities! Of course, the only testing I have done is on, well, the raw material on, er, *myself.* Unethical, I know. It was my call but these might help!" he whispered back.

"Where are they?"

"They are in crates and ready for shipment from base camp."

"How do we get them?"

"It is a long shot, I'll have to try." Christopher needed to come up with a way to escape from their containment and retrieve his specimens and return.

The Scientist looked around the room and surprisingly, found at an oxy-acetylene gas cylinder with a gas torch. It had been stored there carelessly behind a partition. They moved the screen over to the door and anything else they could find to insulate any sound. It was very risky, but they had to do something.

This was the perfect time because they could hear the storm getting wilder outside and with luck, this would disguise their activities. Christopher knew how to use this kind of equipment because he was once involved in building a church in Ecuador a few years ago. They moved the cylinder into position by the wall and ignited the torch.

The walls were made of heat resistant thermoplastic, so they would not catch on fire but the material could not with stand the intense heat generated by the flame. Muffled against the rage going on outside, Christopher worked fast and with clinical incisions, sliced a hole big enough for him to get through. He switched off the torch and knocked out the cut piece with a swift sharp kick.

A gale instantly began blowing inside the opening. Christopher took a quick look outside and into the darkness. Evening had come again, and one could sense the trees waving around them in the noisy storm, thrashing foliage wafting wildly around. Any movement in the jungle like this was dangerous. It would be hard to avoid getting hit by leaves and branches. However, there was no time to lose. Chris stepped outside and without hesitation, stole away into the forest. Rain began pelting down heavily, with thunder rumbling above. Soaked and feeling instantly tired, this rescue had become another nightmare.

****

CHAPTER VII

DÉJÀ VU

Christopher crouched among the wet rich foliage. Small trees shook around him. The forest was becoming more precarious by the minute. Shrubs moved back and forth by the turbulence, and the noise made the conditions perfect for his escape. Christopher's passage went unnoticed in the darkness. He realised he had a mile or so to travel and anything could happen between here and base camp. He knew he had to be quick.

Following the same trail back, he eventually made it. Christopher quickly searched his own tent to find a small portable wallet full of tools. Equipped, he would use a long screwdriver as a lever to open one of the wooden crates that was in the campsite out of sight at a pre-planned pickup point, ready for pick-up. That time had not come yet. These would be untouched and intact.

As the main scientist, he had worked meticulously, collating and packing his specimens away safely and securely. He knew exactly which crate to choose. Each crate was carefully packed with dried leaves for protection. Chris easily chose a smaller box containing a set of specially sealed glass vials and glass petri dishes with growing cultures.

Before recent events, he had used mortar and pestle to create various thick pastes and liquids containing the base ingredients for the synthesis of new compounds, drugs and cures. He had already tested some of their biomedical healing properties and by pure chance, discovered a type of regenerating substance from a new species of fungi. After that, he was able to simply extract the elixir's goodness, testing it on a bad wound of his own—an old one he sustained many years ago while working in Ecuador. It had been a red scar, and was now completely healed.

The elixir exhibited a rapid curing and restorative skin growth ability, leaving no scar tissue. His four-inch scar had healed within a few days of application. It was a phenomenal and natural product, and it wasn't an antibiotic. Christopher postulated that it may turn out to be the next big alternative to the increasingly resistant diseases, and would provide a modern range of new drugs and cures. Just what he had been searching for. This is what he needed right now.

He placed three vials and one sealed glass petri dish carefully inside a spare rucksack for safety. The job was done!

In a moment's time, he was looking around cautiously and avoiding guards as he quickly ran through the turbulent pathway. Soon, he was once again approaching the secret encampment. Seeing the small buildings, he could still not believe they had been built right under their noses. With a bit of luck, nobody would know he had been away. The storm was still providing him excellent cover.

He quietly tapped on the opening in the side of the plastic shelter, and popped it out easily. As he stepped inside, he suddenly looked up. *Oh, shit.* He was looking directly into the barrel of an AK-741 39mm Kalashnikov assault rifle.

"Out for a walk, are we?" a sarcastic tone asked from above. Christopher's spirit sagged because he had been caught. "Do join us," came another soldier's brimming voice from the other side. Chris slowly moved inside, when a long arm grabbed him hard and with a quick jerk, pulled him forcibly inside.

Chris was sent sprawling unceremoniously inside with a *thump*. As he looked up to see who had pulled him inside, something crashed down onto his head. Darkness overcame him as distant sounds of sneers and curses faded.

****

He woke up hours later. His head hurt *badly*. It was pounding like a hammer on an anvil and he felt the blood rushing into numbed cognition. His sight was out of focus. As he came to, he became slowly aware of people and strange voices around him. He *listened*. Soon, he realised the voices were speaking to him.

"Our commander has been delayed. He will want to talk with you." Christopher focused on the strongly built soldier force-feeding him instructions that he could hardly understand. His head was still fuzzy, and he barely acknowledged him. He hoped he would go away.

"Ugh?" Christopher muttered.

"So, these things inside the bag are what you ran off for, are they?" the soldier continued to question him, opening the rucksack and precariously holding up the glass vials in one hand, and his rifle in the other. Christopher and Harjit gasped!

Subdued at gunpoint, Christopher narrowed his attention onto the vials as the big ape-of-a-man attempted to interrogate him, appearing to be preparing to drop them.

"Don't do that!" he shouted, then observed a hardening of the ogre's eye. "*Please*," he said, quickly softening his concerned tone, "I am a research scientist and those are my delicate samples. They are essential medicines that might heal my friend's wounds." Chris pleaded, while realising the change in himself. *My friend? Yes. my friend,* he thought. Christopher felt a strange bond with Mathieson and one he had not felt before. "His condition is deteriorating quickly, and by the hour. This man needs urgent hospital treatment. You must insist this of your captain!" Christopher's eyes were red with warning.

"Please, give me the cultures and allow us to help him," Harjit said. The soldier realised the importance and with a sharp nod, allowed Christopher and Harjit to take the crucial vials to their friend.

"Is it infectious?" the soldier probed.

"No, it is non-transmittable," came the instant reply, "but I think he is going into a coma." Harjit's answer seemed good enough but the soldier stayed a safe distance. He did not know whether her medical analysis was correct. She understood that a wrong answer here could have proved fatal for Mathieson.

They might shoot him if it were a transmittable disease, she thought. *Stupid, that would be too late in any case. If it were infectious, then God help us all.*

Using surgical gloves, the two doctors began administering the paste to the American's wounds. Barbaro and the soldier looked on horrified at the state of Mathieson's infection. It looked ghastly.

"My, God! What's wrong with him?" the small media man could not believe his crazed eyes. The red marks were bad enough, but the poison worse still! But there was something else he seemed more concerned about. "What is that, that devilish white crust forming around the edges of his skin, *tell me?*" he asked. "What's going on?" his voice trembled into a whisper. It had to be bad. "His skin is... Lord, he's turning into one of those ungodly things that attacked him!" Barbaro said, understanding what was happening.

Harjit gently touched the surface of Mathieson's raw wounds. She felt it had become leathery in parts and was getting harder, whiter and crystalline. Showing no emotion, she held her breath a little. *His skin is denaturing and metamorphosing. It is only a matter of time.*

Barbaro stood back, against the wall. The soldier watched as Mathieson's skin transformed in front of them, wondering what could possibly be happening. The media man had jeopardised Mathieson's life by opening his big mouth.

Harjit continued to apply a paste made from a combination of cultures provided by Christopher. She had to try something, anything. Mathieson moaned as she began rubbing the substance onto his wounds.

The next few hours became more harrowing because, one by one, the prisoners, with the exception of Mathieson, were taken away by the guards, and were systematically interrogated about the expedition and its purpose! Everyone was quizzed on every detail and about any artefacts found during excavation.

Haleem the captain, and Hashem his lieutenant, both performed the questioning. They played good cop, bad cop. Now, it was Harjit's turn!

"Ha, ha!" They broke out in laughter. "You expect us to believe this! That there are *monsters* and *creatures* inside the Temple? Look, young lady," Sarvan Haleem joked, "obviously the Temple has deranged your female mind. You don't expect me to believe this rubbish, *do you?*" Sarvan Abdul-Haleem's soft voice suggested incredulity and that irritated her even more. They continued.

"Let's go through it again." Abdul-Haleem smiled. He had a nice face, but she would not drop her guard.

"You are not telling the truth!" shouted the Lieutenant, cutting in.

"I am telling you the truth!" she said, striking the table in front of her. "You just need to look at him! Go and look at Mathieson, *he is dying!*" the girl protested. "If he does not get to a hospital soon, you will have blood on your hands, and a party to murder! You and your men have no right, no right at all to do this! None!" her temper flared. The men stared at each other thoughtfully. *Their tactics were working.*

"Control yourself, woman, watch who you are speaking to!" the Lieutenant threatened. His sharp fiery eyes and long burley beard shook back and forth in anger. The soldier appeared as if he had lost his own composure, listening to an infidel and a woman too. He lifted the back of his hand to strike her.

She braced herself for the impact, but it did not come. Instead, the man banged hard on the table, making her jump. The man was trying to intimidate her, but she calmly tucked her hair behind her ear and did nothing. She would not be frightened or intimidated by these brutes.

"Why are you here?" she asked the bad cop. "You are not Pakistani. Are you Iraqi or maybe, Iranian? Who are you and why are you here in South America?" He ignored and instead, roughly escorted her back to the communal detention room.

During Christopher's questioning, he feared violence would ensue. So, he cleverly responded to their questions as if he were on a TV game show. His answers were quick. Chris suspected that once they knew everything, the expedition would no longer be important. Their captors would kill them by dropping them down into the mines, leaving no evidence. So, he spoon-fed them misinformation.

The soft-spoken Abdul-Haleem did not fool the would-be priest with his polite good manners underlying his menace. The captain persisted.

"How long were you inside the Temple, Christopher?"

"I told you before, I'll not tell you again!" he said, feeling frustrated. "You have kept us prisoners for far too long! All we want to do is go home. We are all really tired." He implored, while running their motives through his head. *They are looking for something specific. But what? Fabio knows more about what's going on.* Christopher knew they were mixed up in something big.

"I will let you go home. First, however, tell me again, how long?"

"Ok, ok we were inside the Temple for two days." The interrogators were sceptical. "*What? Do you not believe me?*"

"No," the man stated bluntly, his eyes hard as pebbles.

"Why not, why all the questions and what is your authority here?" Christopher said, trying to delay the inevitable bullet.

"It was longer than that, *priest.* You are a priest, *are you not?*"

"I am a man of God."

"You were inside over three weeks. Stop lying, you are a disgrace to your cloth!! *Is that not a sin* in your religion?" Lieutenant Jalil Hashem kept pressing him for the answer. "I want the truth! I want it, now!"

"God will be my judge, not you." Christopher answered softly, daring to defy him, although inside, he felt a growing self-doubt in his own sanity and his own faith in God. Everything was being put to the test.

Christopher's mind darted deliriously between supposition and logic.

The evidence, our watches, Mashir's time. Was he right? What happened to us inside there when we were unconscious? How did we ever end up on top of the Temple? Is it possible to "touch time"? Were we away longer than a few days? Why are these soldiers here? Why are we here? There must be more to it, there must! Yeah, Fabio knows much more.

He was brought back to reality when a hard fist hit the table.

"Wake up! Wake the fuck up!" shouted the soldier. Christopher had unconsciously dropped off. The interrogation had been drilling on for hours. But he had fallen asleep, totally exhausted. "We have full authority to be here!" the man shouted down at him. "Anything found inside and around this site is rightfully ours, and anyone caught inside this sacred place is a trespasser!" the lieutenant said, justifying his actions. Christopher lifted his heavy head.

"God has authority here, not you," he said.

"You will draw a map of the inside of the Temple. Here, on this pad of paper. It will determine whether you are telling us the truth or not. I will compare it to the information already provided by the others." Sarvan Abdul-Haleem then passed over the paper to Christopher. "If they are different, then," he mimicked having his throat cut. The young scientist could not believe what was happening. He had no option but to comply. He felt sick as he dosed through waves of heavy tiredness.

The captain might be bluffing. If I give in, then he and Hashem and the rest of his ugly crew will kill us. Sleep forced him to think recursively, then it went again in spurts.

If they have the information already, why don't they go into the Temple right now without us? Get rid of us and be done? What is the purpose of these interrogations? They must need us, for now.

Christopher's body was exhausted and his fatigued mind was at a cross roads. He was unsure what to do next. He had no choice but to give them some information and play their game. Maybe then, if he complied, he would get some sleep. He slowly picked up the notepad and began shakily drawing a basic schematic. he looked up and nodded. They smiled, *good.*

"Very well, look, I need some sleep. It has been a while and *this* is going to take some time. I may not remember everything if you keep breathing down my neck. Why don't you go into the Temple and check the place out right now based on this diagram?" he said, holding up the paper.

"You have specific knowledge, which might assist us more. There are many traps inside. With your assistance, we can move quicker and avoid any pitfalls and traps. You have agreed to help us, correct?"

Christopher nodded again but had decided to draw a map of the Temple incorrectly, thinking the worst, *when they are ready, they will kill us anyway.* His pencil stopped moving. Christopher wanted something in return.

"What about Mathieson? He needs proper medical attention."

"We will see to it," confirmed Sarvan Haleem.

"Sarvan Haleem, this is a place you do not want to enter." Christopher could not explain why but he still wanted to warn the captain even though they were enemies. His men would die inside.

"If you are thinking of drawing the map *inaccurately*, do not," the captain warned sternly. "You will be coming inside with us," he said, while observing his reaction. Christopher's face was full of terror.

"No, you can't!" Christopher shouted in protest.

"Yes, and any wrong turns, there will be *no medical aid for your friend.* So, be under no illusion. My men are not like me, ah, how shall I put it?" he searched for the proper words. "They are not compassionate as I am. Be advised, if there are any inaccuracies in your documented plan, then your friends will be shot." The captain's levelled voice held no illusions to their fate.

"What if I get it wrong? The place is colossal and dark; I cannot remember every turn." Christopher's words came out in accelerated panic.

"Have something for me to look at when I return," he said, leaving Christopher with nothing to bargain with. He had to comply.

****

Time passed, and Christopher worked fast as he jotted down various sketches and diagrams as best he could remember. An hour passed when the soldiers returned with the rest of the team. The captain quickly grabbed Christopher's rudimentary plans and studied them eagerly.

"My superior has ordered me to take you all back into the Temple. It will be your new home for a short while. He thinks that this will help boost all your memories," the captain said. Everyone was horrified.

"Oh, no!" shouted Barbaro. "We cannot go back! This is complete madness! It is too dangerous, you cannot imagine these devilish creatures. You just can't! Those things are inside and *waiting for you too!*" Barbaro shouted, then fell to his knees.

"Get up!"

"You will have to drag us!" Christopher protested more.

"Then, we will."

"Captain, listen to me, please," Harjit said, attempting to reason with him. "We lost two friends inside the Temple, and one at the mines. Surely, this tells you something! Show some mercy for pity's sake. It is inhuman."

"This is outrageous! You can't treat us this way, captain!" Christopher shouted and marched towards him.

Harjit ran to intercept Chris. As she grabbed him, the captain pointed his weapon directly at him. Further protests were futile but tension remained high.

"I have my orders." His monotone voice held no compromise, he was not looking for understanding.

They were outnumbered. A group of twenty soldiers, all fully armed with weapons, began roughly herding them into the jungle and back forcibly towards base camp and the Temple.

The small group of explorers felt a great fear build at the horrors they had witnessed inside the Temple.

They haven't a clue, thought Christopher and would have liked to smile, but smiling was the last thing on his mind because he had taken a great gamble and slightly changed the diagrams. On route back through the jungle, Christopher caught the attention of the captain.

"I urgently need to speak with your commander, captain. Is that possible?"

"My commander will see you inside the building. This relocation is for your own protection," captain Abdul-Haleem advised his guest. He gave a semblance of a smile towards Christopher. *Yeah, pull the other one, pal,* thought Christopher.

Once they passed base camp, they began to climb the many steps of the Temple. The uneasy group reached the first tier. The entrance was guarded by soldiers with AKs, who gave them a cursory look, before going back to scanning the forest. Christopher wondered what they were looking out for.

Their captors ushered them inside the Temple and into room E1L1RM2. It was a dingy room, chartered and already labelled by Fabio's team. Fabio had been industrious. This was one of the few rooms that had been studied in fine detail by them over the past two to three weeks, while Harjit's team mysteriously went missing.

Christopher, Harjit and Barbaro were shocked to see that the rest of the expedition was waiting inside. In the dank candlelight, they looked as if they were on the brink of a breakdown. This was all that remained of their colleagues and friends.

Luckily, Christopher's version of the internal structure reflected some degree of accuracy, having briefly spoken of it with Fabio before being made captive by these henchmen. Once they were reunited with the others, they all began comparing notes.

Fabio believed, as did their new hosts, that Harjit's team was suffering from communal amnesia or severe memory loss, which was due to living off basic rations to keep them alive inside the Temple. How they survived was in their opinions nothing short of a miracle. The professor wondered some more.

I just wish they would tell us the truth. Mathieson had an accident and is not well. They got lost, these things happen, but the rest, my God. The other men are still inside somewhere, dead. Shocking.

Shaking his head, the professor assessed the injured man in disbelief. How could they do this? Fabio knew he would find out eventually.

"You said you found Mashir. We thought he was lost or had run off!" this news surprised Cesaré, the man who was glad to know that the surveyor was still alive.

"He is in good health, aside from being roughed up by those goons," advised Chris, while

Endrissi sipped a cup of coffee as he watched him. Christopher continued speaking to Fabio. The others listened to his story.

"Listen, they think we have something, something fucking important. What other reason can those goons be keeping us prisoner for, eh? Fabio, come on, man, we are not stupid! What are they looking for? It is time to tell the bloody truth!" Christopher said. Fabio said nothing, and his silence was not good enough. Barbaro began shouting irately at him and pointing his finger like a weapon.

"Si, Si! We were all nearly killed inside this place, all because of you! It is more than dangerous; this place is pure evil and you sent us in!" Barbaro screamed.

"Come on, my good Barbaro," Fabio said patiently, fending him off. He needed more time to think, and to consider how to make up another story.

"Bullshit! Fucking bullshit!" Mathieson's voice exploded. The ranger sat up. He had listened to the conversation long enough, wincing as he sat there holding his chest, his skin rasping pain, and creaking like old leather. His gaze cut through the professor with impatience and fury.

"Mathieson!" Harjit yelled, running over to him, "How are you?" She could not believe it. He was conscious again.

"One hell of a headache Harjit, but other than that, I feel not too bad." Turning again to the professor, he said, "Ok Fabio, man, spill the beans before someone else dies or I'll kick your son of a mother's ass." The American meant it. Christopher's remarkable biological paste had worked. Mathieson was back to his old self!

"This is a strange place, and these are strange times, and our expedition is on the brink of greatness," Fabio pleaded for patience.

"Yeah, sure, buddy boy. *Fucking, and?*" Mathieson was enraged. This was the moment of truth

"We heard the rumour of a Temple and roughly where it might be found. The area was completely virgin and unexplored until now. This was my chance," Fabio began. "The Company, ONCOL Corporation, and *your employers*, were in possession of an ancient Spanish manuscript. I have not seen this literature myself, however, my understanding is this," he paused.

"Professor, what did it say?" Christopher asked.

"This manuscript has been deciphered and interpreted. It talks about this Temple and describes a secret place and sacred area in a lost region of Amazonia, right here! Incredible, I know. The main problem, provided that everything is true to this scripture, was *timing* and according to our *acquired scripture,* we needed to be here on *this exact year, and here, we are!*" Candlelight expanded over Fabio's shadowed eyes and harrowed forehead. Everyone was enthralled, all except Mathieson.

"Timing, year, what's in this manuscript? What are you looking for besides this Temple?" Christopher prompted.

"It is key information," he explained. "The key to finding something that has been lost for a very long time. I am not sure what it is yet, something very old and very holy. It is inside here and waiting to be discovered. We did not know where the valley was located. And we were unsure what month this manuscript referred to, but our calculated guess was correct. We were very lucky."

"Why does the time of year matter? It exists, it is here, so convince us and stop the—" Harjit was becoming annoyed and suspicious. This sounded like more misinformation, especially after what had happened to them inside the Temple and his lecture on *The Key of the Gods of the Seven Rays.*

"Bullshit! She means bullshit, professor!" Mathieson shouted furiously.

"Our luck was in finding the *Zaplithowatres,*" Fabio continued unperturbed, "It is their story, their legend, and because of them, we found it, the Temple! Listening to them I knew we had to be close!"

A hushed murmur rippled through the company.

"Why was I not told about all this?" Barbaro pursued the unfolding story. Fabio smiled casually to himself, *Who cares* he thought.

****

The soft shadowy light from the lamps hanging from the ceiling and sitting on the table seemed to calm the disturbed atmosphere. Christopher and the other inmates had not been given any time to wash or change, remaining in their old tattered clothes. Grungy and unshaven, Chris knew, once again, that they were in a tight spot.

"This place is ancient," said Fabio. "And there is rumoured to be an object of supreme importance inside."

"What is this precious thing?" Christopher insisted.

"There is an object of ultimate power and of great symbolic importance here, dating back to before the time of Jesus Christ. Yes, *before our Lord!*" Fabio looked at everyone seriously. "What this power is, I cannot say. All I can say is it exists, and it is here."

"Come on, professor, you can do better than that!" Kees had never heard something so stupid. *My Government should know about his ulterior motives and send him and his expedition home!*

"I know, I know. I realise what you all must be thinking, but we are dealing with an older religion than our own. There have been many before Christ. Think to the Egyptians and the Greeks or the Sumerians, to name a few. Incredibly, the Sumerians, about six thousand years ago, described 'a planet of crossing' in our solar system known as Planet X. In scientific circles or Nibiru, the tenth planet. And this planet was *re-discovered by NASA in 1983!* Which makes the ancient peoples great astronomers."

"I have heard a little about this," Barbaro said. He knew many things about astronomy.

"The civilisation who had built this place also had great astronomers and their religions would be much, much older than any I can mention. So, what is so important about this one, you ask?" Fabio seemed to dwell a little too deeply. "This civilisation, had discovered and achieved many things."

Meanwhile, the large stone room felt peaceful and atmospheric, and no sound other than the sleepy hiss of the paraffin lamps accompanied his tone. The darkness seemed to hug around their candlelight and drew them in closer.

"Just get on with it," Mathieson said.

"Sorry, Mat. The people of this ancient race also worshiped one god. This god is not just some arbitrary or pagan god, these hidden manuscripts were passed on through the ages, and," Fabio swallowed, "indicate that their true god is the same as ours!" This was the first time Fabio had become emotional while watching their stunned faces.

"How?" Christopher exclaimed, finding it all too hard to take in.

"There is much more to this tale than I can tell but as much as I hate to admit it, Christopher, *you did link the Masonic symbols together.*"

"Thank you for telling me something I didn't know," Christopher rebuffed sarcastically. "Why, so much resistance against me, then? You were trying to put me off by discrediting me. You had no right, no right at all." Christopher was disappointed in the professor.

"The implications, you see, were that the Freemasons did not come here, they *left from here.* These people, this civilisation, were the Freemason's forefathers!"

"I knew it!" Christopher said. "I knew they had something to do with it." Then, he wondered, *There must be more to this. We are linked! Who were they and what do they want?*

"These people departed a long time ago, or were forced to leave with their great skills of rock-work, long before Jesus Christ was born. They are what is now known as, the 'Brotherhood' and are understood to be the Masonic Order!"

"Phew!" gasped Mathieson. Christopher raised both eyebrows and waited for the rest. "What links these people to us is found in *these symbols?* I will admit that I was too full of my own Catholic dogma to see it!" Fabio said, admitting his own human fallibility.

"Yes, I was right! Why try and put me off?" Christopher felt betrayed and wanted a proper explanation.

"I apologise unequivocally, Chris. You did outstanding work at the entrance, my dear boy. I am sorry for the mystery and pretence, you understand that I had to be sure, I really did." Fabio began whispering in a softer voice. "The Masonic writings are only part of a larger jigsaw puzzle, and these narratives seem to be *a later development in this civilization*. Before these first Masons migrated to other lands, there seems to have been a more noble aristocracy living here long ago.

"What is their one god, then? Is their one god ours? Theirs came first and is the same as ours and *they* are the true children of God! Is that what you are saying?" Endrissi's hints of hesitation belied a worry that the fabric of his own religion was being unwound by Fabio and made *worthless*.

"I don't believe any of this, Fabio. None of this!" Harjit's respect for him was lost. She could not trust him. "Your explanation is not good enough. Damn you, Fabio, our friends are dead because you had a secret! How can you live with yourself?"

"I know, Harjit. I wish that had not happened. I am truly sorry."

"Sorry? *Sorry?*" Harjit could hardly contain herself. Her eyes were red hot and burning with retribution.

"I know, you are Hindu, and your beliefs are quite different," he continued, as she seared. "This Temple is only a shell." The professor spoke softly. "The real Temple is below our feet, underneath this stone. I discovered this. No, sorry, *we*, discovered another Temple build directly underneath the outer Temple." The men nodded in agreement. "This outer Temple is only a casing. It is a Temple, old and worshipped, but this is not the oldest part. We are standing right on top of the original Temple. It's right below us!"

"Incredible!" Christopher was amazed. Barbaro was beginning to find it all just too unbelievable.

"I do not know anything else except this: the Temple has something that we seek, something we must have. It is a precious thing that links us to our own."

"*Own* what?" Mathieson demanded.

"*Our very own existence.* Its discovery will shine a light towards our true destiny and to our one God." They had not expected this. Was this the answer? *Whatever it was,* it brought only silence to their plight. They sat for a while, gazing into the lamp on the table and thinking about their own existence.

Fabio watched them in the subdued light, considering their chances. Christopher sat in a secluded corner away from the others. He preferred to be alone. He opened his journal and began writing:

Déjà vu,

My Journal 30th October Year 5,125...

I wish to God that we had never come to this awful place.

****

The dark shadows inside room E1L1RM2 were like an obituary, compared to the vibrant life outside. This place was their prison, and an abode more akin to a mortuary, harbouring a quiet blanket of slumbering moods. Everyone was asleep when quite unexpectedly, around five o'clock in the morning, the quiet was cut short. The sound of shouting was getting closer by the second.

Everyone sat up in terror. Something was wrong. They heard the soldiers running towards them. It was obvious there was an emergency.

What is going on, they wondered anxiously.

Judging by the sounds they heard, it appeared that the soldiers were busy building something right outside the doorway.

Dismayed, the group looked at each other warily, waiting to see what was going to happen. An hour later, their door flew wide open and several armed guards came inside, grabbed Fabio and hooded him in submission.

"What! Where are you taking me?" the professor shouted. The others called after them but there was no point. They had seen this treatment before, and the chances of seeing Fabio alive again were not good.

Shortly thereafter, this brutal procedure was repeated. They came in for Christopher next.

"Where do you think they have gone?" Mykola asked, feeling terrified.

"I think we are of no further use to them and we are all being systematically *tak, tak*, taken and shot." Endrissi stammered through his accelerated speech. "They are already dead." His legs were unconsciously trembling.

"Think about any news clips you've seen or heard on TV. Terrorists always split up their victims first and then they kill them, one by one." Cesaré was terrified of the next intrusion and kept looking at the door.

"Come on, you bunch of scared motherfuckers, get a grip. If they wanted to do that, they would have killed us a long time ago. They still need us."

"Do you really think so, Mathieson?" asked Mykola.

"Yea, I do. They must!" Mathieson's confident tone helped.

"Look, the next time anyone comes in we have to hit him! That will be the last thing those swine will expect!" Endrissi said.

"*Now*, you're talking!" Mathieson was grinning from ear to ear. They began planning their escape, knowing the soldiers would come.

****

Christopher had been briskly escorted to a lower level and his hood was taken off for speed, as they neared their destination. With two soldiers in front and three behind, Chris had no opportunity to escape. Each soldier was carrying a sub-machine gun, grenades and a handgun. They had also been kitted out with nasty looking bayonets strapped onto their belts, yet his mind was still on finding a way to escape. He felt his time was running out.

The soldiers didn't trust him and pushed him forward from behind, almost knocking him down. When Christopher turned to protest, he noticed the man's odd-looking tattoo on his forearm.

He had a united red crescent moon and golden star tattooed on his arm. *As I thought,* he thought to himself. This confirmed that these men were not South American. *Drug runners, maybe. There is a sizable Middle-Eastern community in this country too, terrorists. God, that must be it, they are going to kill me. They must be. Do something, anything!* Christopher was trying to think, when unexpectedly, everything went black.

"Umph." Christopher dropped with a groan.

Christopher woke up with a nasty headache—worse than a hangover.

"Ouch!" he shouted. He had a lump right on the back of his head. His eyes began to focus again and began to hear a distant echo of speech.

"Christopher," a voice resonated inside his brain. "Christopher. Are you all right?" The tone seemed to be becoming in clearer and sharper. "Chris, are you ok? Yes, he is coming around now," said a female voice. It was Harjit's.

"Let's help him up," instructed Fabio.

"Wooch," Christopher moaned, standing up shakily with help and looking for his missing colleagues.

Where are they? What is this place? Fuck, what's going on.

As Christopher sobered up, he remembered how Fabio had described a unique white stone structure, found below the Temple. Now, here he was, in this structure, surrounded by the dim light of the candles.

He could see soldiers prohibiting anyone from falling into a dangerous gap in the floor. They were on guard duty. Four soldiers stood attentively on either side of the opening leading into the passageway and entrance. It led out and up to the outer Temple.

He noticed they were not watching them, but instead kept their gaze on the place high up on the opposite wall.

Fabio, Harjit and Christopher stood between them and the inner Temple, surrounded by AK 47s, and waited for something to happen.

Chris turned to see what the guards were staring at. Their wary eyes were transfixed on a three-dimensional stone carving of the Golden Sun-Face, with its seven wavy protrusions. *Its hypnotic,* thought Christopher, moaning a little from the head injury. Sarvan Abdul-Haleem was watching them, and proceeded to walk towards them, stopping in front of Christopher.

"I do apologise for your maltreatment." His tone hardened to a point. "The men who were responsible have been punished for attacking your person." The Sarvan held Christopher's eye for a long moment. But Christopher barely understood, *Apologies, him, them, what?*

"Inexcusable," said the Sarvan. "In defence of my men, they were not themselves. Nevertheless, there are no excuses for lack of self-control and discipline. I also would have preferred no bonds. Please try to understand that, I have my orders."

Chris could see that there was a man behind that uniform, not just a soldier. He had a human side too. He saw it. He also saw that this place was not a place he liked. The captain felt something else but could not, or would not say.

Sarvan Abdul-Haleem did not explain that his men felt uneasy inside the Temple. There had been unexplained happenings, and fatal accidents since operations had taken place inside the Temple.

Each man felt a strange unhealthy feeling within himself, the same dread the expeditionary team had felt and still did. A feeling like a black consciousness eating from within. The civilians understood but could not explain why it seemed that that the Temple worked against everyone. The soldiers kept nervously looking around and into the shadows for something.

Christopher nodded. The captain's short sleeve camouflaged shirt exposed the same tattoo on his forearm.

"Apology accepted, captain. I have some scratches and bruising and a bloody sore headache, but I will live. This place has an undesirable effect on your men, I agree. It's in the air, don't you think?"

"Thank you," the captain said. "My commander will be joining us soon. We should not have too long a wait."

Fabio, Harjit and Christopher stole an anxious glance at each other, a premonition of what might come to be. The expedition leader could tell something bad had already happened, wondering what awful demise could possibly have overtaken his heavily armed soldiers. The professor suspected that they would never know.

"It is good to see you all again, *even you, Barbaro.*" Christopher smiled warmly. The would-be priest still had his sense of humour. The press officer, stared back and smiled too, or did he sneer? Christopher was not sure.

No doubt about it, Christopher was happy to be alive and especially overjoyed to see Harjit again, she appeared unharmed and in good spirits.

Studying the inner Temple structure from where they were standing, with soldiers in front of the gap before them, he noticed a thin line of red tape stretching wide from one wall to the next to avoid accidents.

"I'm glad you are with me Chris," Harjit beamed.

"Well, this is an eyeful and no mistake." Christopher gasped at how spectacular this place looked.

"You two." The captain's tone changed. He had shown them too much already and exposed his vulnerability. Becoming like iron again, he ordered Christopher and Harjit to face the inner Temple. "Stand up and keep facing the Temple. Do not turn around or you will be severely punished." He was not joking. "Please, listen to me, my comrades." He lowered his tone. "You all have one more chance to tell me everything you know about this place." The man waited, then added, "Has anyone found anything, a gem, a medallion or symbolic object of any description? I beg of you to answer truthfully. It would be most wise if you speak."

Christopher could not believe the sudden change in the captain. The captain was deeply troubled. *What is he hiding?* wondered Chris.

"We know very little of this place," Fabio advised the interrogating officer, then turned towards Harjit, Christopher and Barbaro and said, "I am sorry that you all have gotten into this pickle. It is the last thing I ever expected."

"Quiet! And keep looking forward. *Do not turn around!*" he screamed. "Do it or die." The captain's voice implied instant retribution. The group continued to stare at the moat below.

Could he really? wondered Christopher, facing ahead. Suddenly, they heard footsteps coming closer at a smart pace. It was the commander. *The captain does not want us to see the commander. Why?* thought Chris.

All they could do was think of *the PIT, and what did he want of them? He needed something.* No evidence would remain if these animals decided to drop them, *down there.*

Being shot was cruel enough but *sacrificed* by being thrown into the dark void below their feet terrified them more. The commander stopped. The soldier stood right behind them and they could feel his soft breath. Anything could happen.

"Commander, you cannot just kill us in cold blood," Fabio said softly and almost in a whisper of fear.

"Don't test me," the man replied indignantly, his authority appeared boundless and with bad attitude. "I can do anything I choose." his voice was familiar. He spoke in a very good Italian accent, almost native.

"That would be murder," Christopher stated coldly, and was about to turn around to see their executioner.

"Keep your eyes to the front," the captain hissed quietly into his ear.

"We want to know how to get inside this Temple," The commander's friendlier voice urged. "It seems you leave us with very little alternative. I do not want to kill anyone. We are not butchers. The Temple we know has been recently used for human sacrifice. *So, what. do you know?"*

They stood in silence, making that their answer. Each person indulged in their own private thoughts, fearing to speak further. Nobody wanted to be first to die.

Fabio and the others were now convinced that it must have been this commander and his henchmen who had sacrificed poor Doctor Boni Castiglion. Fabio and Christopher remembered the man's limp and eviscerated body, lying helpless on top of the stone altar. It was, them! Not the natives! The commander continued, with more of his mental torture while the cubed chamber waited too and *listened* as the atmosphere began closing in.

"They say that sacrifice creates an energy field, *a "life field",* in and around these ruins. Death of the body changes from one form to the next, alive and then dead. Energy is not lost, but transformed in the moment of *death.* The soul is a catalyst. It remains unchanged but begins a chain reaction, and with simple physics, every action has an equal and opposite reaction. So, *you tell me."* The commander spoke with acid in his tone. No one doubted his cold ruthlessness.

"Yeah, simple physics," Christopher mocked defiantly.

"I will show you *simple physics* in a moment," he fumed, "the next words *you choose,"* he stated firmly, "choose them wisely, my friend."

His voice held vehemence, then fell silent. The pit waited too, to accept his sacrifice.

"Impossible, impossible, No! Sacrifice us, and you will never get inside, never! I will vow to that!" Christopher shouted in defiance towards the Temple. He wondered, *That voice, it's as if I know it. Clever, very clever indeed, using a familiar tone. So, what is he waiting for? He has not killed me. What the fuck is he waiting for?*

"You have one hour, priest. I will return then, and we shall see." The Commander walked away as they stood motionless, looking at the Temple.

Once the commander was gone, the Sarvan ordered food and water, and took out his bayonet and cut their bonds free. He had advice to give them.

"I am sorry for your discomfort. Please enjoy this last meal, *together.*" But somehow, that last note put them off any thoughts of eating! The captain left them to their thoughts.

Everyone sat on the floor, away from the precarious ledge, with their every move watched on by the guards. An hour would not be long and soon the captain would return.

"Those bastards killed Boni. Murdering swine!" spat Christopher.

"Maybe. He did not say that. He only mentioned he had knowledge of the doctor's death, and his understanding of sacrifice. I think he only wanted to scare us," stated Barbaro, as if he understood how to torture minds.

"Well, it worked. I think they did it!" screamed Harjit.

"He'll be back soon, then we'll know," Fabio said, shaking his head.

"Where and what is this place?" Harjit asked, more confused than ever.

"I have been here before in my earlier excursion. My dear girl, when you went off gallivanting through the Temple, I discovered this place with the help of Endrissi Giuliani and Endrissi Bergamaschi, less than a month ago. It seems like ages since then." Harjit and Christopher were pained at this lost time as he continued, "I found it strange then, as I do now. I never thought that I would or could say this. The Temple is a place of real mystery and indeed, if you wait here any length of time, it somehow emanates a feeling of self-doubt inside you. The atmosphere chips at your confidence and frightens mere mortals from being here. This place works and weaves into your psyche." He paused and nodded towards the guards. "Observe them, do you think those guards are overjoyed at being stuck down here? Do you?"

The guards looked scared, *scared stiff.* The soldiers were speaking quietly to each other, some shaking their heads as if debating a conflict or having an internal struggle.

"I feel it too." The others agreed. "It is the same feeling we found in the mines."

"This place is cursed," said Harjit softly, turning and looking around for something she could not explain.

"Those men are terrified, I see it in them. No wonder they're being exposed continually to the Temple's influence. It's not simple physics, it is meta-physics. They take shifts. Watch their faces when they come on guard, they come with complete dread," Fabio added. "I don't blame them either. When we were busy constructing the bridge, none of us liked being inside. We all felt something dreadful might happen, and could not stay inside for very long. It is as if this place was studying our every move and still is."

"How did you manage to finish the bridge then, Fabio?" asked Christopher.

"The bridge was completed by the soldiers," he said, referring to their captors. His face was suddenly turning chalk white behind his beard. That feeling of dread was bothering him. "I sense something weird happening right now, *don't you?*" Fabio's restless eyes were darting from one dark corner to the next, searching for something inside the shadows. The guards too were becoming more restless, panning their AKs.

"No, yes, yes I do!" said Harj, changing her mind quickly. She was scared to look further.

"Oh, yes, I do now, shit!" Chris quickly nodded.

"I feel nothing," Barbaro sneered. Fabio continued apprehensively.

"You know it is strange that this place was as bright as the sun when I came here. Light emanated from all these walls making it hard to see. Then, it all died. For no reason. It just died."

"Weird," said Harjit.

"Si, look at the guards' eyes, they are not watching us at all, their scanning everywhere else. Watch their body language. It's like waiting for an eruption," said Barbaro, almost enjoying the fear.

"This place is a flashpoint," said Christopher, seeing an opportunity to get closer to look below. He walked towards the ribbon barrier, "If we don't find some answers soon, *we will* end up down there. Scared men kill." His voice was hard as steel.

"Watch what you are doing, Christopher!" said Harjit, raising her voice, joining him and holding his arm for balance. When the soldiers heard her, they tried to come in between them, shouting to ensure there weren't any unplanned accidents. But not before they saw below.

"Have a look down there, phew!" Fabio puffed air out, releasing some of his bottled-up tension. "We need answers and quick. Come on, let's get thinking. These markings, they go all around the stone face wall. Even if we could gain access, the front face is sheer and flat. How does it open?" the older man asked in a low voice.

"What is this place, Fabio?" asked Harjit looking up with worry written on her face.

"In ancient days, civilizations tended to build over the original building rather than constructing completely from new. They would build on top and around the location and make the new one even bigger, greater!" Fabio was forgetting for a moment where he was, becoming excited once again, a bit like his old self.

"The stone type of this inner Temple is completely different to the overall shell build," said Harjit. The girl was drawn again into the mystery.

"Stranger than that, Harjit, as I told you, when we first came here, the walls emitted a brilliant white light. It illuminated the whole area, giving the chamber an almost featureless look. All except for the golden carving of a Sun-Face above us and those shadowed lines you see going across the drop. Those were hard to observe, however, they are all quite plain to see in this type of ambience."

"What was that strange light source?" asked Barbaro.

"I do not know where its energy source is coming from, oh and coincidentally, Endrissi dropped something down the gap. A few seconds after this, we were all plunged into darkness!" Fabio remembered their peril at that time. It had been frightening and dangerous. They all began moving back a little, herded on by their jailers.

"The orb in the upper Temple, that must be the source, Fabio!" Harjit jumped to a conclusion. Christopher pressed his lips, not quite so sure.

"The writings on the face must be a clue. Our experience in the upper levels taught us this. Honestly, I know it is impossible to understand. There is something bad, something evil inside this

Temple, *it has been disturbed."* Christopher warned, when unexpectedly, an army radio began buzzing.

They all jumped, what next?

The soldiers at the entrance were listening intently for a moment to excited voices on the other end of the radio, then began talking eagerly amongst each other. They turned towards them with faces that could kill.

Oh, no, thought Fabio. The group's blood pressure rose. They were wondering what was going on. Something else had just happened. Shortly after, quick footsteps could be heard again and were coming from the corridor, when suddenly, a prisoner appeared stumbling through it with a sack over his head. "Oh, shit." exclaimed Fabio.

The man was being marched into the cubed hall, his wrists were tied with rope and he was finding it difficult to walk. They pushed him and caused him to stumble. Everyone was immediately alarmed because they could see the soldiers were intending to push him into the chasm!

"No!" Harjit screamed.

"Wait!" Christopher shouted as they passed by.

"Stop!" Fabio ordered.

"Have mercy!" Barbaro cringed because the execution would be over in a second!

Swiftly, the soldiers kept shoving the prisoner right up to the tape and stopped, then withdrew, leaving him standing there, alone. The figure quivered and said nothing. He knew better. He was teetering on the brink. Christopher grabbed at the figure toppling forward and Harjit instantly supported him. They both saved his life.

They carefully took off the cloth bag from his head and stood back a step to see better. Surprised, Harjit's mouth opened aghast, and softly acknowledged.

"Mashir, *it's, you.*" Harjit's eyes began to water.

"Mashir! I'm glad to see you and *still alive!*" Christopher beamed, giving Mashir a big bear hug like he would his brother, Scott, then quickly began unravelling his bonds. Mashir looked tired and overwhelmed.

"I am most glad to see you all, my friends," he said. The Iranian moved closer to Christopher, whispering into his ear, "I am afraid that I am the transmitter of very bad news. He paused, swallowing hard.

"*Well?*" Christopher's shoulders dropped as if a heavy weight had been put on them. Fabio froze in dread, Barbaro held his breath, but Harjit knew.

"*Our friends,* they are dead." Mashir's eyes looked lost. Christopher's face turned chalk white, while Mashir related this devastating news.

"Everyone?" Harjit's face paled.

"All dead," Mashir confirmed with a nod.

"My, God." Fabio was shocked.

"Listen," Mashir said lightly, "they've been murdered, upstairs." he shook his head in utter dismay at God's lack of compassion, knowing that God did not always look after his own.

"They will pay for this," Harjit said, as she fainted.

Fabio heard Mashir's fatal words and felt pure anger. He wished this mysterious commander dead.

"You bastardos!" he screamed at the soldiers. "You bloody bastardos!"

The soldiers were concerned for the unconscious woman. They checked her out while two other guards restrained Fabio. They controlled him quickly by hitting his leg just enough to make him hobble in pain.

Fabio's silent anger was brooded in hurt. This brutal loss of life dealt him a severe blow. He was ultimately responsible. Sitting down hard, the professor groaned at their helplessness; yet, what could he have done to save them? He was close to his breaking point. *All dead. All dead.*

"I must say a prayer for our lost friends." Christopher felt a great need to speak with God.

Fabio was seeing blood. "You are hurt, Mashir, there is blood on your back." A wound ran across his shoulder blades to the small of his back.

"Yes, ha, ha!" he laughed in defiance. "Unfortunately, the sarvan did not like me too much. Sarvan Hashem takes great pride in his work and a whip in his hands is his most excellent best friend," said Mashir, glaring at the guards.

After this, time passed very slowly as they awaited their own fidgeting for executions, knowing that death might be only moments away. With no sign of the commander, this made their wait torturous, and the only option was to try and work out how to get inside the Temple. They pooled their ideas regarding the symbols together. *Was this really the beginning of the Masonic brotherhood?* There was a missing link *somewhere.* But what was it? Time was running out.

The planetarium at the top of the Temple interested Mashir greatly. The surveyor seemed less sceptical than Fabio on its strange qualities. The Iranian was a much more willing man to accept new ideas for old concepts, bonding thoughts and formulating a new theory for the future. They all had seen or experienced some unexplained happenings, some would say, magic, while others, coincidence.

"So, my friends, how does all this get us inside the Temple? These lines, these grooves on the surface, what are they?" Mashir perused this line of questioning.

"Specifically, Freemasonic. It's the overall linked shape that tells me so." Christopher spoke confidently. "Observe the inner pentagon design. It is formed by the bisecting grooves, but the grooves extend upwards and downwards. The whole drawing completes the symbol of the Masonic Order! It is their symbol. I recognise the compass and square." Christopher remained quiet while the others studied and considered the strange sign. The air was as still as a held breath.

"Tell me more, Chris," Mashir encouraged.

"The compass and square are an architect's tools and symbolize *God as the divine Architect of the Universe*. Studying these symbols and codices, I can unite them, and they make words."

"What do they mean?" Fabio asked.

"I can read them, yes, but they make no sense to me. Evil as it sounds, maybe a sacrifice is required. I have read that this does not need to be human, animals may also do for the release of the life force of energy."

"It happened with Beppi," Barbaro sneered.

"The compass is used to draw circles and represents the realm of the spiritual eternity," Fabio edified. "It is symbolic of the defining and limiting principle and of infinite boundaries. The angle measures the square, the symbol of Earth and the realm of the material. The square represents fairness, balance, firmness. Together, the compass and square represent the convergence of matter and spirit, and the convergence of earthly and spiritual responsibilities. The two symbols together form a hexagram, and you would know and recognise it to be the Star of David!"

"Rubbish!" Barbaro shouted, feeling his religion under threat again.

"Let me continue." Fabio took over from Christopher, "The union of Earth with the heavens, matter and mind, the Freemasons follow the three great principles of brotherly love, relief and truth." Fabio stopped to take a breath.

"It was Endrissi who spoke to me about this shape or design. Endrissi felt the burden too great to keep to himself," advised professor Mancini. Mashir listened excitedly, as he tugged at his goatee beard. He was feeling more enlightened.

"Inside this place, of course, *it is different*," Christopher pointed out. "*This symbol is inverted!* The compass begins below that precipice and extends up to each corner. The square bisects these, as you can see, leaving a central area. Observe the full shape in front of your eyes. The sun is above the grooved apex and the 'Seven Rays' are drawn from it marks to the top of the entrance!" Christopher studied the ancient diagram.

"*The 'Seven Rays'* represent the 'Seven Spheres of Consciousness", Harjit's soft voice continued seamlessly. "*Atala* is the first plane and the world of inner self, *Vitala* is the second and the world of consciousness, *Sutala* is the third and the world of will power, and *Talatala* is the world of mind." Harjit paused to take a breath. The others were flabbergasted that she had spotted a link. Harjit continued, "*Rasatala*, the Astral world of *Mahatala* and lastly *Patala* the seventh plane or the physical world. These are the *Vedantic Planes* and we have yet to learn to manipulate them. This ancient civilization, these dead people, it is they who have mastered these abilities already!" she said. A strange calm settled into her nerves because no matter what happened here, she knew that a higher plane was watching over them.

"All is as God wills it," Mashir concluded.

Outside the Temple, the rainforest agonised. Night had come, when uncannily everything stopped, as if waiting for something unnatural to happen, and when it did, with the first shudder, the atmosphere began getting heavier by the second, transpiring into an unearthly wail. A calling, loud and primal, that pained the silence with an evil scream sailed through the trees, marking this time of a new world. The jungle spoke of its abhorrence, this change, as a lone jaguar hissed its defiance at the flying creature's unnatural presence high above the vale. The Earth started shuddering and shaking violently to these unearthly sounds and screams of, DEATH.

****

CHAPTER XIII

MISPLACED SCROLLS

The earthquake struck hard. The trees, the earth, the foliage — everything was captured in unstoppable shaking motions. Its unnatural undulation caused bedlam throughout the forest. Under the watch of moonlight bleaching its ghostly light and dark shadows across this secluded valley, and the violence seen everywhere, trees began breaking and toppling in all directions. Life watched anxiously on, and wondered what would come to pass in this new world.

Hidden in the juddering foliage the Swiss guardsmen waited. The jungle had once again become a deadly place to live. The Swiss guards dodged every way, trying to avoid numerous trees crashing around them. Lethal vines tightened, then snapped, sending them whipping through the air with a high pitched "twang" flying past them, the reapers slicing and dicing nearby saplings and anything else not fast enough to move.

Concealed men positioned themselves as best as they could in the foliage, just outside base camp perimeter, but no one had expected this chaotic turn of events. From where they were hidden, they could see clearly heavily-armed soldiers appearing sporadically and running on the Temple, bewildered because of the suddenness and unexpected earthquake, everyone watching this instant devastation.

Earth's defiance was over in about twenty seconds, leaving fear, destruction and Godly retribution in its quake. The forest immediately plunged straight into a weird silent lunar illumination that washed full on and over the stone edges and surfaced stone terraces. In this eerie light and frosty silhouette, the campsite lay in tatters. A disturbed calm fell over the forest.

The men from Europe stared out of the vegetation in disbelief. This was a chance. The enemy would not be expecting an attack, as fluorescent yellow crosshairs began moving slowly along the stone terraces. Using their newly designed fourth generation night vision image intensifier scopes, and fitted global eye targeting systems, each guardsman picked out "hotspots".

Easy, steady hands stopped as they electronically marked each victim's neck, on target, *click*, safety off.

Inside the bottom of each scope's view, a tiny green LED changed to flashing amber light, indicating "ready to fire on hold", while eye controlled yellow crosshairs travelled, changing to steady red and locked on. Each marksman took a deep breath in and held it, with their cold minds ready. *Eyes fixed on red, all on red.*

Red.

Red.

In a split second, major Trentino focused and fixed onto the transparent kill button inside his scope, gave a global eye signal to his men's similar electronic weaponry, and with their time perfectly synchronised, commanded they release.

Red on dead!

Thwang! Dull dampened sounds, each digitally controlled with crossbow bolts were released and sent flying speedily through the air in lethal synchronisation at five Km per second, hitting their marks.

He breathed out. *Effective,* he thought. Using the weapon's "dead eye" control, he moved back onto amber and then to placid green. *Click,* the safety was on. The crosshairs once again illuminated on the yellow. Enemy sentries fell dead on all levels. It was time to move.

"Go," the major ordered his men calmly through his microphone.

Running silently, the guardsmen covered the short gap between the perimeter and the Temple. There were no mistakes. One guardsman that was strategically placed had climbed up a tree on a nearby high point and had shot accurately. Two enemies lay dead on the Temple top.

The bordering foliage, forest floor, and the Temple were all bleached in an X-ray blanket of lunar luminosity, its ill-light camouflaging everything. In a few quick breaths, Swiss guardsman, Sergeant Davide Romano of the Eagle Unit, was off and quickly running across the open ground, appearing briefly as a silvery image, blending seamlessly into the jungle floor. This deadly ghost, clothed in silvery white and dappled shadows, soon melted into the Temple stone base and was gone in an instant.

For a fleeting moment, ten out of the twenty men from the Eagle Unit sprinted across the safe border after their sergeant, and like flowing spectres, went assailing up the large steps. When an unsuspecting enemy soldier walked around from the blind side of the Temple on the mid-terrace, he too would quickly suffer the same, ghostly fate as the others.

Red on dead!

Another soldier hastily appeared from the Temple entrance up on the first Tier; this one was suspicious. At first, it looked as though he had mistakenly slipped backwards at seeing his fallen comrade, when a crossbow bolt struck him, shattering through his teeth. The lethal projectile instantly snapped his neck and another stopped his heart. Bolt power!

Survival rate, nil.

As planned, the Eagle Unit was already moving silently and scaling the Temple, and in about five minutes, reached the first tier, with no casualties. This was objective two of *Operation Aequinoxium*. Their holy mission was complete.

Stepping over the dead, the Swiss soldiers, staying true to their motto *'silent in motion'*, began moving inside the passageways. The interior lit up with paraffin lamps, which made it easy to navigate. Pacing stealthily through, with five men on one side and five on the other, they swiftly traversed through and soon reached the first crossroads before another enemy guard stepped out, right in front.

Upon seeing them, the man instantly shouted and lifted his AK to greet them. But no sooner had he done so that two silenced bullets smacked into his skull, leaving his grey and mixed white matter over the walls in a high-octane kill. The remaining special forces of the "Crossbow Regiment" also began entering the Temple as backup.

Another enemy soldier came in from a different corridor, with his machine appearing first around the corner, giving him away. The Swiss hands grabbed it and with great ferocity, pulled hard and caught him off balance. The man fell forward with the weapon and another Swiss guard finished him off, sticking his bayonet right up through his lower jaw and into his skull. The enemy tumbled down into the stone shaft, dead, and hit the ground far below with a clatter.

Major Trentino instantly noted the dead soldier's foreign ensign tattoo on his forearm before he fell: united red and green crescent moon with golden star.

"Watch your step here" he whispered, while quickly peering his head out at the crossroads and surveying the area on his left and right, then finally straight-ahead. Commanding instant action, the major gave snap orders to his men.

"*Sergente Moretti.* You are part of Phoenix. I need you to take charge of five Eagles and go right." The men moved instantly with a nod. "The next five, move ahead a little, then stay put. Prevent any outflanking manoeuvre. *Sergente Romano* you take five more Eagles, then go left. Everyone, keep in contact. The rest of Eagle Unit, stay here. I'll need your support to keep this key position under *our control.*" The men saluted sharply. "Phoenix, come with me. We are going down that fucking hole!" they all affirmed silently. "Stay close and remember, there are civvies inside here."

On their way up the corridor, the birds of prey knew the element of surprise was over. They were all inside with no casualties, and the major strategically split his tactical units, which was essential to locate the scientists quickly for a decisive rescue.

Phoenix abseiled down the shaft in a rapid descent. They had plenty of practice with this technique. In his crackling communications microphone, he calmly advised his men, "Go with extreme caution, if the prisoners are in any danger, standoff and report their location. I will take over and negotiate their release!"

Once the soldiers had entered the superstructure, it was not long before their specialized electronic communications equipment started to malfunction and fail.

Trentino knew that the *Osprey Unit* could only be hours away from meeting them here, although their exact operational status was currently unknown to him. Colonel Greco Rossi, the overall commander of this operation, was coming with Osprey. Trentino knew that the commander's hi-tech mapping equipment would be of no use here. Inside this superstructure, communications from the outside was near impenetrable!

"Keep going," ordered Trentino. Once he and his men reached the bottom of the shaft, he said, in a soft whisper, "And *no explosives*." He did not want any civilian casualties.

Elsewhere, the lit-up passages periodically cast varying degrees of light over the walls, showing weird inscriptions in the shadow. However, the men gave them no second thought. They were uninterested in the mysterious runes. Those things were for the academics, *not soldiers!* The Eagles were on the move, rapidly flying along one of the passageways. They spread out while silently dropping onto the floor, and came face to face with their mortal enemy.

The United Islamic Forces!

Upon seeing the Italian Swiss guardsmen, the Islamists knew they had no chance of survival as their bodies instantly absorbed silenced rapid firepower. Blood and tissue jetted out through their pin-cushioned bodies, and most men fell to the ground quietly in a mess of blood and bone.

Unfortunately, one wounded Islamic guardsman managed to raise the alarm, which sent a high-pitched alarm all along the passageways.

"Fuck! That's done it," swore Sergeant Davide Romano, quickly stepping over their deadly handiwork. "Look, they all have that bloody same tattoo. What the hell is an Islamic force doing here in South America?"

They moved faster inwards and heard something ahead. It was *the enemy!* Using only hand signals, the Swiss guardsmen decided to backtrack by going along an alternative route, exiting the focal passageway. Knowing this would be a risky alternative, they arranged three men in front and two keeping watch at the rear.

What is that noise? Romano heard a low sound coming closer to him, like a rolling stone. *What is it?* Then, he suddenly realised what it was.

"Grenade!" he screamed in warning. The men dove to the floor as a fire fight began in that instant.

Flash! Bang! An enormous flash wiped out the corridor in dazzling light and immediately stunned their senses, their balance reeling in an already billowing smoke-filled corridor.

Flash! Bang! Another one went off right in front, blinding them. Grenades were designed to stun and confuse an enemy in smoke, sound and light.

FRRRRRRRRAK! FRRRRRRRRAK!

Mechanical sounds from numerous AKs sounded as they fired at them, with bullets spraying widely across the corridor.

FRRRRRRRRAK! FRRRRRRRRAK!

Bullets were everywhere, whizzing in all directions at them.

FRRRRRRRRAK! FRRRRRRRRAK!

The AKs were dealing out death from the dense smoke.

"Ahhh!"
"Eaaagh!"
The first two Swiss guardsmen were dying in the hailstorm of lead and blood, their guts

flying in all directions. The men were dead, and Romano could not believe that among all this human carnage, he was still alive. He began scrambling behind the bodies of his lifeless comrades, knowing this cover would not last long.

"Get out of their kill zone!" Romano screamed to whoever remained. He quickly fired from his Beretta SCP 90/100 gas-operated magazine fed assault carbine, and immediately hit several enemies.

Breathing hard, Romano quickly attaching his barrel adaptor to launch his rifle grenades. However, his instructions were to *not* to use this weaponry inside the Temple. The risk to civilian life deemed too great, so his odds of survival fell near to nil.

"Fuck," he cursed, remembering his orders. He then resigned to another plan. There was no telling what strength of force they were up against. He expected this adversary to be brave and ruthless, their distinctive and unmistakable ensign tattoo proved that pedigree.

They were not a death squad, or terrorist group. He recognised them as a hardened and elite Islamic fast reaction force, from the combined United Arabian and African countries. A new force that included the emerging Arab and African democracies, formed from seed after the Gulf conflicts, already well-known to the Swiss guardsmen.

The element of surprise gone, and with no cover other than smoke, the remaining men retreated, crawling quickly back just as another barrage of bullets came after them, ricocheting death into another guardsman.

Umph. Part of his head blasted off. The rest retreated further, and taking a defensive position further down the passageway, they readied themselves to repel the enemy. Losing all ground they have gained, the Swiss pushed right back to the crossways. Stalemate.

They needed to hold them at these crossroads. Sergeant Romano switched on his analogue radio, knowing this to be more reliable than that new digital crap.

With his men in another section of the Temple, Sergeant Moretti headed along a shadowy corridor. This way was the same as all the others; each dimly lit. Unexpectedly, an opening in a wall presented itself. It was a doorway into another similar passage.

"Another bloody maze Sergente," said an unimpressed guardsman in a low tone. The soldier was not wearing his beret. He had a marine haircut, long sideburns and red mosquito bites all over his face.

The sergeant got a quick look inside. "Let's stick to the lit passages. If we detour too much, we will end up disorientated and lost." The risk was too great and dangerous to navigate.

****

"Signore," said the radio operator. The guardsman just received vital information. "It's Sergente Romano, his Eagle Unit has met a formidable resistance and has been forced to retreat, taking up a defensive position at the crossway with our re-enforcements."

"We need to find those civilians. Let's go." He looked ahead. This bad news added impetus to the major's mission. *Islamists. Swiss Black-Op mission. A rescue. What's this really about? Somebody knows more,* he thought. *Let's get them out alive!*

Everyone crouched down and moved swiftly along the curved white sides of the convoluted stone passageways, continuing with caution, checking and moving, checking and moving, each acutely aware that any stone outcrop was a potential ambush.

****

The general alarm had not reached the section held by the Islamists. As the Eagle Unit quietly approached the enemy stronghold, they were unaware of the Christian intrusion.

"Hostiles ahead, Signore," whispered a guardsman, holding up four fingers, twisting his hand and leaving one finger. "Heavy machine guns and a nest."

Ahead, the gunners were stationed and ready behind their machine gun nest. They had not spotted them, and from where the Swiss guards were, could see that the enemy protected themselves by what resembled a stack of sand bags, most likely filled with forest dirt.

"Heavy machine guns. Those guys are expecting big trouble." This readiness and preparation puzzled Sergeant Moretti. *Surely not us*, he thought. *They could not know we were coming, not yet. If not us, then what? What are they fighting?* The guardsman was looking for answers he could not possibly fathom.

He was suspicious of the Islamic garrison. They seemed too well prepared. It was obvious they were expecting an attack of some kind. It was curious to think that they may have been involved in some unknown conflict already. They were afraid of something else. *Head hunters, drug traffickers? That might explain their readiness.* Unconvinced, Sergeant Moretti looked unsure, because he already knew that their own colonel had his own heavy machine-guns coming too and enough weaponry to start a third World War. *What is going on here?*

The enemy sat prepared with an "M2HB 12.7mm .50" calibre heavy machine-gun on a tripod stand with short chrome bore barrel, able to fire at a rate of 750 rounds per minute and the Islamic garrison's weapon of choice. A killing machine normally used against air targets.

"These guys mean business." The Sergeant's tone sounded like failure. In the dimness, the Eagle Unit crouched motionless on each side of the corridor, looking at the deadly arsenal. Enemy guns covered a central position and were aimed up the corridor where they were hiding. Behind the M2 nest, a large stone door remained closed. *The scientists.*

"They do not know we are here, *not yet,*" said Moretti softly. "It looks like there has been trouble already," he added. "We can't rush them, but we might be able to outflank these guys." Moretti spotted another way. "Inside there, that passageway. Move it!" he snapped his order quietly.

Knowing that any hesitation would bring certain death, the sergeant and his men quickly backed off, and went for the cover under a dark shadowed opening in the passageway.

Inside, it looked as though it might have once been living quarters, with large bits of broken furniture lying around the dark room. It joined onto a small corridor opposite and into other additional and similar rooms; all built along this smaller passageway.

I only hope the hostiles don't kill the prisoners because of this detour, Moretti prayed to himself, while leading his men through the dark room. Their night vision was operating well enough to aid them, but some of the hi-tech components were already beginning to malfunction inside the Temple.

The Eagles moved fast from room to room, attempting to negate the M2 machine gun nest. Soon, they arrived at another exit. These walls looked as though they had a bigger stone construction, leading into yet another uninviting dimly lit passageway.

Taking off his night goggles, the sergeant was spatially aware of his surroundings, and the soldier could roughly judge the distance and position they were in and from the M2 nest, which was hidden somewhere within this warren of rooms and passageways.

He calculated that the enemy would be close by. Sergeant Moretti was right. One soldier discretely protruded a small miniature camera into the next passageway.

There it was, the nest! He counted his targets behind the barrier and it looked like there had been a new development as well. The enemy soldiers had just received bad news, and were talking in excited voices. They were alerted to their ingress and were now in direct communication with some of their own forces, who were currently engaged in a firefight, attempting to repel Swiss guardsmen further up the Temple. The Islamic soldiers looked poised and in the highest state of readiness.

"Si, they are busy bees, sergente, and it looks like the party is about to begin," the smiling corporal advised his sergeant. Both men had camouflaged faces. The machine guns were pointed away from them in the opposite direction. They had outflanked the nest, which was exactly what Moretti had calculated.

"We are going to enter that large stone vent. *Look above you. See it?*" He pointed over the man's head. "The hole is big enough for you to quietly negate the ventilation system and come down either inside the room and behind that nest or somewhere else that gives us a better vantage point."

Sergeant Moretti stood on a piece of old furniture to the grill ventilation, which was about ten feet off the floor. Lifting the heavy vent upwards, he began shining his torch down the dusty way. Inside, clear of obstacles, he believed that this plan might just work. The soldiers understood.

"No obstructions that I can see," confirmed Moretti. "Ok, men, the usual drill, you two, go through and press the green light in your communicators when you are in a good position. I will reply with the red indicator."

"Then, signore?"

"Then, we wipe them out. *All of them.* Get going and good luck."

Saluting, the men were off and were soon crawling along a dusty ventilation shaft, which routed them and kept them unseen across the corridor. It took them away from their targets. Using head torches this time, the Swiss got closer to some weird noises up ahead.

The stone tunnel soon met a crossroads of sorts; a congregation of the system, like many others throughout, like a star hub. Here, the acoustics were the greatest, and the sounds came and went. This was a lonely place.

To go any further, the men carefully lowered themselves into the hub area and into soft dust, a place just less than ten square metres, where the hollow woodwind noises converged together in a benign airflow, but strong enough to cause a mad orchestra of woodwind and odd pipe acoustic effects, its shallow air blowing white dust around them.

They found themselves waist-deep in a fine soft dust, their head torches showing swirling patterns all around them, some periodically settling in small piles on top of the smooth surface, before being whipped up again in a dynamic cycle.

If the dust had been deeper, the men would have suffocated, but it was manageable and the men quickly traversed through the substance. From here, small tunnels went in all directions—straight up the vertical structure, straight ahead, left and right.

"What is this stuff?" the Corporal asked.

"God knows. Which way?" the other soldier was unsure which route would be best to take.

"This place is a complete maze, man." The corporal's light beam shot up the vertical shaft. "It goes up for miles!" Both men were astounded by the sheer scale of the construction.

"Come on, this place is giving me the creeps." The soldier pushed him on, urging the other to keep moving.

The air flowing along these tight pipes was creating weird moaning sounds throughout the tunnel system, and low hissing noises occurred where air passed slowly through different vents.

Occasionally, the dust got caught in their lungs, making them cough spasmodically. The air carried a stale and rotten smell and soon, they were quite thirsty with the dry white powder covering their lips. Dust flowed lightly around in the air and through the desiccated tunnel system and in various locations. The white powder became piled up like snowdrifts or lay thinly spread on other surfaces. Dust coated all the walls of the vent system, breaking off when touched.

Lifting themselves up and out of the hub, the surface felt quite slippery like cosmetic talc. They were once again crawling on all fours through another tunnel. The dust coated their white faces and with no idea where they were going to end up, the men kept on moving.

****

The Islamic garrison was now fully aware of the Swiss guards' arrival inside the Temple, and with the element of surprise gone, they waited in a state of high alert, aware that their deadly adversary had breached their security.

The United Arabian and African forces would not be expecting any help being that they were so far away from home, and realised their Holy Mission was to be completed alone. In the short time of being here, the Islamists had already searched parts of the Temple to find the *misplaced scrolls* and the fabled *object of power.* Unfortunately, all those men had not returned.

This loss of manpower was a severe setback. With three squads of soldiers gone, this loss depleted the commander' s ability to complete his own mission. He needed support, and assumed his men were incapable of using their personal communication devices. Lost or killed. He understood that they were all expendable. They all were. All except for the civilians. *I need them to stay alive.* The commander needed to know their secret.

The commander understood that his quest now rested on a knife's edge with the arrival of the Swiss guards. His mission was on the brink of success and failure. The commander had planned well, delegating operational tasks to his most trusted officer, Sarvan Haleem, and holding the high ground, his forces were strategically placed inside the Temple. He still had an ace card to play.

The commander stood with the scientists and soldiers next to the inner Temple. As a well-read man and scholar, the commander knew this was the place spoken about in the *"Misplaced Scrolls".* He understood that these ancient documents had been stolen by the infidels centuries ago.

This area was secure, or so he thought. His military control was complete and went right up to the first Tier. The upper level was held strong by his men against the Christian soldiers. The infidels had arrived, but he also knew that time was running out, the time of *Qiyāmah!*

Perplexed, the commander was concerned that there was still no obvious way to enter the inner Temple as it was completely sealed. The civilians gave no secrets away; they too did not know how to enter, that was now obvious to him. With no answers, the fate of him, his men and his mission would be a dark one.

So, it was written, unto the end of the world this place would be evil. He and his men were the "Best and the Chosen". *I must not fail,* the commander thought as he waited for an answer to his dark thoughts.

It has come, yawm ad-dīn, 'the Day of Judgment', and as-sā`a, 'the Last Hour' is very close. Failure is not an option. Allah, what am I to do? The commander prayed for divine guidance. *My mission is well organized. Spanning many years, many lives had been lost in this time and are always in conflict with the "Crossed Sons". Infidels. It is the prophecy.*

His answer was right in front of him, the archaeologists and scientists remained alive and still his main hope to enter.

In the "Misplaced Scrolls" it states that "resurrection will be followed by the gathering of mankind, culminating in their judgment by God", or so it is said, he reminded himself.

Going through the words recursively in his tortured mind, the commander firmly believed the prophecy would happen while interrogating the civilians. To extract any information from them proved most difficult. The world depended on him, and these civilians. They too were unsuspectingly, "the key" to this prediction and now, a myth had become reality. Could he further persuade them to cooperate? He had no choice, he must.

****

CHAPTER IX

ENTER THEN MY APRENTICE

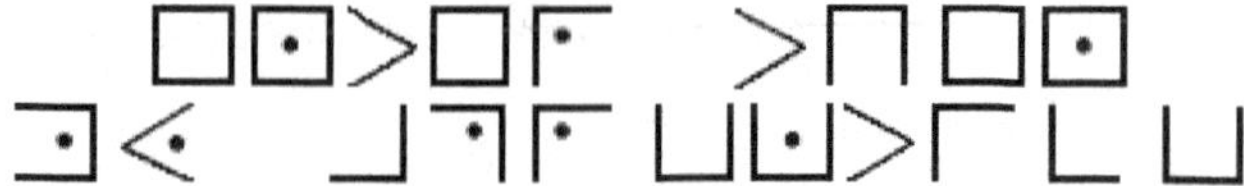

Waiting anxiously for a sign, Sergeant Moretti looked at his watch. It had stopped. He guessed it had been ten minutes since his men had climbed into the ventilation system. They had travelled about two hundred yards through, going in much further than first imagined, and far beyond where they wanted to be.

His men, who were close to the rear of the main living quarters, saw a dull tone of yellow and orange light coming from inside the room, filtering through a stone grill. One of the guards stretched up, struggling to see and what they could see on the floor were the prisoners, covered under sheets. Dead.

"Killed," he exhaled deeply. After a moment, the sheet moved. "No, no, I've got it wrong, thank God, they are alive!" the Swiss had thought the worst, but fortunately, the people were only sleeping. At last they had found them.

The guard could see two Islamic soldiers standing inside the dim room, and both appeared to be very edgy, as they paced up and down. One of them was communicating quietly into his radio. It looked like he also was having problems with his device. He looked frustrated as he shook it vigorously to get more life from the object.

"We can take them," he whispered.

"No, there may be others in the adjacent room. The prisoners will all be killed! At least we know they are here and alive."

"Affirmative on that, come on, let's get back and report."

The men retreated, quickly crawling their way back. Air wailed wantonly. They could hear the weird hollow woodwind sounds of air movement resonating along the tunnel shaft system to greet them.

Without hesitation, the first corporal lowered himself down inside the hub area again, standing once more waist-deep in white dust, which puffed around in small clouds. He was about to speak, when without warning, something blurry dropped directly on top of him as the other corporal waited to enter. The other soldier stared in disbelief. He was horror struck at what he saw.

"For God's sake!" he shrieked.

A horrible white creature with a great mouth engulfed the man's head and part of his shoulders. His blood poured down and covered his white dust-covered body, which shook in agony!

The soldier dropped to his knees and screamed from inside the white creature, then collapsed and was instantly buried under a pool of white dust. The dust turned deep red and pink with blood. The corporal behind him, committed to his route, could not prevent himself from dropping inside too, along with it.

"Agh! What are you?" he called out in disbelief, as the odd-looking animal stared up at him. The thing was slobbering on top of the fallen man, its white crusted body slurping copiously, and looking in all directions with excitable eyes. It crunched, fatally muting the soldiers screaming.

The corporal felt sick at sound and sight of this thing killing his comrade. He quickly pulled out his black Beretta.

Bang! Bang! Bang! Bang!

He rapidly shot bits of the creature's crusted armour off.

"Bastardo! Bastardo!" he kept screaming at it, as he rapidly emptied a full magazine at the creature.

Its hard casing cracked open in the fury of bullets, showing its gutsy internals, mixed with human body parts. Its dry exoskeleton simply disintegrated against his most effective weapon.

Disgusted at the bloody mess, he managed to steal a quick look towards his escape route, and moving quickly through the dust, he turned around in time to see another creature dropping down behind him from the vertical shaft.

His heart almost exploded with terror. As he tried to get away, another cloud plume erupted when a third creature landed into the drift of powder, causing a smoke screen of white dust. He could no longer see.

"No!" he shouted, and leapt to the other side of the hub. Using his spring-loaded legs pumped full of adrenaline, he launched himself up and into the exit tunnel to safety. But, it was too late. The creature caught hold of his leg.

"Eeeagh! Eeeagh!" he screamed in agony.

Brave as he was, the screaming corporal was sucked slowly back down and like quicksand, sank into the bloody dust. The corporal could not get out. There was no escape.

****

The corporal's sudden scream, pushed on by a violent blast of hot air, was sent travelling rapidly through the stone ventilation system. The walls and shafts collapsed into the cubed hub, as the blast incinerated everything inside, burying the men and creatures. The vent was completely blocked. The detonation was complete.

The first sign of trouble was the screaming and gunfire coming from the vent system. Sergeant Moretti was alarmed, and immediately went over to the opening, looked inside and listened to the horrific dying screams. A few seconds later, an almighty explosion came shooting towards him.

He ducked down from the vent, as the incinerating air blew out a mixture of red cinders and charcoaled black dust. He stood hunched over while it scorched the air above him. He instinctively switched on his radio. He needed to report back to the major and tell him he had failed.

"Moretti here, two feathers are down. Status, civilians are not secure, I repeat, civilians are *not secure*. Signore, the enemy remains in control."

****

Deep inside the cubed chamber, the Islamic commander was entranced in prayer. He mulled it over once more.

Allah, it is a race against time to see who will find this sacred place first. These people do not have the right to arbitrarily take whatever they want. This place and all its possessions belong to Islam. It is a holy Mosque, our faith shall be the most powerful on this Earth and all will look towards Mecca, Medina, Jerusalem and MalisIblis. This is the Seventh Pillar of Islam, the true way to God and the way to Jannah, Paradise! Praise to Muhammad!

Sarvan Abdul-Haleem reorganized his rapid reaction force, positioning them along the in-shots of the walls, each man in an excellent defensive position set against a determined enemy — the Christian invaders.

Haleem knew that his commander had complete faith in him. The officer knew that a structure like this would be to their advantage, against the aggressors. The commander was in prayer, and he could see him close by, listening to everything.

Allah, Medina is the site of Muhammad's tomb, MalisIblis would not be his. Ah, Muhammad did not create a religion but was the restorer of the original and uncorrupted monotheistic faith of Adam, Abraham and others. Praise to Muhammad.

The commander knew they needed to stay hidden. The men were ready and waiting, barring the pathway ahead into the inner Temple. Haleem and ten soldiers held the cubed chamber. No one would be leaving until the commander got what was already theirs, written by law. The darkness would not win.

The scientists stood next to the inner Temple. Fabio was concerned about Mashir. He seemed to not be listening to them, and appeared dazed and distant, as if in a trance or in a prayer.

"This is a real puzzler. One thing is for sure, if I find out how to get inside, I am not letting those guys know, because then our usefulness will be over," stated Barbaro bluntly to mooted agreement.

"Barbaro, if you don't, then they will kill us anyway," Mashir said as he came to life and out of silent prayer.

"Aren't we being too optimistic? We do not have a clue how to get inside," said Fabio angrily.

"Not strictly true, Fabio." Christopher spoke calmly and made them listen. "Things *we do know* about this place," he emphasised, "is that this is a magical place." He glanced at Fabio looking cynical. "I know, I know, Fabio, you find it hard to believe. But believe me, you must. The evidence is here, you have already witnessed it. This place crosses the boundaries of Christian religion. It is like the Devil's own house." his tone became apprehensive.

Everyone watched Christopher with uncertainty, not knowing what he had in mind.

"Say what you have to," Fabio ordered.

"We have sadly lost many friends in this God forsaken place." The memory made him falter, and he paused briefly. "It is by no mere chance that we have come to this place and at this exact time. *My belief is this.* We have all been guided here for a very good reason."

"God forsaken, si! And yet, this guidance must be God's will and our justification too! Whatever is inside there," Barbaro intervened rudely agreeing with Christopher for the first time, "must be very important, whether it is *a precious stone, a treasure or even the Holy Grail!* Who knows what it might hold inside."

"What are these soldiers doing here, what do they want?" Fabio asked. "This is a scientific expedition and here we are, prisoners!" The professor was feeling exasperated.

"You may be wrong about that Fabio," Mashir countered. "All is as God wills it. These soldiers are here for the same reason we are." The Iranian put for a new argument. "They have been sent whether they know it or not, like us. Sent here by their masters, whoever they might be. They are here to claim the same prize. Maybe they have more right to be here than we do, I do not know. We are all foe and friend alike, assembled together. This is the time, my friends." Mashir knew more, and a calm understanding settled into his frayed nerves.

Again, the prediction.

"What do you mean?" asked the professor.

"We were here first. It is our claim," Mashir whispered.

"I agree." Barbaro was in an agreeable mood.

"A Temple within a Temple," Fabio stated. His mind was back onto the problem at hand. The professor knew this sort of construction occurred within the INCA civilization, attempting to bring the discussion into a more focused and scientific line. The atmosphere seemed set as their guards drew closer to listen to the professor. The soldiers were intrigued and nervous. Harjit began to speak.

"Examine this place, it is as strong and dominant as a castle with the moat before it, with no water. Instead, a gap, which is replaced by a deadly and unfathomable drop. The slopes prevent anyone from climbing back up. It is more than formidable, because there does not seem to be a way in. It's a death trap."

Christopher chose to remind them, "Recall the inscriptions outside the Temple?" He slowly and meticulously transcribed the same Freemasonic words.

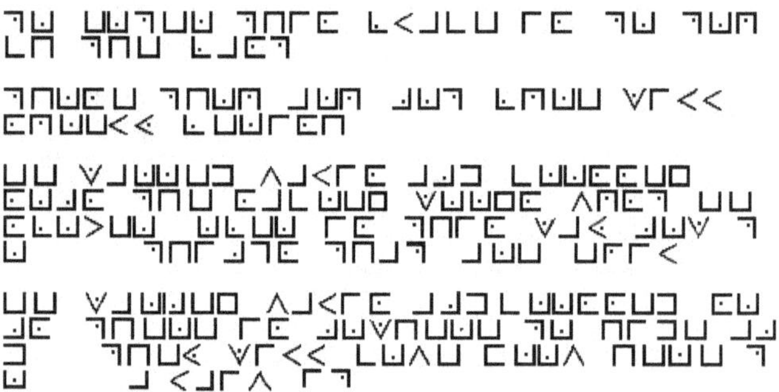

He began to quote the first paragraph of the scripture.

"To enter this place is to touch the past. Those thou art not pure will surely perish. Be warned malis and crossed sons the sacred words must be spoken. Open is this way now to things that are evil. Be warned malis and crossed sons there is nowhere to hide, and they will come from here to claim it. "

"Strange words indeed." Christopher contemplated their meaning.

The guards looked at each other, the men openly petrified after listening to Christopher's immortal words. Christopher felt that if they could have run away from this place, they would have.

Fabio and Barbaro held their breath.

Mashir bubbled with unusual excitement as he watched the priest working it out.

"Tell me, Chris. What are you thinking?" asked Harjit.

"Taken literally, Harj, if we were to enter this Temple, we would go back in time. Maybe, it's a type of bizarre museum. And, those of us that are not spiritually pure, would die. In a nutshell, that is what it means. This next part is more difficult to interpret." Christopher seemed more perplexed but Harjit intercepted his struggling thoughts knowing what had happened to them. She sensed something more.

"Chris, listen. Listen to me! I understand what it means. *'Be warned malis and crossed sons, the sacred word must be spoken'*. Well, if we rearrange the word *'malis'* it means *Islam,* and *Sons-of-the-Cross!* So, both, Islamic and Christians will or must stand together as one, right here and right now!" Harjit said.

"What, why should we?" Barbaro swallowed hard at her crazy notion.

"Surely not," said Fabio flabbergasted.

"Harjit, well done!" Mashir nodded with respect.

"Yes, Mashir, you are Muslim and Christopher and Fabio are both crossed sons, as is

Barbaro. I suppose some magical words *'must be spoken'* to enter. I really am guessing now, I have no real idea about that." Harjit put together what she believed made sense.

"Never!" Barbaro screwed up his face in disbelief.

"This is the very place," Christopher reminded them of the carnage at the Temple entrance and their escape. "How can there be any doubt of the power of words and prayer?" This time, it was his words that silenced the press officer.

"Magical words, they are," Harjit said. "It looks like evil has an opening or a route here already, remember *'Open is the way now to things that are evil'*, a way to enter into this world, our world? Mine, in Shiva the Destroyer, or your Christian one, the Devil, Satan. Who can say?"

The chamber was completely silent except for the sound of laboured breathing, nobody spoke, so Harjit added.

"We have been given this message as a warning." Harjit's expression was solemn and her voice grave.

"We cannot escape because *'there is nowhere to hide'*, we will all die," Fabio continued. "They will come and claim it. But, what is it and who are they?" Fabio wanted to know more.

"The object of great power," Mashir advised. "It must be inside there, what everyone has come to claim!" he said, pointing to the inner Temple.

"Who are *they*? Who is coming to claim it? Christian? Islamic or something or someone else? Who?" asked Christopher and dreaded the words he had spoken. *Who are they?* Swallowing bile, he felt nausea come over him.

"No, I cannot believe this. It would be hopeless if we take these words too literally," Barbaro said, trying to rationalize, everything. He was a willing and ready sceptic when it came to other religions.

"What day is this?" Fabio asked irrelevantly.
Christopher did not hear him and continued reading and speaking his interpretation.

He began to quote the second paragraph of the scripture.

"To enter this place is to touch the present. Powerful thou are in prayer if not pure thee will surely perish. Be warned malis and crossed sons those before sacrificed their souls to him and were overcome and they were all destroyed. It is purely evil so do not falter in vain pursuits."

"Another message. *Now*, is the *present, here, today!* Only the pure will survive, *non-sinners*, other civilizations, their souls sacrificed. *Our people* have been sacrificed, and *something evil approaches.* MY GOD!"

Christopher's mind went from prediction to premonition.

"Go on, Chris," Mashir encouraged.

"Some great evil is coming our way. We need to prepare." He looked pale and it seemed as though someone else was speaking through him, like a clairvoyant. He continued narrating the given scriptures.

Not stopping to take breath.

"To enter this place is to touch the future. The three ships will sink alone. Comradeship, membership and friendship fine, as is the might of arms but will not be enough alone against his hordes. Remember the presence and humble yourself to, to one god with patient perseverance, faith and prayer. All will be tested, and so look east north east from Malisiblis for help as Iblis Smite surrounds you with despair."

His prophetic words were crystal-clear, making Mashir's lips tremble and the Islamic guards' muscles tighten with heightened tension. Their trigger-happy fingers prepared to fight an invisible enemy, and with crazed eyes full of fear, their mechanical weapons moved from left to right, as if tracking an unknown force. But, mechanics and bullets were of no use here. Right now, it seemed as though anything could happen as Christopher continued.

"The future of the world, 'ours' and the 'next one' and much, much more will end here. We will need to stand together or sink alone. That is what it means, 'comradeship', 'membership', and 'friendship' to what?" He stopped, and tried to understand and comprehend further.

"Chris, don't you see? It is the fraternity, the brotherhood of Freemasons!" Harjit's excited words helped him see the light.

"*'Might of arms is not enough'*, so guns cannot win against the enemy mass that comes to meet us. We must look to the *'North-East'* for help. *'Iblis or Islam smite surrounds us with despair'*? Mmm, I am not sure what that means. Islam smite and despair. Does this refer to the guards that are holding us prisoner or something *else?*"

"No, Christopher, it is not my Islamic brothers that will kill. What *'Smite'* gives reference to is still unknown to us. What I do know is that the guards will not kill us. Something much, much worse approaches!"

"You suddenly seem too trusting of the guards, Mashir. Look at those trigger-happy brothers of yours. How much worse can it get?" Christopher measured the Iranian with doubt.

"They do not look very happy to me, my friend." There was a sudden hardness in his eye as though he felt judged.

Christopher was not finished, and continued to narrate more. The strain between them was building.

"To enter this place is to go to nowhere and is also to this land. Where time is nothing and time is everything. The lost link is found, so must be taken, as unified it must never be by them, or all is lost for all time, and purification, illumination and glorification, will be never more."

And, finally the last paragraph spoken:

"Say the word nasom, and enter to meet your soul, or be lost and forever in nowhere."

"*Smite* sounds like the name of a thing, or," he said, pausing as he looked at Harjit.

"Or a dark angel," she added.

"Or *the Devil*, as you said, Harjit," offered Mashir, supporting her theory. "It is the 30th of October, maybe that is important too." Mashir now answered Fabio's earlier question. "I have more, my friends. I have other inscriptions from within the pentagon centre."

At that, they looked at him questionably. Why had he not said anything about this before?

"Why have you not told us this?" Fabio asked. He became immediately suspicious of Mashir. Then, a few other things seemed wrong about this normally mild man, looking at him with his new words that implied a peril yet unseen, a peril about to happen. Something a mere surveyor could not know.

Mashir explained, "I have written it down."

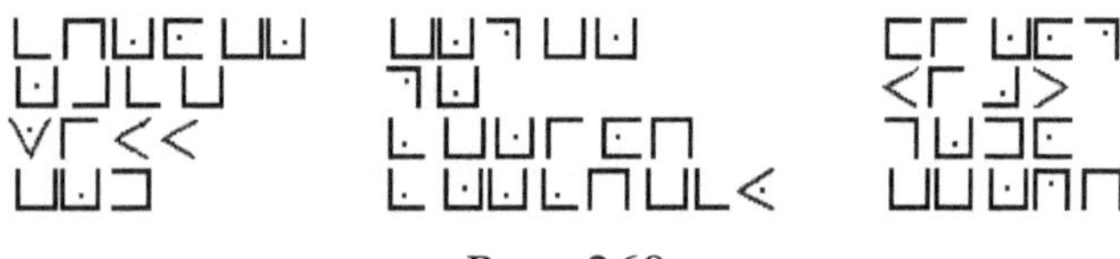

Everyone was unaware of many tall and slender *invisible shadows* inside the large cubed chamber, like a stewardship they solemnly oversaw it, the ones that had watched Fabio and his men before when they had first discovered the inner Temple. This was important. They were listening too. The shadows had always been here, inside this ancient place. Gathered together for this moment. The shadows, and the humans waited for a *Ceremony to begin.*

****

"As you can see, these are three blocks of words," said Mashir. "The *"Three Degrees"*. These can be read in two ways: in rows and in columns. What do they mean, Chris?"

Christopher studied the words closely. Miraculously, and in an instant, he deciphered them. The bio-technologist took out his small notepad from his shirt pocket and scribbled them down in plain English, then showed them to Mashir.

"Well?" Fabio wanted to know. They all did! "What do the words mean?" The leader was completely captivated, just like Hyram Bingham must have been when he discovered the great peak of Machu Picchu last Century, the Inca City in the sky, back in 24th July, 1911. He felt that same feeling of elation and sense of pride. His work vindicated, Fabio looked seriously at Christopher. Both men were triumphant.

Speaking so that everyone could hear him.

CHOSEN	ENTER	FIRST
RACE	TO	LINK
WILL	PERISH	GODS
END	PROPHECY	EARTH

"Look at the words and phrases, *they all have meaning*." Christopher said. "Follow the words down each column and fill in the blanks. A chosen race will end. Enter to perish the prophecy. First link to God's earth."

"What can this mean, my clever friend?" Mashir knew Christopher too well. *He is the one*. Mashir nodded with admiration. But it was the professor who cut in first.

"Now, try interpreting the text by reading it from left to right as one long continuous row," Fabio said excitedly because he now saw what Christopher had already worked out. The professor took the lead, "*The chosen, enter first, race to the link, will perish Gods, to end the prophecy of earth*."

Professor Mancini was always one to make things difficult for Christopher, but nevertheless, he had always strived for the truth. The group watched the professor's face as a gradual enlightenment showed. He must have seen these words before. Glancing momentarily at the others, he realised he'd been found out. They waited for him to tell his dark secret, his truth.

"Well, professor, it seems as though you have something else for us." Mashir said.

"Si, the old manuscript, I have seen these words before, back in Rome, but I believed it only to be a dream, like looking for the Holy Grail, but then the trail has led us here. An inspiration for any archaeologist or explorer. It is quite a remarkable find, if not impossible. It has been sent to us by God!" Fabio looked at Mashir, his face astonished at the interpretation. It confirmed everything to him, especially his own right to be here!

"Is there anything else you would like to tell us, professor? You now seem to be a step ahead of us." Barbaro was angry because he was completely in the dark, the powers in Rome had excluded him.

Christopher stared in disbelief at the professor, realising that he must have known all along that the symbols in the Temple were Masonic. *Mancini, had to know!*

"You are a Freemason, am I right?" Christopher blurted with annoyance.

"No, I am not, and these are not Freemasonic symbols, they are far older. The Masons adopted or were guided to use these for their own purposes." It seemed as though Fabio was holding back more information.

"Stop splitting hairs, Fabio!" Harjit snapped at the professor, knowing that they all needed to pull together and trust each other. "Why not tell them! The parable that Christopher spoke about earlier, those words seemed good guidance to what we should do right now!"

"Ok, the three ships will sink alone. Comradeship, membership and friendship, as is the might of arms, but it will not be enough alone against his hordes. These words are the 'Three Degrees'. Standing here together, right now, is us! We are the three ships!" Fabio stated bluntly.

"Islamic, Christian and Hindu all the great religions of man, there are others like Judaism, Buddhism and others. However, with a Freemason, it is a way of life," said Christopher, concurring with Fabio's mooted nod. "Freemasonry is not a religion, it is more akin to a catalyst. It is a way to find God. Look over there, at the wall." Christopher said, pointing to the large wall in front of them. "See, the star drawn from the grooves? You can see it as the Cross of David, and as all Freemasons should know, can be extrapolated from the square and compass of Freemasonry. The star represents Judean *εάqnov*. We, are the ones chosen as brothers together as predicted in the prophecy."

Captors and captured alike were all spellbound at this revelation. They all listened silently as the girl took over with her own pin-dropping prophecy.

"To interpret the prophecy, all will falter like a sinking vessel, but not if we have comradeship, friendship and membership to the brotherhood bonding everyone and everything we hold dear to us, together. All religions and all countries need to pray and fight against this. This evil horde that comes to take us!" Harjit's tone dropped to soft whisper. "There is still hope, I think." More than intuition, she had felt this unknown dread many times before, but now she knew for sure that a great evil was on its way. They all did.

"You are very astute, Harjit." Fabio said. "I have looked at the scripture time and time again. I still do not fully understand it. I too believe that we are all here together, not only in the "Three Degrees" but also the five, Christian, Islamic, Judean, Buddha and Hindu. Remember, Mathieson is wounded, but the man is with us too. He is Jewish and is part of this battle as well."

"The five," Harjit smiled softly in covenant with him.

"Only the pure will survive, non-sinners, other civilizations, their souls were sacrificed and died as something evil approaches," Christopher repeated. "I agree. We do not have a lot of time left. Feel it, there is tension in the air, as if it hinted thunder. And, the thunder will be great!" Chris began speaking the quoted parable of the third paragraph.

"Humble yourself to unity to one god with patient perseverance, faith and prayer. All will be tested, and so look east north east, from Malisiblis for help, as Iblis smite surrounds you with despair."

"We must unite. Unite all our forces, all our peoples, all our religions, Spirits and look to the East-North-East from the Temple, for help!

Iblis smite surrounds us, but we will not despair. We will meet despair head on! Put your faith in God! God will prevail!"

The frightened soldiers gathered around him as they were attracted by the strength coming from his powerful words. They had been listening closely and on the edge of panic, but knew that the unity of their spirits might prevail and save them.

"Words. have influence in this place and are linked to God," said Harjit.

"Or the Devil, for he is here too, and make no mistake of that!" Barbaro quickly countered. "Remember those things above, those devilish creatures, have you all forgotten what lurks inside this awful place?" Barbaro balanced her view.

Her revulsion answered his question.

"Devil be damned, he is not here, not Kali, Kroni or your goat devil, only their minions! No, because the demon of all is on its way! We have already spoken the enchanted word 'NASOM' and in those conditions at the time, everything went crazy! Maybe we have to say them again, maybe there are more words of power we must discover, *magic words we need to open this place.*" Harjit concluded.

"Indeed, we need a sacrifice. The riddles will then unfold, my friends," Mashir said. He seemed oddly prepared for such an event.

Christopher stood firm, looking at the white stonewall in front. He was standing on a rougher stone surface underneath his feet. It appeared to be made of the same type of crystalline white stone—just as hard and dense as the granite that surrounded them in the great cubed hall.

Kneeling for a closer inspection, he could see a slight difference in texture. He then used his hands to feel the chiselled-out surface below him. The surface was the same non-colour to the stone floor and made it almost indistinguishable to see. He swept his hands slowly over the rough surface, believing that it was another message. The others looked down at him questionably. The bio-technologist continued to touch what might be numbers and text. Quickly using a black felt-tipped pen from his top shirt pocket, he marked the grooved lines, highlighting them for everyone to see them.

He first drew an outer line that formed a pentangle and then marked the text within the ancient symbol. Christopher stared at the familiar writings. Taking out his pocket Bible, he held it in his left hand and placed his right hand on top, saying the following powerful words.

"Here is the bond from Osleiotect.
Only the pure may enter within as this is a
dominion of Nelumakragas.
The linkage of life beacons to linkage of death.
Hold your left hand supporting your sacred words.
Right hand resting thereon.
No further you can go.
Enter then my apprentice."

After the words had been spoken, the temperature began to drop acutely, and it became cold, increasingly cold. In seconds, their environment became more like an ice cube.

"My God," said Fabio. The sudden change made his skin pimple and body shake. The place felt like the Arctic.

Simultaneously, everyone began to feel an invisible external pressure, squeezing on their freezing bodies.

They all looked around anxiously, wondering what would happen next.

When abruptly, loud machine gun fire began breaking the atmosphere like a giant type writer gone mad. Gunfire in multiple staccato delivered instant violence from somewhere inside the passageway behind them. The group jumped in fright and surprise.

All hell broke loose. There was shouting and shooting, mixing death and luck in fateful blasts.

FRRRRRRRRRAK! FRRRRRRRRRAK! FRRRRRRRRRAK. FRRRRRRRRRAK!

The Islamic guards' weapons were firing just inside the corridor and other fully automatic gunfire created *new type written noises* — its mechanics pitched much higher, coming in ricochets from the passageway.

It was becoming more like a shooting gallery inside the chamber. Their lives were hanging in the balance.

Attackers were using three second sharper spurts and some bullets were getting through and striking the wall of the inner Temple with metallic sounds.

The group of fearful explorers was hunched over, as the Islamic guards turned around anxiously to watch the tunnel entrance. With the shooting getting closer by the second, the soldiers next to them began shouting and screaming orders.

Machine guns were now firing just beyond the entrance, accompanied by a few sudden explosions and dense smoke. The fumes moved along the inside of the convoluted passageway.

Soon, the gas began spreading slowly inside the cubed chamber, where they stood. The Islamic guards readied themselves to thwart the incoming and determined enemy.

Their AK47 100 round drum mags were levelled and ready to spit death at any adversary who dared to enter. The soldiers ran over to reinforce the breached area. Combat inside was imminent.

Mashir and the others, except for Christopher, looked around at the unfolding events.

"What is going on? Who is shooting?" screamed Harjit.

"Maybe those creatures have found a way down?" Barbaro's terrified face stiffened with fear.

"A rescue," Fabio stated optimistically.

"Come on, Christopher!" Mashir shouted. "If we do not get inside right now, we never will!"

The distressed bio-technologist was confused at the ensuing mayhem around him as he listened to Mashir screaming.

Mashir was sweating despite the cold and was losing his composure and self-control. For the first time, Christopher saw his friend panicking.

"Gentlemen, I must hurry you," the Sarvan said, directing his weapon towards Christopher. "You must gain access to this inner Temple. I can no longer guarantee your safety." While checking his AK, the man was getting ready for close combat and needed Christopher to complete what was expected of him. His weapon commanded him to do it now or die.

Smoke was twisting inside the passageway. *They're going to kill us when we open the Temple,* he thought in a moment of truth. Swallowing hard, he turned and stared into Harjit's eyes.

"Chris, I love you," Harjit said softly from under her breath, "They are going to kill us if they cannot get inside the Temple, and if not, what is coming down that corridor most likely will!"

The girl needed hope but expected no mercy at the thought of the mad creatures scuttling their way down to meet them, or whoever else might want to kill them.

"Come on, Chris, get us inside, it's our only hope!" Mashir pressed. More bursts of rapid and frenzied machine gun fire ensued.

FRRRRRRRRAK! FRRRRRRRRAK!

The Sarvan's men started coughing inside the chamber and a few others joined from the corridor beyond, while the irritating smoke curled around them.

Leaving the group, the captain sprinted over to see how bad the situation was for his men who were engulfed in gas. His soldiers were coughing semi-spasmodically, while holding their battle positions at the entrance.

"Enemy, sir," the soldier was spitting to clear his throat, "they were on us before we had a chance to repel them! The crossed sons have come again, and the infidel foe is very determined."

Crouching down, the soldier quickly updated his officer, as bullets ricocheting around them, forcing them to hunch down with more smoke engulfing around them.

He had no option, and commanded his men to fall back and take a last defensive position deep inside the cubed hall, along with the scientists. They would die together and if the bullets did not kill them, then the intense cold would. The temperature had dipped to below zero, and ice was already forming all over the stone surfaces.

Retreating to where the prisoners stood, the last of his men lay down next to the scientists in a defensive semicircle, with two in front and two pairs on either flank, with their tripod and barrel machine guns ready to spit God's wrath or glory in a crossfire one last time. The other soldiers were standing and breathing heavy from the back. They were ready and resolute in their purpose. They were strong in spirit. None of them would die easily. They would fight hard to keep this haloed place. It was theirs. They stood waiting proudly for their mortal enemy to appear from the smoke. This was it.

****

CHAPTER X

GATEWAY OF THE GODS

Captain Abdul-Haleem stood in front of his men. The captain, with no shred of a doubt, believed it was their divine rite to be here. Over the centuries, it had always been a race against time to find this place, the Temple. The man wondered doubtfully, *Are we already too late?* He stared questionably at Mashir and then at Christopher. His eyes were almost looking for guidance. Suddenly, from the smoky passageway, a muffled voice called to them. He turned to meet the threat.

"We belong to the Ninth Degree Paracadutista Special Forces Assault Regiment," the voice shouted with authority from the smoke, "And I am the Commanding Officer, Maggiore Trentino! My force is superior in numbers and I have come for the release of your prisoners! They are here in good faith, a civilian force with full authority from the Brazilian Government."

Negotiation had begun.

"You do not belong here, Maggiore!" the captain shouted loudly, rebuffing the major's intension. The commander of the United Arabian and African countries remained silent, while watching the dispersing smoke and planning his next move.

"I am in control of the Temple and have taken full authority. The civilians were granted permission to be here by the government. You have not. Lay down your arms," he ordered seriously. "Sir, I would like your terms for their release and your surrender." The major said, making his case and his intentions clear. The Islamic soldiers readied themselves inside the large hall, and in answer, reloaded and cocked their mechanised weapons loudly. A heavy silence ensued.

"I am Sarvan Abdul Haleem of the United Makka countries of Arab and African States, Islamic Special Forces," the captain said, identifying himself and his own authority.

"Give it up, Sarvan!" the major shouted sharply from the smoke.

"Our rite here is a just cause!" replied the Sarvan. "It is Allah who has overall sovereignty inside this Temple, major, not you nor these civilians!" His voice grew stronger in defiance. "We will not surrender!" His frosty breath formed a weird frost all over the walls. By this time, everyone was shivering from the cold.

The Swiss commander said nothing. Each adversary was completely indoctrinated, both knowing that any further attack would end in the killing of all the civilians—a risky strategy and one that would also jeopardise entry into the inner Temple.

"You must surrender and save any more bloodshed! There has been too much spilled already," The major appealed to the Iranian captain.

"We are here, and this is our holy shrine by Rite of Allah! This place belongs to my people as stated in the Parchment of the Lost Scrolls! You can observe that our guests are in good health and will remain so long as you retire your men from this place immediately, Maggiore!" the Sarvan demanded.

"I cannot do that!" The soldier was solid as stone.

"You and your forces are not welcome here, Maggiore!"

Minutes passed slowly, and both combatants had taken casualties, so neither was of a mind to give up their personal goals. Fabio had an idea.

"Sarvan, please give me your binoculars, there may be text on the face of the inner Temple entrance. It is too far away. It's like the text Christopher is standing on and I think it is also inscribed on its surface."

The Sarvan nodded smartly, giving him his binoculars. This could be a game-changer. Unsure, Fabio looked desperately for an answer. His keen eyes searched for a way in, aware that he did not have long because the hard frost was beginning to spread everywhere, even onto the Temple's surface. Its thickness would soon make it impossible to read. The professor studied it for a minute, while the tension increased between the combatants. He could hear guns being cocked and readied again for a fight to the death.

"Christopher," Fabio urged with fear. "Quick, man, *quick!* There are masses of tiny symbols on top. They are nothing like what we have seen before, the entire surface is covered!" Fabio's voice was faltering, as he stared blankly at Christopher. The priest took the glasses and immediately began scanning the white surface area.

"Not quite, professor. There are similar symbols strung together in a particular geometrical structure, but it is strangely familiar to me," Christopher said, sounding relieved.

"Well then?" Fabio demanded. He could not take much more of this suspense. *God, its freezing in here,* Fabio thought. He was shivering and the chamber was like a freezer. Fabio's teeth were chattering. *Something is meant to happen.*

"These ancient people are far more advanced than our own civilisations. *They know our language.* These people have tried to communicate with us throughout the past centuries, if not for thousands of years. It's incredible! These images that I can see, and Harjit can corroborate this," his eyes scanned along the wide surface, "these lines I am looking at right now, *my God,*" Chris gulped hard, "I have only seen them at the end of an electron microscope! I am observing the human genome right now."

"Let me see, Chris, let me see!" Harjit insisted, desperate to see this astounding observation with her own eyes, her body was shivering but for a moment, the intense cold was forgotten in her over-excitement.

"Harjit, please concur. I observe twenty-three pairs of chromosomes as seen in humans, including the X chromosome, plus mitochondrial genes seen over there on the left of the pentagon door and also seen on the opposite over to the right side of the door. These markings resemble a long length of 'left handed' and 'double stranded' alpha helix. On the right, is another alpha-helix, incredible." Christopher briefly explained the genetics, while quickly handing her the binoculars.

"By the *Trimurti of Brahma the Creator* I do recognise this. At least these patterns and the tiny graphic. They are almost transparent images of the master map gene sequence, but I am not sure what build it is. We would need to 'highlight' them to be sure. There is too little time to analyse them and the others. The recombinant possibilities are quite staggering." Harjit was mesmerised by the sheer scale and impact of their fantastic discovery.

Mashir and Sarvan stared at each other, both in hypnotic thought, both unable to understand genetics but realised how astounding a discovery like this was. Fabio gasped hard, while Barbaro blubbered quiet curses in denial.

"This will reshape everything," stated Christopher. "Our own being, links to our own creation, our own Genesis." Christopher's voice was holding no compromise, knowing that this discovery had Biblical importance. Why else would Christendom and Islam come together head to head? This was no chance meeting. It was meant to be.

****

Everyone was shivering involuntary, as the physical atmosphere inside the cubed chamber had become Arctic for no explainable reason, or was there? Christopher's words of magic had triggered some sort of chain reaction in some mysterious esoteric ceremony. So, was it really by chance or preordained? Nevertheless, the ceremony had started but it was incomplete, an essential ingredient was still missing. It was now eleven fifty in the evening on the thirtieth of October. The time was right and everything was set.

The major, in command of his soldiers, the *'Cross of Light'* Crossbow Regiment shouted over again to his opposite number.

"I would respectfully request that I speak with you face to face sarvan!" shouted Trentino.

Captain Haleem watched the dispersing fumes while casting a quick glance at his prisoners one by one. He thoughtfully left his gaze firmly fixed on Mashir.

"Let me see you then, major, come out of the smoke! I give my permission for you to come forward." The captain agreed.

The major stood out from the smoke, took off his gas mask and walked forward, with his men appearing a few seconds later as the gas lifted away at his back. He saw them squat down and they were ready on either side of him, with machine guns fixed ahead.

"Sarvan." the major said, watching his foe's cold body language.

"Yes, major, come forward unarmed so we can speak. The last thing we want is any collateral damage. We are not barbarians, despite your judgement of us." The captain agreed. He knew that their mission would fail if his prisoners were mistakenly killed. Right now, he needed them more than ever because of what had just happened.

Major Trentino walked confidently out from the corridor and into the large and dimly-lit cubed hall, studying the group of shivering people and seeing the Islamic soldiers all heavily armed in a defensive circle around the prisoners.

The captain opened his top collar aggressively, exposing his own gold chain. He pulled it down tight to show it proudly and display his own pedigree in battle, showing off his distinguished medallion of the 'United Crossed Sword' before his cocky adversary. His challenge to the major was clear.

Captain Abdul-Haleem then moved forward to meet the major. The Swiss guardsman was tracked by AKs every step of the way. If there was any hint of deceit, they would shoot first and ask questions later. The major was not to be trusted.

The men stood a few metres apart and saluted sharply, regarding each other suspiciously and what the next moments would bring. The cold expressions between them displayed nothing. Underneath this game of chess, both men had respect for each other's combative abilities. They were both elite. A fitting match for each other.

The major immediately recognized the united red and green crescent moon with golden star tattooed on the man's muscle-bound forearm. It was the same ensign he saw earlier, that of the United Makka Arab and African countries. His eyes were briefly drawn to his shiny medallion as the Sarvan came closer. This was given only to those who have served Allah in battle, showing great bravery and intelligence against many foes and had survived martyrdom.

The captain also wore his family's golden bracelet on his wrist. An heirloom that he believed gave him luck. Captain Abdul-Haleem began his deadly game of chess, where they both would try to control the centre.

The Christian's move, thought Abdul-Haleem, as the major watched the Sarvan's stony face.

"You are far from home, Sarvan?" observing his rank, the major's preamble started the clock. One, *White Pawn moves e4.*

"We both are, major. My mission here is holy and I have orders to seek out and return the final Lost Scripture to Makka." One, *Black Pawn, e5.*

"What is that exactly?" the major asked in ignorance. His breath blew frostily into the freezing air. Two, *White Knight Nf3.*

"It is the lost holy documents and a sacred book that our Prophet Muhammad spoke of in his secret works. It was not widely known about, as the masses would not understand them at that time. They were stolen from him by the infidel and lost. Despite vain attempts of rediscovery, they were lost and never found." Two, *Black Knight Nc6.*

"It seems to me that you have strayed a little off course by coming here." The major smiled with a hint of superiority. Three, *White Bishop moves to Bc4.*

"*You too* are far from home, major and have come here, killing my men unlawfully!" His tone was harder than concrete. Three, *Black Knight moves to Nd4.* His voice was judgemental, and his eyes with filled with disapproval. Plainly, he wanted the major to leave this arena.

"Si." The major paused. "Accept my apologies for your lost brothers." Then, his tone hardened, "My men too have died. My place here is unambiguous. I have my holy orders direct and clear, they are to recover our people safely and make this area secure, returning any possessions back to His Holiness. This place and his children are now under his divine protection, and I am his cross." The major's bold words defended his position. Four, *White Knight moves Nxe5.*

The captain expected this strong stance and it was exactly what he wanted to hear.

"Interesting, major," he said, recognizing his 'crossbow' insignia, "It is more than just coincidence that we are both here, is it not? For the same reason as I, however, you want to steal the book of sacred words as other Christians did before you!" Sarvan was adamant. "Is this not the truth?" Anger pulsated inside the bulging veins in his arms and forehead. It was not easy holding back, but the captain remained composed. Four, *Black Queen moves Qg5.*

Major Trentino knew that the captain made sense. His own superior, the colonel was the officer who had guided the Swiss units to the Temple and only the colonel knew the full facts to why his elite force was sent here. The major had not been told why, other than this being a rescue mission. The seed of doubt sewn inside the major's mind was now germinating.

Smiling again, with eyes like acid, the major recognised the divisive tactic played by Sarvan Abdul-Haleem to unhinge his purpose, so he refocused on his orders.

"Listen, I want those four civilians and the rest of their party." His tone was insistent and his patience was fraying. Five, *White Knight attacks Nf7.*

"I will make a deal, major. You may have them but then, you and your men must retire, leaving all your possessions and you must not return. The captain spoke with complete lingual control. His steady soft tone spoke with complete authority and ownership. In his mind, the game was not finished, mentally positioning his Bishop. Five, *Black Queen in position Qxg2!*

"So, now, we have a problem, Sarvan," said the major. "What this expedition has uncovered belongs to us. It is law." Coming to the end of the parley. The Chess clock ticking, Trentino waiting for a response, Six, *White Rook Castle's and defends Rf1.*

"Major, please, we do not want any additional bloodshed, we are not murderers or delusional martyrs by which all our people have been branded. Be clear. My men and I are prepared to meet Allah this evening with you. Do not underestimate our purpose and determination. Everyone will die."

Sarvan Abdul-Haleem spoke with cold precision and ruthless lucidity in a bold move. Six, *Black Queen Attacks, Check Qxe4+.*

"Do not believe him, Maggiore, his band of cut-throats have already murdered the others!" Fabio shouted at the major. "Mashir told us of their murder, our friends are all dead!"

The major's rock-hard eyes narrowed into slits, searching for the truth in Abdul-Haleem's.

When unexpectedly, Mashir called out too. Mashir knew that violence between both adversaries would be swift and everyone's mutual annihilation would be certain. There was a final move to make, when Mashir stepped in and intervened.

"I am not sure! This place is evil. It works on our minds, all our minds, my mind too! Even now, it tries to undermine all our people!" Mashir's tone trembled in panic. Everyone was confused at his interruption. Mashir was unsure of what to say next.

Christopher, for the second time in a few minutes, saw a man he no longer recognised. The surveyor's whole-body language was somehow different. What was happening was not normal.

"You said," spoke Fabio, looking astonished at Mashir, while thinking to himself, *Why would he lie about something so serious? Mashir's behaviour is unlike him!*

"I said," Mashir looked apologetic and timid, "that they might be dead, *only that!* I am not sure anymore! Sorry, professor, forgive me." Mashir's tone regretted his confused words. "It's this place, it gets to you. It made me lie." Mashir lied again.

"Well, captain?" Trentino furrowed his brows and expected an answer from the captain. The game was over, but the clock was still ticking in this duel of wits. Both men understood that this was the defining moment for all.

"They are alive, major." The captain spoke calmly and in truth. "This man is mistaken." His eyes held the major's laser eyes. "I cannot allow you to take them. My men cover you and you are already aware that my forces hold other key positions within the Temple." The captain was still in control and this time, he smiled peacefully at the major.

"You are outnumbered, Sarvan," he stated simply.

"Numbers do not count in here. These passageways are built for defence." Sarvan Haleem spoke the truth.

"We managed to get this far." Trentino's confidence matched the captain's smile. None knew the exact strength of each other's force. Each duellist was determined, stepping one step closer to mutual destruction.

"This place is evil, major, have you not felt this yet? I have lost many men inside. It will kill your men too. Your elite guardia will not avail you. None will return from this place. It is so written," Abdul-Haleem stated hard as iron, and for the first time, looked grim.

"The will of Christ be done, sarvan Haleem." Trentino's hot words were condensing like a Genie in the freezing air around his face.

The major began slowly moving backwards, keeping his eyes fixed firmly on the captain. Their game was nearly over. Seven, *White Bishop retreats to defend his King of Kings, Be2.*

"Major, I ask you. Have you not already seen things, unexplained things in the valley or felt the despair inside here? I think that both Christ and Allah have forsaken this place, don't you?" he stated fatefully. Seven, *Black Knight moves finally and Nf3# 1-0.*

Checkmate.

The captain gave the Swiss guardsman a stark last warning and for all concerned, combat was inevitable. An unexpected cold tingle began running through everyone's body, making them shiver at exactly the same moment. They all felt it spreading slowly through them as if an icy spirit had embraced their souls before death.

Trentino shivered stiffly, perceiving the impact of captain's final parting blow of words. The icy feeling made his eyes narrow more, searching this time for some invisible enemy around him, just like the Islamists had because they already knew this feeling too well, a queer unnatural presence.

And with these dark thoughts imprinted into his mind that weird image came to him again—he had not forgotten it. Trentino recalled that gigantic bird of some kind, an evil looking thing, its memory wiping away his confidence. This was something he could not understand. It was illogical. It was impossible. The major remembered the colossal featherless bird. He saw it through his scope when his unit had just bordered the vale of Iblis for the first time. He saw its vile unnatural ugly form. Trentino's confidence was peppered with uncertainty. *What is this place? Surely none of this is real,* he wondered as the creature DEATH haunted him.

The conversation did not take long. The pressure was mounting between both officers. The straining atmosphere, albeit polite and firm, was dry as a tinderbox. Moving apart, their chess game over. The peculiar hard frost was adhering to the walled surfaces and was spreading across the stone floor towards the corridor. Everyone watched the strange phenomenon and were afraid to guess what was happening. *Again, the prophecy.*

Christopher quickly took the binoculars to see what Harjit had described. The bio-technologist's articulated mind worked swiftly as he toyed with several possibilities. Mashir suddenly shivered. He was observing Christopher and realized he had seen something new.

"Chris, my friend, what do you see?"

"To the right, the genetic patterns are almost like our own, except there is another extra two chromosomes—a total of twenty-five pairs! The base geometry matches my knowledge and the atomic representations are drawn in Masonic symbols." *What the hell is this place all about?* he thought, frowning in confusion. "It is clearly an intelligent civilisation we are dealing with and another species altogether, not human. They lived here thousands of years ago. This writing remains for us to interpret its meaning. This is a big IF.

Even if the Spaniards or Portuguese got this far, which I doubt, they would not have gotten any further because their knowledge was restricted by dogma and doctrine, let alone lack of scientific knowledge that we have today."

"Si, doctrine would have prevented this as blasphemy in any case," Fabio concurred.

"They failed at the first hurdle because of the alignment on the Temple top. These events were not to occur for another five hundred years!"

"And?" Mashir prompted Fabio.

"Yes, this is the place, here and right now, Mashir, right NOW!" the professor knew there were too many coincidences. "This is the correct date, correct time, correct year and correct Temple!" Fabio clarified.

"There are faint words, other words of a different shape, and tiny symbols that are harder to see. They were blurry and I could not make them out. They were inscribed within the genome itself. Look, just below the Seven Rays." Harjit was trying to describe what she had seen as best she could.

"I know." Christopher nodded grimly, and did not say what those words were, but he dreaded them. He tightened his lips. *Were they words of wisdom or words of power?*

Fabio had an idea. "Say the words again, Christopher, then add those words to the end of your narration," he instructed. There was very little time left. It was twelve o'clock in the evening. The Swiss guards withdrew to take their final positions and were ready to attack. The enemy captain gave his men final words of encouragement before engagement.

Christopher readied himself to recite the faded words on the wall. He took a deep breath, then stood on the same spot where the first script lay underneath his feet. He began:

"Here is the bond from Osleiotect.
Only the pure may enter within as this is a dominion of Nelumakragas.
The linkage of life beacons to linkage of death.
Hold your left hand supporting your secret words
Right hand resting thereon.
No further you can go.
Enter then my apprentice."

Something was missing. Christopher hesitated, and did not say the final words.

"Nothing is happening, Christopher, you have not completed it! Come on read it again and finish it this time, read it all, man! Read it all!" Mashir's accelerated voice was blaring at Christopher with urgency, with only seconds before a firefight would ruin everything. "You must!!!"

"Harjit, let me look at your watch." Her watch was the most reliable.

"Oh, Chris, no don't do this." The girl was terrified for his safety.

"Please," he insisted softly, "Count-down to exactly twelve o'clock."

"Sarvan," Christopher ordered, "give your bayonet to Mashir." The Sarvan looked doubtfully at Christopher but quickly handed the long blade to the surveyor.

"Well, Chris, what do I do?" Mashir asked with a fraught look of apprehension, as he accepted the blade from a Christian priest's hands.

"Mashir, trust me. When I read the text again and right to the end this time, it completes the magic with blood. Timing is critical. Cut my hand at that moment, and I will recite it a third time and then pray to God that there is nothing else I need you to do." He looked him right in the eyes. "Wait exactly to the second on midnight, then cut me. It approaches, so get ready." He looked at Harjit's watch. "You have exactly sixty seconds from now. Don't be late." He encouraged his friend, but Mashir knew the power of blood.

"Words of power, too," Mashir stated respectfully, as he took the razor-sharp blade and readied himself. "Are you certain that you want me to do this thing to you?" His hands were trembling at the thought of cutting him, and if this did not work, Chris's intimation was clear on the third narration. Kill him.

Christopher knelt on top of the words below him and held out his hand and began again, loud and clear. Harjit counted the seconds down.

"I will pray for you, brother." Mashir feared the worst for his friend as Christopher read the text one last time with pure clarity, and this time, completed the sentence.

On that exact hour and that exact second, Mashir cut the hand of Christopher. The priests blood burst out and began to flow across his hand. The magical fluid dripped warmly onto the pentangle and sacred words below him, turning the stone a crimson colour. Chris placed his left hand on top of the rough stone surface and held his pocket Bible in the other. While they waited and watched, Christopher recited the sacred words for a third time.

"Here is the bond from Osleiotect.
Only the pure may enter within as this is a
dominion of Nelumakragas.
The linkage of life beacons to linkage of death.
Hold your left hand supporting your secret words
Right hand resting thereon.
No further you can go.
Enter then my apprentice."

He followed it with the last words from the genome, saying:

"Sacrifice and saviour!"

Christopher was completely drained, then got up wearily upon completing the unknown ceremony. His bloody hand was self-evident. He looked at Mashir.

Suddenly, he heard something, something unnatural. He was the only one who heard it. It sounded like a hushed murmur of distant and close chattering of strange voices. He could not comprehend what it was – the shadows. He looked at Mashir who raised his bayonet.

Both military officers detected a change in the cubed hall too, they sensed an unbalance of nature. It was as though they were tuning into a lost radio station. Then, the signal came in clear and focused and tuned into everyone inside the hall.

Mashir's raised hand stopped mid-air. Both officers recognised the imminent danger to everyone. They had felt something like this before during the earthquake not too long ago.

The fatal words had been spoken, ones that had never been spoken before. A silent dialog began, heard only by Christopher. These mysterious mutterings were becoming increasingly more clear. He was listening to conversations inside his own mind.

The voices of the silent 'watchers' were speaking to each other above and around him. Christopher attempted to understand their outlandish language. Their excited voices echoed inside him when suddenly, the enclosed area felt compressed, squeezing tight around them as though they were in a pressure chamber.

The frosty atmosphere began to enclose around them. Ice coated everything, living and non-living, and the temperature plummeted even more. Everyone's clothes were hardening fast. The soldiers stood ready to fight, but what?

What did they fear? There was terror in their eyes. It was uncanny waiting for something to happen, while gradually freezing to death. Frost coated the walls, floor and ceiling. Harjit looked fearfully at Christopher staring upwards; Chris mesmerised by the moment and listening to those who spoke from above. She motioned to touch his frozen body. She felt anxious at his apparent lack of awareness.

"Leave him, Harjit, don't touch him. He has been chosen to open this doorway." Mashir's teeth were chattering in the intense cold. He was acutely aware that Christopher was in a trance. His safety depended on finishing what he started alone. Harjit could kill Christopher if she misguidedly touched him, and like a rejection, stood back.

"We are all going to freeze to death, captain, if we stay here!" shouted the major's blue lips while he waited with his shivering men.

"You are right! This is uncanny!" the captain replied.

Fabio was frightened but in awe of this unique event that had never been witnessed before. Nothing like this has ever happened to him before in all his explorations of ancient tombs and pyramids.

Suddenly, all the flamed torches around the room quickly diminished, and the room darkened ominously. The temperature dropped even more, when the crystals of ice began crunching and crackling tighter together. If they did not leave in the next few minutes everybody would be dead.

The major recalled that he and his men had felt something strange like this before, earlier, when he and his men first approached the Temple. It happened a few seconds before a terrible explosion occurred that sent everything in the jungle into chaos.

Without warning, Christopher snapped out of his trance, pallor pure white and beard iced over in hard crust, his senses truncated by cold numbness. He looked around with suppressed dismay for reassurance, while trying to gather what was going on. His body was shaking involuntary.

Fabio had chosen well again. The professor could not believe the younger man's superior intellect, drawing on all that he had discovered, and to be standing here together for this moment. The professor spoke to Christopher softly, not wanting to draw too much attention to them both.

"I have to say, my boy, I admire your tenacity for learning and mental capacity. You are gifted." Fabio spoke earnestly, almost apologetically, which was very unlike him. "I was wrong about our ideas. However, I was right about one thing." He paused, looking satisfied. "I was right to bring you here on this expedition. We could not have gone any farther without a key to get inside the Temple."

"But, where is this key, professor?" Christopher's teeth were chattering.

"It's here, right here," Fabio stated quietly, "Because Christopher, you *are* the key!" The professor smiled in complete admiration. Christopher's frozen face cracked a smile back at the leader's own icy beard. It was the professor's way of apologising.

"Professor, nothing has taken place." Christopher felt awkward and undeserving of Fabio's approval.

Everyone was shivering to death.

On the opposite wall, 'The Seven Rays' began emitting a weird radiance, and everyone felt its immediate heat too. At first, a glorious warmth. The temperature instantly rose, then became uncomfortable and melted the frost away in a few seconds. The intense hot rays were another extreme force, as it evaporated any water that was left of the melting ice.

Remarkably, the ice was gone. It was as if a transparent energy pulse had travelled unseen across the whole area, causing the naked torch flames to begin spluttering back to life.

The moat stood in front of them, and as if from nowhere, a flame ignited and turned into a deadly ball of energy.

Some groaned in fear, while others were speechless or cursing epithets at it. There it remained, floating menacingly above the empty void, and with each passing moment, intensifying in strength before them.

They stepped back. Some already knew what might happen next, as they had been witness to a horrific conflagration like this before — that of the librarian, Beppi Genovesi. He had died a horrible death, while giving them a way inside.

But that energy ball in front of the outer Temple's property had been much different to this. It was like all uncontrolled events — furious and uncontained and created out of an electric field and alchemy. This one, on the other hand, was controlled. Its energy was twisted in a controlled expectancy and was created out of a flaming sun. It needed more alchemy to complete its purpose.

The intense ferocity of raw energy roared while the sun hung suspended before them. Sweat ran down their roasting brows and scorching faces, and nothing remained of the frozen conditions.

Unpredictably, the walls of the cubed chamber were suddenly becoming overly bright, generating the same white intensity seen first by Fabio and his fellow team members when they had first discovered this place weeks ago. Everyone was rooted to the floor. They were paralysed. These unbearable events were happening too quickly for their numbed minds to catch up.

The time to run and hide or make peace had passed, with this uncanny illumination bathing everything. Everyone was waiting for something. Judgement.

Oh God! Is it really happening? Christopher wondered. *It is going to happen again, just like with Beppi, it must!* Christopher knew someone must die, and that person was him. The prophecy would greedily take him. With fate impending, its next victim began praying that it would be a quicker death than poor Beppi's horrific sacrifice.

Please deliver me, oh God, quickly into your arms.

****

In this last moment of life, Christopher shook nervously as the flames streaked down at him like a flame-thrower. Suddenly, Fabio jumped in between them, knocking Chris forcibly over and sending him sprawling across the floor.

Professor Mancini was instantly struck with the raging force of fire.

"Aaaagheeee!" Fabio shrieking loudly.

Christopher turned around to see the flaming man.

"Fabio!" Harjit screamed. Her voice was blurred against the roaring flames.

The ball's ferocity instantly wrapped around his body, enclosing him in what appeared to be a mighty fiery claw. The man screamed in agony, his body writhing and wriggling in pain.

The fiery fist held onto Fabio, then picked him up with some esoteric magic, and rotated him slowly as though he was on a spit, then inexorably pulled the helpless man into the waiting inferno.

A gasp went up from the all soldiers and scientists caught up in this macabre spectacle. Fabio was covered in a cocoon of flames.

"Professor!" Christopher shouted.

The dead man was suspended for a moment longer as the ball of flames consumed his shaking rag doll-like body. The professor's body popped and burst into a hissing mess of evaporation and the flaming orb imploded with a weird sucking in of air. Everything was gone with a whooshing noise, leaving nothing, except a horrible burning smell. Professor Fabio Mancini, Expedition Leader, was gone.

"He is dead. Phew." The major was bewildered at the orb's destructive power. He recognised this as his own personal failure, unaware that he could not have prevented what happened and that the Prophecy had claimed another life

Christopher sighed sadly, his head dropping in mixed emotions of guilt and anger that Fabio's life had been sacrificed to save his.

Everyone struggled to come to terms with what they saw, stunned at the extreme violence, and speechless that such an impossibility had come to pass.

A blue light began flooding into the chamber, dulling down the whiteness to nil. This uncanny blue luminescence dominated the room.

Christopher looked up wearily, trying to assimilate its meaning. His jaw dropped, because before him, he saw a secret doorway move slowly and grittily backwards, then stop. The stone door waited further inside for a short moment, then slid dryly downwards and out of sight.

Behold!

Unearthly echoes started coming out from the open entrance doorway. Everyone cringed at the strange and frightening winnowing winds that were blowing out from the guts of the inner Temple. This was bad. This was worse.

Christopher shivered. They all shivered. Something evil lurked inside. At last, the doorway lay open, awaiting their arrival. This was their way; the only way, and it would take a lot of steel to enter it.

Christopher got up, staggering on with his heavy head tilted forward to his chest, half toppling forward towards the pit. Unbalanced and dutifully drained by the exertion of these esoteric events, Christopher appeared disjointed from his mind, heading hypnotically towards certain death.

Still in shock, everyone watched him as he walked towards the gap and blued-out doom, all except Mashir. Mashir moved quickly, aware of the imminent danger and grabbed him hard, stopping him from joining the ill-fated Fabio. The Iranian caught him just in time. He pulled him away from the moat, and gave him a great bear hug in brotherhood or love. Fabio was dead, but his friend was still alive.

"Chris, my brother, this, is not your fate," Mashir said, shaking his head.

"A strange light, I see, and a strange wind, I hear. *What does it all mean?*" Haleem looked around apprehensively, then over towards its source. "It is evil!". Captain Haleem's tone was fearful, as if an obscure death foregathered in his mind while the winds from Hell kept whistling, causing his eyes to water. Everyone was bathed in this mysterious and magical blueness.

"Christopher, I am glad to see that you are all right. You are our saviour. You are, our saviour!" Mashir thanked him repeatedly.

"Fabio was the sacrifice. It should have been me," Christopher mumbled, near to tears, shaking his head sadly. "It should have been me."

"A true martyr indeed, he sacrificed himself for us." He looked seriously at Christopher, "Please, rest for a moment, my friend, you have been through too much already."

"We all have," replied Chris weakly.

The cubed hall was bathed in icy blue luminosity, generated from the mighty and shiny sun face in front of the Temple wall. Strangely, they could see what they were observing.

This was what the professor had spoken about—the lost and sacred Golden Disc toned into metallic blue, the glowing blue light spoken of in the legend of, '*Arama Maru*'. When according to legend an ancient shaman transgressed from Earth to another world through an open portal in a blue light. Like then, here before them was the same light emanated from the keys golden disc and skull face glowing brightly. Sadly, the great professor Mancini was not here to witness this spectacle.

The golden disc radiated a cold blueness. This was real magic. And, there was no question of the importance of where they were standing, because this place was truly known as:

"Puerta de Hayu Marca"
or
"Gateway of the Gods of the Seven Rays!"

Behold!

Their pathway was open and waiting, and in all this time, the eerie winds blew their foul windstorm at them, challenging humankind to enter if they dared.

The Swiss guards that had crouched at the entrance to the cubed chamber were witnesses to these extraordinary events. Too dazed and partially shell shocked, they got up and started walking cautiously forward towards their equally-stunned adversaries, the United Makka Arab and African forces. Everyone was relieved that what had happened was over, leaving only doubt for the future. Fighting between each other now seemed futile.

Both officers stared at each other without speaking. Each man completely bewildered at what had happened and in all their years in military service, none had ever seen such a strange power. They both understood that they had achieved what was required: entry into the Temple with no further bloodshed between them.

The unnatural winds kept blowing into the cubed chamber, its organ-like acoustics sung songs from the dead. Everyone looked for courage within themselves and wondered, was this place really and truly the Gateway of the Gods?

****

CHAPTER XI

I AKYARON

"Are you and your men all right, major?" the captain asked his counterpart.

"One casualty. I am unhurt, thank you, captain." Trentino looked at the captain. "It is right that we should be here together. Both our forces have paid heavily with their blood," said the major. Captain Abdul-Haleem accepted the bold statement with a quick nod.

"Your acknowledgement is noted, thank you, major."

"I see now that this is much more than the rescue mission I was led to believe," said the major. "If we choose to work together, we might survive." The captain agreed, but mutual trust was something else, knowing he would have to watch this major closely.

The major's mission orders were explicit, but the goal posts had completely changed. His colonel was not here to advise him and the main contingent of Swiss guards was still making their way through the jungle and were behind schedule. Undermanned and out of moves, the major felt that for now, cooperation would be the best plan.

"The Temple lies open. The scientists are free to go, major. They can choose their own fate. I am sad for the loss of the professor. He was a very brave man." Sarvan Abdul-Haleem felt the group's loss. "They need go no farther." Looking at the major for his collaboration, major Trentino gauged Abdul-Haleem with unspoken thoughts.

The captain seems genuine enough at this professor's death. I cannot trust his kind, especially since the way ahead is open. The colonel will deal with him later. At present, there's another matter. It is still possible that the captain has executed the other civilians. I need proof one way or another if they are alive. If not, then I'll kill him. For now, we work as a team.

The major decided to play a waiting game, briefly he had thought to take advantage of this situation, but he could not afford the civilian risk. The doorway was open.

"Captain, I will go inside first, I have too," said Christopher.

"Christopher, you are very weak, rest." Harjit tried to protect him. "This place is deadly. You must rest, Christopher, please." Her eyes began to water.

"My friend," Mashir insisted, "I will go in your place. Both you and Harjit rest here, the way is far too dangerous. Barbaro and I can enter, and report back in no time. These other soldiers will wait outside, and Abdul-Haleem and major Trentino can enter with us for our protection. It is still a civilian expedition." Mashir's voice sounded more like orders.

Mashir had always been the talented diplomat, and when his flowing tongue spoke, everyone listened. It seemed the sensible thing to do. The surveyor had been with the expedition from its early stages and he would keep Barbaro from pocketing some priceless artefact.

"Did you see it? Did you see that horrible claw of fire ripping him in its fiery fist? Clawing Fabio to death?" Harjit could not hold her emotions back any longer, crumpling and crying, it was obvious, she could not take much more.

Distraught, Christopher reacted by comforting her in his arms. There was no shame, no ridicule. They wanted to disbelieve everything they had seen, everything that had happened and make it all go away. He whispered in her ear as they both cried, then lifted his head to speak to the surveyor.

"Everything is falling apart, *Mash.*"

"I will take over, Chris. There is no shame in it." Mashir respected his friend.

"Sorry, Mashir, no, no, thank you," he said, wiping away tears. He grew more defiant.

"But." Mashir tried to persuade him.

"No buts. Fabio sacrificed his life for me. He saved my life. I must go inside to finish this thing."

"The doorway is open," Mashir said. "Listen, Chris, you are weakened. It is too dangerous and," he paused, choosing his words carefully, "inside that place," he whispered, "you will fall."

It was clear that Mashir wanted to dissuade his entry, so much that Christopher sensed Mashir had overstepped his authority and friendship since his words were beginning to sound more like an order than a request. *Why are you being so insistent?* He thought with a hint of suspicion.

He stood up with tenacious and gritty determination. He saw something different, something intangible about Mashir. Something had changed in Mashir's manner, and he sensed an unspoken barrier between them. *Is the Temple doing this to us?* He wondered.

"I am going in!" Christopher's mouth spat icicles. His mind was made up. "And you, will not stop me."

The tension eased slightly between the men. Mashir felt Christopher's will strengthen and become irrefutable like a tornado. He had tried his best to prevent him from going inside but Chris's character was solid and unshifting.

"You may come with me, major and those scientists that are brave enough to volunteer." Captain Abdul- Haleem did not want to jeopardize further bloodshed. He decided that a compromise was best, *but on his terms.* "Your men and mine shall remain outside and be ready to come to our aid if required." He glanced over at the entrance. "Can you ask your men to stand down, please?" he urged. He quickly nodded to his own soldiers, who immediately obeyed, shouldering their military hardware.

"No problemo," the major quickly agreed and smiled. "We can have a small bridge made to cross this gap, pronto. We will gain entry in next to no time." He looked over at his subordinate. "Make it so, sergente," he ordered. The sergeant saluted and set about construction.

Christopher felt more at ease. His body sagged from its defiant position as did Mashir's, who stepped aside to allow the priest to walk closer to the opening. Everyone listened to the weird wind coming from nowhere.

Is there a message in its howling? wondered Mashir.

The Sarvan walked over to stand with Christopher.

"If the upper Temple is anything to go by, we might as well be entering the ends of the Earth," stated Abdul-Haleem.

Relationships and tensions had improved from what they had been only minutes ago. At least for now, everyone would work together. Later, they would kill each other.

It would take hard work and a lot of patience, but they had a common goal. Mutual respect went against the grain for all combatants, but they would just have to gulp hard and get on with it.

Instructions and orders were given by the officers. Everyone needed to be tolerant and respectful of each other. It would not be easy, given they were all from very different cultures and religions, each group knowing only to distrust the other's intentions. Oh, yes, it would not be easy.

The officers secretly agreed between them that if they did not return in three hours from entering the Temple, the final instructions were that both combatants would blow the place up completely. Destroy it! But the major held vital information from them. He had something completely different in mind than total detonation. His own orders were different from their agreed truce, and another Queen to play in his new game of chess. Checkmate, game over - *The Colonnello.*

A narrow wooden bridge was quickly constructed and positioned over the thirty-foot gap, and straight into the entrance of the inner Temple. The bridge was built with rails to assist their short crossing. It was not their imagination, but the turbulence seemed to increase and grow, as if the Temple knew they were about to embark on the next part of their soul-destroying mission. The winds seem to be asking them who they were or telling them to stay away. Everything looked uncanny in this crazy blue light.

Whowoooo... Whooooo... Who... youuuu...

"Where is that bloody weird noise coming from?" Abdul-Haleem kept staring into the dark gateway, with dread in his eyes.

"You already know. It's coming from *nowhere,*" Christopher stated with an inward shiver.

"We are going to find out, come on Sarvan, lead the way." The major prompted the other officer to get a move on.

The precarious winds came at them head on, sweeping forcibly out from the hole, and threatening to push them over into the deadly chasm below.

Haleem balanced himself against its might. Christopher came next, walking unsteadily, then Harjit came close behind, shielded by Chris. Mashir walked in next, then Barbaro, crouched down and tentatively crossed step-by-step like an infant. Trentino watched him and the rest of the column ahead and with unshakable resolve, tightened his lips and began his own crossing at last.

As they crossed over, the blueness underneath changed into impenetrable darkness. Abdul-Haleem looked down into the gap and knew it was not a good place. His focus tried to penetrate its endless shadows, his headlamp illuminating only so far. *This is the Palace of Iblees, he thought.*

He felt a disturbance in his thoughts. *What is that?* Could he see something? But what? A reflection, a little pinprick of light squeezing into his view, a reflection. *There it is again!*

"There is something down there," he said and guessed that something covered the gap at a much lower level. His vision was not strong enough to distinguish what it might be.

He was right. There was a metal mesh, long and extensive, with vicious razor blades positioned in every direction. What for? The answer to this question waited below in the darkness. Something much older had been moving since the explorers had returned and after Carmello fell to his death in the mines. It lurked in the depths, in the endless caves, in blackness. A physical barrier. It could not pass, not from here, not yet.

No mercy was spared to anything that crossed the blades, they remained by its makers a formidable Bastion. They were blades that could shred anything that either fell or crawled up from those darker places. An old threat remained caged. It waited until the right time to emerge — and it would be soon.

"Don't look down, don't look down," Barbaro kept repeating under his breath when it was his turn to cross over the pit of darkness. Sporadic gusts seemed to be pushing and pulling like an ill omen.

Before entering, the captain turned and spoke to the others.

"This is your last chance to turn back. There will be no disgrace!"

"You need not go any further, Christopher." Mashir continued to try to persuade him not to go on.

"This is my way." Chris was not going to turn back. *Why does he keep wanting to stop me?*

More determined than ever, Christopher dug in and entered behind the Sarvan through the pentagon-shaped doorway. The wind blew harder and harder! The young man's hair had grown long, and was waving wildly around in the turbulent air.

Thankfully, they all made it safely across without mishaps, and now began guardedly descending into a more shadowed and lonely place. From the other side, the soldiers watched them disappear, some making the sign of the cross, with others prayed to Allah.

The large entrance opened into a similar shaped tunnel in a subdued and uncanny light. The light had changed again and had become more moonlight, its wattage barely helping them negate the steep stairs downwards. They switched on their headlamps.

"The way below is very steep, so be careful," Abdul-Haleem boldly advised. His headlamp not strong enough, so he switched to his more powerful battery.

His torch lit up the immediate area and further down the deep passageway. Looking around, the walls and steps appeared crystalline white and completely polished to the touch. It would be so easy to miss a step and fall, especially against the ceaseless unrest of air howling like a supernatural symphony of woodwind instruments around them, a tuneful sad lament and more foreboding like a final warning.

Abdul-Haleem pulled his cap down tight onto his forehead. He was full of gritty determination and purpose. He strapped his sub-machinegun over his shoulder, and looked at the others' shadowy faces following him. He straightened himself up, ready for the challenge below. The Sarvan began leading the group downwards into the bowels of the main Temple, ready for the fight.

Their breathing was becoming heavier and more laboured with effort, the descend proving much more difficult than anticipated. It was hard to see with the strange light, and intense concentration was necessary to prevent them from falling. The hard winds took their toll on all of them, mentally and physically as they continued their trek.

They heard sounds that resembled the roar of the sea, and eventually, reached the bottom where a codex imprinted doorway waited. It was closed.

They stood in front a triangular doorway, looking puzzled. The doorway was fourteen metres wide and similar in height, and on either side, fourteen mummified bodies stood upright and still. They were not human.

The mummified things seemed to stare at them in judgement. With uneasiness, the intrepid team cautiously moved between mummies. There was no going back.

"Well, here we are!" Barbaro struggled against the gale that tried to take his voice away.

"I do not like it here!" Harjit said, terrified.

"Not a good sign!" Abdul-Haleem agreed, screwing up his vexed and furrowed brow, as he shouted against the disturbing unrest. The barometric pressure was fluctuating. It dropped again and the winds knocked them all down.

"We have to take extra care here, Sarvan, for what lies behind that doorway is what I, we, seek!" Mashir said.

"Where is that bloody wind originating from, Christopher? I still cannot see its source. Is it blowing from the door? It is quite literally, a dead end! How can this be?" Harjit jabbered nervously.

"It comes from *nowhere,*" he answered flatly. *Again, the Prophecy!*

They did not want to dwell on it any longer, and who could blame them? They approached the closed doorway, when without warning, they heard the sounds of stone on stone. The doorway began to slowly slide downwards, until it was gone.

"Too easy." Abdul-Haleem reserved his judgement.

"Mmm, that's what I'm afraid of," Mashir cautioned.

Moving guardedly, they could not see inside. Their torches were unable to penetrate the blackness beyond, no matter how close they got.

"You were saying?"

"Mmm."

The wind stung their faces. Their nightmare continued. Harjit could not forget those vile mummies, petrified and gulping hard, she wondered what could be inside that black void. Her imagination was making her shake.

Sarvan Haleem steadied his killing machine—a sub-machinegun, an AKSS-100 'shorty' assault rifle, outfitted with a PBS silent fire device and a BS-1 silent under-barrel grenade launcher. He had the real deal.

"I am taking no chances, major!" The officer had lost too many men to the Temple. His missing soldiers had gone somewhere inside the superstructure and never returned.

The supernatural turbulence seemed to intensify the howling noises. The winds swirled around them as they walked towards the vortex. Its intensity was increasing and they struggled to stand. It was impeding their mission further.

Could it be that it did not want them to enter, with those creepy dead things standing guard to stop them? Strange. Surely these mummified things would be light as a feather and easy to push over when the group stepped inside the vortex. The vortex from *nowhere.* Suddenly, without transition, it stopped.

Startled and mystified, they all froze as though they had stepped on top of an explosive device. Anything could happen next.

"Piss easy, Haleem," major Trentino smiled, breaking the ice. He had other plans as he walked forward to be at Abdul-Haleem's side. The major was sporting his favourite weapon too, a Sig Sauer SSG 30000 sniper, fitted with the Laser

Optronix DME 30000, keeping them both in very good company.

With Harjit's torch in one hand and his in the other, Christopher saw that his torch light was being absorbed into the black hole. He would not let her go, no matter what, before they stepped into nothing. Barbaro followed along like a puppy dog behind Mashir.

Everyone took a deep breath, as though they were diving under water, then walked into the dark interior. It felt like nothing. Once inside, their torch light worked fine. It was as if the darkness had only been a black film, no more than a millimetre thick!

The relieved group quickly fanned around to cover what seemed like a wide area, illuminating everything as much as possible. The room was quiet as a crypt. There was no sound and no wind.

"This is a strange place indeed, my friends," Mashir said warily. He had expected nothing less.

"This is not a Temple." Harjit felt her chest tightening. "It is a tomb." The girl was spooked and shone her torch, watching out for the slightest of movement. *Those things could be anywhere.*

"Indeed, very strange," Mashir whispered vigilantly, surveying everything around. Captain Abdul-Haleem moved slowly along their left flank, with the major on their right. Each soldier's senses heightened to a hair-trigger, ready for any eventuality.

An unexpected threat could come at any second and from anywhere, and so they waited.

They could see inside the Temple, at first unsure of the structure, then perceiving that it seemed built with four walls. Each wall measured exactly forty metres long and tapered inwardly to form a hollow pyramid to a point exactly forty metres high. The walls on either side were in the directions of North, South, East and West.

Looking up, multiple beams rose to the ceiling. They saw colours. But of what? Suddenly, they realised they were looking at pictures. They were gigantic murals and so life like too. The images were drawn on each sloped wall and were frightening. This place had to be created by someone powerful, but who?

"Oh!" Harjit put her hand to her mouth in shock.

"For God's sake, what are they?" Christopher stood back, staring at each enormous eye. Each was lidless, and had a different shape painted on each centre. Each was finely detailed with lush rich paintbrush strokes and specially designed intricate markings. The largest surface coated in dazzling white and surrounded each large iris.

One iris was coloured a deep fiery red, another a chilling blue. The next was painted in a startling green and the forth was coated in an intense and vivid yellow. All unnerving, all judging them. Each triangular was wall decorated in a wonder of rich coloured mosaics of incredible detail, surrounding each colossal eye. These gigantic eyes felt so real that it seemed as though they moved slowly. It all felt very unsettling. The Temple huge, it dominated all that it watched.

They continued their search. Notably, there was much evidence that the walls were once covered in thick vines, which suggested the building had been breached some time ago to allow this foreign host inside. Having nothing to feed on, the organic matter had long since withered and died. The group observed the remains of fallen debris scattered on the patterned floor. Underneath this dead vegetation, the stone floor was patterned with black and white squares, like a chessboard.

Christopher took a deep breath in and shone his torch on the pointed ceiling. Its apex was undistinguishable, almost two dimensional. Bewildered, he saw a central great eye looking straight down at him. The eye joined all the walls seamlessly together. But there was life in this great eye, its surface was dancing with gems in torch light.

An all-seeing eye, he thought quietly to himself as the light echoed back in numerous shades of sparkling green reflections.

The fairy light illuminations continued to dance madly. It was an incredible spectacle. It appeared to be made of an infinite number of precious stones like emeralds and the iris appeared to be made of rubies.

Enthralled, he stood there transfixed with the others, guessing that the transparent crystal pupil of the eye must be made of a gigantic rock diamond!

At this second, all their torches struck the eye simultaneously, giving out and immediate and extraordinary explosion of crystal light. A blast like a starburst lit up the Temple in wonder.

"How magnificent!" Christopher said.

"Wow, by Trimurti of Brahma. It is wonderous!" Harjit gasped.

"This is what we have come for, my good friends." Mashir said, captivated by the scale and awe of it all. "It is indeed, a sacred place."

"It must be worth the heavens themselves!" Barbaro was fascinated. "Oh, how wonderful it all looks! Priceless!" To Barbaro, this was no tomb, it was a treasury!

"I wish the others were here to see it." Harjit was suddenly feeling melancholic, as he remembered the cruel sacrifices that was made to get them here.

All the eyes were staring down at them like the Gods in Mount Olympus. This place could be like a scope to another world, and maybe it was. When the light stopped abruptly, darkness once more took hold again in torchlight.

There was still much more to see. They moved slowly and could see a complex structure located off to their right, quite near to the wall, containing many designs and small sculptures. These drew Mashir to them like a magnet.

Meanwhile, Sarvan Haleem had already walked on cautiously ahead of them all. He was not so easily impressed. The grand spectacle could wait, he had a job to do. Alerted, he suddenly stopped.

All around Sarvan Haleem lay the missing, the dead. He looked grimly at this macabre scene of bones and metal before him. A very tall race, nobles clad in golden chainmail and yet, not of that type of elemental metal found in this world. Gold would also be too heavy and too soft to use in battle, unless it was only for dress display. This metal was not gold or for dress. It was very light. It had a hint of rusty red, giving the metal its flexibility and strength.

Whatever had happened here happened a very long time ago. None of the explorers who came over to inspect this atrocity could tell just how long it was when these sentinels had fallen. All lost in some lonely battle eons ago. Among the dead, lay pieces of bone from strange animals or beasts they must have had fought against in their desperate struggle.

More in evidence, were those large ugly and unearthly warriors like the ones discovered in the upper tiers, all dead and mummified. Everything inside this place appeared completely desiccated. The dry atmosphere inside the Temple made sure of that.

The Sarvan counted no less than a hundred of these golden knights. They lay as they died against this great host. In the darkness, it all looked so final, so very sad.

"*Why?*" Christopher whispered.

"Who are they?" Barbaro wanted to know more.

"Mmm, a last stand," Sarvan guessed, seeing the weapons strewn over this battle scene.

"Phew, looks that way, captain." The major agreed nodding watchfully.

"Even with their superior intelligence, in the end, it came down to this. Brute force and mindless hatred." Harjit's eyes relived her ordeal in the upper tiers. "Right, everybody. Watch where you are walking," she reminded them, "these creatures are dead, but they can, still kill!"

"Grazie, giovane signora, ah, what shall I say? Thank you, young lady." Trentino was appreciative of the heads-up from Harjit. He tipped his finger off his beret.

"Harj is right. We lost a friend upstairs and these ugly looking warriors are still killers." Chris paused, looking at the aftermath. "I believe that this fight took place long before what happened upstairs." Christopher's attention to detail was striking. He could see the difference in body composition to those above, and postulated further. "This battle occurred at a different time, and a different year," he guessed.

Mashir wandered off exploring elsewhere, uncaring for his own safety, while examining a strange looking circle of tall figures, sculptures and stone artefacts.

These objects would uncannily move or glide to the side, opening a way through when he approached them, and revealed a large stone table within. He kept quiet with unspoken thoughts and said nothing to the others.

Allah, help me in this strange place. What is on the table? the Iranian thought to himself as he walked inside the circle of figures.

****

The immediate danger passed for the main group, provided they kept away from the dead warriors. There was a lot to see, in fact too much, as the explorers began to move apart and unconsciously split their investigation over the large area.

Harjit side-tracked while observing the floor over to her left, quite close to where they had come in, near the entrance. It was difficult to distinguish because of the pattern, but there were outer steps leading to the floor at a lower level. Going down the large steps, she saw more inscriptions on each. Harjit could easily see that these were of a completely different type of scripture or codex. She examined them more closely, but was at a complete loss.

The soldiers covering each other's positions, flanking left and right through the bones, walked ahead, scanning the entire area. Christopher was unaware that Harjit had drifted away from him; he was too preoccupied, when out of the darkness, something else came into his view, something the others had not seen.

Saying nothing, Chris walked slowly towards it, when without transition, steps appeared unexpectedly in front of him, elevating upwards to another stone floor, and one at a much higher level.

Stepping up and almost without realising it, he found himself above the height of the others. Christopher passed through a sort of transparent skin. It felt slightly cold as it touched him like a whisper of air, its surface sliding smoothly over him. He closed his eyes, then opened them in surprise, finding himself moving through from the blackness of the inner Temple and into a completely different place — a place of shimmering silver vertical strands. Chris was completely mesmerised. *What is this place?*

Struggling to see where he was going, there was some comfort in knowing that the others were not far away, so he continued. *What harm could it do?* The vertical silvery lines wafted back and forth like a tapestry of traps caught in a light breeze, but no air moved it. Christopher looked around bewildered. *Where are they?* Everyone had vanished! He was suddenly all alone as a grey mist appeared.

"Oh, Lord Jesus Christ, please protect me," said Christopher on the verge of panic, while encouraging himself. *I must go on.* Willing himself against the unknown, "*I must go forward!*"

Coping badly with the silvery drapes, the priest prayed for godly defence as he approached the intimidating grey mist.

Entering the dense cloud, Christopher's torch made things worse. The cloud changed and appeared brightly all around him as if floodlights were suddenly switched on. The light was blaring, and was blinding his way in all directions.

he jumped in surprise. His eyes and face immediately felt dry. All the moisture had been soaked up into a moister humid atmosphere around him.

Losing all recollection of where he had come from, Christopher, feeling disoriented, was quickly and hopelessly lost. He kept on going, even though there was no way of telling how to escape. Blinded like this, he switched off his torch and the blinding light ceased, leaving him standing in a dim containment. What he discovered next was worth every moment of taking the extra risk as the mist began to clear.

Christopher hesitated, then his mouth opened wide in awe. Something quite unexpected appeared in front of him. He blinked to clear his eyes and clear his mind to take it in. Were his senses right? *Yes!*

A massive throne!

****

As he walked steadily closer towards this mysterious stone-seat, he wanted to discover more. He had too. The seat was similar in structure to pure red sandstone. Upon closer inspection, Christopher could see how carefully carved with fine detail the throne was. Switching on his torch again, the throne sparkled whenever the beam struck the internal stone crystal. In front of the throne, stood a large altar which appeared to be made of the same stone-type.

On the stone table sat large golden candleholders, tarnished by age, with their long candlewax melted and flames long gone out. The wax had flowed and stayed stuck all the way to the floor.

By now, Christopher was breathing faster. The excitement and anticipation was bursting in contrast to the silence inside here which seemed eternal. Then, the mist dissolved away completely, revealing its secrets. He gasped quietly.

In the tranquil peace, as the throne unpeeled of mist, there sat a tall figure, watching him.

A great figure indeed. A noble frame wearing a crowned golden helmet with metal nose protector and metal jaw guard to match. It appeared to be a tall nobleman, his massive frame sitting alone in the darkness.

The helmet was laced with an intricate silver metal art design and with what appeared to be words and symbols bearing a detailed insignia of a crescent moon. There were numerous tiny ruby jewels and a deep red star at its middle, glinting with life from the reflected torchlight. This ill-fated noble had been dead for a very long time.

Dignified, he wore what might have been a rich red leather tunic, bearing the arms of a noble house, with a small cross positioned inside a star and both symbols encompassed by a larger sickle moon.

A thick brown belt was strapped around his waist and held his long sword. His tunic was pulled over his light chainmail, the metal lace made of a more intricate and richer metal made from wire loops, different to the other soldiers they had seen here. This made this noble special.

The protective suit was crafted using elaborate esoteric metals. It gave the appearance of gold and silver with bronze like interweaving links. These special metals provided the wearer with a kind of magical protective property, proving to be much harder and more durable than most tempered steels or synthetic hardened plastics known to modern man.

An army of these warriors must have been a most formidable force indeed and yet, here he was, dead. No magic, in all his fine protection, helped him. This super-warrior killed by an ill-fated poison arrow. It sought to find a weakness under his armpit and there it lay inside him.

A mitt made of similar chainmail protected one of his hands, while the other was bare and exposed. A great sword lay across his lap as if placed to rest. His large hands and exceptionally long fingers, rested on top of a cracked leather-bound book, with the page lying open.

Christopher held his breath. His excitement was hard to contain. With wild eyes, he quickly scanned the page in view.

Last mortal words! he guessed. The Nobleman wanted to say something. The ink was faded with age, making it hard to read. *It is a strange complex language and with curiously curved end symbols. What do they mean?*

Christopher unconsciously absorbed these surreptitious words. *These are important words. Some symbols are strangely familiar to me. I should know their meaning.*

Experiencing a strange eccentric feeling in himself and carefully turning over the cryptic page, there appeared to be the noble's last scripture, judging by his weakened writing. It looked as though it was scribbled in weaker patterns of symbols that looked more familiar. He recognised them now.

The nobleman's ink appeared to have run out, and changing his message into red freemasonic symbols, it was instantly recognisable. *My God, and blood written.*

"It says," Christopher spoke in the darkness:

"I am wounded mortally and thee have come my Osleiotectian brethren.

Thee have come of age and I speak in the common tongue.

These are my final words.

The universe is cracked.

Our last stand is over, the Race of Nelumakragasians and I Akyaron, Lord and Prince of my people, is no more. Too many of the enemy came when we were weak in this distant outpost, this doorway from Nelumakragas. My lineage is finished.

Know then this, evil are the Preyweeps, they too are now dead for I killed their breed.

This way is weak, and the doorway is now ajar as thee now stand before my downfall, the enemy can and will return and claim it, the Link.

This Link is flawed, broken, and it must now be taken from here to be remade as one chain. Never yield this link of power. I gift this Link to God to thee my Osleiotectian brethren. Flee from here like the winnowing winds that greeted thee and join the Link of Light to the others and remake Gods Chain.

God's Chain was created by the great geometrician and became the Chain of Existence. It governs everything bound by universal laws. These laws are already disintegrating because the Chain is unmade. God was weakened by the schemers, the dark lords and their devilish angels. The unnamed one, made this weakness within the Link so breaking the chain. This allowed the darkness to grow. God was able to save order in the universes by spreading his broken Links of power in spacetime and place dimension until the prophecies come of age. Now.

You have entered here, by a doorway, a path. It is open to Osleiotect, this place you call Earth. Time has weakened God as the Links are taken by the darkness. They are becoming so powerful God cannot prevail without the help from his children, kindle hope and restore order. You are chosen.

The darkness does not hold sway, not yet. Unless they bind Gods Link in their own fashion.

Be warned, the dark lords will now come. They are destroyer of worlds!

The path will be lit for thee, know that it is perilous. If you fail, then chaos and the ending of your world will be. Mine will follow and God will be no more.

The links must be made strong again or all existence is lost.

God speed your path, for ours is forgotten."

Christopher sighed hard, staring up at the giant nobleman, his melancholic tale had been told. He saw a scrawled glyph on paper, which depicted a Temple broken and on fire, reminding him of the late professor's lectures about Mayan glyphs, one like this meant or described a burning Temple and how it signified the end of a bloodline.

A fine metal chain, most likely worn around his neck, now lay broken in the noble's bony hand as though he had torn it off. Then, something else caught his eye. A special talisman. A charm that was richly coloured with what must have been an enormous blue sapphire and sliced with an esoteric rune. *A cut of magic!*

Inside, there was a green emerald that was slightly smaller and of similar curvature. A sliced precious stone arranged with artistic design of crystal green on its crystal blue surface, its middle inset with a red ruby slice and a rhomboidal diamond at the apex. It was a work of art. It was breath-taking and priceless. All the gemstones were set into a pure silver base metal, not native to this world.

Unseen to Christopher from where he stood, was an ancient "House Crest" stamped into its back. Curving along each stone rim, on the inner curve, were ancient words. *I can decipher the message!*

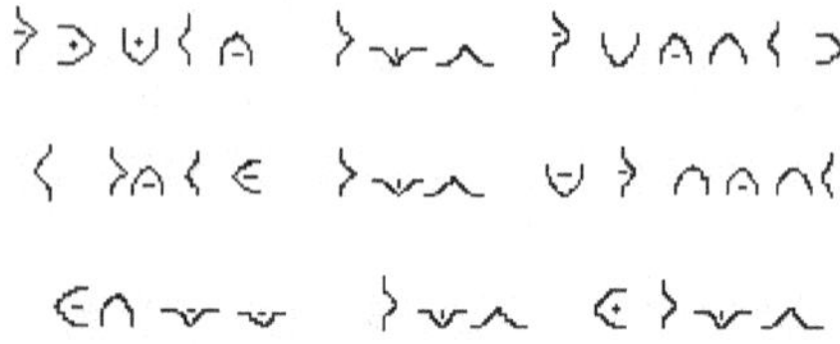

Christopher's eyes opened even wider. *I know what it says!*

Power and Purity

Earth and Spirit

Link and Land

Tightly gripped even unto death, there was something else. Something appeared fused into this noble's fingers. *What is he holding?* It looked like a large round silver metal link. He wanted it. There were tiny letterings, invisible to the naked eye. Here was the *missing link* that the noble forewarned about in his blood-written message. *It must be special. There is no telling if I will come back.* Looking around uncertainly, like a thief protecting his bootie, Christopher grimly prized the precious link from the nobleman.

"I have it!" Christopher raised his voice. His first impression was strange. The link felt heavy. He quickly placed it into his zipped pocket. It needed to be hidden. He somehow knew this.

How strange. It still feels warm? As if the fossilised fingers still had life!

No sooner had he had taken the link, Christopher heard something speak to him in an outlandish voice, strange and polite — it was almost regal.

"Two others lie hidden and protected in this world. The Link of Death and the Link of Nelumakragas. Find them first. They are the footpaths to God's Chain."

"What? Who said that?" Christopher was shocked and turning around. There was no one in the room aside from the dead nobleman.

Christopher began to panic. "Get out of my mind." He tried to gain control of himself. *I do not understand what all this means.*

Suddenly, he stared back at the nobleman and gasped. *Oh, shit. No fucking way!* He did not want to stay another moment longer. His imagination made him believe that the nobleman was... when without warning, he blacked out.

****

"Christopher! Christopher! Wake up!" Harjit was shaking him vigorously. Slowly coming to, Christopher felt sick. Harjit continued shaking him awake. "Snap out of it! Where have you been? Christopher, listen, listen! Where were you?"

"Here, right here. I was always here!" his mind was racing trying to catch-up, his stunned concentration finding it hard to hear Harjit properly, his fuzzy unfocused thoughts were mixed. "I did not go anywhere."

A dream. He was trying to make sense of his fast-evaporating memory, and was attempting to make sense of what he could remember.

"You were not here a minute ago!" she blared at him. Harjit saw Chris appear from nowhere. She had been standing and turned around, startled to find him with her!

"We have to go," Christopher ordered, "we have to leave right now. I cannot explain why but please, believe me, I know this!"

She looked at him awkwardly. "What do you mean, Chris?" Harjit's brow creased.

"Don't ask. We must leave immediately, now!" Christopher held her and looked around in his scrambled head. More mystified than ever, Christopher saw nothing of what he experienced, except stone steps. Harjit could not see them. *Is this still a dream? Dare I step up again?* When suddenly, excited shouting interrupted them from across the Temple! It was Mashir.

"Over here! Over here!" Mashir interrupted, calling them. He had found something important.

"The others are not ready to go," Harjit answered Christopher bluntly, "I said to you that we should go from here weeks ago, now the others will not leave!" She could not understand his wanting to leave the Temple like this, and without explanation. "We have been in here only a short time and we need some answers. Don't you, Chris?"

"Harj, I cannot explain. Listen."

"No, you listen and get a grip. Come and see what Mashir is up to. He has found something very important."

Christopher felt resigned. There was nothing he could do.

"Over here, Chris, Harjit!" Mashir called out once more. They all ran over to him.

"What's going on?" Harjit asked first.

"What have you found out?" Abdul-Haleem asked, looking down with genuine interest.

"It is a map of some kind. Only Allah truly knows where these places are." Mashir seemed puzzled. "Several ancient maps. Look, this a type of fortress, a city, mountains and many other land markings on a smaller scale and look over here. In this other map, the land looks massive, like a new continent! "

Mashir was keen to study these but for the moment, there was not enough time for detailed work when Barbaro came to the rescue with his camera.

"What scale is it? This might be the size of Italy or just as easily be the size of a continent like South America or larger." Barbaro spoke with more of a statement than a question.

"Observe the sea. It expands along the full length of the land to the East, a line of fortresses over this Northern region, large mountains and forests to the South and West but what is that area to the South and South East? It looks like a darker featureless region. They call it 'Douerim' *I think*. I somehow managed to translate it myself, Chris." Mashir smiled casually with pride.

"Well done, Mashir. I see, yes, you are right, Douerim it is," Chris confirmed.

"It might be a new city that they planned to build here, except for the fact that something happened along the way. Er, they got killed." Mashir seemed overly pleased with himself. "Some catastrophe ties in with these events. Their map, however, is very inaccurate. In those days, I believe that these people could not have known their local geography."

"Eh. Why, I cannot agree. Their measurements of the night sky and the stars are very accurate. We have seen their advanced technology in the observatory above. You are wrong, Mashir. The maps must be accurate." Christopher judged. It was impossible to get the local geography wrong and too much of a mistake to make. There had to be something else, some other logical explanation.

"Christopher may be right," Barbaro concurred, wondering where these observations could be.

"It is the map of another world!" Christopher stated bluntly. "A world much different to our own, and one we know nothing about, until now." The bio-technologist seemed to know, while thinking to himself, *What the hell is going on?*

For a moment, the air was still as a held breath as the idea of another world sunk in. The group thought about the life-changing implications this could have on humanity.

"You mean a new world! And you, Christopher Hrycuik, *you* are like our very own modern-day Christopher Columbus!" the major stated factually but smiling with some scepticism.

"The map looks unfamiliar. Look there, it looks like some sort of scale." The captain seemed unsure.

"No. I think Christopher might mean in a *different universe.*" Harjit looked at Christopher for confirmation.

"Yes, I do." Christopher nodded to Harjit. "As difficult as this idea is to believe, all this—all these events that have happened and are happening to us right now—are happening for a reason!"

"My men have not come here to listen to some crazy bullshit story like this," said Trentino, annoyed at the scientist's stupidity.

"Please, major, sarvan, listen to me." Christopher asserted to get their undivided attention, placing great emphasis on his next words, "We, must leave here and right now!"

"What do you mean?" The captain probed. *Is this a trick?*

"Things are in motion. Things that cannot be undone. They are happening this year, this time, and right now!" Christopher gave everyone a fraught look of apprehension.

"You have our attention, young man. Why exactly should I do this?" Trentino asked.

"Somehow a bond exists here in this Temple between our world and theirs." He looked at the map. His tone conveyed sincerity. "We are all in immediate and imminent danger and something of great evil approaches. We must get out of here, now!"

Mashir stared at him with a flat expression, very unhappy at what sounded like a rant from someone he respected. It was very bad news to Mashir, because he was not ready to leave. This was a place of extraordinary interest and he wanted to find everything. However, he knew his friend well enough to know that Christopher believed in himself. Doubt seeded into his uncertain mind. Mashir needed to decide what his best course of action would be.

Chris has been right about everything else. I am not sure if he has gone completely mad this time or if I should heed this warning. It might be wise to leave for now, then plan for a return on my own.

"You are my friend, that is enough," his tone was confident, he trusted him implicitly. "But, what evil approaches?"

"Please, Mashir, everyone." Christopher did not know how to explain.

"All is as God wills it." Mashir said.

Major Trentino and the Sarvan were happy to leave too. After all, this was once again a civilian expedition. The others too were relieved, knowing that they would be returning to base camp and the safety of the forest.

****

CHAPTER XII

THE FLYING CENTIPEDE!

>⊓⊔ ⊏Ŀ‹⌐ ⊔⊓ ⊔⊔Ŀ›⌐⊓⊔⊐ ⊔

The air was still and silent as they cautiously exited the pyramid to go back into the macabre dusty corridor where the mummified things waited patiently in the murky shadows, some with remaining teeth that smiled in their direction, while others with mouths stuck open in a frozen scream.

Their senses were heightened. It was easy to get out. They approached the mummified things, when suddenly, the winnowing winds hit them again, blowing as hard as before.

This time, however, the wind was coming from mouths of the mummified things, their ghostly materials fraying into long ribbons, wafting about and emptying their lungs of dead air.

"Get the hell out of here!" Trentino shouted. With no more prompting from the major, everyone instantly ran, while the gale kept gluing around them, shoving everyone outwards and away from where they had come from. The howling scaring them all the way back to where they came from.

Maggiore Trentino stood his ground for a moment longer at the bottom of the stone steps, turning defiantly towards the howling winds and stared right into them.

They all ran up the steps. Nobody wanted to look back. They climbed up as fast as possible, leaving the pyramid far below; this place wanted them no more. At last, they could see a brightness above. The light was coming from the entrance to the lower Temple.

The team suddenly appeared at the top doorway, looking out again at the cubed chamber, and screwed up their eyes from the brightness. They saw the Moat directly in front of them and the bridge across where the soldiers waited.

Something is wrong. Both the major and Sarvan intuitively read each other's minds. The military figures across from them looked agitated and apprehensive, feeling the increased turbulence coming along with them.

The soldiers' eyes held the heaviness of a death watch when they unexpectedly appeared. Surprised, the soldiers gathered close to the gap's edge while one by one, Christopher and the others took a turn walking precariously back across the bridge re-joining their waiting comrades.

Immediately, they all began talking with renewed enthusiasm, except for Christopher. He remained detached in his own thoughts. He had a dark secret to keep.

The Temple played with people's mind so easily, but in the bio-technologist's case, a new influence was affecting his judgement and thoughts. He touched his talisman softly. "The

Link" hidden inside his breast pocket. *I found it! I will tell them about it in my own good time.*

The soldiers were relieved to see their officers emerge along with the scientists. Trentino and Haleem sensed the tension. Standing on the opposite side of the soldiers, everything was held in blue light inside the cubed chamber.

"Thank fuck we are out," Christopher eventually sighed.

"You know, Chris? This gives credibility to whoever built this place. They knew we would come someday." Harjit said.

"Christopher," Mashir said, "some of the lost teachings in the Quran also describe some super-being. 'The Lost Children of God'. It is said that their home might be *found in our time,* in some distant land near the Earth's middle." Mashir was keen to tell of his religious teachings and beliefs. He continued enthusiastically, "In other words, here at the Equator. Don't you see that Allah had already spoken of this in his lost teachings? Listen to me. Those who cross to this place, will find 'the power', a piece of the Earth which bonds us to the cosmos and to God eternally!"

Christopher had never heard Mashir talk like this before. He seemed more knowledgeable than ever. But, there were those who did not agree with his words.

"You are ill informed, Mashir." Barbaro refused his open doctrine. To consider these Islamic teachings in his company was pure blasphemy! He rejected him with a sneer of disrespect, "If you say these things are in the 'Lost Teachings' of the Quran, then it follows that those 'teachings' are no longer lost?" Barbaro was venomously unimpressed.

"Mmm, I meant 'lost' *loosely*, my good friend, Barbaro." Mashir was unperturbed by the Christian's vain attempt to discredit him and his religious beliefs.

Listening to Mashir had unsettled Christopher. *Mashir has not been straight with me, he has changed. He has been hiding these things, these new ideals. Mashir has lied on numerous occasions and is no longer the man I have known over the years! I know him well enough to see that. He sees more.*

Once they were all safely across, the officers listened to their subordinate's individual reports with interest.

"Buona mattina, Signore, good morning," the Sergeant saluted Trentino, "I am glad that you have returned. You have been gone too many hours. It is o-seven-hundred and the Sun has just risen outside." They looked at the major for fresh orders.

Sergeant Moretti had returned from his failed rescue attempt to release the captured scientists in the first tier, the ones that Mashir had lied about. He had said they had all been executed, but Trentino did not know this. The sergeant, now stationed at the inner Temple, had something urgent to tell the major.

"Signore, the men are wondering when are our reinforcements are due to arrive."

"Sergente, we have not been gone that long."

"Signore, with respect, you have been gone seven and a half hours!"

The major looked at his watch. It had stopped. *My God, my watch stopped inside there. The time too!*

"Signore, I am receiving disturbing reports from outside the Temple."

"What reports?" his tone was hard and certain. He needed to know what was happening.

"There is going to be trouble." The Sergeant's tone sounded urgent.

****

Outside the Temple, dawn broke with a beautiful sunrise over the rainforest on the thirty-first of October. The four Swiss guardsmen who stood at the front entrance on the first tier were immediately rewarded by this sight. The men watched the breath-taking view in awe. But, the natural beauty was not the only thing these men were observing.

Below, at the base of the Temple, two other Swiss guards were shouldering arms on the first steps of the south-face, both on sentry duty and were scanning the jungle's edges while debating their untenable peace.

"This place does not feel right," one guardsman said. Both guards watched the forest suspiciously.

"It feels like death," the other added.

"Rain is on the way." The looked around to see two UMCAA soldiers coming out the Temple behind the Swiss guards standing on top.

A lukewarm truce still existed between both warring factions; both Christian and Islamic forces following direct orders, each waiting to see when the ceasefire would end, with both sides already having lost brothers. The UMCAA forces continued to hold the Temple in two areas, as agreed to be their base, whereas the Swiss guards held the junctions to the first tier and bottom tier.

UMCAA troops had been allowed safe passageway through to the surface, each man escorted by the Swiss. A verbal agreement and a pledge was made to give each other mutual respect for the moment; although, it was more like mutual distrust. It was true to say that each viewed the other with profound suspicion. They were all allowed to shoulder their weapons, this way, they would remain unharmed.

Another two Islamic soldiers appeared behind the others from the Temple mouth and everyone looked out jointly towards the mighty green mass before them.

"My comrades," corporal Jansher Dilawar said kindly to the Swiss guard, "do you have any water to share with me, my friend?"

"Si, here." Private Hernán Narváez threw over his plastic canteen with a friendly smile.

"Thank you," the corporal said, catching it. "This is a terrible place."

"I do not mind it," Private Narváez replied contrarily. He loved conditions that were unnatural to others.

"It is the flies and especially those bloody mosquitos!" corporal Bianchi added to the general conversation, smiling too and showing off his chipped front tooth. The soldier took off his beret, wiping the sweat from his buzz cut, with its zigzag pattern cut into his scalp. The man had short sideburns, and for his hard exterior, it somehow seemed to suit his chiselled face.

"The air here is much better than inside," corporal Dilawar gestured, putting his finger horizontally below his nose. "The Jungle is full of oxygen; it makes me feel great!" He inhaled deeply. "Aagh! Goooood!"

The Arab was feeling much better. He expanded his chest, when unexpectedly, the other Islamic soldier slapped his stomach.

"Oooffph!" Dilawar bent over and rubbed his stomach, while laughing. Everyone joined in on the laughter. A simple thing like this somehow seemed to defuse the uneasy awkward mood.

"What's your name?" corporal Bianchi asked.

"My name is Sarjukhe Jansher Dilawar and this is Aadil, my comrade." Corporal Dilawar looked at Aadil, who was speaking to another Swiss Guard. "It is good to get out of that place. The Temple is oppressing and unhealthy."

"Si, same here," Bianchi agreed. "We have come for one thing, to take our people home. I am

Caporal Bianchi." The corporal spoke plainly to Dilawar.

"Yes, I understand your position, corporal. Our men and I are simple soldiers of Allah. We are here for a different reason and one which we do not yet know, only our commander, and the Sarvan and of course Allah himself understands the whole truth of our Quest."

"We have not seen your commander yet. Where is he?" Bianchi asked, becoming friendlier towards his adversary, whereas Narváez could not care less. Narváez might have to slit the man's throat by tomorrow. He smiled at the idea.

"Inside," Dilawar answered, nodding towards the entrance.

"Inside where?" Narváez probed with little interest and a parting shot, "The coward."

"Just inside." Dilawar was no fool. He could see he was a menace.

Insulted, Aadil threw back his canteen at the private, giving him a steely stare. Narváez was ready to pitch it back.

"No, no, please, the private did not mean to trick you!" corporal Bianchi tried to quickly smooth over Narváez's lack of etiquette. "Apologise, Narváez!" he insisted.

There is nothing better than a good fight in Private Narváez's psychotic makeup. Dilawar did not flinch as his smile turned into a sudden sightless killing stare, He stayed glued onto Narváez's blunt look.

The Islamic soldier's flat face held steady when Narváez smiled again. Dilawar breathed steadily with no illusions between the two gladiators, knowing there would be only one winner.

"We have lost many brothers inside this tomb," Dilawar stated bluntly.

"We have lost fine friends to your AK bullets!" another Swiss guard called out angrily from the side. The men displayed less caution and more mistrust. The peace between them was hanging on by a thread.

Narváez being a troublemaker was hoping that in the next few moments, his sabre rattling would prompt corporal Dilawar to a fight and give him somebody to kill.

"You executed helpless men, civilians that were doing nothing wrong! You're a bunch of cold blood sadistic bastardos!" another Swiss guard said taking sides.

Aadil got ready to pull his bayonet out, as both factions were quickly siding off.

The Swiss guards at the Temple base heard the angry exchange of voices above them, and saw the soldiers squaring off and shouting abuse at each other. There was only one person cool and level-headed enough to win: the troublemaker, Narváez.

Corporal Jansher Dilawar felt awkward to say the least, as he looked at corporal Bianchi with incredulity when he mentioned the scientists. The fragile truce was disintegrating with the touch paper ready to explode.

Yet, Corporal Dilawar had always been a clever negotiator; his Sarvan had taught him well. The corporal was destined to be a ranked officer after this mission. He could handle this flare up. Smiling again, he began speaking softly.

"Listen, listen, please, my friends. I will ask my commander and see if you can visit your people. This will prove to you that they are not dead. Believe me, they are still very much alive. We have not killed them. Try and be patient, it is this place." He looked disturbed at the thought. Lowering his voice so that only the men close to him could hear, he said, "It works on all our minds, corporal, it is an evil thing, and if we are not vigilant, it, will undermine us all."

"What do you mean? Why have you not allowed us inside to see them already?" a soldier fumed, missing the point completely.

"Orders," came the blunt answer. "Many of our men entered to explore the Temple," he shook his head in regret, "but no one ever returned." The corporal conveyed sad sincerity. "And, I too have lost good friends inside this place."

Corporal Dilawar gave his subordinate, Aadil Muhammad, an order to speak with his lieutenant or the colonel, his commander, about getting permission to enter the Temple. He would honour his word and arrange for the Swiss soldiers request to go inside and visit the civilian quarters. The soldier promptly saluted and departed into the Temple.

"We will see." The atmosphere thawed immediately. Narváez stopped smiling and lost interest. There was nobody to kill.

"Strange things happen here, I have felt them too," agreed corporal Bianchi, "We all have. I admit to being," he nodded his head, "not quite myself." The corporal, unable to explain his disturbing thoughts, looked up at the Temple's mouth.

"It is a strange place indeed," Jansher Dilawar settled. "Corporal Bianchi, they say that whoever enters this place will never leave." Corporal Dilawar looked down with hatred at the jungle, his angry eyes challenging it with his mind. *Will it claim us all?* he wondered. His remote thoughts detached momentarily, and he was speechless. His eyes began to water as corporal Bianchi turned with an unsettling sigh to look at the surrounding forest with him.

****

Time passed slowly, and by now, at least twenty soldiers had come out onto the Temple platform, on the first tier. They were all fed up from being stuck inside so long. Some sat relaxed with their legs dangling over the edges, and their sub-machine guns strapped to their shoulders or sitting on their laps. They were taking it easy and drinking water. It was strange to see the different uniforms together. The dappled greens and browns of the Swiss guardsmen, and the speckled yellow, rusty reds with green mosaics of the United Makka countries of Arab and African troops.

"Smoke?"

"No thanks, corporal."

"Where do you come from, Dilawar?" asked corporal Bianchi.

"My home is in Iran. I was born in Falayarjan. It has a population of two hundred thousand, to the West of the City of Esfahan. I do miss my family, very much," said Jansher Dilawar in a friendly tone. "As you are aware, the Arab forces and African Islamic countries have united for common good and economic stability, which is on a par with your European countries."

"I thought Iran was democratic now?" stated Bianchi.

"We are. Our governments have established this new relationship for mutual good of Allah, even our brothers in Iraq who have been enemies since the last century. Even now, there are tensions between us. It will take many generations to resolve all our differences. I pray that we will keep trying. They too are now entering into this unified Islamic World, so we will see."

"At first, I thought you had come from the Brazilian government with that different ensign. You know, this is the first time we have come so close, face to face, to speak together. What on Earth are your men doing here, in South

America?" he frowned with disbelief. "Surely you cannot expect to get out of here without the Brazilians knowing? I would have thought it to be the last place on Earth to find combined Islamic special forces."

Bianchi looked even more confused by the incredulity and courageousness of his men. Jansher Dilawar saw respect in corporal Bianchi's eyes and approachable manner.

"That is our advantage, corporal. We can move around the world easily, my friend. There is a large population of Muslims in San Paolo. In and out of countries is not a problem in one such as this. I am not giving anything away by telling you that we are here to find something very precious and most sacred. I have trust and belief in my commander. He is guiding us, even though I personally do not know what this thing is that we seek." Dilawar spoke candidly and honestly with the corporal. Corporal Bianchi stared at the Arabian soldier and at his incredible story, thinking it was not so different from his own.

"I must compliment you in your mastery of the Italian language, it is so very, very good, as good as mine and almost as if you were born to it! You speak with a natural tongue. In fact, all your men do, they are exceptionally excellent!"

Jansher Dilawar looked startled. For once, he was almost speechless. *With my dialect!* and *Just like his own!* and *They are exceptionally excellent!* Dilawar cast a look fraught with apprehension, wondering if it was another trick. *What is he talking about? We do not speak Italian, none of us!*

"I believe you joke with me, my friend. I cannot speak a word in, eh, your Italian! I have to say, I am surprised, it is you, corporal, it is you, who speak to me in my own language and with great dexterity! You jest with me, I think, mmm?" Laughing, he studied Bianchi's confused expression, while trying to work out the guards gambit. *What game is this Christian playing with me? What has he to gain out of this futile deception? To make me out to be some idiot?* "I cannot speak a word of Italian."

"You are speaking it now!" Bianchi insisted flatly.

"No, you speak in my own *Farsi* or as you know it, the Persian language. Are you feeling unwell?" Dilawar looked more than concerned.

He was beginning to get the impression that all this talk was a hoax to gain some advantage, or was he trying to make a fool out of him? The other soldiers who were listening to this crazy conversation started taking an interest, looking at each other in complete disbelief, beginning to mouth louder.

"Si, these guys think that we speak Arabian, ah eh, no, let us call it Farsi!"

No provocation was needed as the Swiss guards and the Arabian African soldiers were all standing once again and shouting at each other. Everything good had disappeared in the space of seconds and crumbled into madness. It was impossible that each person could understand the other's language fluently, as if it were inherent to each person. Narváez smiled.

Each soldier grew increasingly more frustrated. *Had they all become mad?* Who was who in this insanity? Instinctively, everyone was deeply disturbed by this apparent "new ability" to understand each other, and how it had taken them such a long time to even recognize it. Was it a deception?

"Listen! Quiet!" Dilawar shouted over everyone's irate voices, waving his arms and hands downwards, trying to calm the dispute.

"Men!" Bianchi held the Swiss back.

"We must try and accept what we have discovered about ourselves. This is a gift given for a good reason and we must use it to our advantage!" Dilawar was trying to understand.

"No gift!" The corporal looked unsure and attempted to re-evaluate his men and himself. "It's this bloody place, it is the Devil's work."

"I cannot ignore what has happened to us." Corporal Jansher Dilawar's quiet voice spoke volumes.

Bianchi looked around, "*A gift for a reason.* Well, whatever that reason is, it sure looks like there is going to be trouble ahead." He took the field radio from another Swiss guardsman.

"Yes, we must be vigilant," Dilawar agreed.

Meanwhile, two soldiers down at the jungle's perimeter watched the events taking place outside of the temple. The two soldiers, Cattaneo Pugliesi and Mancini Bellucci quickly unlocked their weapons. Bellucci radioed in for intel. They needed corporal Bianchi's immediate status.

Reception inside and around the Temple was nothing short of sporadic noise, its speakers crackling into life.

"Bellucci here, what is your status, over?"

"Bianchi speaking, situation is green, stand down, soldier."

Distracted, the soldiers below were completely unaware of something very important, something that had just happened. The jungle had changed. It had become deathly quiet and that was not normal.

An unnatural silence held its breath, when from somewhere inside the dense foliage, the silence was broken by only one sound — the sound of a strange buzzing noise which was louder than a hornet.

"Signore, is there a problem?" Bellucci asked. "Do you need our assistance?" looking up at the Swiss guardsmen on the Temple, the Islamic troops were outside because of the truce. This situation could go either way.

"There is a lot of confusion up here, everyone is a little edgy *but*," glancing diplomatically at Corporal Dilawar, "status here is not critical, I repeat *not* critical. I'll handle it."

"Affirmative, Signore, Bellucci out." He turned off his radio and switched his immediate attention to the annoying buzzing noise. He looked around to see where it was coming from.

Fucking strange. That noise is the only sound coming from the forest, nothing else. "What is that crap?" Bellucci saw something moving about a hundred yards away. "Aha! There it is!" he stated, while attempting to focus on a blurry object dancing about in the sunlight.

The thing appeared to be the size of a small bird. It was slowly rising off and hovering shakily above large colourful shrubs and blowing in the air. It was off in the distance, jiggling about the tree line.

"Mmm, nice colours," Cattaneo Pugliesi said, taking note of the wildlife. "maybe it's a dragonfly or something like that. It's too small to be a bird, and it's too big for a hummingbird. Mancini, what is that thing called?"

Their attention turned completely onto it, the insect was hovering just above the massive red and orange shrubs with large flowers, wide open and in full bloom; an ideal habitat for pollination.

It seemed to swirl about as if getting caught in the hot turbulent air and started fluttering around in a sort of mad erratic circle. The men watched it hypnotically as it darted up and down, displaying itself in a mad frenzy above the plants, as it tried to readjust its balance, almost as if getting ready to take control of its flight. With little effort, it was suddenly off and moving fast in their direction. With curious interest, the soldiers stared, numbly transfixed by its random and rapid approach towards them.

"Screwed if I know. Hey that thing is coming our way!" Surprised, Bellucci hunched his shoulders. The insect was accelerating rapidly, flying like an arrow, with the wind aiding its flight path. The creature was bigger than they thought. Within four or five seconds, its blurred image shot right past them with an angry buzzing following it!

"Shit! Look at that thing, phew!" Pugliesi shouted as it sped past him. It had been only a blur, then the insect stopped in the mid-air, as if slamming on its airbrakes and considering a new flight plan. It remained hovering in one place.

Then, it turned in their direction and starting coming at them once more.

"Watch out, it's attacking us!" Pugliesi shouted and within a second, it flew by, missing them again.

"Hey! It's well pissed off!" Bellucci warned.

"Si, listen to it, its annoyed!" Pugliesi agreed. The buzzing was getting angrier than ever.

Caught off guard by the sheer speed of the thing, it had surprised the soldiers, but they were now ready for it. It had stopped again in mid-air, waiting to attack them once more.

The men knew that this time it had become a menace and the last thing they needed was another sting in their backsides. Both men already been bitten too many times by vicious bugs. Sure enough, it was coming back for another go. What they at first thought might be a colourful bird, had turned out to be something quite different.

The loud buzzing noise was generated by long and short transparent shaped wings. Its aggressive looks appeared to defy nature and belief.

"Insect!" Bellucci called out.

The thing was bright orange with what looked like a long thin armoured body like a lobster, with numerous long legs spreading out from the main body. It was like a genetic mutant!

"It's a bloody flying centipede!" Pugliesi spat at the pest.

Yet, it appeared to have two large ugly insect heads, one at each end, and long proboscises dangling with needles sticking out from both its faces.

From a safe distance, it swirled close-by and as if unsure where to fly next, it closed in little by little. The men knew it was watching them with its bright two-toned fiery red oval eyes, looking and searching for a weakness.

"Watch out, watch out!" Bellucci warned.

"It's not a songbird!" Pugliesi called out, as it hovered closer than ever around them.

"You are right it's not! It's getting too close, watch out!" Mancini Bellucci pulled out his long bayonet and lunged at it, only a few feet from him!

Swishhh.

His blade swept right past the thing, the fast-moving creature dropping easily underneath his razor-sharp blade and surprisingly flying up at a steep angle, just beyond his reach.

The insect flew past Bellucci and attached itself lightly to Pugliesi's exposed back.

The insect was no heavier than a feather but Pugliesi began to immediately scream like a crazy man, trying to shake it free! He tried to throw it off, but the thing had attached itself to him like tar.

Its hair, like sticky barbs, was already splaying widely over him, and its long legs were digging into his combat jacket, gluing onto it with a sticky substance that was adhering fast. Once on, it was not coming off.

"Ah! Get it off me!" Pugliesi screamed frantically and spun around like a mad dog trying to grab at it with his arm. "Get it off me!"

Bellucci came to Pugliesi's aid with his bayonet in hand.

Upon seeing him approach, the ghastly-looking creature suddenly spat at Bellucci with a nasty red fluid that jetted out from its long proboscis, causing his eyes to mist over.

"Merda! Merda! Bastardo piccolo!" Bellucci cursed loudly, while rubbing his irritated eyes. Fortunately, the main jet missed him.

At the same time, the maniacal creature bit into Pugliesi's back, exactly where it had already made a small hole in his garment. In a split-second, its reflexive proboscis invisibly retracted, jabbing in again, and this time, biting in deeper.

The creature's lightning fast mandibles bit him a hundred times a second, while it inserted a local anaesthetic into him, numbing the immediate area.

Pugliesi yelled out in anguish. Its speed of attack took both men by surprise.

"Get it off! Get it off me!" Pugliesi shrieked in disgust and panic, and in an instant, the armoured creature retracted its fierce mandibles, re-introduced its sharp proboscis, and pierced straight through his thick combat jacket and right into the man's back. It slid inside him and forcibly extended the tubular weapon down and deeper below his shoulder blade, and into his heart.

Like a fine needle, it easily penetrated his heart, and the sharp proboscis suddenly erupted straight out the front of the man's chest, creating a horrible squelch in a fine powerful jet of blood. Pugliesi's eyes were fixed in open surprise, and he dropped dead on the ground.

Still stuck on the man's back, the creature's furious wings kept buzzing madly. It wanted to escape from its victim and move onto its next, having done its wicked deed. But it was trapped by the dead man's body. It could not get away.

Bellucci had just enough time to swing his bayonet down and across the scaled body and cut it in half.

"Ah, thank God!" he sighed, but it was not dead. It continued to attempt to break free from the dead man's body.

Unexpectedly, it managed to pull itself off and apart. Bellucci watched as both pieces flew frantically around him.

"Merda! Merda! Merda!" he shouted, as the insect's body parts spun uncontrollably through the air, rabid to get at him!

Bellucci moved in and out between the two body parts flying around him, desperately trying to avoid getting hit.

From the top of the Temple, the soldier's watched the crazy Tango and knew it could not go on forever. Bellucci was fending the body parts off, when suddenly, both bits surprisingly struck each other, and glued themselves together, creating a macabre superbug.

With no time to use his handgun Bellucci repeatedly slashed with his blade until the creature suddenly broke apart again in a game of Russian Roulette.

For about twenty seconds more, each batted for supremacy when unexpectedly, an abrupt gust of air blasted over them, lifting the insect parts high up and blowing them far away into the forest, landing out of his sight and somewhere to die.

"Pugliesi!" Bellucci shouted as he ran to his fallen comrade's side. "What the hell have we gotten into here?" He checked his pulse. There was none.

Bellucci threw his beret on the ground in disbelief. Death in under a minute. Bellucci sat down exhausted, staring up at the Temple for help and an answer.

****

During these deadly developments, a Swiss guard had radioed from his strategic position on the top of the Temple into the inner Temple to Sergeant Moretti inside the cubed hall, just a minute before Trentino and the scientists appeared.

"Eagle to Phoenix, Eagle to Phoenix, over!"

"Phoenix to Eagle, you have my full attention, what is it, soldier?" Sergeant Moretti quickly acknowledged the impromptu communication.

"There has been an incident near the forest perimeter. One of our men is injured. I have sent assistance, and there is something else, signore."

"Speak!" Sergeant Moretti snapped. He knew this news would not be good.

"I am not sure, signore. Something is gathering, something is forming not too far away from the Temple, something like a mist," the soldier replied in an uncertain tone.

"Jesus Caporal Bianchi, get a grip of yourself! Have you not seen a Jungle mist before? This place is a fucking cloud forest."

"No, sergente, it is not like any cloud I have seen. It is very different, and it's forming just above the trees and expanding around the valley. So weird."

"How?" he snapped. "What is wrong with you, soldier?" the sergeant's temperament was beginning to crack.

"It is black, signore, completely black and moving like it has a purpose. A cloud does not move like this one. If you saw it, sergeant you would understand what I mean. What kind of mist is as black as night?" His conversation was interrupted by furious hand signals from his men below at the Temple base. "Signore, signore, I have more bad news."

"Si?"

"Pugliesi is dead." Corporal Bianchi's tone was solemn. He looked out apprehensively from the first tier and at the new and ominous threat coming over the distant tree line. The black mist began moving in.

****

The explorers had emerged from the inner Temple as major Trentino finished listening to his sergeant's update.

"Thank you, sergente. I will need a burial detail. We have lost six men and now Pugliesi. Arrange it and take the bodies just beyond the jungle perimeter. Bury them out of sight."

"Si, signore," he saluted and quickly left the cubed hall.

"Sarvan Abdul-Haleem. Where is your commander, one of the scientists informed me that your superior officer was going to interrogate our people? Well, where is he or has he run away?" Trentino was in no mind to play more games and needed to see that the other scientists were safe.

"He has gone into the upper areas of the Temple with some other men. They have not returned," the captain lied.

"I would not expect to see him return," Christopher stated bluntly. Both officers turned and looked at him curiously.

They listened to his unbelievable recollection of his initial exploration of the Temple, and both men were speechless at Christopher's tall tale, especially when he told them about their encounters with monstrous creatures inside the Temple. The battleground and deaths of his friends, leading to their own unbelievable escape. It was just too much to take seriously.

Harjit and Barbaro nodded in irrational agreement. The picture looked bleak for anyone gone missing inside the Temple, as Christopher continued trying to explain events.

"There are things at work here, supernatural things that we cannot understand or comprehend."

"Sarvan," the major spoke, "this speech recognition thing, it has been reported to me, I have only now been informed of it by my own men."

"And?" the captain prompted.

"I hear it too, don't you? Do you hear me speak in Italian or in your own voice?" the Sarvan nodded. Trentino continued, "I hear you in my language. All languages are seamless, they are all the same." He paused to consider the mysteries they had already witnessed. "Should we really be so surprised?" Major Trentino tried to understand and accept.

"Yes, major. I am listening to you in my language." The captain was troubled. "Why should we all being gifted with this thing?" he asked, knowing that Allah had good reason for the Temple's presence, and to exist in this prophetic year in all its legacy and inheritance.

Christopher burst in angrily. "Don't your soldiers get it yet? This place here, the Temple, is your Interpreter. That's right, the TEMPLE! Believe me, there is a strange power at work here, one which we cannot even begin to comprehend. Its influence is all around you and I tell you again, what happened to us is the TRUTH!" he demanded their acknowledgement.

"It is a testing time for us all," Sarvan agreed but Christopher accentuated.

"If we stay here, we will all surely die, we must leave this place, right now!"

To anyone that did not know Christopher, the bio-technologist looked and sounded completely insane, and maybe he was; maybe they all were.

"No, Chris, none of us are leaving here until we have seen the other scientists." Harjit said. "If they are dead," she paused, shaking her head, "we are not leaving them inside this forsaken place! You are next in command of the prisoners, Sarvan! Your commander is missing. So, that leaves you in charge. I demand to see them!" her face was flushed.

Both men did not want another battle on their hands, yet each would do their duty blindly if need be. Beads of sweat began running down the captain's face, the officer was clearly under pressure.

****

"Gentlemen, come on, please, calm down. There is no need for this unpleasantness." An agreeable soft voice broke in. It was Mashir's easy tone.

Everyone turned to look at him. Both military combatants shifted their eyes from each other, unsure what he had to tell them, and what right he had to defuse this duel. Harjit looked as surprised as Barbaro and Christopher. Mashir was a man full of purpose and surprises. What was this one?

"Signore, I am quite calm." Trentino's eyes stared stone cold and ready. The captain regarded the surveyor thoughtfully.

"Everything is fine." Mashir seemed certain and twitched a nervous smile. "I am certain of this."

"What, how?" Christopher found this hard to swallow.

"It is not as bad as we suspect," Mashir's voice was patient and relaxed, just like his usual manner, "these soldiers are not murderers, you can see this."

"That's not what I heard," Trentino said.

"These soldiers and the Sarvan are not terrorists either! These are not the black days of the Nineties or early Millennium. These men are modern and proud, spiritual soldiers, and professionals like you! Listen to me. It is against the 'Will of Allah' to murder innocent people." Mashir's melodic accent cooled the searing tempers of the combatants.

Mashir seemed in control, he had the advantage of a skilled negotiator, a bit like the captain, but better. The surveyor had many talents.

"I want to see our people. I do insist." The major persevered politely.

"Very well." The captain shrugged bluntly and steadily eyed Mashir. The captain, Abdul-Haleem, acknowledged a silent agreement, almost as if a heavy burden had lifted from the captain's mind. "Follow me, please." Sarvan Haleem gestured, leading the way.

"Thank you," major Trentino saluted. On the way through the stone corridors, the captain had something to say.

"Your men and civilians should all leave here, major." The Sarvan continued talking whilst marching on quickly. "This place," he paused, "I know it to be in imminent danger. Please take your people out of here now and save them, there is not much time."

Trentino knew that with his objective secured, he would be able to leave, but the captain seemed to be withholding vital information. Regardless, it would not matter because his job was done here.

"Sergente, organise the regiment to assemble outside the Temple, and once the civilians are safe, we will be leaving."

The Sergeant saluted and set off quickly to systematise the Swiss guards' immanent departure.

"We shall stand firm here as your rear guard," the captain commanded his men. All his men knew that Martyrdom might be expected, to aid the Christian retreat.

"A rear guard. For what?" Trentino asked.

"The Prophecy." The captain shrugged matter-of-fact, while marching off quickly with Mashir and the others. They all moved quickly through the convoluted alien passages, leaving the brightly lit cubed hall behind them.

"What are we running from, what do you fear, Mashir?" Trentino wanted to know more of his thoughts. "As you know, my job will be done once I have you and all the other scientists, and you seem very well versed. I do not know what this immediate danger is. What more can you tell me?"

"I cannot say, but Christopher has warned us," Mashir answered, looking at Christopher's troubled face. he wondered about the bio-technologist.

What does Chris know? Where did he go, earlier inside the Temple? He is hiding something. I know him too well. He is always talkative, but not so now. He is too quiet, as if he is sulking. Chris is holding back the truth, I think. Maybe it is the Temple's influence. I cannot rule that out either. Christopher does not know my suspicions. I believe he has a precious item on his person, an artefact and the symbol of power and a great wealth, he got it there, he must! This explains his mood. How can I get a hold of it?

****

Eventually, they came to the shaft. Steadily, everyone climbed up a permanent and extremely long rope ladder. It was generally agreed that this shaft had once been an ancient elevator, it had not moved since first descending with Fabio and the other's weeks before. It took a while to reach the first level to where the cross path was located, and from there they could go anywhere.

Most of the soldiers departed on their way outside, while the major, sergeant and the scientists continued following the captain and his troops further along the codex-carved corridor. Mashir walked next to Christopher.

"Where is it, Christopher?" Mashir whispered quietly.

"Where is what?" Christopher was puzzled.

"You know, whatever it was that you found inside the inner Temple, come on, you know." Mashir did not want the others to hear him pressuring Christopher again. "I sense that you have a secret to tell. Tell me, what did you find there?"

"Nothing." Christopher was irritated at his prying. "What are you talking about?"

"What is it?" Barbaro butted in, listening from behind. Mashir and Christopher ignored him and walked further up in front and away from the media man's ears.

"My friend, I know you found something inside the Temple. Why are you hiding this secret thing from me? Let's face it, we need not tell the others," Mashir insisted.

Unemotional normally, Mashir's lazy right eye closed and opened again, giving away some of his underlying concern; he sensed that Christopher was holding back.

The soldiers continued ahead with Trentino up in front with the captain heading along another passageway towards where the captive scientists would be. Mashir pulled the bio-technologist's arm hard.

"Speak."

"Look, Mashir, I cannot talk about this right now," Christopher replied curtly but could see Barbaro closing in again. "I have something, yes, you are right about that. I will not speak of it here."

"We have been friends too long to hold a secret with each other."

"I have a metal-link, made of what looks like pure silver. It has some peculiar properties when it is close to you and when you hold it. Even now, I feel its warmth as if a chemical reaction is still exciting the metal in some way. I think this may have been the same object Fabio was looking for."

"Maybe, Christopher, maybe."

"It is really strange," Christopher explained, "and comes with a feeling. Shish, I cannot speak any more. The others will become very suspicious. I just do not know what I am going to do with it."

"Ah, then you have this thing on you, my friend?" stated Mashir. By now, Barbaro was too close, and may have heard some of the story.

"It is time to go," Christopher said, cutting off any more talk of the matter, and ran to catch up with the front of the group.

****

At the end of the corridor, the UMCAA forces prepared their heavy machine guns for action, when the group rapidly approached. Once they recognized who they were, the Sarvan ordered them to point the nozzle up the other corridor to where their fellow comrades had recently gone missing. That was the next place to watch—an area already compromised.

Some unknown enemy lurked beyond. The captain and his Scimitar guards were expecting trouble, and continued their fearful watch. Trentino could see the strain written on their faces.

Two Scimitar guards squatted further along on the right corridor, keeping checkpoint there and were ready to scout ahead if needed. Earlier, they had been no further than the end where a stairwell was located. From that location onwards, it was quite literally a "no man's land".

A few brief words were exchanged at the barricade and the soldiers saluted letting them all through. The major prepared himself to deal swift judgement.

I will have to be quick. If the prisoners have been executed, then this is a double-cross, a trap!

Unseen, major Trentino silently unclipped his Beretta 98FS "Brigadier Elite" pistol with its heavy slide. It held twenty rounds, more than enough for the immediate job. Two extra Islamic guards had slyly tagged behind their group as escorts. The major sensed them, but he did not look at the extra baggage. *Piss easy,* he thought.

The captain was first man inside the makeshift living quarters, closely followed by Trentino, whose eyes were darting quickly from left to right, scanning for anything vital. A trick, potential weapons, anything, and committing it all to memory.

They walked quickly through the large room's buttery illumination. Their smoky shadows in candle light were cast across the large stone block walls along with the few lamps hissing there like pressure cookers. The rudimentary ventilation system was also hissing slightly in unison; its vents seen up in the walls.

As they got closer to the room, they were grimly expecting to see their friends' dead bodies inside. *They must be in there,* Trentino surmised, knowing that the Sarvan would need to take them out soon.

Suddenly, a voice spoke to them.

"Who are you?" it challenged from behind them.

"Endrissi?" Christopher almost burst into tears at seeing him, "My, God, it is you!"

"Endrissi!" Harjit called, stunned at seeing him.

"Fine, I'm fine. We are bearing up." He was surprised to see them.

"Where are the others, signore Bergamaschi?" the major needed an instant answer. "Where are your companions?"

The major knew all their names and faces implicitly, his homework was meticulous.

For the geologist, this was the first time he saw the Swiss guards.

Obscured in the semi-darkness, it was too easy to miss out this adjacent room where Endrissi had appeared from. Staring at the major, Endrissi hesitated. *Who the Hell is this?*

"Fine, and who are you?" he said to the major, cautiously watching the military.

Unexpectedly, Mykola Castrenze and Sebastiano Potenzia joined them.

"Where is Mathieson? Is he all right?" Harjit asked.

"Mathieson is worse." Endrissi nodded to where he came out from. "Follow me."

Sarvan and his men looked uneasy going inside. Trentino was on alert for anything.

The sizeable stone room was divided into small sections with partitions for privacy. Kees Acampilchtl lay resting in one section and Mathieson lay quietly on a camp bed alone inside another. It felt cheerless.

"Oh Mathieson. Let me get you fixed up, Mat," Harjit said.

She checked him out, all the while trying to stay positive, but clinically, his condition seemed hopeless.

Mathieson's skin on his face and arms had become an off-whitish colour. Swallowing quietly, her suspicions were rekindled. His skin was dry and powdery and flaked off to the touch, dropping onto the ground like dandruff and revealed a scaly white dermis underneath. Harjit kept her shock hidden.

"It's not as bad, Mat, we're going to get you fixed up." Her confident tone was quite remarkable.

"He has some sort of infection, a disease," Endrissi spoke quietly into her ear, "The guards will not go near him. They are too scared."

"Mashir," Christopher tugged the surveyor's wrist and held it firm. "I thought you said they had all been killed, executed?" Mashir swallowed a groan, while Chris bore into Mashir's soft eyes. "Don't get me wrong, I am relieved to see them alive! I made a mistake, Christopher, a big mistake. It's my fault and I cannot apologise enough. Sorry, my friend. It was what the guards said to scare me into talking and giving them what they wanted."

Christopher narrowed his eyes suspiciously, "I trusted you," he said, shaking his head in disappointment. "Sarvan, my intension is to leave here with all my friends immediately." Chris was in no mood for debate.

"I insist. My reinforcements are not far away from here." The major played his ace card just in case the captain was having second thoughts about their release. "We will be extracted within the next few hours."

Captain Haleem smiled at the major and Sergeant Moretti. He too had an ace card to play. His Scimitar guards outflanked the Swiss guards, and their Scimitar AK sub-machine guns were already pointing directly at them.

Outflanked, no way, the major thought.

A split second was all it took, to move quickly and with no sound, the regiments moto 'silent in motion' and going to the side of the captain. The major bringing up his bayonet pressing its point lightly into his competitor's throat. A split second more and the captain would be dead!

****

"Major," the captain stated sincerely, "We have no quarrel, I have already been given permission to allow all our guests and your men to leave here. I am a man of my word. We have been waiting for our commander who is lost somewhere inside the Temple. I wait for his safe arrival. I have been keeping your friends secure inside here. It is for their own safety." his voice conveyed honesty. "Be aware, it is also unsafe to be outside in the forest. The Temple is now the safest place."

"I doubt that." Harjit's face showed deep dread at her haunted memories of what lay somewhere inside the upper tiers. She did not favour his superior's chances of survival either.

"You said he is lost?" Trentino was still holding the lethal point to the man's throat.

"Yes." The captain swallowed as a bead of sweat ran down his brow. He did not know if the Swiss guard was going to let him live.

"Order your men to put their weapons down, captain, then I will lower my knife from your throat." The major bartered, he did not fully trust the Islamic soldier.

"Look below you, major." The captain was holding a pistol underneath, pointing straight at the major's belly!

Page 382

As quick as a gunfighter, without anyone noticing, the captain had already slipped out his handgun, swivelled it horizontally from the hip, and took the major's lethal advantage away.

The major looked down and saw their mutual destruction. He would join the Sarvan in death. Knowing his responsibility was with the civilians in mind, *stalemate,* both men lowering their weapons.

"You and your people are free to go, signore." The captain holstered his pistol securely.

"Thank you, captain Abdul-Haleem." Trentino turned to the girl. "Harjit, can Mathieson be moved?"

"Unless there is some place to take him, I would not move Mathieson. At this moment, he is under shelter. The captain is right, this is probably the best place for Mathieson to be looked after. We keep him here until rescue arrives." She lowered her voice. "He is in a very bad shape."

"I will be calling for assistance once we get out of here. There is little to no signal inside the Temple. Reinforcement is scheduled to arrive here in a few hours, final extraction in twenty-four. Be ready."

"Great," Christopher acknowledged. "If it is acceptable with Sarvan Abdul-Haleem, with his men's aid, the best plan would be to keep Mathieson under Harjit's medical attention until then. I will leave and go look for my bio-medical samples at base camp. The *paste* I made has not cured Mathieson. With more, or if I can refine it, he has a chance." Christopher was eager to get going.

"Are you in charge suddenly, Christopher?" Cesaré was annoyed at these new arrangements, causing an awkward silence between them. Leadership seemed up for grabs. The others were not yet up to speed with the events.

"Where is?" Endrissi asked tentatively.

"Fabio was killed," Harjit gently informed him, "He died in the lower Temple."

"He died saving me." Christopher felt a heavy burden press on his shoulders, and he dropped his head in guilt.

"Not Fabio!" Sebastiano was shocked.

"No, this cannot be!" Endrissi's face paled. "How?"

Harjit seemed relieved to step down from the team leader position in favour of Endrissi.

Endrissi had always been officially second in charge after Fabio but Christopher and others knew his mind had been unhinged, albeit in remission. But, since Carmello's death over at the mines, the geologist could crack easily again under pressure.

"He was an arrogant son-of-a-bitch. I will miss him." Mathieson's voice unexpectedly joined them! Everyone turned around, amazed at hearing Mathieson's dry throat crackling as he spoke. The ill man slowly turned his head with a smile, his neck joint clicked as though it was bone-dry.

All this time he had been listening to them. Harjit immediately helped Mathieson sip some water.

Christopher left immediately with the other scientists, with Trentino and his men tagging along to protect him.

Why are the Islamic forces still here? Why did they not want to leave too? Surely there is no point in staying any longer, unless they have not completed their mission!

Everyone was happy to be outside again. The sun shone on their faces and they welcomed the freedom, in contrast to the dingy and stale confines of the Temple. The site of copious green forest immediately lifted their hearts, breathing the fresh air with the knowledge that soon they would be going home. At the entrance, Trentino spoke seriously to Christopher.

"My men will escort you and your colleagues down to search the tents and take whatever provisions you need. This forest has become deadly. We will all assemble at base camp." The major calmly advised the younger man. "Extraction will be in twenty-four hours. Everyone who wants to go, better be ready."

****

CHAPTER IX

THE BLACK FOG

The major tracked his men and the other scientists below, and the group moved quickly down through the terraced steps. Now, his vision began slowly scrutinizing the forest perimeter. The military man was proud of his Sig Sauer SSG 30000, fitted with the Laser Optronix DME 30000. He could easily shoot a mosquito with pinpoint accuracy over great distances.

Trentino knew that somewhere out there in the vale was Colonel Greco Rossi and his men. Osprey should be here right now. Colonel Rossi, also known as Chameleon — that was his call sign. Rossi was late.

No sign of Osprey, they're overdue! Rossi must have had to detour from the rendezvous point. If he does not arrive in the next twenty-four hours, they'll miss the pickup schedule. Extraction is on time.

The soldiers electronic "blips" were configured for the Swiss guards, who had no choice in the matter. He had never needed any electronic gadgets in his past missions, after all, the man was a natural survivor. Electronics and their use was the decision of those higher echelons back in Vatican City and their tin pot generals who wanted ultimate control of the battlefield. Trentino and Rossi detested their distant courage.

There was a better chance of the satellite communications working outside. So, the question for Trentino was, who was watching Osprey's progress? Were they online? Although, the mission orders were still the same: no contact with the outside World. The forest had been sporadic at the best of times for electronic gadgetry, so with any luck, his leaders might be blind as bats. Like Rossi, didn't need any of this new technology to do the job.

"What do you think, Maggiore?" Sergeant Davide Romano from the Eagle Unit sighed. The soldier was anxious that "Chameleon" was overdue. The scar on Romano's face looked angry red. It had become irritated due to the jungle climate.

"Chameleon will be here soon," Mantis stated confidently. "He's been late before. Osprey will make it before we go." the major turned and nodded over to another guard. The radio operator gave him the radiophone.

"Phoenix to Buzzard, Phoenix to Buzzard. Come in Buzzard, over." The major stared directly up into the blue sky as though it could help. He listened to a non-committal electronic hum, and the annoying squiggle of static interference continued noncommittal in the airwaves. The major was hoping to contact their air lift. He tried again.

"Phoenix to Buzzard. Phoenix to Buzzard, come in Buzzard, over." He finally gave up. *Damn interference!*

"Signore?" Romano asked expectantly.

"Ok, Sergente Romano, I will go with the corporal and a few men. Head down and track due South for a bit. This structure is causing complete havoc with our devices. I'll get better reception out there."

"What about the civilians, Signore?" The sergeant wanted his orders.

"When we manage to make contact, we will provide the coordinates to land on top of the Temple. We will get everyone and their mothers up there, including our Islamic chums if they want to come. Unfortunately, we have the extra space," he paused as he thought about his lost comrades and the civilian fatalities, "there will be room for us all."

"I do not trust them, Signore."

"We have to stay ready at all times, Sergente. What is our op status?"

"Out of our thirty-five feathers, signore, five were dropped in the fire-fight and one fell not too long ago down there at the base, attacked by some fucking super-bug. The scientists have lost seven people out of their expedition." The sergeant gave him a quick body count: thirteen.

"I reckon that our Islamic brothers had about the same numbers as us right now. We killed about fourteen and there are injured men on both sides, but only scrapes, most were outright kills."

"Signore, if the colonnello arrives while you are gone, could we capture them and turn the tables?" Romano asked.

"No, soldier, these Scimitar guardians will die first before that happens. I cannot risk the expedition. That cost is too great. We have our prize, the civilians. Our mission is complete." The major saluted him. "Sergente, you look after the civilians, I will not be too long. Right, I need six soldiers and the buzz-saws." He ordered a small team to come with him. The major knew that they would all be out of the jungle very soon, once communication was re-established with their pickup.

****

Major Trentino and a hand full of his birds-of-prey were already moving swiftly along the main track, cutting down foliage. Soon they were about a kilometre from the base camp perimeter. The jungle had already reclaimed most of the foliage, forcing them to cut heavier strokes than he had expected.

The forest dampened much of the noises and every now and again, they could hear water flowing somewhere in the distance, each time becoming louder. They were cutting more of the dense foliage away, when the volume unexpectedly switched up a notch. Major Trentino and his men suddenly found themselves right in front of a powerful torrent.

Like pulling back a heavy curtain, with the vegetation gone, the white-water instantly deafened their ears and surged past them, with such force it could wash away anything! It rushed downwards with great ferocity, making them feel dizzy as they watched it flow. The water was as unstoppable as a tornado battering off the banks. It kept going on its escape through the forest. There was no telling when streams or rivers or flash floods appeared in the forest. Its destination, a place much further than they could see, cutting and eroding deep gouges through the vale and feeding into the larger rivers and tributaries far beyond here.

This is a God forsaken place, the major thought to himself.

They found themselves in an opening inside the dense green foliage, with the natural light penetrating through the branches from the high trees above. The sunlight reflected beautifully off the foaming white water below them, making it look startling and fresh!

They stood above steep banks, with freezing water splashing up and onto their faces. They looked downstream to where the water raged away. The group could only shout at each other, since their voices were drowned out against the inexorable fury of the bouncing stream battering off the near banks. The force of nature was immense as it went on thrashing past them. How could they cross this natural barrier? The major stood back inside the foliage to get away from some of the noise and tried to contact the extraction crew once more.

"Phoenix calling Buzzard!" the major shouted, while taking off his beret to wipe sweat from his brow, showing off his styled dark hair that was swept and gelled back like a model. That was his thing. Killing too. "Phoenix calling Buzzard! Phoenix calling Buzzard! Do you copy, over?" He repeated his call. The noise of non-committal static was useless, "Come in Buzzard!" Trentino's tone sounded more frustrated this time because it did not look good for the mission.

The major stared up into the blue sky with his piercing green eyes, praying for a reply from God. Surely somebody is out there, when without warning, the static broke.

"Buzzard One to Phoenix, we read you Phoenix, over." A reply came from the pilot's crisp and clear voice. They were through.

"Yeah!" The men's cheer echoed through the forest. The wait, the frustration and tension all broke in an instance, and everyone looked upwards and congratulated each other. Their extraction was secured, and it would be on time. The major smiled, his composure held intact. He still had a job to do. He still needed to get these civvies out of here and back to base!

"Phoenix and Eagle are ready to fly. I repeat, Phoenix and Eagle are ready to fly, over!" The immediate evacuation status was set.

"Copy on that, Phoenix. What about Osprey, over?" the pilot needed to know his full cargo.

"Osprey has no wings, I repeat Osprey has no wings." He paused in the silence, then added, "Over!"

Static and silence were the only sounds heard on the airwaves. The major waited patiently for a reply from the pilot.

A poignant moment. The jungle could disorientate even the best of navigators, yet there was still a better chance than not that Osprey would get there in time.

"Copy on that, Phoenix." The clear and polite tone of the pilot broke through the static. The pilot had assimilated the lost unit and knew the next in command's rank, sticking to the pre-assigned "call signs" he would not break that type of protocol over the communication.

"Phoenix to Buzzard One, Phoenix to Buzzard One, we need an "evac" on LZ Pink Flamingo, coordinates on my electronic flare, over!"

Trentino switched on the red gadget. The equipment was about the size of a flat rectangular box, six inches by nine, known as electronic flares, e-Flairs or e-Buoys, their transmission set on a 1600-2850 kHz range, with a power beam and optional sound alarm.

Unknown to anyone other than the rescue pilots, this signal was amplified from their helicopter via the GEOSAR satellites and monitored by Geostationary Earth Orbit Local User Terminals.

"Buzzard One to Phoenix, we have received your signal, our Buzzards are far out, E.T.A. eighteen hours and closing."

"Affirmative," acknowledged Trentino.

"I have an interruption signal, Phoenix, hold on. Transmission has a security override on it. I'm passing you directly, signore, over and—" when a rude voice truncated the pilot's mid-sentence.

"Phoenix, this is Apostle on the line, do you copy?" a man's cutting voice came over the airwaves.

"Si, I copy you loud and clear, Apostle, over." the major replied. Apostle was straight from the Vatican, Rossi had mentioned that at least.

"This is Apostle. Do you have the "Golden Egg" and is it undamaged?" Trentino sensed stress in this unfamiliar voice that bordered on controlled panic.

"Si, signore, the eggs are in the nest, but a few are broken. Over," he answered curtly.

"You are not listening to me, Maggiore?" The voice snapped back. "The Golden Egg! Do you have it?" the voice sounded incensed with the officer's lack of clarity.

"Sorry, Apostle, I have no data on that, over." The major replied bluntly. He waited for an immediate rebuke knowing that this answer would be unacceptable.

The major didn't know what Apostle was talking about. Trentino's mission orders were search and rescue, nothing else. The scientists' code word was "Egg". He didn't know anything about a "Golden Egg"! Rossi, his commander, kept certain secrets on a need to know basis.

"Phoenix, have you had contact with Osprey, over?" The ill-tempered voice sounded suppressed as if this time whoever Apostle was, he was not wanting recognition.

"Negative, over."

"Phoenix, these are your new orders. Locate the "Golden Egg" and return it to the hatchery for pickup. Find it back at the nest. You must have it secured before extraction is available."

The major's face changed into a deeper shade of red because he knew exactly what Apostle meant. No air ticket home unless the "Golden Egg" was found. Blackmail was not what he bargained for.

"Apostle, our eggs are damaged and we need immediate extraction." He tried to urge whoever was at the end of the line to reconsider the wounded. "We need immediate medical assistance!"

"Phoenix, listen carefully. The "Golden Egg" must be found and put into safe incubation and returned to the hatchery before your extraction. Check all the Eggs in the Nest. I must have it."

"Signore, I insist, we need immediate evac now!"

"You will find it first. I have utmost confidence in you, Mantis. This is Apostle, over and out."

"Signore, we have injured—" when suddenly, he was cut off. Mantis felt bitter. He was distraught at knowing he had let all his men and the people of the expedition down. He was now committed to a mad search for something he knew nothing about. "And what does this fucking Golden Egg look like, shit-face?" he said to the static and blue sky.

His new orders were unshakable. Apostle was clearly putting everyone's lives in serious jeopardy. The bottom line was, nobody was leaving until this object was secured. Apostle seemed convinced that one of the scientists has some precious artefact on them, the "Golden Egg" and Apostle wanted it. Why is this thing so important? The major wanted it too.

"Buzzard to Phoenix," suddenly the pilot's clear melodic voice came online. "E.T.A sixteen-forty-five hours at LZ Pink Flamenco, we have your "e-Flair" just coming into range on my scope. You are being received loud and clear. We will pick up your "e-Buoy" nearer the LZ."

"Buzzard, what's that playing in the background?"

"Oh, that? It's 'Painted Black'. You know, the 'Stones'. I love those guys!" the pilots voice turned clear and professional once again, "Good luck, Buzzard One, over and out."

Trentino needed to get back, and at this moment, anger was as pointless as hope in finding this object.

Compromised like this by Apostle demonstrated a disregard for life, the mission had suddenly changed, because the civilians and his men had just become disposable. He had lost enough men on a *so called* rescue mission while pondering what kind of thing was more important than the civilian's lives! The major knew nothing of the real reason for the mission and the link to God was Apostle's ultimate goal.

"Operation Aequinoxium" the coded mission name given by Apostle for the major's black op, all else was expendable including the civilians.

"Ok, men, I want you six to stay and clear this site. Make it large enough for a helicopter to land on. I am going back to the Temple while you lot chop this place down. Use the power-saws we brought with us. The electronic buoys are now planted, and the Helicopter is heading here, so get tore in. I expect this place to be cleared ASAP. I am heading back to base."

"Si, Maggiore!" the men acknowledged him but nobody was happy because in front of them stood plenty of wood and forest felling was a Goliath-like task!

Mantis smiled, his disappointed thoughts unspoken and said in his fashion. "*Piss easy*, boys, piss easy."

On his way back, Trentino racked his brain to remember if Rossi had ever mentioned this object.

Shit, what is this Golden Egg? the major thought, as he hacked furiously at the greenery, steadily heading back to base camp.

That Pratt Apostle, the swine, he suggested that one of the scientists had something of vital importance. The egg? And that means searching each member of the expedition! They will not take kindly to a body search, trading one gaoler for a warden! This will make me no better than those Islamic's! Where the fuck has Chameleon gone to? Maybe he already has reached the Temple.

****

Christopher entered his tent inside base camp, searching his frugal accommodation. This was luxury compared to the Temple. Immediately, and with set purpose, he began looking for his specimens and samples to help Mathieson's illness. He also wanted to privately study the strange object he had been carrying for some-time, and now was his chance.

The others were inside the large marquee, gathering various things they would want to take home with them. Unzipping the inside of his jacket pocket, Christopher felt for the strange artefact, and brought it out cautiously. His eyes studied the silver link with deep curiosity. It seemed smaller somehow from what he remembered.

Watching it, his distorted eyes reflected off its shiny surface almost like they were not his. Strangely and disappointedly, the object did not seem to be anything special. Unknown to him, its physical and chemical properties were subservient to its hidden esoteric qualities.

Puzzled, Christopher tried rubbing it, squeezing it, rotating it and examined the object at every angle, scrutinising the thing, using his pocket magnifying glass. He found nothing. *What is so special about this thing, this link?*

Consoling himself, he recalled the facts again: where he found it and the strange and mysterious circumstances under which it had been gifted to him. *From the hand of the dead, that must count for something!*

For now, he would have to keep it safe until he could figure it out more. Disappointed and groaning with muffled lamentations, he deeply regretted that Mashir knew that he had it. Christopher was caught between choices. *Maybe I could keep this as a memento for my old age. Why not? It has been given to me. It's nobody else's. It is mine.*

The priest was more confused than ever. *No! It must go back to His Holiness. It belongs to him. It's his treasure. This thing is not mine to keep, but then why should it belong to any one man?* He wrestled with his thoughts and in the end, decided he would take it back to Rome. *I will keep it, for now. It leaves me with a strange feeling.*

Christopher had been feeling odd since it came into his possession. He felt very unlike himself, and now while holding the link, it made him feel happy, contented. All his worries did not seem so big anymore. *Why worry?*

Shrugging at danger, the priest spellbound. Already the power of the link influenced his mind like a drug, making him feel euphoric. The Scientist experimented with the mysterious object some more. He tried to polish it using his hands and noticed a strange rash had appeared on the surface of his skin.

Mmm, I must be allergic to its touch, he thought. When he held it, he felt oddly more conscious of everything around him and more aware of his surrounding environment. The link was beginning to expand his mind.

Christopher bit his lip to make sure he had not fallen asleep. *Am I dreaming these feelings? These special thoughts are very real. Lord above, I am changing.* He looked up and could see right through the canvas material of his tent, as if it were made of transparent polythene!

His attention moved to something else, another influence on him—a warning. His perception became mixed with intuition, and it gave him an acute awareness and special insight for imminent danger. This new ability settled firmly onto an image inside his mind. He now understood that something lurked below his hat lying on the tent floor next to his pillow, something dangerous. It was becoming opaque and more transparent.

The rash on his hand suddenly became wildly red and very sore, but Christopher swallowed the pain. He saw something moving underneath his hat. He immediately recognised it as the same small spider that had attacked them inside the Temple.

This link is a gift!

He quickly brought his torch hard down onto his hat like a hammer.

Thump! Thump! Thump! He tried to flatten the spider.

I know it is there. He carefully lifted the hat and saw the spider smashed to pieces underneath. The spider had been there waiting for him. *How did it get there? Someone has tried to kill me!* Christopher could not understand what was happening to him and yet it all felt so natural. However, what this new ability did not answer was, who wanted to kill him? *My God, who is trying to kill me?* With grim realisation, his survival had taken on a new dimension.

As he looked though the semi-transparent tent before him, he could see Barbaro's opaque figure coming out of the large marquee and walking across the muddy ground towards him.

Suddenly, the metal link changed in appearance. The atomic level became colourless, and blended transparently in his hand. His eyes widened in panic.

My God, what is going on, what is it doing now?" It's disappearing on my hand! It is still there, I can still feel it! Hot. It feels hot, as if some chemical reaction is occurring sub-atomically.

Defying physics it had weight but no mass, no physical body to see. It was invisible. The link's transitional state frayed between *dimensions*, and the link had vanished. He put the invisible weight into his pocket and zipped it shut, just in time.

"Are you organized yet?" the media man unzipped the doorway wider and entered without asking.

"What's wrong? You look flustered, is there something wrong?" Barbaro suspected something. *Christopher was not quite there! What is wrong with him? Is he unwell?*

"I cannot find my specimens anywhere inside here. I will need to look inside the crates."

He pushed past the media man and headed quickly to where the crates were stored. He looked at the disarray of wooden boxes. Some had fallen and had rolled during the strange tremor that had occurred last evening when the Swiss guards had arrived.

The campsite was now in a complete mess, but the smaller tents were saved! The larger mess tent was damaged but had been quickly repaired and reconstructed by the Vatican guards.

"Ah, here they are!" Chris was happy to find them. He opened one of the environmental pods and peered inside. "Excellent, the specimens had grown more, developed and matured as I had hoped!"

Christopher's plan to make some sort of paste for Mathieson's wounds would take a few costly hours to synthesise. He would have to work against the clock. With each minute, Mathieson's health deteriorated.

Inside the large tent, the bio-technologist quickly organised himself, mixing his samples into a muddy light brown and green paste inside his makeshift laboratory. He blended the paste into a rich pomegranate coloured extract, and it resulted in a potion that was not so far off an old alchemic recipe, one synthesised by the natural elixirs.

The link told him this new product would be a life-saver. He felt the link move inside his pocket. It gave him the ability to see through materials like a tent, a hat, maybe anything. It gave him the ability to feel his surroundings in a different way.

He had no scientific explanation for this object's paranormal qualities. Was it sorcery or a sixth sense?

It would not stop pulsing inside his breast pocket. The throbbing increased as though it mimicked his heat beat. Christopher imagined it was speaking too him, like an enchanted communication device, urging him to do something, but he could not tune in to it — not yet.

Then, a sense of great dread pushed nausea up from the pit of his stomach. If Harjit were here, she would have prescribed strong anti-depressants and beta blockers for him. Was the link attempting to warn him to leave this place? This is what he felt. He wondered how much more he could take before cracking.

Christopher deliberated whether he should keep the ancient treasure. Apprehension washed through his mind. He could not control it. He understood that his behaviour was altering, and he was powerless to stop it. But he didn't know whether it was the Temple or the link behind this change.

I must hide it for safe-keeping. There is no telling what might happen next! This must be what those UMCAA troops were trying to find, they believe in some lost scrolls but now I think, it must be this link! They still do not understand what it is they are looking for because they have asked too many questions already! I am not sure myself what this thing is. Its power seems to be growing. I shall take it with me later and God protect me.

He looked around cautiously to make sure he was alone. Christopher went back to a pod, and placed the invisible "Link of Power" inside and carefully touched it one last time. He then covered it in moss and earth. He was convinced that it would be safer here than on his person, knowing that if some accident or worse befell him, then the box would be sent to the Vatican. It lessened his guilt.

****

Endrissi was making coffee for the others in the mess tent, while the Swiss guards kept watch around base camp. The scientists were warned to stay close to the local confines of the marquee and not to go wandering off. There were no arguments with that, after that horrific and fatal attack of that unnamed flying insect.

The Swiss guards also kept a lookout from the Temple top, watching everything that moved below, including the UMCAA troops, aware that they still held the main areas inside the Temple. That seemed less important now that they had retained the safety of the scientists. Trentino was somewhere inside the jungle, heading back to base camp after leaving his men working on the trees, but the goal posts had shifted again.

The Islamic forces also oversaw the surrounding rainforest. They watched it with dread because even though there was a sunny blue sky, something curious was beginning to develop in the surrounding forest. An uncanny dark fog was making its presence known above distant trees, the black mass shifting in from the South. Oddly, while the sultry winds were blowing Southwards, the dark low cloud did not. Instead, its gloomy formation moved in the opposite direction.

Bizarrely, even at this far distance, the fog could be seen steadily coming towards them, getting closer, and growing in from the direction of the vale entrance. It was travelling in a Northerly route, right up the valley towards them and beyond. However, now it seemed to be taking a wider berth, its black saturation making inroads on the West and East of the vale. They could see that in time, it would eventually encircle them.

Unknown to them, where it encroached into the forest, the birds stopped singing, instead flying off in fright. The monkeys too, they halted their ceaseless screeching and instead, jumped and swung as far as possible, away from the abnormal phenomenon. The blackness was bound by an unnatural fear, and everything moved fearfully away from its path.

A new noise started coming through the rainforest, a new sound echoing its presence to everything—a distant buzzing. It was heard where Trentino's soldiers were working. His men were busy clearing the trees and making the new landing zone. Crazy high-pitched noises could be heard, along with more guttural ones too. At the Temple, the sounds of tree felling were coming in loud and clear at different degrees of pitch and speeds.

The guardsmen toiling hard at the landing zone "Pink Flamingo", they were clearing the way. The six were soon joined by three additional men, and all with chainsaws. These power-tools were provided by the Islamic force and expedition stores. The extra men made the hard graft a little bit easier.

At the LZ, tall trees and overrun foliage were being cleared and the trees felled mercilessly; they needed to move fast as time was critical. After some time, a wide semicircle had been made, pushing the forest back. The annoying racket and clatter of chainsaws on tree bark kept going, biting deeply and all the time the trees screamed sawdust and death.

Zzzzzz, zuzzzzzzzzz, zzzuuzzzzzz, zuzzzzzzzzz, zzzzzzzzzz zzzzzzzz.

Their human presence here was like a blasphemy to nature in such a beautiful place, with timber felling, sending trees crashing into the nearby stream, and into a place where Mother Nature washed it away in its fast-moving rapids. Sweat pouring from their brows, the major's men watched, feeling satisfied as the logs bounced and bobbed out of sight.

"Thank you, God! We are nearly finished here!" one man said, wiping sawdust and dirt away.

"Si, I am glad. These mosquitoes are fucking torturing me!" The men were fresh pickings for the dirty flies, as they feasted on them.

"I want to fight. Not cut down bloody trees!" one soldier complained.

"You must be a complete idiot," another soldier said, glad that the shooting was over.

"I am up for a murder and the bloodier the better for me," he boasted. "So what's the big deal about killing a few Islamists, eh?" Private Lucie's psychopathic tendencies simmered through his boyish looks. He smiled at this thought. The other man looked disgusted, but it was pointless to argue with him.

After working for another few hours, the men were utterly spent and were glad to stop their petrol-driven chainsaws for a rest. But, the savage flies gave them no respite, dive-bombing and biting them. The place infested. Then, for some inexplicable reason, a few minutes later, these pests were gone.

"Merda, those damn pests are gone!" Private Lucie swabbed sweat away from his bitten brow.

"Same with those flocks of birds up there." They looked up and saw a mass migration of birds flying North. The sergeant then spotted something else. "What is that on the river, that black Shit?" He narrowed his eyes suspiciously.

Curiously, they stared at a strange black fog-bank. It was massive like a giant wall and black as tar. It had silently appeared from *nowhere*, and now it was here.

They watched the black mass gather on top of the river, then it stopped and seemed to wait. When they would take their eyes off it, it would encroach some more. The men were left wondering whether it had moved again. Quickly and gradually, it stopped and staggered forward, and went weirdly against the direction of the wind. It moved as though it had purpose. Its speed caught them off-guard, when it began flowing quickly. It no doubt was moving again.

Their wary eyes followed the rapid blackness as it glided smoothly and quietly up the river, its outlandish presence chilling them because the water had been clear, bubbly and fresh just a moment ago. The forest had been lively with life, but now, the sunshine had disappeared and there was nothing but an ominous blackness and fear.

The fog moved on silently and quickly, and it brought something else with it—a foreboding atmosphere. This was unlike anything they had ever experienced or seen before. The fog looked peculiar because it seemed to be angular and too well defined, more akin to a black wall than a fog-bank. Thinking it would come all the way, when it stopped again waiting.

Out of their view, further inside the trees, and too high up to see from where they were working, the fog stretched from the floor and reached up to a higher height, just under the treetops. Where the fog displayed a strange flattish surface, to which it would occasionally percolate from its straight edge, then suddenly sprout or throw up into a convoluted puff or streak of blackness. There, it would wave around madly like a limb and settle flat again for a period. Other than that, most of the wall sat still.

The men could hardly believe their eyes. The fog's definitive edges seemed to kiss the surface of the river, giving the illusion of the turbulent stream disappearing into some sort of black hole and almost as if a mouth was swallowing it up.

The blackness stretched unseen, going much further into the forest, much further than they could imagine and by this time, it dominated the expanse next to where they were felling, right to the edge of the clearing.

The men had no time to lose, this unusual fog spooked them badly, adding impetus to their work, they cleared away the rest of the foliage just to get out of there. With their heads down, they gnawed heavily into the tree bark with their chainsaws, buzzing through bush again and again. The noise echoed across the large clearing. A short time later, nobody saw the fog move.

The chainsaws stopped abruptly, their distrustful eyes looked steadily upwards. Each man was speechless as they looked up to see its height. Their necks hurt from reclining so much. The fog was right above them.

It had stealthily shifted closer to them like a shadow. A straight wall of blackness stood twenty metres from them, and it dominated everything. They staggered back.

This naked black wall stood sharp and defined while their fearful eyes watched in disbelief. A massive body of blackness. The surface was smooth now and extended from where they stood to the distant riverbank. Seeing it up close, it appeared to be something quite different, not a fog.

"When did that crap move again? Shit!" Lucie spat on the ground. He knew what he was looking at was not natural. He took a deep breath. Alarmed he instinctively picked up and loaded his machine-gun.

"That stuff has come from, *nowhere!* It looks so bloody odd, completely black. Look here, guys." The sergeant decided, enough was enough. "Our job is about finished, a few more trees will do it and we're out of here, so hurry up!" The sergeant swallowed hard, surveying what was left of the landing zone. His mind was more preoccupied with this new intrusion.

The sergeant hoped it would not cause trouble with the landing in terms of visibility, wishing that the lustreless substance might blow away before their extraction tomorrow.

Bloody hell, the wind's going the opposite way and that mass is not dispersing. Maybe it's some huge chemical gas release. Oh, who the fuck knows. It's not blowing away. It can't be a normal fog.

The electronic buoy was still transmitting as expected, so other than this, there should be no problems finding them.

The soldiers were looking increasingly unsure. They didn't know what to make of the uncanny spectacle. There had to be a logical reason because whatever it was, it was not natural.

Lucie thought he saw something inside it, and pointed his weapon at the fog. All they wanted was one thing, for the sergeant to give the orders to leave. The sergeant picked up his chainsaw and said, "Just a few more trees."

The buzzing started.

****

At base camp, the men heard the wailing sounds from distant chainsaws, and visualised the bringing down of more tormented timber. They were happy that the guys were working hard and getting the new landing zone ready. The LZ could not be more than about a kilometre away and within easy reach. The sultry heat made everyone feel tired on the walls. Some yawned, quite bored, listening to the noises as the lazy sun beat down.

Bzzzzz, bzzzzzzzzz, bzzzzzzzzz, bzzzzzzzzz, bzzzzzzzzzzzzzzz.

"Those guys are too keen. How long have they been gone, it must be hours? What are they getting up to?" Endrissi said.

Endrissi was desperate like the others to leave this place, and his carefree attitude was only a smoke screen for his fear. He had seen too much. At that moment, everyone heard distant staccato of machine-gun fire.

Everyone got up to see where the noise was coming from. Could it be the LZ? The buzzing of chainsaws never stopped, not even for a moment when just as surprisingly, the guns fell silent. Then, more abrupt sporadic bursts started and came within earshot.

The shots sounded a little closer this time, when once again they stopped. The only noises heard again was the buzzing of the chainsaws.

Immediately, the soldiers began mobilising, quickly gearing up along the terraces, some taking cover behind bushes on the steps, while others moved down the steps to reinforce base camp. Soon, everything was ready to meet any new threat.

Other Swiss guardsmen ran along the first-tier, meeting up with UMCAA troops coming out from inside the Temple. Everyone needed to see what was going on.

"Gunfire, Sarvan!" a UMCAA soldier saluted his Sarvan at the Temple entrance, awaiting orders. The Sarvan assessed the danger.

"What is going on, major?" Abdul-Haleem demanded of Trentino, expecting a quick explanation, and suspecting his Christian reinforcements.

Trentino replied curtly. Back from his earlier trek from the LZ. "Gunfire, yours more like."

"Not mine, we are all here." The captain stared coldly at Trentino. The major rolled the dice on various possibilities.

"I could ask you the same question captain, have you more men hidden down there?"

By sounds of it, my men are still cutting those bloody trees, Trentino thought. He listened for the chainsaws, and upon hearing the buzzing, it was confirmed his men were ok, and getting on with his orders. The gunfire must be someone else thinking that his guys would return soon. *They might come back in with Osprey.*

Major Trentino knew the colonel was out there, somewhere and surmised that the colonel's unit was closing in from the South and might be neutralising more Islamic insurgents, which would account for a fire fight.

"Which direction did the gunfire come from, soldier?" the captain asked one of his men.

"South, somewhere inside the forest," said the alarmed Muslim guard.

"Your squad, major?" the captain enquired unfavourably. "They went out to cut down trees for a landing zone, did they not? Should I be expecting *more* visitors to our Temple?" The officer felt let down, badly misjudging Trentino. The man had seemed like an honourable soldier to him.

"There is something else, Sarvan," his heedful subordinate continued. "A dense black fog has been reported and is progressing up the vale!"

Anything was possible. Both men measured each other up for a quick obituary. The Temple was once again a Tinderbox. Trentino stared emotionlessly at the captain, when more firing started again in the forest.

****

Yesterday, Swiss guardsman, Colonel Greco Rossi, officer in charge of Operation Aequinoxium, had to take a large and unplanned detour from his route, because at the time a deadly mass of ants was in his way. There were highways of them. They were all crawling quicker than a fast-flowing river. The treacherous creatures ate everything in their path and claimed one of his men's lives.

The satellite navigation equipment had developed peculiar technical faults too, and the data provided by it was giving the wrong information. It was a beta system, a prototype, which was said to be, state of the art technology. It had played a key role in misdirecting them right up the wrong valley.

Thought as much, I told them this kit was shit! The colonel was seething. *And now, these continual errors in transmissions, these crap coordinates have made any measurements of our locale worthless. I have lost contact with both Trentino and mission control.* The officer looked up to where the sky should be. Chameleon was totally pissed off. He saw nothing but branches and leaves. Wiping his vexed brow, he thought, *Bloody techno-freaks and power-mad generals putting this hardware onto us to test. We're being used as fucking guinea pigs. My men's lives are at stake here. Typical!*

Events had gone badly so far for the colonel. What else could possibly go wrong? Moving on, he and his men eventually reached over the top of some high ground. This was when an open area unexpectedly appeared — the vale.

"At last, we are back on track!" Rossi looked relieved. Below, he saw a natural clearing that had appeared among the trees, giving a view towards the elusive Iblis vale. Tightening his lips, he nodded ahead to his men, while thinking, *I should have followed my instincts from the beginning.*

He was late. Colonel Rossi knew it. He did not know this area or where the valley was for sure, until now. There had been no previous measurements taken to work from. Moving blind, the vale could have been ten miles or more in the wrong direction. Now, he had found it, without the technology. In any case, the vale was only a dot on any map inside Amazonia. His mission depended on linking up with the rest of his command.

Osprey had arrived at the vale before the mysterious black fog closed the gap. There was only way one in and one way out of the Iblis vale.

Rossi, a born survivor and natural tracker, observed something and it made him very suspicious. He saw evidence of too much troop movement. His very keen eyes could spot it and not all due to his men. Large areas of green foliage had been trampled flat, which indicated they were not alone in the forest.

A trail, si, I expected that, but not so much trampling. Mmm, sloppy. Hunching down, he observed the unexpected tracks for a moment, then looked up and saw the Temple. *My God, it's colossal!*

"Check your weapons," he ordered smartly. *Trentino is a useful soldier, he will know what to do.* Chameleon was confident in Phoenix's abilities. "The tracks are not Swiss." The colonel signalled to the rest of his Osprey Unit, leading his men down into the vale with their heavy weapons. They were late.

****

The Vatican and Muslim guards stood side by side in an uneasy truss, contemplating this new development. The sporadic gunfire to the South had stopped. Looking further South, they could see that a strange black mass had formed and had already closed the Southern gap and had taken away all the greenery.

From this expanding body, it crept slowly and ate up the green hills in all directions, more so now on the Western and Eastern slopes. Soon, they would meet the vertical rock faces on each side of the secret vale. If it continued, they would eventually be enclosed. It couldn't be a natural phenomenon. The men realised this with growing trepidation. Their "Death Watch" continued.

What kind of cloud or fog would move against the wind? They shook their heads with mistrust at the ominous black formation. When it started heading towards them again, some pointed and others readied themselves. Their day of judgement approached.

They will come first and SMITE.

It was the Prophecy.

High on the terraces, cold shivers began running up the spines of the men. Many soldiers spoke openly about their worries as they watched uncountable numbers of uncanny puffs of gassy black shapes appear. Weird protrusions came from the top cloud, extensions of the black fluffiness below. This silenced their murmurs.

Long prongs of gaseous blackness kept randomly appearing like long arms and claws, protruding out and above distant treetops, then slowly sunk down and disappeared again into the black fog. This meant that this so-called fog was much closer and was hidden just below tree level. There was no telling just how far in it had come.

From this distance, the black fog was still miles off. It looked like it had of millions of tiny arms blowing up and down in the air, moving wildly around. Soon, the men would be standing alone, on a stone island.

"It is a very strange sight," the captain said, while lowering his binoculars. His distinguished medal, the "United Crossed Swords", was imprinted boldly on his golden bracelet, its metal catching the remaining sunlight and reflecting its shadow onto the Temple wall. "There is darkness within it," said the captain, then paused thoughtfully before speaking again. "This evil fog will be here by night fall."

"It's yet another fucking odd thing in this place," stated the major, scowling at its curse. He knew by now that nothing in the vale was normal.

"You and your men, major, need not face this thing." The Sarvan's tone hinted regret. "We will face this fate on our own." He spoke to his men, with the knowledge that the Christians would be leaving.

"Sarvan," a boy said. He was a soldier and no more than twenty years old.

"Yes, soldier?"

"What are we to do?"

"We wait. We wait here until our commander gives us orders to leave," the captain stated bluntly.

"Sir, by then it will be too late."

"We must put our faith in Allah. Allah knows our true destinies," said Sarvan Haleem, holding the boy's shoulder and shaking it solidly in comradeship and equality. The boy was afraid, but his faith was stronger.

"Praise be to Allah," the boy replied.

The captain sighed. He could not hold back the tide. He shrugged casually, then nodded confidently to him with hope.

"Now, go to your station, my Scimitar guardian, you and I will await our fate together." The boy smiled back and quickly disappeared.

"Face it, captain," said the major, "your commander will not be returning. You should assume absolute responsibility and leave this place. Come with us. What do you fear from that, cloud?"

Trentino reflected recursively because he too had witnessed a weird vision.

That strange flying thing and it's grim mating call, one that reverberated death around the vale. The major suppressed a shiver. And now, this fog held something inside. He felt it too.

The captain regarded him thoughtfully for a moment before speaking.

"What do you fear, major?" he honestly wanted to know and smiled warmly.

"Failing."

"We all must be prepared for that."

All will shake in terror. *Again, the Prophecy.*

****

Earlier, and seconds before the gunfire began.

Inside base camp it had been a quiet moment up until the shooting to the South began. Christopher sat inside his tent and wrote in his journal. This was important to him because as much as possible of the expedition's journey had to get back to civilisation. It would not take long.

Once done, he would take the elixir up to the Temple.

In the distance, he could hear the waning sounds of the chainsaws buzzing. The felling of the forest continued. Unexpectedly, his heart jolted as it pumped harder in sudden shock at the sounds of sharp sporadic gunfire. Christopher stopped writing and looked up in shock.

Alarmed by the sounds of conflict, he could hear distant running of feet and soldiers shouting and getting closer. Chris finished, then put his journal safely away inside a small rucksack, along with his latest cures and specimens. Emerging from the tent and strapping his rucksack on, he did not quite know what to expect.

Christopher saw a charge of soldiers running fast in various directions. Some were sprinting right past him, while others were shouting orders; those were the men sent down from the Temple. Others were moving camp gear and taking up defensive positions.

Everyone scanned the forest, with their synchronous sub-machine guns levelled, watching for any unusual movements.

What is going on out there? Bloody shooting! Christopher knew that nothing good would come of this place.

Crazy! I hope to God that the helicopters come soon. This can't go on.

The gunfire was replaced by a peculiar quiet, a hushed silence that dampened the natural life. Again, wildlife suffocated into silence as the forest took another deep breath in.

Silence, then shooting, and my God, I feel something else! Christopher's survival instincts told him to go.

"Run! Get out of here!" he shouted to the men on the ground, waving his arms widely in the air.

Everyone waited. Nobody could understand why the scientist was shouting like a lunatic, when the ground began vibrating. At first, there was a deep rumble, then it got louder. Something was approaching at high speed.

My God! It's not an earthquake.

As unstoppable as a tornado, deep rumbling caused the ground to vibrate. The noises closed in rapidly, screeching and squealing, and unseen activity was getting more and more irate! It seemed as though every animal imaginable might be heading their way.

The troops could only think that the noise was the same freakish phenomenon they witnessed last evening when they saw the Temple in the moonlight. It happened then too.

In that ghostly moment, when they emerged from the forest edge, the forest had held its breath, like now, just before the earthquake struck. Yet this time, it was different.

The darkness of the forest came in waves of rampage with every passing second. The closer and louder the noises came, the spreading of alarm became greater, adding to its power.

Everyone heard the snapping of branches and the collapsing of trees. Maybe it was a flash flood, but that was unlikely. Their nerves were fraying, waiting, anticipating the worst, with no option but to listen to an oncoming tsunami of sounds surging through the crumbling foliage. The men could only guess what was approaching.

Sweat ran off their brows as they stood straddling their automatic machine guns. They aimed them steadily in the direction of the noises closing in. They were ready for anything, but not this.

Loose on the hoof, crazed animals suddenly burst open the foliage perimeter like a huge tidal wave of beef. Animals of all shapes and sizes flattened anything and pulverised everything! Out they came, howling in terror, running blindly screaming at them, snarling and biting at anything standing in their way.

The men could not believe their eyes. Everything was happening so fast around them. They watched the rampaging exodus in bewilderment.

Flocks of birds flew above, escaping from the woods, and displayed the same insanity heading up the valley, squawking and whistling away into the air in panic. From apes to anacondas, frogs to flamingos, nothing stood still, not even insects — they too were buzzing off in swarms over the campsite and beyond. The terrorised animals continued their headless stampede through the forest. None would tarry from where they had come from.

Monkeys began dropping down from the trees, their tails high like tall antennae and jumped in disarray, all screeching insanely and running around senselessly at high speed.

Some wide-faced monkeys came snarling and spitting at Christopher, like rabid dogs. Christopher stood like a plank of wood not wanting to move in case this provoked them, when suddenly, he found himself in the middle of a riot of yelling primates, screeching on all fours past him.

Driven by sheer terror, the monkeys were darting this way and that, some falling and rolling under heavier animals and were crushed instantly.

A mother ape with her baby went rocketing past him, battering through some stunned soldiers, the men falling to the ground as the barrage of animals continued. No bullets could stop this mayhem.

Soldiers were standing bravely shooting the oncoming stampede in the hope to change the flow of the terrified animals, while others had no option but to take cover behind dead carcasses. But even this was ineffective under the hoof. Those guys had no chance. The outer perimeter was compromised in seconds. The soldiers who did not get out of the way in time were simply trampled to death or torn apart by a mad ape before the animal was shot dead. Many animals climbed the Temple steps to get away. Some were easily thwarted by the men shouting at them, while others were killed.

Something had made the forest animals crazy, as though they were being chased by something unnatural. It had only been minutes and already most of the mayhem passed. The mass rushed beyond the Temple. Later on, there would be no escape, save for those that could fly or climb sheer rock. The rest would soon perish, trapped inside the Iblis vale — the Devil's Valley.

****

CHAPTER XIV

CATCH OF THE OSPREY

Colonel Greco Rossi and his Ninth Degree Paracadutista Assault Regiment entered the vale and were moving on quickly through what was once dense greenery. Based on the trampled foliage, they rightly assumed that a mighty stampede, or some sort of mass migration had occurred not too long ago.

They all could hear the distant tectonic rumble of fleeing animals. The colonel squatted down and felt the ground. A distant vibration was going North.

"The animals are heading up the vale," he said.

Colonel Rossi's cold blue eyes scanned for clues. They all knew something had happened here, something unexplainable. Rossi wondered what could have caused this unusual panic. What were the animals running away from?

Nowhere to hide. *The Prophecy.*

Staring ahead through the devastation of fallen trees, it looked like a scene out of a battleground. His men did not stop, and everyone quickly moved in small groups of three. One man in the lead was flanked by a second soldier, then the third Swiss guardsman. Each would then move quickly in front of the stationary first soldier and in this way, the Paracadutista Special Forces covered the ground quickly and efficiently like a revolving human spiral. This S.A.S. type of flow and formation meant they protected each other in all directions as they continued. The Unit could go in any direction as a group protecting the smaller ones, while each soldier protected their own smaller sub-group formation.

"Some sort of stampede, signore?" a guardsman said in a whisper.

"Yes, it might be something to do with that black fog we passed earlier, it seemed to be emerging from inside that long crevice, a fissure of some kind? It did not look natural, now did it? Maybe that's what spooked them?" The colonel's low melodic accent disguised a feeling of impending danger. The fog had been flowing out, but they were ahead of it, leaving the weird gas somewhere behind them.

Rossi knew that they must reach their destination sometime today. As a soldier, he was always ready to assimilate each new situation as it arose. He needed to make appropriate decisions, knowing that any further delay may have fatal consequences for the civilians at the Temple.

Rossi kept his primary objective, the "Golden Egg", from Trentino. Orders were orders.

His subordinate, Major Trentino, reminded him of himself when he was a young soldier.

Luckily, Rossi's acute sense of survival alarmed him to this navigation error, compensating and backtracking for ten miles through this unforgiving forest, then up the very steep ascent before climbing down into the cloudy vale. They had only just made it through before the black fog closed the gap behind them.

"Si, colonnello, it was bad luck with that useless new navigation system. Back to the drawing board for the boffins, eh?" The soldier spoke quietly, as they all headed towards the Temple.

"What was that unnatural black fog, signore?" the other man whispered. "It felt really weird being there. I am glad that we were not too close to it coming out the fissure like a strange smoke."

"No idea, but the way it was fuming out of that hole, I don't think it was going to evaporate any time soon. It'll not be far behind us at that rate and might be an escaping poisonous gas," Rossi whispered. *Too close for comfort*, he thought retrospectively. "Forget it, at this pace, we'll soon reach the Temple." The colonel did not mention that he felt the same impending dread. Something inside told him to keep away from the fog. Like everything else, they too were trapped inside the vale.

Once the valley mouth was sealed, the fog had already risen almost above the trees moving wider and up the vale. The men kept on moving, leaving the black threat far behind. In any case, the colonel did not expect to return this way. With the rumblings gone, the vale became unnaturally still and silent.

Colonel Rossi was determined, in mind and spirit, to never fail again. He loaded his Beretta SCP 90/100 assault rifle, with the additional grenade launcher barrel attached. His eyes were filled with wild fire.

Rossi stopped quietly and gave the signal for his men to halt. In the distance, they could hear strange buzzing sounds.

Their keen eyes scanning the area ahead of them. A large clearing had appeared directly in front, filled with strange looking green rusty brown tapered stacks. Termite mounds.

Strangely, the smooth surfaces of all these mounds were covered with thin zigzag-shaped yellow flashes. He estimated there were at least a hundred or more of the tall cone-shaped objects, all equally spaced between each other. It looked to him that more of them extended further into the forest, beyond the clearing. The true scale was hidden like an iceberg.

"What is it, colonnello? Do you think there are head-hunters behind those things?" a soldier whispered cautiously, sensing his commander's hesitation to go through. With the mind of an instinctive killer, Rossi gauged their survival against time.

"No idea, soldier, everything in this damn place is strange."

"Can we detour, signore?" he asked.

"We cannot reroute again. Take the shortest path first," he stated quietly. A sudden hardness came into his eyes, and they held no compromise. He surveyed the odd-looking cones before them, thinking, *They're like bloody tank traps.* "Stay with me, move fast, keep light and we will be through them in no time. If anything jumps out. Shoot it."

Rossi gave the signal to move. "Stay close to me, son." He was off and immediately covered ground fast. He quickly started weaving in and out through the strange funnel-shaped objects, with his men doing the same.

The tall obstacles were like towers and there were many. It was difficult to manoeuvre through them. The men tried to keep their formation, but it proved unworkable.

After about five minutes of weaving in and out, it was impossible to keep everyone together. Now, with no clear view, Rossi could not see his men, except the younger soldier who was in his group and who had kept up with him.

The colonel stopped. Using his unique indigenous bird call, he signalled his men to get closer and regroup in his locale.

Rossi was confident that he could rely on his own instincts and disciplined training; he had been in situations like this many times before. However, in this case, he was wrong.

Both soldiers breathed heavily as they looked warily around. There was nothing but cone-shaped mounds everywhere!

"There must be hundreds of these things, signore," the younger soldier stated. Then, a few more soldiers appeared. Sweat was pouring down all their faces.

The sunlight was beating down without remorse, and it was becoming another hot sultry day in the rainforest. The colonel looked at his own Osprey Unit. Twenty-one determined men gathered as best they could, reassembled in another defensive formation and surrounded their commander. He proudly looked at them all, fearing a hidden enemy. They all smelled the same danger. Unexpectedly, Rossi perceived an illusion of movement.

What was that? He looked behind his men. *Shit.* He sensed movement in the mounds.

"Ambush! Down!" Chameleon screamed a warning. Like lightening, he raised his Berretta carbine and started shooting at a mound.

Rossi shot rapidly while his men lay flat on their bellies. Their commander's bullets struck many targets, but already it was too late.

Unexpectedly small horizontal slits in the mounds surface opened and horrible wide green eyes with yellow dots began staring out hatefully at them. They were everywhere.

Instinctively, his men reacted and began firing.

Frrrrrrrak! Frrrrrrrrak! Frrrrrrrrak! Frrrrrrrrak!

At the Temple, the Islamic and Christian soldiers began assembling outside, looking out towards their distant gunfire and watching the forest.

"Signore, behind you!" a soldier screamed at Rossi, staring at the alien object behind his commander.

Rossi ducked as something passed over his head and flew straight through the soldier's chest. The boy yelled in agony.

Total mayhem ensued and death once again showed up unexpectedly. Some of the mounds disintegrated into a heap with bits of the hard surfaces being blasted off by brutal fire power, the cones breaking apart. They could not believe what they were seeing.

Before them, these coned surfaces changed structure, almost as though they were regenerating right in front of their eyes. As bullets ricocheted off their polished surfaces, they could hear an awful gurgling noise from something inside them. Colonel looked around at the bloody mess and disintegration.

"Follow me, men, come on, this way!" Rossi's tone was hard and certain.

Obeying him, they all began sprinting and firing their weapons as they ran, flying on "a wing of a prayer, diving and dipping between numerous long darts, some flying past and around them narrowly missing the men by inches! Some darts striking and rebounding off other coned structures following his lead, even so, it would be a miracle if they made it out!

An unknown enemy had been waiting. The colonel shouted directions to his men as they ran.

"Paracadutista regiment, turn, and head west! To the west! This way, over to those trees!" Rossi pointed his machine-gun and gave a quick burst, when some transient obstacle appeared in his way. He struck it with a flying front kick and knocked it over. He kept strafing left and right and straight ahead and by now, was charging at full speed.

Frrrrrrrrak! Frrrrrrrrak! Frrrrrrrrak! Frrrrrrrrak!

His weapon was blazing. Rossi ran and saw an opening beyond.

His men looked at him questionably as more of those damned obstacles stood ahead of them. Rossi looked back from where they had come from. It looked like they were trapped and going forward was the only way out.

Rossi's looked wildly ahead; they had somehow found themselves right in the middle of the real trap. He was now fully committed to his new target, the distant trees.

It looked unattainable, so he dug in undeterred as he always did, when unexpectedly, he saw something else.

Closing the distance between him and the trees, a solid horizontal line of cone structures assembled in front of his target like a firing squad.

Sprinting faster, he saw them mesh together to form one solid wall of death, but the trap was not complete, not yet. He continued charging.

Some soldiers were falling, while others floundered in a hail of long darts, sinking into them in the few short seconds that passed. It was then that Rossi and his soldiers suddenly saw their enemy's weakness.

When the cone structures moved, they changed from a hard, protective armour into a flexible cloth textile, like a large cloak, which allowed them to move. In that second, they were exposed, and only then could they shoot their lethal darts.

The Swiss guardsmen charged at the wall of cones, watching warily for the moment of transition. The distance between them and the barrier was closing in fast.

Hundred metres.
Eighty metres! Two seconds.
Sixty metres! Four seconds.
Forty metres! Seven seconds.
Twenty metres! Ten seconds.
Rossi fired his grenade launcher. Dead ahead. "Aaagrrh!" Rossi screamed.
No seconds.
Impact!

Boooom!!! Crashsssssh.

Everything around him was in flames.

"Si! An opening!" Like a bulldozer, Rossi smashed through it and shouted a war-cry! "Aaaaaaah!" He blared at the enemy. His mind was set on destruction. Kill everything.

His plan had worked! Colonel Greco Rossi and his men reached the edge of the clearing, but he had been unfortunate as two long darts had already wounded him. Adrenaline kept him going.

Rossi felt nothing, the penetration was no more than a few thumps. His instinctive sense of survival drove him through the bloody debris and flames.

"Osprey, this way, this way!" He guided his men and defied failure. "Over to this embankment, come on, men!" his sheer determination knew no bounds, as he looked grittily downwards and into a green hollow, like a trench.

Rossi tied to wave his men into the dip below the ground that lay ahead, as numerous darts flew overhead.

As he kept running, Rossi quickly realized he was alone. All his men had been cut down. Even the young man who had spoken to him earlier. He lay dead with a dart in his chest.

The boy lay massacred like the others. Rossi was determined to survive. *I will make it.* He had done it before.

He moved quickly along the deep trough, when he heard something. Rossi pivoted his body around, with his rifle at the ready, when a long thin spear with a vicious curved blade at its end hooked his ankle.

With a quick jerk, he fell and dropped his rifle. The blade cut deeper into the back of his foot, making him wince.

He found himself on his back staring upwards at a large cone that was towering overhead as it quickly finished its transition. Out stepped a large fighter wearing a heavy cloak.

Everything happening so fast. *Kill the fucker!* he thought.

Then, the warrior who had caught him with the curved blade approached. The warrior's neck was thick because he had two backbones.

Rossi tried to quickly pull his side pistol out to shoot the big warrior's helmet off his face, but he was injured and could not lift his arm. They had pinned his arm down with three sharp darts. The darts came from inside the warrior's arm. Rossi stared at the rotating limb in disbelief. *A natural weapon, shit.*

The warrior's arm opened even wider, revealing the revolving organic weapon, like a Gatling gun. Unbeknownst to Rossi, the warrior's natural weapon could only grow a set number of organic darts within a given time. But the warrior felt best when butchering an enemy. This warrior was bred for close combat.

Rossi stared upwards. Two fighters had appeared around him to watch like spectators. The warriors were wearing strange helmets and their bodies were covered in armour. Colonel Rossi knew that his last chance at survival was his machine gun, but before he could reach for it, the warrior sensed the soldier's movement and pinned his other arm down coldly with another long spear.

Taking off his protective gauntlet, the warrior bent down to gloat and without a word, a telescopic finger with a vicious sharp point extended smoothly outwards from its claw.

Knowing that his life was finished, Colonel Rossi attempted to scream but even this last indignity was not allowed to him by his enemy. Rossi's mouth opened when the stiletto-like point pierced his voice box and continued on through the ground. No sound ever came out.

****

CHAPTER XV
BLOODHORT

Chaos reigned around base camp. Christopher looked on as if he were not taking part, watching men scattering for their lives, while all hell broke loose in the forest. The bio-technologist stared numbly, his mind transfixed at the unstoppable stampede — hoofs and heavy bodies battering everything and soldiers shouting. All he could hear were muffled sounds.

"Come on! Get out of here. Move it! Fucking move it!" a soldier kept screaming into his blank face and shoving him hard, again and again. Christopher then snapped out of his inactive state, realising the soldier's warning and what it meant.

"Head for the Temple, NOW!" Christopher, like a peculiar dream, found himself almost floating as he ran for his life.

Christopher looked to his side and realised he was running side by side with Barbaro. Both men were going with the flow through the disintegrating camp, dodging every obstacle and every animal to get to safety.

Animals and men ran for their lives, fearing the unknown.

The tents and tarpaulins were torn, and everything was bulldozed out the way. Wooden crates and boxes moved about and appeared like floating like rafts in a great flood.

They could hear Sergeant Moretti firing his automatic machine-gun to sway the direction of animal flow. This worked enough to allow the two men space to reach the stone steps of the Temple.

Christopher, with little time to take stock, could see that everything else appeared to be heading beyond the Temple, up North. He breathed heavily, it was not over yet. He and Barbaro quickly climbed up the Temple steps, with some animals behind them.

They now had competition. Orangutans and other primates were with them, all with the same instincts, all screeching fearfully and gnashing angrily at them.

Caught in this hairy crowd, Christopher lifted his arm to shield himself from an oncoming orangutan, when suddenly it was blown away. Its pirouetting bloody body flew through the air and fell heavily onto the steps. A cracking shot from a high-powered bullet killed it instantly. The other primates scurried off at the sound, jumping down from the terraces and running out of view. Below, most animals had already parted East or West around the Temple, like a fast-flowing river, the main surge on its way further up the vale.

Christopher and Barbaro were utterly spent. They had just made it to the first tier, and fell down from exhaustion among the soldiers. A few baboons unexpectedly made it too.

They came from somewhere close behind them, leaping and stepping onto their backs and jumping all over the two men, tugging and screeching loudly before running blindly through the entrance and into the Temple.

Instantly, each baboon appeared again. The primates were suddenly even more spooked, and ran back outside, screeching madly and disappeared as they headed North!

"Have you seen Mykola and Sebastiano?" Christopher asked Barbaro, frightened for their safety, "Where are they?"

"I do not know. I did not see them running," Barbaro replied, "The last time I saw them, they were inside the marquee." Both men looked down with disbelief to what had once been base camp. Nothing was left standing.

The bedlam and racket of stampeding animals quickly passed like a distant thunderstorm, seamlessly replaced once again by that same continual sound of sawing — that familiar buzz of metal on wood, floating through the sultry breeze.

Bzzzzz, bzzzzzzzzz, bzzzzzzzzzzzzzzzzzzzz.

"There's that noise again." Barbaro looked at the forest. Through all the mayhem, the soldiers were oblivious to what had happened, and incredibly, they were still not finished.

"Lucky bastards." Sergeant Moretti looked out at the forest.

"The Christians can't hear a thing with those buzz saws going," the Islamic soldiers said.

Distrust between both troops seemed to be a bit more tolerant after having experienced the mutual danger.

"Hey, Christian!" the captain shouted at the major. "Can I offer you our assistance to find any injured?"

"Si, I would be honoured to accept your kind offer, Sarvan." Major Trentino looked at his counterpart in a renewed light.

"Your thoughts my friend, what could have scared those animals in such a manner?" the captain asked.

"It might be that," he paused momentarily, turning to stare at the black fog closing in. "My guys are still down there. I need to bring them in." Trentino was worried for his soldiers' safety. The Sarvan understood and nodded. Like a noose, both men apprehensively watched the unnatural fog tightening around them.

****

The soldiers were quickly assembled to rescue the wounded people below. As they neared the bottom of the Temple, they could hear the horrible sounds of hissing. Everyone stared uneasily at each other. They could see the ground moving like water.

"Wait! Stop, go no further," Sergeant Moretti snapped, watching with disgust. All over the forest floor, an infinite number of snakes writhed—snakes of all shapes and sizes wriggled and spat at each other. "Damn nation, God what now?"

The exodus was not over. The whole forest floor had come alive with serpents swarming all the way from the base of the Temple and out to what once was the safe perimeter. The ground was replaced by a moving carpet. Large spiders, beetles and insects of all species were also on the march. Even the smallest of creatures of the forest were running and tiny as they were, it was there time to get away.

The men stood high on the tall stairs while the creatures kept slithering past them, some were fast, others not so, and all were heading around the Temple, the easiest path away from whatever it was that was driving them mad.

Any hope of finding their friends still alive was dashed by this sight. Who could survive such a slithering storm? Christopher thought that the only thing that could cause this mad panic were ants—lots of them. That would explain it.

"They are being chased by ants, that might account for this," Christopher warned.

"We have to wait. The snakes are moving on. When they pass, you have to be quick!" Moretti said.

The creatures were moving away but not quick enough, it was taking too long. Thirty minutes seemed like thirty years for someone to give aid. In all this time, they didn't hear any groans or calls for help. All human life was dead.

Christopher began to move through the wreckage. Collapsed tents and tattered canvases lay all around. In the aftermath, the smell of smouldering logs hung distastefully in dying wisps of grey smoke, lingering over a wide area from where embers miraculously still burned. Everywhere was trampled into stinking pulp in the decimated camp.

Barbaro looked disgusted, stepping into the mess of mud to assist the rescue. Christopher was surprised as he believed this selfless act was quite unlike him.

Christopher beheld the scale of destruction that lay around him. Slowly moving on, stopping again and tentatively raising another canvass, he waited. He looked below for a long moment, then swallowed hard.

His face became chalk white. Below the tarpaulin lay the broken bodies of Cesare and Mykola. Christopher fell to his knees and wept.

After a few long minutes, Christopher jolted himself upright, wiping his moist eyes. He gathered himself together, remembering another purpose.

Where is the pod with the link? In this devastation, Christopher was caught between focusing hard and blind panic. *My God, oh my God, where is it, where can it be?* Like a man possessed, he had to find it. *If I have lost it, all this death will have been for nothing!*

Christopher could be seen scurrying around like a crazy person around the camp.

"What are you looking for, Christopher?" Barbaro asked softly, he interrupted Christopher's progress. Chris looked up surprised to see the media man standing there watching him. Behind Barbaro, some soldiers were placing the dead bodies onto stretchers. The deceased were destined for a secluded burial place. The details were overseen by Sergeant Moretti.

"A box, one of my environmental chambers, a small one. I left it in my tent," Chris answered. He was frantic.

Christopher felt an uncontrollable loss, as if the object had a weird hold on him. He unexpectedly dropped to his knees in despair.

"Si, it is a great loss to you indeed," Barbaro agreed with a sneer but his tone was apathetic. *Quite a drama for a simple box.* "I can see that," Barbaro hissed quietly.

Christopher was immediately on the defensive. *What did he mean by that, has he picked it up? Has he stolen it from me?* Christopher's face got redder and almost burst with rage.

"Sebastiano and Mykola, they did not have a chance down here," Barbaro reminded him and began walking away.

The man looked genuinely disheartened. His attention was on the crosses being hammered into the ground in the distance by Moretti's detail.

Some other graveside crosses had been previously erected there for other dead comrades.

"Si, you are right," said Christopher, feeling a pang of guilt. Such a selfish thought. Yet, he knew the artefact was much more than an object or simple pendant. He had witnessed its esoteric qualities and it had been gifted to him.

"You should say a prayer for them. They need you now, priest." Barbaro's tone was as hard as a gravestone.

Barbaro is right, Christopher solemnly thought. He agreed and took out his prayer book.

****

"Right, you two," came a hard voice from behind, "go back up to the Temple. No more can be done here." Mancini Bellucci, the paramedic from the Phoenix Unit, ordered them to move on.

Christopher had not found the pod. He hesitated to leave, when without warning, a blurry object shot right past his face.

What the? Something hard struck the soldier in the eye, and Bellucci fell backwards, screaming. The soldier was holding a sharp wooden dart in his hand.

Strangely, there was no pain or blood, only shock and a feeling of deep pressure as its weight pressed on the underside of his eye. A long dart was lodged in the socket. Remarkably, he could still see. On the ground, the soldier began firing his machine-gun behind Barbaro and Christopher.

"Go NOW!" he shouted brusquely at them, as he fired again into the forest from which weird noises started coming from the tree line.

From multiple places, noises, echoed along the full length of the jungle perimeter. They were in deep trouble, both men knew that. Staring at each other in disbelief, both remembered when they had first heard it; the dead creature warrior inside the Temple.

A handful of soldiers arrived quickly, coming to their aid and threw themselves onto the ground, lying spaced out in a semi-circle around them and their injured comrade.

By this time, Bellucci lay propped up with one elbow. Only a small amount of blood was coming from his eye. He was lucky to still be alive. The dart had not penetrated his brain.

Playing for time, they all began shooting into the forest at some hidden enemy.

"Get it out!" he screamed.

"Bloody hell, Barbaro run, man! Get out of here!" Christopher yelled while trying to pull the arrow out of the injured man's eye socket. At first, it would not come free. Christopher placed his leg firmly on the man's chest and with both hands, yanked the arrow out of the paramedic's face. It came with a disgusting squelching noise. Bellucci yelled out in anguish.

Bellucci's face became swollen and blood ran from the cut. Christopher quickly applied a temporary field dressing from the soldier's medical kit.

"Grazie, signore, thank you." Bellucci got up and insisted he stay with his comrades.

"Ciao, signore." Bellucci picked up his weapon and immediately opened fire again in short bursts.

"Get going, signores, we will cover you!" Sergeant Moretti offered his protection and ordered them to leave.

Chris hunched his shoulders. The sounds of simultaneous gunfire almost burst his eardrums.

Whatever had shot the soldier, their gunfire seemed to silence the strange sounds coming from the trees. Maybe this enemy knew nothing about guns.

"It must have been bloody head hunters. We are sitting targets here. Unless you two want to end up with your heads on top of a Pigmy spear move it now!" the Sergeant insisted.

"No, sergeant, come with us," Christopher pleaded, "You and your men cannot win this thing. Believe me, this enemy is no Pigmy, this enemy is not even human!" Christopher's tone sounded urgent.

Both men examined the long dart and were certain they had seen this foe before.

"Believe him, Sergente Moretti. We have seen the creatures that fires those darts," Barbaro confirmed.

Sergeant Moretti smiled. *They are humouring us, stupid civvies.*

The Sergeant knew it was a big risk to enter the jungle and the native's territory.

"Get going, signore, and you too, signore," he said to Christopher and Barbaro, "the Temple has played too long on your minds. We will give you time. Return and join the others in the Temple, it will be safe there. Go."

The civilians were on their own and he had a responsibility to his men. They passed beyond the tree line, and out of view.

****

"Right, let's not hang around here, Barb, *come on!*" Christopher used the man's nickname and for the moment, set their differences aside. They climbed fast and as they approached the first tier, an abrupt burst of sub-machine gunfire came out from the forest. They both stopped and looked down.

Another bullet burst. Then, the sounds of a rattle of castanets. Barbaro and Christopher grimly looked at each other and started running. The gunfire burst again, followed by shouting. Sergeant Moretti's clear commands could be heard. Then, an explosion.

The jungle suddenly went eerily quiet. From the Temple, everyone saw smoke rising above the trees. The men would not be returning.

Christopher and Barbaro arrived out of breath, the concerned soldiers ushering them behind their makeshift barrier built of wood. They had been busy, very busy, and in this short time, both factions worked as one army taking provisions from inside the Temple to build a makeshift barricade. A barrier built like a thick fence all along the first tier terrace on the South side. This would protect the Temple interior. Now, they stood together, both Christian and Islamic forces, the men spread evenly along this level and ready to fight together in a new alliance.

"What is happening, Maggiore?" asked the Sarvan.

"It's critical, captain." Trentino replied, as he observed the forest through his Laser Optronix DME 30000 on top of his Sig Sauer SSG 30000 Telescopic Rifle.

"God knows," said Christopher, standing next to them. "Sergeant Moretti and his men went into the forest, hoping to skirmish the enemy."

"The enemy, what enemy are you talking about?" the captain wanted to know more.

"Our new enemy," Christopher said and told him what had happened below at base camp. "The sergeant believed he was going after head hunters. He and his men saved our lives. We warned him not to go. Unfortunately, he would not listen."

"Dead." Trentino understood.

"You heard the gunfire, Maggiore!" Barbaro cut in. "You all did!" trying to make them understand what they were dealing with.

"Can you not keep your men under control, major?" the Sarvan was angry because his soldiers had gone into the jungle without direct orders from their commanding officer.

"Hang on, captain, they saved Barbaro and me!" Christopher protested. But both Trentino and Haleem knew that this lack of discipline was foolhardy. It compromised everyone's safety.

"This depletes our numbers severely." The captain snapped in retribution, his words like a verdict.

"They bought us time, arsehole! Those brave bastards saved us!" Christopher was livid.

"Listen, captain, we will be leaving here very soon, so do not worry about your depleted numbers. You will be alone." Trentino paused before shouting at him in anger. "And those depleted numbers were. MY MEN!" his eyes were watering.

It had been an act of bravery, there was no question. The tension was rising again between the troops, each soldier not quite knowing why the men in charge were arguing.

The Temple's influence once again was undermining any sense of reason. It hacked at the human mind, gnawing through any moral fibre, draining self-belief, and nurturing dissension. That's what it did.

"I do not believe it." Christopher's eyes widened when astonishingly, Mashir appeared from around the Eastern wall. "Mashir! Mashir! You are still alive! Thank God."

Mashir's face lit up when he saw Christopher's smile once again. The priest was standing between the two feuding officers like a referee, as both soldiers stood eye-to-eye like duellists.

At this second, anything could happen. The dice was thrown, and a clash of cultures was inevitable. However, there was a small ray of light that might help them and get them over their inherent differences - *a common language!*

They did not realise it but at last, something was working for them, something gifted on their side. Arbitration and self-preservation was in their favour, they just had to see it.

"The others, where are they?" Mashir asked.

"Only us," replied Christopher sadly. "Harjit and Mathieson are inside the Temple. Mathieson is in bad shape. The rest are," Christopher's smile vanished, "are gone, all gone." He paused to think about all those who have died. "So many, dead."

Suddenly, the captain was taken down by a swoop of the captain's foot. This was a powerful Martial Arts manoeuvre.

Haleem sensed the man's move too late. He attempted a counter with a straight punch to his forehead but having lost his footing, the Sarvan's strike was blocked easily by the edge of the major's hand.

The UNCAA officer's spontaneous strike failed. The force of the major's ankle sweep left him collapsing on the ground with a heavy grunt.

"Infidel!" Haleem shouted, as he scrambled on the ground at the Christian's mercy!

"Major, no!" Christopher called out.

"Sarvan, get up and give your apologies to the major," Mashir snapped. "Do it, now!"

Breathing hard, both men immediately stopped fighting. Captain Haleem got up slowly, red-faced from embarrassment.

It had only been a momentary lack of discipline but it was enough to unbalance their already frayed relations.

The major had lost his composure too because of the lives of his men who were dear to him, and as hard as this was to accept, this uncontrolled aggression was unacceptable. The Temple could undermine everything.

"Give your apologies to the major right now. That is a direct order, soldier," Mashir commanded.

"My humblest apologies, Major Trentino, forgive my mistake." Swallowing hard, Haleem apologised. "I forget myself." Captain Haleem saluted his combatant. The major reciprocated the salute smartly and withdrew.

Captain Abdul-Haleem turned around and stood to attention saluting Mashir.

"Your orders, sarhang!" he obediently said to his colonel, the commander.

****

"What is happening here, Sarvan?" Mashir asked. Christopher looked on even more confused.

"The infidels are not to be trusted, sir." The captain simply replied.

"We are all in this together, captain Haleem. Trust them, or we will all fail. Is that clear? Regroup the men and bring them to me inside the Temple. Keep two Scimitar guardians outside as lookouts. Observe anything unusual from the forest, and get them inside quick, time to report. Understand?" Mashir expected obedience.

"Perfectly, Sarhang!" the officer saluted and left. The captain quickly rallied the UMCAA troops. Christopher was red in the face.

"What the fuck, Mashir or should I call you commander?" Chris said. "How can you be one of them? You, owe me a fucking explanation!" Christopher demanded.

"My sincerest apologies, Christopher, I am—" Mashir was cut off mid-sentence.

"A double-crossing liar, comes to mind!" Christopher sliced.

"I am Sarhang or in English, 'Colonel' Nabeel Khosrau, the commander in charge of these UNCAA Special Forces. They are known as 'Scimitar guardians,' Mashir said proudly.

"Yeah." Christopher was unimpressed.

"There is not enough time to explain things, Christopher." He paused briefly, as he weighed the risks for imminent threat. "You should go inside with the others for your own safety. I must organise my men, with the help of the major and his Swiss guardsmen. There is still a chance to get out of here alive."

"Danger, danger be damned! Why, why, why? All the stories, all the lies, Mashir, oh, er, Nabeel is it now?" Christopher's eyes ignited with instant fury. "This deceit it is just so bloody dishonest. And all this time, you were a spy. I've known you for years. I trusted you as a friend!" Christopher shouted.

He still could not grasp what was going on with this latest admission.

"My name is a noble one, and royal in Persia. I am not dishonest." He paused, choosing his words carefully. "Chris, please listen and try to understand. Sometimes, we must do things. This situation is not what I wanted," he stated, while scrambling to find some common ground with the bio-technologist.

"And all this time, you have been playing us like fools!" Christopher stated. "You, you are this real commander, the one that is meant to be lost inside the Temple."

"You are upset, Chris." Trentino could see the bio-technologist's hostility.

"Yes, yes I am!"

Trentino looked at Colonel Nabeel Khosrau in a new light. *This man Khosrau has prevented a fight at a critical moment. Maybe he has what we all need right now, namely, unity. Let's see.*

"Yes, Maggiore, I am who I say I am. Here are my credentials, signore." He pulled out his identification papers that revealed his stamped photograph with a silver shield and crescent moon imprint, along with a golden star for each country united as with the newly formed UMCAA flag.

"Mmm, I see."

"I am, in charge of these soldiers, they are my Scimitar guardians." Mashir somehow appeared to stand taller.

"Impeccable."

"Thank you, major."

"Si, whoever is out there," Trentino eyed the forest again, "it looks like we will have to fight them together, Colonnello Khosrau." Major Trentino saluted his brother soldier and superior officer — the Islamists, his unlikeliest of allies. Mashir, AKA, Colonel Nabeel Khosrau had shown his true colours.

"We will die together, major as 'Crossed Sons' and 'Sons of Allah'. We unite as one, against a great evil that approaches this holy place."

"And just what, are we here for, Mashir?" Christopher asked.

"It is foretold in the lost tablets," Khosrau said casually, "All is as God wills it, my friend, even unto death." This was his hallmark expression of unending bond of friendship and hope. Christopher was not so sure. The only way to survive was to put their differences behind them and unite forces in a fight to the death and in universal brotherhood.

****

Later, inside the Temple's makeshift living quarters, Christopher stood next to Harjit, as they studied Mathieson's deteriorating condition. The diseased man was sleeping quietly. His chalk-white skin was covered in a light amorphous powder, the dust much more widespread. Harjit was listening to his slow heartbeat with her stethoscope.

"Christopher," the girl spoke softly in a whisper, "I don't think he'll last much longer."

"It has spread quicker than I had imagined, but I hope to God you are wrong, Harj." he replied.

"What has been going on outside?" she asked. "The soldiers inside are worried."

"I can't believe it. All this time and the years I've known him, Mashir is their commander!"

"All a disguise. How can Mashir be a spy, a charlatan?" Harjit was unable to compute it all.

"He has been grooming us for years! It's simple. Mashir needed me to find the Temple and guide his men here."

"Why, Chris, why?"

"Good question."

"He must have disappeared while we were stuck inside the Temple. Leaving the two guys inside base camp alone. A perfect opportunity to rendezvous with his men and bring them here!"

"Not quite, Harj, his soldiers were already hidden not too far away from base camp. This jungle is so dense they could do it without us knowing. When we came out of the Temple, they followed us. I think they have been inside the forest for a while." Christopher smiled and laughed a little.

She looked puzzled, "What is so funny?" Harjit asked.

"It's too bad."

"Chris, whatever are you talking about, what's too bad?"

"Mashir didn't get what he has come for."

"Come for? And what is that exactly?"

"What a fool I've been! He is here to find the 'Last and lost scrolls of Muhammad'. Unfortunately, by mistake, I told him that I had found the object told in the tablet."

"Chris!" Her voice was like steel, "More secrets! Why did you not tell me? What do you mean, I don't understand? What object? Tell me and tell me right now!" her whisper was colder than frost.

"I discovered an object inside the inner Temple, just before you helped me, remember?" said Christopher. "I was dazed. I would have told you then, but you would not listen to me, you were more interested in Mashir and those crazy maps he found."

"I remember. Oh, sorry Chris, forgive me for doubting you." Her eyes watered.

"What else do you remember, Harj?"

"There was no sign of you as if you had vanished. I looked for you, when I turned around and suddenly, you were there. You simply appeared, my God! You appeared from nowhere! Like magic. Come on, Chris, and tell me the rest."

"You will never believe this."

"Try me."

"It is an object with unusual characteristics, to say the least. I do not understand what this thing is yet, but it is a complete enigma."

"Nothing would surprise me anymore. What does it look like?"

"Sometimes it looks like *nothing*." He paused, considering the strangeness. "I observed its strange lustre and composition changing before me. It disappears and somehow camouflages itself, and yet, it is still there. I can feel it. When I first saw it, its natural appearance was as a silver metal link about three inches in length with a polished surface. This *sacred object* is not made of real silver, it's made from something else. It is an artefact of crafted metal of a type unknown to me. I think it was made by some dead and ancient race from many years ago, before any of our own civilizations came to exist."

"Or created by a greater power," she said. "What else, Chris? Go on."

"It is a metal undiscovered on this Earth with peculiar properties and abilities."

"Abilities?"

"Yes, abilities." Chris then told her what happened in the tent with the spider and the events that followed.

"This is incredible! Impossible, Chris!" Harjit exclaimed.

"I know, I know but look around you. There are many mysteries and impossibilities here. This place defies all boundaries of experience. A type of metal that I guess is found deep inside the mines. These people dug deep, so very deep. Call it a new element or substance, I do not know." His tone conveyed sincerity. "I know this is all so unscientific, I also know it is totally unbelievable. But, it is true." Christopher looked around to see no one was close by listening to them speak.

"This must be why everybody wants it. Where is this thing?" Harjit needed to see it.

"I bloody lost it." Christopher swallowed hard.

"Lost it?" Her face dropped flat. "Lost it, how?"

"I put it inside one of my environmental pods for safe-keeping just before all Hell broke loose down at camp. I lost it in the fucking stampede! I need to go down and find it before Mashir discovers I have not got the link." Christopher was holding something back.

"What if he decides to take it? Mashir thinks you already have it? What have you not told me, Chris?" Harjit sensed his hesitation

"I must find the link again! Our pickup is on its way, you must be ready, but I cannot leave this place until I find it. Too many people have died for this thing."

"Is there anything else I should know?" Harjit could not take much more suspense. "What are you not telling me, Chris?"

"Someone tried to kill me."

"What! Who?"

"I do not know. A spider from inside the Temple was placed under my hat lying in my tent. It had to get there somehow."

"That's terrible. It must be one of our team. We are the only ones that saw these creatures," concluded Harjit.

"I must find the link and bring back those special herb pastes for Mathieson's wounds."

"It is too dangerous on your own! At least ask for protection from the major and his men. What if those warriors are waiting down there for you?" Harjit's heart was racing. "Why you?" she asked. "Why does it have to be you?"

"I do not know why." He felt so lucky to be in love! Christopher looked warmly into her large brown eyes. They gripped his heart as her stunning beauty captured him at that moment.

He kissed her softly. *Forgive me, God,* he thought, knowing God saw his sin. Her sweet lips kissed him tenderly.

"Chris, I have seen Barbaro, Mashir, you, and Mathieson. Are we the only ones left from the expedition?" she asked.

"It's just us, Harj. We are the only ones left."

"Where is Barbaro? I thought he came inside with you?" She suspected he was up to no good.

****

Page 459

Suddenly, loud banging noises were heard outside the living quarters. Hectic activities surprised everybody inside. It sounded like a building site with metal banging and the Islamic soldiers shouting irate orders at each other.

Everyone knew this was no drill.

"Oh, Chris!"

"Harjit, I need to see what's going on."

"Be careful."

Christopher cautiously opened the door into the dim passageway. Soldiers in front of him were busily dismantling their heavy machine-guns and barriers and loading them onto wheelbarrows.

"Harjit, Harjit. There's more trouble, stay here. I will find out what is happening!"

"Be careful, Chris!" her forlorn echo chased after his running feet.

Only two people remained in the lonely stone room, with the heavy doors left open. She was alone with glyphs looking on from the large stone blocks for company. The only sound that could be heard was the constant hissing from the lamps.

Harjit quietly walked back over to observe Mathieson and his calcifying body. Feeling his wrist and hardening skin, she sighed a whisper, "Oh, Mathieson." She could still feel a pulse. With unspoken thoughts, she groaned softly with tears washing in her eyes.

****

Christopher emerged from the Temple and was immediately struck by how windy it had become outside. It seemed as if a storm was approaching. In front, soldiers were working hard, quickly relocating sandbags and machine guns from inside the Temple. Like clockwork, this heavy weaponry was almost mindlessly and rapidly assembled and re-positioned behind the barriers, ready to be used.

Orders were flying in every direction, sending soldiers purposefully about their duties, checking and re-checking defences along the Temple walls. Alarmed, he instinctively knew there was going to be big trouble. The men had no time to be nervous. Soldiers were also being deployed strategically above, stepping cautiously around the Temple top at the highest vantage point to keep a lookout.

From the high Temple top, the true scale of entrapment could be seen. The fog's weird undulating black wisps lifting menacingly upwards, then dropping to sink back down and out of sight below the treetops, only to lift a minute later.

The Temple top covered such a large area the soldiers could only be spread very thinly around its fringes, enough to warn the main defence.

Christopher stood on the first tier and thought, *All this for what?*

"Christopher, this is no place for you, my friend! You should go back inside to the safety of the Temple while the major and I work. Please."

Colonel Nabeel Khosrau looked genuinely troubled to see him. His immediate duties demanded his full attention when another heavy machine-gun arrived.

"Mashir." Christopher tried to speak.

"Over there! Soldier, put it over there!" Mashir was preoccupied again, shouting orders.

Christopher looked around at the mayhem.

What a big mistake I made with him? Christopher thought, unsure of everything. Both groups of men were very busy securing their areas, working fanatically and getting ready for the hidden enemy.

The major came briskly and walked towards them, while hailed by his radio operator.

"I think we might have until sunset before those natives' attack," Trentino stated, speaking directly with Khosrau, then turning and talking to the radio operator. "Any reports, soldier?" he asked the subordinate.

"Signore, the fog has not moved any closer, it seems to have stopped completely. It encircles us, holding off to about two or three miles in every direction from here. All is quiet."

"Too quiet," Trentino replied, touching his small Bible inside his breast pocket.

"The darkness has cut us off, my friends," Colonel Nabeel Khosrau stated bluntly.

"What do you mean, cut us off? It is only a bloody fog! The head hunters are the real enemy. They are silent and stealthy, and it is they who have cut us off, not a bloody fog. So, give me a break, Colonel Khosrau. Extraction is imminent and my offer of a way out of here still stands."

Strange as it all looked, major Trentino seemed confused at the Islamic apprehension placed an unfounded importance on a low cloud formation. The natives were hiding inside, no question.

"I know this makes little sense to you, major. The black fog appeared from nowhere. It has encircled the Temple and is exactly equal distance all around from us. This as you can see, and feel is a strong wind. Yes? The cloud should be over and beyond us by now, like any normal cloud. Not sitting out there against the winds. It waits there." Mashir felt a primal instinct grip his heart.

"Waiting for what? Waiting for what, colonel? What are you afraid off?" The major was becoming increasingly disconcerted.

"Believe me, this is not a natural phenomenon, my good major."

The major could see this too. The cloud did not move along with the turbulent air. *Maybe there is a rational explanation, something meteorological?*

"Before I hear any more crap from both you soldier boys, listen to me." Christopher was in no mood to be ignored any longer. "We are not dealing with simple head hunters with blowpipes.

I have already heard and seen what those fucking types of weapons are. What I heard down at base camp is different from a bloody blowpipe. I have heard those Castanet sounds once before, inside the Temple. Yes, that is correct, right here."

The men in power stopped talking and listened intently. Both men knew he had been inside the Temple. He deserved this recognition and their time.

The bio-technologist gave a short historical account and demise of his fallen comrades, Aléssandro and Sebastiano while exploring the upper Temple.

"I am sorry for the loss of your friends, signore. Providing I give you the benefit of the doubt, what do these warriors want?" Trentino probed.

The commanding officers both waited to hear if Christopher could provide this answer.

"Benefit of the doubt, benefit of the doubt? *How dare you, major!* My friends were killed inside there!" Christopher unleashed his fury. "I can't believe your cold callousness. For fuck's sake, major, you were having a set-to with the Sarvan for the same bloody reason. We have all lost friends."

"My apologies, signore, you are right. I spoke out of turn."

"These things have been here before." Christopher wanted them to know. "They were here a very, very long time ago. I believe it is these creatures who built this mega-structure or invaded it. Once again, it is they who come." Christopher's tone was hard. "A warrior race and this is their temple. We now stand before them and they have come to claim it!" Christopher did not expect them to understand but had to try. They needed to know his secret.

"What is '*it*' exactly? You are not talking about the Temple then, are you?"

"Correct, major."

"Yes, Chris you said to me." Colonel Nabeel Khosrau's tone implied peril.

"Oh, then, I thought I was speaking to Mashir and not Nabeel, and in trust." Christopher rebuked.

"My humble apologies, Chris, but try to understand. Our religion has known about this legend, and '*it*'. Here, this Temple is a sacred place and is written in the '*lost Tablets*' and known about for a very long time. I," Nabeel coughed awkwardly, "*We, you, me, the professor, the major – everyone,* we are all destined to be here."

"I trusted you." Christopher swallowed.

"I know." Nabeel paused. "It was so difficult living my life as it was. Being your friend was and is an honour," he said with warmth in his tone. "I knew this day would come. Fate and faith in Allah is greater than any friendship but this is my mission. I am bound by my faith to do what I must."

Nabeel wondered, *Is he still my friend? If not, it is the will of Allah.* "You have something that we need, Chris, you have something of *great power*."

Christopher gulped and lifted one eyebrow in consternation at the loss of the link. "It is not in my possession. It is down there," he said, looking at base camp.

Christopher recalled the stampede and the death of more friends as he stared hopelessly towards the forest.

A new feeling washed over him, a place that had been his home for months loomed below like a dead zone, threatening their demise.

"You lost it?" Nabeel asked.

"Shit," the major said, narrowing his eyes.

Ah, this "power" must be what Apostle seeks too, the so-called "Golden Egg". The Scimitar guardians want it too! Crazy, looks like we are all here for the same thing. They will try to keep it. My orders are clear, no fucking way, we're taking it.

"I need to get medicine for Mathieson. I will locate the link at the same time," Christopher stated.

"Bloody hell, Hrycuik. It looks peaceful enough from up here but if you go down there, you will not be coming back, signore! I do not want to lose you too. You are in my care now and my responsibility." The major's voice was resolute.

"You cannot stop me, major. I must go, for all our sakes." Chris showed no emotion. He did not feel brave, in fact, Christopher was scared to death.

"I see." The major looked to Colonel Khosrau for help. "We need some volunteers, Colonel Khosrau."

Two Islamic soldiers immediately stepped forward and saluted him in respect of his rank and martyrdom.

"We go together, signore Hrycuik," the major acknowledged. "I will see you back safely."

"Count me in too," a voice came from behind them. It was Barbaro, the unlikeliest of people. "Do you think that the Holy Father wants you to go without the official office? Not so. All for one, Maggiore!" Barbaro smiled at their mute surprises. Barbaro had always been underestimated.

Khosrau wanted to go with Christopher but knew that a commander must stay and prepare for attack. *If they do not return, the link will fall to me. If they do come back, I will take it.* Khosrau let them go.

"Ok, men, I will head first. You two soldiers take my flank, Christopher come next and Barbaro you bring up the rear. Before we go, signores, take these weapons." Trentino gave each civilian a firearm for their own personal protection.

"I don't know how to use this," Christopher stated bluntly.

"Grazie, Signore Trentino." Barbaro was happy enough.

"Safety off, point and pull the trigger. Think of it as your computer mouse, signores. Just, point and click your mouse finger. *Piss easy,*" he said wittingly.

"Wait! Chris, in case your mouse fails." A tender female voice came from behind him. Christopher turned.

Harjit! When he saw her, his eyes instantly lit up. There she was, the girl of his dreams, standing there at the entrance by herself. *So beautiful.*

From behind her, she brought a surprise for him. His sword. The one Christopher had used inside the Temple. It was special to him. She had been keeping it hidden and safe just in case. This was the time.

"Thank you," Chris said tenderly.

"This is yours," she said with a warm smile. The major laughed a little as Christopher displayed his sword proudly.

"It's a gift from a once great Lord." he said, remembering who had allowed him to have it.

Harjit placed her soft hand on Christopher's face, searching deeply into his eyes for the right moment. She kissed him softly as tears welled up in her eyes.

"Look after yourself and come back to me," she said.

"Harj." Christopher was lost for words.

"Chris, I will love you till the day I die."

****

CHAPTER XVI

BATTLE FOR THE TEMPLE

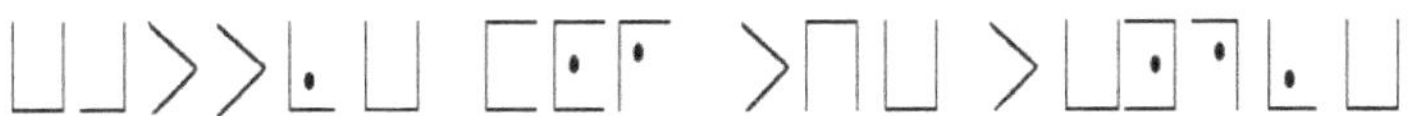

As they were about to head down the stone steps, the major and the others suddenly stopped in surprise, when a new enemy slowly emerged in a line, stretching along the perimeter of the rainforest. These were the First Cohort of Hsals Slaugohtŕ. These were no head hunters!

Defiantly, this new threat stopped and stood waiting as they watched and judged this human alliance for obliteration. The soldiers winced quietly, as they stood high on the stone terraces. They could not believe their eyes. A new army had arrived to reclaim what was theirs — the Temple. Like giants, they stood at eight feet or more.

So, it was inside this lonely vale, a place hidden deep within Amazonia, that the greatest war known to Mankind was about to begin.

With the initial shock gone, the men attempted to gauge their foe for strengths and weaknesses. They observed that their opponents were protected by lightweight black body armour. It looked hard and protective like any efficient high-tech body armour found on the modern battlefield. These assailants had helmets to match. Each warrior wore a long green cloak with thin yellow zigzag stripes wafting in the strong breeze. They wore light sandals and their limbs were protected with black metal shin and arm guards.

Through narrow slits in their horizontal visors, menacing saucer shaped green eyes with yellow speckled dots stared venomously up at the defenders. They held long swords, vicious tridents or spears in one hand and a round black shield in the other. The shield bore a blood-red claw ensign on the front. Hidden below their helmets, these formidable legionnaires had thick dark green leathery skin, with a yellow zigzag tattoo etched into their faces, giving them an individual characteristic — a name or rank scar that matched their long overcoats.

These warrior creatures were organised and built for battle. The army started banging their shields, taunting the soldiers on the Temple, the noise reverberating around the vale like thunder. This was a place made for hell.

"Well, major! It looks like we did not have to wait as long as you thought. They have come ready and are prepared!" the colonel shouted.

The major's search party had stopped not far down the steps to observe the enemy. Lowering his powerful telescopic lens, the major's jaw tightened and he began speaking to his small group of volunteers.

"They are not human."

One of the biggest antagonists took off his helmet, displaying a devilish looking claw for a hand, its middle finger retracting inwards. Each warrior had a vicious stiletto knife-like finger in each claw. It was a natural weapon and one that could extend to about twelve inches or more. It was lethal and ready to slash or stab a victim in a split second, then retract just as quickly. The warrior showed his black horned teeth. Negotiation was not an option.

"They are afraid, my lord," said a burly warrior urging his monstrous leader.

"The human soldiers fear us, my liege," said another. "We should attack now."

"They shake in terror," said Cohort Praefect Anghur Naglutre. He was their leader. The Praefect took a deep breath in, and stepped out in front of all his warriors.

He lifted his black visor to study his adversary. His large saucer-shaped eyes were designed for night but his genetic makeup meant he could focus closer than any of his warriors could. His sight was specialised for long distance.

The Praefect instantly found himself drilling upwards and directly into the major's determined telescopic eye, right in front of the major's crosshairs.

Cohort Praefect's reflexive eyes widened as he saw the white flash of light.

Without thinking, he tilted his head slightly as the high velocity bullet went flying past his heavy jaw with a ripping sound!

"Urg!" The bullet was followed immediately by another one, striking hard into a large shield that had been put in front of the leader by his bodyguards.

The leader moved back cautiously into the safety of the trees. He had underestimated his adversary. That mistake would not be made twice.

"There is no escape for humankind," growled the Praefect. "They will all die."

"Shall we kill them painfully, my liege?" asked an inflamed warrior.

"What other way is there?" another warrior said, laughing.

"I will take back this place for my master. Cut them to pieces!" he hollered. "The way is now open for us, so the "Bond" has is already been found by humankind. They have it! They have our master's Bond! It is pulling him to it." The warriors around him became more excited as they listened to their leader. "Kill all the protectors. Cut them down to pieces! Find the Bond and bring it to me."

Shouting an almighty war cry and pulling down the visor of his helmet, he released his warriors for the fight. The large battle group sprang into action, and warriors who lay hidden suddenly joined them, charging out from the forest and attacking the Temple walls on all sides. The forest had transformed into a battlefield from the middle-ages.

****

"Missed the bastardo!" spat Trentino, enraged that the enemy commander had narrowly avoided his assassination. "Ok, men. Here they come, get ready!" he shouted calling his soldiers to arms.

Suddenly, a multitude of black creatures came charging out of the trees and began immediately scaling up the place of worship with a carnal carnivorous vehemence.

Even for the tall creatures, the huge stone terraces presented a formidable barrier, as each required the help of another to climb the walls.

The main attack was coming in front. It was breath-taking to see these vile creatures sprinting the way they did up the stone steps, covering the distance to the first tier at frightening speeds. The steps tapered inwards the further up the incline, making their ascent increasingly more congested and hindering their insane charge. It slowed their bulk down.

"Soldiers of Islam! Ready!" Khosrau shouted down, while aiming his "Shorty" assault rifle at the converging hordes below him. Then, he nodded to the Sarvan.

"Open Fire!" Captain Abdul Haleem called the order. His heavy machine gun units immediately released a wall of armour piercing rounds into the enemy. The major's special forces also blasted on command with everything they had.

The Temple was ablaze with an onslaught of enormous firepower, and the noise was ear-splitting, with gunfire shooting downwards in every direction. Smoke and brimstone could be seen everywhere. The forest watched and listened.

Automatic gunfire and the heavy machine gun bullets began raining down into the vile creatures, bits of limbs falling off. RPG launched grenades that detonated right into the charging legion, delivering their explosive power and sending more guts and gore everywhere. Strangely, a yellow-purple fluid flowed out of the wounded creatures, as they lay in anguish on the steps.

However, instant incineration was not enough. There were just too many. Fast, mobile and determined, the creatures replied by using lethal darts and black bolts fired from strange weaponry, hammering back their own death-makers towards the human garrison.

The major and colonel—Christian and Islamic—all brothers in arms were firing in unison from the different stone tiers.

Many of the evil looking creatures had little chance against the RPG explosives and high velocity bullets speeding through the air to meet them.

The lighter machine gun bullets were not as effective, and did not manage to stop the grotesque brutes, despite magazine after magazine being emptied. The projectiles bounced harmlessly off their specialised body armour or simply cracked its surface. The soldiers above tried to find their weaknesses instead.

Not so lucky were the warriors who were met with uranium tipped bullets from the heavy machine guns, as they pierced and found a mark through their armour, obliterating the creatures easily.

Bodies fell everywhere onto stone in piles of bloody bone and gore, the carcasses piling up, but the assault kept on. The enemy was gaining more than just a foothold. Astonishingly, despite the firepower and explosives, the Temple walls remained undamaged.

Over on the West, groups of warriors, who appeared to be archers, came out quickly from the forest, and readily released deadly salvos of bolts onto the Temple, sending a deluge of lethal rain into the men's makeshift barriers. The Vatican guards flattened themselves to minimize their target areas, while firing as best as they could against the suppressing fire. Many bolts found their mark and the enemy climbed up further.

"My magazines are getting low!" a soldier shouted desperately.

"Here, have these!" another threw a spare at him, but the enemy numbers were too many.

Archers released their powerful black bolts from their crossbows, which came down onto the West wall. The bolts plunged into their bodies and within minutes, all Vatican guards were dead.

"West wing! West wing!" shouted Colonel Khosrau, alarmed at the lack of gunfire coming from that position. He moved as quickly as he could. It would take time to get on top. On there, he looked down onto the battle. Now, he was in a great vantage point.

"A decoy!" Colonel shouted down.

"It's a decoy!" Trentino heard his allies warning, repeating it to his men fooled by this frontal assault.

By this time, twenty or more of these murderous warriors had scaled the wall up to the first tier. They glared fiercely at the distracted soldiers who were reloading magazine after magazine into the surrounding mayhem.

The creature army on the steps stopped their direct charge and stood there.

The sheer power of Trentino's sniper rifle always found a weakness in their armour. The rest of the creature fighters feint assault was stuck about two thirds up towards the first Tier because of the human defence, allowing time for the Colonel on top to turn his attention and help repel the assault on the west wall with his handheld RPG!

On the busy Temple top, desperate gunners were sprinting, confused from the South side to the North, and ran quickly past him and the altar, making a detour around the huge observatory building to get into a better position and stop the enemy from overrunning the Temple.

Pre-occupied, the Colonel stared at the men below, fighting on the tiers. He bellowed a huge war cry that resounded amid the smoke and dust underneath.

"Allah is with us!" The Scimitar guardians lifted their heads proudly. They were inspired. Colonel Khosrau stared at another mass of cruel creatures assimilating into a new formation to attack again. The ferocious warriors lifted their weapons to target the human forces.

"Check your targets and fire at will!" The colonel shouted.

The enemy heard the man's foghorn commands coming from the top, sending him an angry salvo of bolts that went flying at him. Most of them went swishing past him but some of his men were not so lucky.

Incensed at this, Khosrau answered with his own volley of bullets and rocket propelled grenades, which immediately exploded in and around the damn creatures.

Colonel watched as they blew up and flew through the air, when unexpectedly, more lines of fresh creatures appeared out of the forest perimeter. With no end in sight, the men's hearts sank.

By now, some of the creatures had gained a precarious foothold on the first level terraces, fighting hand to claw against the soldiers. Others lifted their out-stretched arm to aim at the men, opening their disgusting limb to expose their fleshy internal organ with deadly consequences.

Inside it, the rapidly spinning organic mechanism worked by shooting out a salvo of organic thorny missiles under high pressure from its internal organic tubes. The limb was lubricated with a brown fluid and dripped like saliva out of the arm each time it fired its deadly dart.

The whole thing was a repulsive spectacle to watch.

Now, fighting for their lives on the first tier, deadly darts flew by, killing soldiers left and right of the major. The warrior was ready to take him on too. In that split second, Trentino found his mark! That killing advantage was also their mortal weakness, their arm exposed! A bullet through their raised arm shot into their bodies each time, made them think twice about using this vicious body part to fight. A creature born and bred to use it, now feared the major's personal touch.

Too many, too many, the major was assimilating the scale and determination of the enemy, while long black missiles zipped past him.

He dropped instinctively, rolling rapidly along the stone wall and out of the way, as several darts missed him.

These close quarters found Trentino still holding his rifle after his dive, the soldier spinning around into a squat position and ready. Trentino rapidly fired his weapon in this bitter battle to live. His shot knocked two of the armoured creatures clean over and off the terrace.

His trusty rifle won again as he watched the merciless warriors growling in their own agony. *Piss easy,* he thought defiantly, but as he looked around, it seemed hopeless as more warriors were running to meet him.

On top of the Temple, Colonel Khosrau and his men kept blasting away with a murderous onslaught against the invaders.

Trentino fell when one of several warriors came charging along from the West tier, knocking him right over. One warrior was on him like a rash.

"I am not going alone, you bastardos!" he cursed, as he pulled out a grenade.

He sensed more devilish creatures speeding past him, as he struggled with the beast, trying to survive against the large brute on top of him. He saw that some of the enemy had reached the top of the structure by way of the Eastern wall.

A valiant stand, yes. The human demise was inevitable. The Temple was lost and quickly overrun.

Meanwhile, *"DEATH"* soared high above within the hot air eddies, the creature moving quietly and unnoticed in the heat of battle. It watched with sad eyes from a distance.

Ghoulish creatures lay in gory filth among the dead and dying bodies of bold Scimitar guardians and the crusading crossbow battalion.

Yet, some resistance remained in the Temple, a place not quite taken, where the brutes eventually managed to drag themselves wearily to the top, their deadly arsenal on the unsuspecting troops still defending the North side.

"LUYRU!" one grotesque creature screamed in triumph using its own guttural language—a language only heard by its own depraved kind. It spoke in low-pitched notes, mainly acoustics, outside the scale of human frequency, below 10 Hertz.

The Islamic Scimitar guardians could not hear the impending threat. A salvo of bolts and long darts quickly struck them dead.

Other creature warriors continued their run on both sides of the observatory, overwhelming any remaining opposition, who were fighting in every direction.

"Death to the devils! Death to the devils!" Colonel Nabeel Khosrau kept calling, anger sharpening his fine features. "Death to the devils!"

HSALS SLAUGOHTŘ had taken the Temple.

****

Trentino was tumbling and twisting jerkily, trying to avoid several vicious attempts to stick him with a determined trident, the weapon causing sparks to fly off the hard-stone surface next to him.

As the death fork quickly came back for another stab, the major automatically pulled out his bayonet and caught the trident fork right in front of his face. The warrior forced the sharp points and the bayonet back towards the major.

His bulging eyes watched as the sharp prongs inched closer. Sweat poured from every pore, as he held the fork only inches from his throat while the fighting continued all around him.

Heavy machine guns fired their lethal sprays at the colossal brutes, trying to keep them away from the Temple entrance.

The major, delirious with cold rage would not die, as he fought for his life against the immense weight.

The major was losing the battle, as the trident moved ever closer.

He could see the insane creature's yellow speckled eyes staring at him with a rabid frenzy through its visor. Its large claws gripping the long metal shaft.

I cannot hold it, Trentino thought, as he struggled. *I must hold it, I must.* Only a minute more and he would be dead.

Trentino, AKA Mantis, saw a second warrior coming towards him with a weapon held high to strike. The weapon looked like an Egyptian khopesh. The warrior ran in to finish him off, when without warning, another sword unexpectedly swung across, decapitating the creature.

The creature's head flew off like a kicked football. In the same swift action, the double-edged sword flashed with blue edges striking and slicing on through the armoured flank of the dominating warrior above Trentino.

Shocked, the major stared up dazed and in disbelief.

There stood Christopher, wiping the creatures blood away from his sword. The Sword's blue edges still blazing with a mysterious energy.

Smiling, Chris extended his hand down to the relieved Swiss guardsman, breathing heavily. Mantis felt utterly spent but still managed a cheeky grin back at the man who saved his life.

"Handy with that little sword of yours, Hrycuik," said Trentino.

"Piss easy, major," Christopher said smiling, repeating Mantis's own signature saying while helping him to his feet. "Piss easy."

****

On the Temple top, Colonel Nabeel Khosrau and the remaining men were still desperately fighting for survival. The creatures were far too many, and were coming at them from every direction, fighting and forcing them to stand on the edge. Below them, the drop was ten feet to the terrace below.

"Over the top men!"

"Watch out, colonel!" a Swiss guardsman warned when a mighty creature swept its sword at him. The guardsman quickly shot into its bare leg with his pistol. The creature fell in agony with its leg broken. There was no time to spare, are more creatures continued to charge at them, as they jumped down.

"Ok, men. Lob your grenades over! Let them cook!"

The men hugged the wall for protection, when the explosive discharges of their grenades erupted, deafening their ears. Sudden heat blasts hovered above their heads.

One soldier stood on another's back to see what was above them, only to get his head sliced off.

Immediately, more warriors jumped down onto the terrace below in quick pursuit of any surviving humans.

Colonel Khosrau watched as the adversaries landed on the stone around him, the creatures laughing arrogantly. The colonel knew he would have to make a stand right here.

From behind their visors, the creatures' faces changed from gloat to grimace when they realized the man was not for running away. Surprised at his determination, they fumbled when they saw him charging them.

In this defining moment, the Scimitar commander showed his true worth, as he jumped onto one of the creature's enormous thighs and using it like a springboard, catapulted his body up like a gymnast into the air and quickly striking the creature bang on its neck with his instep.

This sudden Karate strike pushed the immense warrior over, and its huge body knocked into the others at the same time. Like a domino effect, the beasts fell off the side of the terrace together and crashed into a heap below, killed by their own weight. Then, he had another idea.

****

Trentino and Christopher stood deep in blood at the front entrance, with another creature falling near them. The utter carnage of a battlefield lay everywhere. Multitudes of body parts were strewn over the Temple in senseless destruction. They looked down at the steps and across the terraces quite bewildered. The battle was lost, and their hearts were racing. Their minds were full of questions. Why? Who were they? What are they? And most importantly, where did they come from?

They gripped their weapons tightly once again, and prepared themselves. Horrified, and unknown to humankind, the defenders were standing witness to the start of the next World War.

Suddenly, from the top of the Temple, massive blasts began detonating in succession. They hunched over every time a huge explosion occurred. Two, three, four detonations and more. The men below simply lost count after ten.

Trentino imagined what the devastation would be like on top and what thousands of fiery ball bearings would do to an enemy.

"Anti-personnel mines?" Christopher asked the major.

"No. Explosives positioned all around the top," Trentino replied icily, "These Islamic duderinos have laid C4-based explosives up there, a trap ready for any helicopter landing and rescue. The little shits really wanted to take us out, but they were not expecting this kind of company, were they?"

Armageddon lay before them. Creatures with grotesque ogre-like faces and large heavy jaws open wide displaying a mouth full of sharp black teeth. With lifeless large eyes with no lids, the creatures could only stare with pure hatred for Man.

****

Islamic and Christian soldiers fought together in the most unlikely of unions, but fight they did. Men of different faiths and ideals bound together in life, most now lay dead amidst these devilish things. Yet, hope remained as the battle continued where pockets of human resistance were still fighting on. Both men watched in horror, so close like this they could see perfectly red symbols imprinted on the side of their black helmets, some with three "///" strokes, while others only with two "//". They assumed the markings to be some form of ranking.

"I owe you one. Thanks, Christopher," the rescued major said. "What kind of sword is that anyway? Looks like something out of the bloody Lord of the Rings or Star Wars, signore!"

"Si, major, and I've become quite adept at using it."

"I noticed."

"Anyway," Christopher said over-simplistically, "I do not know how to use this gun."

"What are these evil looking things?" Trentino asked.

"Major, do not move any closer to that creature, it is dead, but they can still kill, years after death."

The major recoiled, careful not to take any chances.

"So, all that you spoke about inside the Temple is true?" He reflected soberly at the scientist's insane stories.

"Damn right."

"God help us."

"Their kind have been here before, or something like them at least." Christopher advised.

"What else can you tell me about this scum? The more we know our enemy, the easier it will be to defeat them." The major needed answers.

"These ones are different to the creatures inside the Temple. Those ones have legs like large long ostrich, mutated or bred into a different position. Also, their skulls are a different shape. These ones have legs like ours, except much longer." Christopher was equally astounded that these assailants were different from the ones he had seen previously.

"Anything else, Christopher?"

"The other warrior creatures inside the Temple had something in common with these. They all have three clawed fingers and a curved talon for its thumb, good for gripping and slashing."

Both men looked down at the dead carcasses for measurement and bone structure.

"Thoughts?"

"Those large lidless eyes are common too, but the other differences between them are quite distinct. I think each must be a different species. I'm guessing that it has evolved since the first days of conquest of the Temple. Maybe these ones branched in another evolutionary path." Christopher hypothesised.

Trentino looked even more surprised, "It doesn't look much like the ones we saw in the lower Temple either! Those ones wore chainmail and looked more human except were much bigger. They were Goliaths!"

"Yes, these alien things undoubtedly have been here before. I would say, twenty-five thousand years ago!" Christopher postulated. "When man in Europe was still running about in caves. Maybe even further back than that. I cannot say. Possibly hundreds of thousands of years ago. God only knows?"

"It is unbelievable!"

"Well, it is they who are responsible for the demise of those other warriors wearing the chainmail. What that race belongs too, I cannot begin to guess!"

"They want what we don't have, and right now, they think we have it or think it's up for grabs inside the Temple. Basically, we are in the way!" Trentino stated bluntly. "They want what I know is to be the 'Golden Egg'."

"The Golden Egg?" Christopher raised an eyebrow.

"Si, I know, I know, signore, it's code crap. Look, I could get court marshalled for saying this, but shit, who the hell cares out here! My new orders are to secure this thing. The one problem is, I do not know how to find it."

"You mean the link? A talisman of sorts? I agree. The link is an enchanted object with peculiar qualities of unmeasured power."

"You know of this thing, signore?" his honesty worked.

"Sure. It is down there somewhere in the mud just waiting to be picked up." Christopher pointed at the base camp. The flattened ruins looked uninviting. "And major, I have to get it back before these beasts find it first!"

Christopher knew that in this hour of darkness, he must find a way—a way to secure this ancient and magical relic again. The major listened to his plea, when unexpectedly, they heard a familiar voice.

"Chris, and you too major, I am glad to see you both alive!" Christopher and the major immediately stopped talking, and turned around to see Colonel Nabeel Khosrau slowly walking down from steps above them.

His ripped shirt and bloodied trousers bore witness to his hard fighting.

"Mashir!" Christopher exclaimed in surprise.

"Khosrau!" Trentino was happy to see the commander.

"We saw them off, my friends. We saw them off." He regarded both men thoughtfully.

"Colonel Nabeel Khosrau, quite a party eh! I heard Christmas crackers being pulled up top," he said, referring to the recent explosions.

Shaking the major's hand, both men eyed each other thoughtfully, as equals.

Nabeel turned and quickly grabbed Christopher and hugged him hard. Both men brothers once again.

"Come on, get back behind the barrier at the entrance, our guys still hold it in safe hands," said Trentino, quickly moving along the first tier, and staying alert for any sign of pursuit. The fighting had stopped. The explosions had done the trick.

"Thank Allah, I see some of our men have survived." The Colonel looked bleary-eyed at the devastation.

"Nasty," Trentino stated. Disturbed by Christopher's prodding, the creature warrior's head turned lifeless on the ground and displayed a logo on its helmet which was shaped like the Temple.

The living soldiers were quickly accounted for. The total was thirty, with ten Swiss guardsmen and 20 UNCAA special forces. Looking out at the devastation, the enemy had paid a heavy price.

Christopher turned around to see Harjit! Her face was chalk white. She was overwhelmed at the sight of all this death and destruction.

"Harj," said Christopher softly.

"Oh, Chris. I'm so glad you are not hurt." She hugged him.

Upon hearing the groans coming from the injured men, Harjit immediately began saving the wounded.

Colonel Khosrau again posted lookouts onto the Temple top. A few men were stationed at the entrance and were ready with heavy machine guns. Other guards moved cautiously along each wall wary of any new threat. The forest waited once again.

The forest had become so quiet one could almost hear a twig snap or bush rustle.

The smoke from the battle rose high above the trees and Temple top. The smell of death quickly pervading the air in the humid atmosphere. No vultures or vermin appeared, as a queer brooding silence settled. Yet, the buzzing of those saws could be heard again. They never stopped. The small detachment of Swiss guardsmen was remarkably still at it! A race against time, they must have heard the battle, gunfire and the explosions. Knowing better than to stop until the job was done, their orders were crystal clear. This was the only way out. Many good friends had been lost and any bravado they once had, fizzled out. Everyone wondered if they would live to see a new day. The defenders' lonely thoughts turned to the landing zone and rescue. It gave them hope.

****

"What are we going to do now? We are doing the same thing as we did before, staying here and getting our backsides kicked!" corporal Bianchi moaned to an Islamic counterpart.

"We must have faith in our true destinies, my brother," he answered sincerely.

"Si, we may die here but we'll take more of those things with us." He pulled out his pistol and sucked air in through his broken tooth. It was a sobering thought to know the enemy was down there, in the forest.

"Our leaders are consulting together inside the Temple and planning for our extraction." The Islamic guardian reassured corporal Bianchi.

"I hope they do it fast. It'll be dark soon," said Bianchi. He took off his beret to wipe the sweat from his brow, then fixed his eyes grimly to the forest and the queer black fog. *What the fuck is that?*

****

Inside the Temple, hissing lamps spluttered, yet provided enough light to perform minor surgeries for the wounded. Two soldiers were guarding the entrance to the room and this time, it was for her genuine protection.

"How is Mathieson, doctor?" major Trentino asked her. She took the major's arm gently and walked slowly away from her patients.

"Mathieson will be dead by tomorrow morning if we do not help him right now."

"I see that his skin has turned completely white? Jesus, what is wrong with him?" he asked.

Harjit described how the expedition scout had saved their lives and fought a wild life-form somewhere deep inside the Temple. His acute condition could only get worse.

The major tried to imagine what had happened to the scientists further inside the Temple. He shook his head knowing how inadequately prepare he was to get these people out. Not to mention the communications message via satellite from someone called Apostle. And where was his commander, Rossi? Trentino could only wonder what this place really was, and why it was so strategically important.

Sadly, there was little she could do to help, except try and give Mathieson water, make him comfortable and talk to him even though he was unconscious.

"We have to get out of here." Khosrau was concerned about their next move, when quite unexpectedly, he heard humming.

Christopher began to sing.

Amazing Grace, how sweet the sound,
That saved a wretch like me.
I once was lost but now am found,
Was blind, but now, I see.

When we've been here ten thousand years.
bright shining as the sun.
We've no less days to sing God's praise.
then when we've first begun."

Christopher finished the full song with tears in his eyes.

"That indeed was stirring, my friend." Nabeel smiled warmly, his spirit lifted and yet, he felt sad, and his eyes watered too. He had missed listening to Christopher's songs of late. Nabeel still appreciated those fine words and verse even though he was a child of Islam.

"God looks upon us all. *I know he is here,"* said Christopher, staring skywards.

"I agree."

"Thank you, Mashir. It is one of my favourite songs. I have been long gone from my own church. It gives everyone hope and if not in this one, then in another."

"It's time to put your cards on the table, guys," said Harjit. She could no longer suppress her unspoken thoughts. "What do those things really want?" Harjit wanted to understand more of their enemy and who better to ask than both commanders?

"Colonel Rossi, my commanding officer is coming with reinforcements," said Trentino, trying to reassure her, "they will be able to help us. He is better equipped, and will be bringing heavier armaments. He will be with us very soon. In addition, our extraction is on the way."

I have some questions for Rossi, too, the major thought. Unfortunately, major Trentino did not know that the Osprey were all dead. Without warning, Mathieson's voice broke the tension.

"Water. I need water." Mathieson was regaining consciousness and speaking with gritty dryness. Surprised, Harjit moved like lightening to help him. All questions would have to wait.

Slowly and gently, Harjit lifted his heavy head, hearing his neck scraping like sandpaper, which sent a sickening shiver up her spine, while Mathieson, with great effort, began sipping the water.

"How are you, Mat?" asked Nabeel Khosrau, concerned at his deteriorating state.

"Mashir, you son of a bitch! What the mother are you doing back?" Mathieson surprised him. Everyone looked astounded at how alert and conscious he was.

"It is good to know you are becoming better, my friend." Mashir was sincere.

"Fuck off mother fuck!" retorted Mathieson in his usual style. The ex-navy seal would not accept his ill health, turning his head like a slow ratchet to see the room. His movements produced a low grating noise like stone on stone, flaking off his hard skin. Mashir was shocked to see him this way.

"Cards on the table, yes. Why not man, come on." Mathieson insisted, pushing for answers, just like Harjit. He wanted to know too.

"Allah wills you all to know this. Where we stand, is the Temple as written in the legend of the 'Lost Tablet' and tells of a Holy War against unfaithful Christians." They listened quietly as Nabeel Khosrau began speaking.

"Huh, this is going to be good," Mathieson tried to laugh.

"In legend, Jigbir or the angel Gabriel gifted revelations in the cave of Hira to our great inspirer forewarning about a great enemy on another land mass at the end of the world, the valley of Iblis. The tablet which no longer exists describes this Temple, a Temple of Islam. It is here. In history, the Quran mentions the name "Iblis" eleven times, Iblis is the name described to us as the 'tempter' better known in your religion as the devil. During the Arab raids in the seventh to ninth centuries the Emir, Ibrahim conquered the failing Roman Empire, and in 902 with the fall of Tauromenium in Sicily. However, the Emir gained access by the way of Saracen Gate or Cuseni Gate, destroying monuments and churches. He put many women, children and old men to the sword. The girls were bought by the Caliph to populate the harems of Bagdad. All others were sold to mingle with the Mediterranean people and the Arab race. Bishop Procopio was sacrificed and his heart was eaten by the Emir. The Emir was said to have the scrolls with him during the conquest."

"Yuck!" Harjit was disgusted.

"Must have been a real hungry motherfucker. Ha, ha, ha," Mathieson said, laughing, but his voice seemed different somehow. It sounded hollow or woody. Mashir smiled and continued his story.

"That's the history and here's the rub…"

"What rub?"

"The scriptures were stolen from the Emir as he feasted on his enemy. These scrolls were then stolen and lost, hence the name the *'Last and Lost Scrolls of Iblis'*. The Infidels escaped and no one knows where the sacred scrolls ended up. Hence Christianity know of these things too."

"Less of the infidel stuff, Mashir," Christopher was annoyed at his degradation of religious views.

"Apologies, Chris, as you know, it is only a history lesson. The Caliph called it Almoezia, but on the night of Bishop Procopio's death and according to the legend, the firmament also wept for the dreadful massacre of Tauromenium. This was an Arab domination that lasted for two and a half centuries." Nabeel paused for breath. "During that night, in Ago 10, 902, the sky was illuminated by a storm of Meteorites." Nabeel looked at them wide-eyed. "If all this sounds confusing, remember that the scrolls speak of this place, I mean, this Temple—the 'Temple of MalisIblis'"

"Quite a history lesson it is too," Trentino broke the silence, not quite knowing what else to say.

"So, here we all stand together, as Prophesised!" Nabeel Khosrau spoke again, his words honest and sincere. He believed in the Prophecy and knew his words to be the truth.

"False Prophet!" Barbaro screamed. "It was an unholy massacre in Sicily by the heathens and a great loss of our martyr Procopio! The Light of God is ever watchful, and he took the scrolls. They were not stolen, for a great evil was done to his children!"

"As you wish, but *we* have tried to find these lost teachings for centuries, looking here and there, and always falling short until recently, er, when only a few years ago..."

"Go on, Khosrau," the major was captivated by his story.

"There were rumours, and once again, we heard murmurs that in a place of rain and forest, these lost words could be found. A place of deep learning and knowledge of the path to God. Some call it the 'Doorway of the Gods!' Our unfortunate late friend, professor Mancini, knew a little of this legend. He called it 'The Key of the Gods of the Seven Rays'. However, unknown to him, he was manipulated by others and was used like a pawn." Nabeel spoke deliberately.

"Rubbish! This is no chess game!" Barbaro blared and resisted this new prophet and a traitor, who now calls himself Nabeel Khosrau. Barbaro did not want to hear any more of this blasphemy.

"Our intelligence runs deeper than you know." Nabeel Khosrau watched his attentive audience. The major moved closer to him, and lowering his voice, Trentino whispered into his ear.

"*Colonel, I recognised your hand grip. You and I are both in the fraternity, are we not?*"

"Ah! So that is why you are working together?" Christopher overheard. "And indeed why you are both here. It's all making sense now, you are both Freemasons." Christopher watched them. The priest had his own secret thoughts. *The ones known as "Osleiotectian brethren". How extraordinary!*

"Clever, Chris!" Harjit spoke up.

"We both have allegiances to our own peers, our Holy Governments and to one single God, quite correct," Trentino concurred.

"We are here by design rather than chance, my good major, and not by luck or fraternity. We have come to seek and take back this thing to our masters," the Islamic commander stated openly.

"And which leader would that be exactly? Yours or mine?" the major asked.

"I do not think it matters, we are here together to fight this battle and above all else, we must take this object back home. I would prefer to take it back to Mecca, but this choice will not be ours too make, major."

"Oh, I think it is," Barbaro said. He would not accept a chance decision.

"Christopher told me some things about it," Harjit said, "but to be honest, I am confused to what this thing really is. An object so important to kill for is abhorrent to me.".

The Freemason link is too much of a coincidence. They may or may not know what it is, but this brotherhood, has a bigger part to play in this mystery than even they understand. Christopher thought.

"I think it is God's 'Link to Earth', also known as 'The Link of Osleiotect'." Christopher was sure. "It was written in the prince's own blood, and I quote: 'Our last stand is over. The race of Nelumakragasian and I, Akyaron Lord and Prince of my people, is no more."

The group was in awe at what Christopher said. Even the soldiers were entranced. The men of both faiths gathered quietly around him. They wanted to know more. What was so important about this thing, this link, that was worth dying for in such a lonely place? What had the priest found out? What did he know? All their lives had been placed on the scales by God, waiting for his judgement.

"No, don't stop now, go on, mother fuck! We all want to know why we are here. You seem to have God's ear, so, what is God's grand plan for us?" Mathieson was not being sarcastic or joking, and at this poignant moment, felt somehow much closer to God than he had ever been in his turbulent life back home in Detroit.

Here, inside this Temple, Mathieson seemed at peace and strangely felt that it was his own Mount Sinai. *Maybe this Temple had not always been an evil place.*

"I do not understand this myself, Mat." Christopher replied to Mathieson's question, as Christopher tried his best to explain. "I do not know why these things are happening. When I was inside the lower Temple, I went through a peculiar dark veil. At that point, I could not see anything inside. This was when I encountered something very strange. A dead figure."

"I'm still listening," Mathieson said, lifting his tone to ensure Christopher would tell all.

Christopher went on to tell them of what he saw in the strange tomb inside the Temple.

"We must go and get this link, right now! Immediately!" the Vatican official rudely demanded.

"I agree, I need to locate my medical supplies too, that is, if I can find them." Chris looked over at Mathieson, "I'll find the supplies and I'll find the link."

"Yeah, hurry up, man. I've a motherfucking big hangover here!"

Turning sharply away so that Mathieson could not see her, Harjit's eyes filled with tears.

"Mmm, that will prove very difficult," Nabeel Khosrau's said.

"I hate this place, it is evil," she stated with passion. "I would prefer not to be here at all. I know what lies inside this place and would prefer to take my chances outside. Chris, you understand, don't you?"

He said nothing at first, instead, took her hand and pulled her gently and firmly away from Mathieson's earshot. Mathieson once again drifted back into semi-unconsciousness.

"Mathieson needs medicine, Harj, I must go," Chris said with tightened lips. "I will be very careful, and while I'm gone, you must do the same. Promise me? I will return and with a little luck, we will all be airlifted out of this place very soon. I know that the major will see to it. The Temple up top is large enough for a helicopter to land. This place is huge and easy to spot from the air. Try not to worry, Harj, we will get out."

"Oh, Chris."

"I must go."

"Mashir! How long do you think we have?" she asked.

"No idea, Harjit," Nabeel stated candidly. "Once those murderous devils regroup, they could attack before nightfall."

This news knocked the stuffing out of them and their morale took a tumble with despair. Then again, that was the way of MalisIblis! Even now inside the walls, it was still working on each of them.

Harjit turned back to Christopher, "Not long, then." She could not take her eyes off Christopher and he kissed her tenderly.

Trentino stepped in from the shadows. It was crucial to say something positive to everyone—soldiers and civilians alike. His eyes caught the light of the lamp and sparkled hopefully.

"We still have a good chance," he said in a positive tone. Then, he began to explain how they would escape.

****

In the wake of such ferocious fighting, death and silence hung over the forest like a plague. The Iblis vale took another deep breath in, and another hour passed without incident. Dead and mutilated bodies lay littered on the steps and terraces, from the encircling forest perimeter to the Temple top. The whole area was a dead zone. Meanwhile, human eyes kept watch for signs of their return.

Trees and leaves were repulsed by the stink of death and decay, and the rainforest had become a place with no birds, no animals or insects. runoff or gone berserk leaving it denuded of animals, not even scavengers. It seemed as though Mother Nature was under attack herself.

The distant buzzing and cutting of timber was the only sound one could hear. It did not stop. Hope echoed throughout the offended foliage. It ıs as if nature felt offended by evil. With no heart, the rainforest's breathing stopped and the air was, still.

Christopher, Sarvan Haleem, Private Narváez and a radio operator quietly left the relative safety of the Temple. The team descended inconspicuously down the Northern side. The men crawled slowly through large shrubs and green brown foliage, thankful for the newly formed biomass from the past weeks that provided them with cover. Their camouflaged gear blended in. Chris wore clothes, borrowed from a dead Islamic soldier, and it was as though God had bonded both faiths together. The group knew what to do, carefully zigzagging from bush to bush, as the boy priest prayed silently all the way for divine guidance.

****

They will come first and SMITE.

It was the time of the Prophecy!

The enemy had left only a few legionaries of HSALS SLAUGOHTŔ behind as lookouts, and knew it would be enough to watch the trapped Osleiotectian Garrison. The first Cohort, badly bruised and beaten, retreated about three miles away to rendezvous with the main fighting force, the Prime Legion. It waited for their return. Four thousand troops, an expeditionary force, were stationed and ready to move on command. HSALS

SLAUGOHTŘ had returned to Osleiotect and this time, they were here to stay.

The Prime Centurion, and leader, stood and waited for them. He intimidated all that he saw, and patience was not a quality he admired. He was a warrior beast, massive in muscle, and was about eight-feet high. He was also bigger and the strongest of his kind. He was a born leader with an inherent anger and brain for battle.

The Praefect arrived and presented himself immediately to the Centurion. Power emanated from Prime Centurion *Zirkic Kgnash* of the Legion—the power of pure evil.

Zirkic Kgnash was like most of his race, with a peculiar triangular shaped head, which was wide and almost flat at the top, and an angular face with a pointed chin. Not wearing the same black armour as the First Cohort, Centurion's medieval attire included a heavy leather green tunic that covered his thick torso, and a wide leather belt to hold his sword. Black chainmail underneath the Tunic protected his body and head. As an accomplished strategist, his orders were simple: take the Temple and secure the link.

As fate would have it, this was the same mission the Christian and Muslim forces were on.

Acknowledging his subordinate Praefect, the Centurion displayed no welcome, instead regarded him thoughtfully with a hateful glare. Prime Centurion dutifully saluted his Praefect with a tri-clawed gauntlet made of a black chain metal.

"What is the report on the Osleiotectian forces?"

"We have probed the Osleiotectian defences, my Primus Kgnash," he said as he bowed at the Centurion, the Praefect then immediately stood to attention.

"And?"

"They have machines that have destroyed many, my Centurion. We have weakened them greatly."

A hundred or more remaining legionnaires of the Praefect's first Cohort and own race stood stoically in formation proudly behind him.

Primus Kgnash seemed satisfied. He had no second thoughts about his Praefect's casualties. He was a merciless monster hardened by his years of battling and bloody campaigns. To him, this invasion was the beginning of a new adventure.

"What of the "Link of Osleiotect? Do you have it?" he snapped, while staring cruelly at his Praefect.

This link was the key objective for his master. Bowing his head again, the Praefect replied cautiously.

"No, great Prime Centurion Kgnash." Praefect clearly understood that any ill-favoured news was punishable. Primus Kgnash made a quick sign.

Quickly and brutally, all the Praefect's remaining warriors were immediately overwhelmed, bound and gagged! Their Praefect watched the mayhem, and did not dare show any sign of emotion. Silent and still, the Praefect said nothing.

"It is not any fault of yours, Praefect, that your First Cohort was not strong enough and inferior to my task," the Prime Centurion began to walk. With a flicking talon, he indicated for the Praefect to follow him. The Centurion was scheming. *Fear is a great motivator for the Praefect, I still need him for this expedition.* The Praefect followed on. Kgnash growled. "You failed," he said, looking back at his subordinate. Death was certain as his black soul.

"Apologies, my Centurion." The Praefect realised that this trap had been well planned and executed by Primus Centurion, and knew that the Primus would only use his failure to goad him even more.

"I have no further use for them." Their death warrant was sealed as he pointed his talon at the surviving warriors.

The Praefect's wire-bound warriors were brutally taken away, scuffling. A hundred warriors all destined for the pit—the deep crack in the Earth. Failure meant certain death. Something awful waited to feast on them down there.

Primus Zirkic Kgnash had a deep scar on his right cheek from a previous skirmish. As he took his helmet off, he sniffed at his subordinate's company. Kgnash and his warriors were of a different race to that of the Praefect. The Centurion had long legs and a massive torso.

Zirkic Kgnash was, by breed, a "Preyweep" and as such, hated the Praefect by nature. Kgnash had been bred by genetic design by his lord and master. The Praefect was naturally born, a "Ráevil", and a different species.

The Praefect unfortunately had been placed under the Centurion's direct command. The Praefect was born off "Royal stock", so the Centurion could not arbitrarily just kill him, not yet. He chose instead to make him suffer. Kgnash hated the Praefect.

"I will give you a proper Cohort of Preyweeps to lead."

Taking the Praefect with him, Primus Kgnash walked taller than his own *"Bloodhort"* Legion, moving quickly through the forest, and inspecting his many formations of legionnaires. His troops were all well trained and ready to march. This Spearhead Legion was assigned to retake this outpost on Osleiotect!

Arrogantly, Kgnash strutted confidently with the knowledge in his own ability and that of his "Bloodhort".

Each Bloodhort warrior displayed a red triple clawed logo on each side of their helmets, and wore chainmail with a green tunic on top, a long cloak of greens and browns with yellow flash stripes. The cape was designed to be draped over their shoulders when they were not in combat. Their unique attire would provide them with remarkable properties for defence or in battle, shelter with an ability to change appearance and camouflage into the jungle's environment.

The only insects fluttering around were a swarm of mosquitoes, which emerged from damp pools. The bugs hummed around them and bit at their thick skin, trying to suck at their poisonous blood. For those successful, they began flourishing with excitement, flying quickly off in madness, then died. This new forest creature was not too its taste. It's blood was a serum of death. The mosquito had not yet adapted to this new animal.

A mosquito kept buzzing in front of Kgnash. The Preyweep looked indignantly at the trivial pests and drew in his throat. With a gutsy snort, he suddenly spit out a large amount of sticky spray, and the hovering insect fell dead onto the forest floor! Prime Centurion Kgnash looked around and gave the order for his legion to move on MalisIblis!

****

CHAPTER XVII

WE ARE GOING TO WAR

Christopher was foraging more like a berry-picker than a scientist around the camp's grounds. The man was inspecting every piece of wreckage shrew about, all the while staying vigilant, since attack could happen at any moment.

The guards lay flat and perfectly still on the ground in wide flanking positions on each side of him while the continued his search. No sound was heard from that dark green interior except the distant cutting of trees. The men were edgy, with their machine guns trained on the forest perimeter.

Warriors and creatures lay lifeless all around them. Christopher did not look at their mutilated carcasses because they looked so disgusting with their wide lidless eyes. They made him feel sick. Like walking through a mine-field, he had to be very careful not to prompt a Salvo by mistake.

Scavenging below bits of tattered tent flysheets and frayed ropes, Christopher decided to use a tent pole to lever some crushed and broken crates that had been flattened into the muddy forest floor.

He groaned at yet another grim discovery. A battered and bloodied body, sunk deeply into the forest floor.

"*Kees. Poor sod.*" Chris whispered to the dead man. "Why, God?" Christopher cursed. His faith was tested to the limit. Without warning, the foliage burst open.

Huge Ráevil soldiers in black armoured bodies leapt out from the forest, and were hammering towards him. Standing up, Chris could not move. He was frozen. He could not take his terrified eyes off them. Three big brutes came at him with battle-axes raised high, ready to strike.

The Swiss guards and Scimitar guardians saw the threat immediately. At lighting pace, the creatures moved towards him, when the soldiers opened fire.

Everyone watched helplessly as the bullets ricocheted off their tough armoured bodies.

"Get them! Get them!" Christopher was horrified.

His survival instinct kicked in and he remembered his sword and gun, and fumbled to take both of them out.

Without warning, Christopher felt a thin jet of hot air pass by his ear. Unexpectedly, the assailant that was furthest away stumbled and skidded into the mud, head first. Christopher began blinking rapidly, trying to take it in. His eyes stayed glued on the runners in front.

The closest attackers were completely unaware that the last one had fallen, and continued charging straight at Christopher.

Chris gulped in surprise when both attackers fell awkwardly, plunging into the thick brown green Earth, in an explosion of mud followed a split second later by two sharp cracks fired from what sounded like a distant weapon echoing off the treeline.

This gave Christopher a chance to get ready to defend himself. Without thinking, Christopher hunched over.

Agile as lions, three more warriors came springing out from the forest perimeter, only to trip over debris and fallen warriors.

"Crack! Pitumph." The sound made from the same weapon and another clean shot piercing bang through the front of the Beasts helmet! The Beast dropped hard with the sudden impact of a precision bullet blowing off half the helmet at the same time.

"Crack! Pitumph." the next fell just as certain, and just as dead but the last Warrior was by now right on him!

Unexpectedly, a Swiss guardsman stood abruptly up in between him and the last brute, the Legionnaire automatically using his round shield in an enraged fury swatting the guardsman away like a fly!

This giving the warrior time to consider its own danger against this puny human with a sword, stopping only yards away from the

Scientist, thinking again whether to continue its attack. Sensing danger, hesitating, turning quickly to look back at the safety of the forest, when its astonished eyes saw all its comrades fallen, killed by a hidden enemy!

Furious, it twisted again to face the small man with the strange blue sword. The warrior raised its battle-axe with only a few paces to go and viciously swinging it in a wide sideways curve to strike Christopher; when another Crosshair from a rifle lined up against its Visor. Red on dead.

"Crack! Pitumph." The Legionnaire continuing its whirlwind twist in the air going backwards and falling heavily, its head gone!

Smoke rose from Trentino's rifle, his sharp shooter viewing the headless warrior lying in the mud.

Christopher's heartrate accelerated as he watched the killing. He scanned the perimeter, looking for the elusive major. *Thanks, major, wherever you are.* He and the other men wondered where the major was hiding. His life-saving marksmanship had saved them all.

"Hey, Barbaro, what the fuck are you doing over there?" Christopher spotted the press officer. The man appeared suspiciously from behind a damaged crate.

"Looking for that thing you described, the link."

"Well," he asked Barbaro, "have you found it?" there was no time for niceties.

"No."

Christopher was relieved that the Vatican official had not found the link. *It is not for him*, he thought reticently. Nevertheless, the group continued their fruitless search. A little while later, they stopped as they anxiously peered into the forest and at the sound of distant drums.

"Holy Father, what is that noise?" Barbaro asked. They waited a few more seconds.

Boom, boom, boom.

"Sounds like far-off drums?" Christopher said.

Boom, boom, boom. The drums came a little closer.

With no more time to lose, they continued their frantic search for the link. Finding it had been hard enough before and now, nigh impossible.

A minute later, more drumbeats began to join in an insane percussive madness. Closer! It all sounded so crazy! Then, they heard something else. It sounded like the breaking and felling of massive trees, when strong horns began blowing loudly too. More drums were added to the percussion and were communicating together. They were coming.

"Bloody Hell. Drums! What is going on?" a guardsman asked.

"They want us to know," Barbaro replied, scanning the forest.

"Know what.?" the soldier asked.

"They are coming," Christopher expressed exigency, "There is very little time left. Come on, keep looking!"

They all continued looking when a cold voice began speaking to them. The men looked down surprised to see someone moving in the undergrowth.

"I could have killed all of you." The major had come down from the Temple some time ago to watch over them, standing up from behind a thick cover of red and green shrubs with bright orange flowers.

"Signore!" a guardsman stood motionless, amazed that he had not seen the major.

"Major!" Christopher gasped.

"Always be on the watch, *all of you!* Drop your guard for a moment on these bastardos and you will be dead."

The drums continued.

"Signore," the radio operator said, "I have just received a message from the Temple guards, they say," the soldier stopped to listen to the communications.

"Si?" Trentino prompted urgency, he needed to know.

"Movement has been detected around the perimeter to the South and East! I have tried to reply, signore, but."

"Spit it out, son."

"The transmission has been cut." his voice trembled.

Whatever they were dealing with here, the enemy were organised and intelligent. *Who could have cut the communication?* Trentino wondered.

The young guardsman tried to disguise his nervous hands, shaking his earpiece vigorously to sort some equipment malfunction. Instinctively, all the men crouched down in unison. There was very little time left.

"Ok soldier, you get back up and instruct the commander that if he and his men want to live, tell him to get everyone out of there and up onto the top deck of the Temple, *no messing* now! E.T.A. will be from the "Nest" in one hour! Synchronise your timepiece with mine, soldier. Check!"

"Check, Maggiore!" he affirmed as both men synchronised their watches.

The sounds of war drums rolled on and on. They sounded like growing thunder.

"Anything else, signore?" with uneasiness the radio operator waited.

"Inform him that we are heading one Km due South to DZ, our drop zone "Pink Flamenco", I have already briefed him on that position. Our boys are still out there. Your extraction will be immediate after our own pickup. *Be ready.* Give me the radio, further in, it might work better. I'll need it then to speak with the extraction force. Right soldier, get going and..."

"Signore?"

"Good luck." Trentino smiled calmly.

"Godspeed, signore." And with a short salute, the soldier was off like a wildcat, taking with him explicit instructions for the commander in charge, Colonel Nabeel Khosrau.

"Christopher! Haven't you found this thing yet?" Trentino asked.

"What about Mathieson? He needs my help, major?" he said, ignoring the officer's demand.

"Help him once we get picked up. We'll drop in on the top of the Nest. Mathieson will be waiting for us there."

"The Nest?" asked Barbaro.

"The Temple." Trentino snapped.

"He won't last." Christopher said, thinking of Mathieson.

Christopher knew the major was waiting for him to move. He had very little time left. *I cannot do this anymore, I can't!* Christopher was at his breaking point.

"Come on, signore, snap out of it!" Trentino said, seeing the scientist's internal struggle.

Where is it? Christopher nodded smartly, his mind kick-starting again like his heart, the adrenaline pumping faster, sending more colour back into his face. Under severe pressure, he was in danger of panicking.

The flight or fight response kicked in and he knew this was his last chance. He lifted another heavy tarpaulin, and peered underneath. *There it was!*

By chance or by design, there it was, his environmental crate. He knew it contained the *"Oncol Safe Pod"*.

With relief flooding through his veins and the pod positioned securely as it should be inside, Christopher pulled away the tarpaulin.

"Ah, this is it! This is definitely it!" The pod was synthesised using a light rigid semi-carbon material, and it made the black casing super-hard. Eagerly looking inside, he took a sharp breath in. Something was wrong.

He examined the chamber indicators. *Oh no! Something is seriously wrong here!* He observed its status. *Amber!*

"What's up?" Trentino asked.

"It is still intact, however, I expected it to be either broken or on the green, not on amber?" Amber meant the seal was open.

"So?" Trentino challenged, "Is this not what you seek?" he demanded.

"What do you mean, Christopher?" Barbaro interrupted.

Trentino and the other soldiers were becoming more anxious. They wanted to leave the area but were being held back as they watched Christopher pressing a few buttons on the pod, as he pressed in the code to open the secure container.

The samples were inside, but, the indicator status on amber meant that the fine delicate balance inside the pod had been disturbed, and the environment inside was no longer acclimatised as it should be. Chris's eyes searched for a clue on the electronic log seen on the LCD display. He nodded and confirmed it had already been opened by someone else, today.

He looked around in hope the link had been dropped, but he could only draw one conclusion.

"It has been stolen," he stated, staring at the major. It was obvious by who. *Mashir!*

"What!" Trentino needed answers too.

"The "Link of Osleiotect"" he paused with a tightness in his throat, "the link is not here, it is gone, major."

"What! Check it again!" Barbaro demanded.

"We must get back to the Temple, major. I think Mashir, no, *I know* that our ever so trusting Colonel Nabeel Khosrau has stolen the link, the 'Link of Earth and Light'. It must be him!" Christopher's face was a deathly white.

Distracted, Trentino listened but his attention was on the forest.

What is that movement at the far side of those trees? Something is out there and that noise, that cracking of branches. It's not Colonnello Rossi. He's always silent in motion. The Chameleon makes no sound.

The major was completely unaware of his superior officer's murderous death by HSALS SLAUGOHTŔ. A black mood came over him.

"We have company." Being outside the Temple, the powerful and more conventional analogue Radio began crackling into action. "Phoenix to Buzzard One, Phoenix to Buzzard One, do you copy, over?" his steady and calm tone broke through the airwaves.

"Buzzard One to Phoenix, we copy you. Molto bene, good to hear from you again, Phoenix!" the muffled voice of a pilot breaking was mixed with music in the background. Trentino could hear the wailing ghost-strings of a British rock group. "Buzzard One to Phoenix what is your operational status? Over." the pilot asked.

"Phoenix to Buzzard One, Phoenix needs immediate "evac" from rendezvous point Pink Flamenco. In addition, there are other fledglings waiting for pickup on the top of the Nest. I repeat more fledglings are on the Nest and waiting for pickup. We have not secured the Golden Egg. Over."

Trentino and the others were watching the forest, alert and wary.

"Buzzard One to Phoenix, how many fledglings are there ready to fly? Over." the pilot tried to ascertain his pickup.

"Two fledglings are here, one other Phoenix plus an overseas bird plus me, that's five birds in total. We are on our way to pick-up, Pink Flamenco. Only two other fledglings are inside the Nest, referring to Harjit and Mathieson. One is badly wounded, possible contagion and needs immediate medical attention. Phoenix and Eagles are waiting inside the Nest, their wings are good. Over."

"Has Osprey landed on the Nest, over?" the airman enquired.

"Negative, Buzzard One, Osprey has not landed, its wings may be broken. No flight plan for Osprey at this time." Trentino was gritting his teeth.

The major knew the odds were stacking against Colonel Rossi, as the drums rolled ever closer. *He's late and will be left behind. Bloody orders. This is a shit life,* thought Trentino, realising there was a good chance now that Osprey would have to go it alone.

"Affirmative on that Phoenix, understood." The pilot's voice sure, "We have just picked up your "e-Buoy" at LZ, Pink Flamenco meaning the helicopter knew exactly where his men were to be found. "Buzzard One E.T.A. there in twenty minutes. Copy?"

"Copy." Trentino replied.

"Buzzard Two, I repeat, Buzzard Two is heading directly to the Nest on reconnaissance and will be at the Nest first, E.T.A, less than ten. Copy."

"Copy on that Buzzard One. Buzzard One, there are unknown birds to be returned to the Hatchery from the Nest. Can you accommodate extra? Over?" The pilot was aware of the additional foreign UMCAA troops and understood they might need a ride back to the air-forces main base, code-named, "the Hatchery".

"Affirmative, Phoenix, if Osprey is not ready to fly, we can pick up your extra birds and fly them all to the Hatchery, safe and sound. Over," he confirmed immediately.

"Buzzard One, be aware that this area is compromised, and poachers are in the wild with deadly force. Copy."

"Copy that. We are prepared to use deadly force." He was ready to attack if need be. "You should know that both Buzzards have lost long-distance satellite communications with "Apostle" since arriving in this region," the pilot advised. "Apostle will not know our flight paths or status until after your mission extraction. Over."

"Affirmative, Buzzard One. Over." The major was glad to know that Apostle was wingless, and that heavy firepower was on its way. "LZ is clear for landing. Copy?" All they had to do was reach "Pink Flamenco" in one piece. Trentino for once felt that fortune was turning in his favour.

"Copy on that, Intel. Stay safe, Phoenix. This is Buzzard One, over and out." The pilot smiled confidently and closed transmission.

Capitano Eliyah Bonifacio, the pilot captain, immediately turned up the music to hear better. "The Stones". *Ah, perfect for flying!* The Buzzard dropped altitude to smoothly hug the treetops, while accelerating faster. The captain switched on automatic kill mode.

****

Prime Centurion Kgnash's Bloodhort had been standing ready, and assembled in square formations within the forest.

It had taken two days to assemble and organize his spearhead legion of Preyweeps in the rainforest. Primus was sent in the smaller Ráevil strike force to measure Osleiotect resistance. Once again, he would re-establish their power on this outpost. The Citadel on Osleiotect was ready to fall.

For this purpose, Primus Kgnash reflected on his lord and master's history and previous overthrow and subjugation of this part of Osleiotect. His master could never forget the importance of its link and as foretold, the gateway again had been opened.

Unshackled by time, his species would be able to come and inevitably claim it. The timing right for the Temple to reappear, and with the sun's rise to be misaligned inside the obelisk allowing the darkness to take hold. The Link taken by the humans allowed it to appear like a beacon. The link, like a living thing had been waiting through generation to generation and untold aeons to pass, for fate would now play its part in the future of the cosmos. The waiting was over. *Again, the Prophecy!*

Centurion Primus Kgnash was born at the right time to rise through the ranks and become Primus. Selected by his master, he welled in arrogant superiority, watching his mighty legion, with this purpose always in mind.

It is I, Primus Kgnash, "The Chosen" to return to this outpost. The Bastion of Nelumakragasian is ready for taking. I will then take the great power held inside there and keep it for my master!

Primus then studied the human weapon taken from a dead Swiss guardsman, the NATO 7.62x51mm calibre machine gun, swivelling the 700 rounds a minute weapon in his evil-looking claws. *Mmm, a strange-looking fire tube.* Sticking the rail under his armpit and quickly taking aim upwards into a sparse tree, he gave it a sharp long burst.

FRRRRRRRRRRRRRAK!

Three trapped monkeys quickly dropped onto the forest floor, bouncing like rubber balls. The primates all suddenly released from their lives. The Primus could use any weapon. Born to kill, born to conquer; he was not impressed.

"Bach!" he spat in disgust at the puny firetube. "No, we enjoy killing slow and close. Do we not, my fighting legion?" he hollered at them, throwing the human weapon away, as he raised his double-edged battle-axe in his clenched claw

The legion was immediately energised. He did not need these Osleiotectian killing machines. HSALS SLAUGOHTŔ had returned. The forest erupted like a volcano, sending blood-curdling calls throughout the forest.

The humans could not hear their voices or their calls of war, but the animals could—the few left alive, the ones that were in hiding after the stampede — they could hear their unnatural toned frequencies.

All indigenous animals sensed a devilry at work here from these gelid beasts, those that had not escaped, tuned in and kept quiet. The animals could hear the alien communication and foreign pitch, and it drove them mad. For some, it was too much and they broke out in panic, but were soon killed, while others hurtled themselves with insanity into rocks or blindly into trees. This was the same fate destined for Humankind.

Primus called to his legion, "Sound your horns and beat your drums, we are going to war my HSALS SLAUGOHTŔ!" He then turned to his subordinate. "Praefect, take your new cohort and move it to the North East. Avoid the approaching Demongoyle Bog," he warned. "I will take my Bloodhort North and West to MalisIblis. Go!"

Ready with his main force of HSALS SLAUGOHTŔ, Primus set out to kill, his battle legion shouting and banging shields amid the horns and drums of war. His blood thirsty legionaries marching off in fast formations, breaking and killing everything that trod in their path, with the drums of death rolling on before them.

****

Out on patrol, a soldier caught a peculiar movement at the tree line, a flurry of activity close to him. He warned the others.

"What is that?" he whispered, anxiously peering into the foliage. The guardsman instinctively crouched as did the others. They were acutely aware of rustling noises of bushes and trees. Further on, there seemed to be more activity happening on the South perimeter.

Trentino's small group automatically dropped low and tight. Hidden below the dense foliage, their survival instinctive. The air felt electric, and the men waited there silently for a short moment, when all hell broke loose.

Suddenly, out from the forest, hundreds upon hundreds of creature soldiers started pouring in from all around the perimeter. A sea of huge bodies was seen sprinting at the Temple, when suddenly, countless numbers went crashing right past them. The group was hiding and as luck would have it, these warriors were ordered not to stop. The enemy had only one thought in mind. Take the Temple.

Trentino's team had been completely cut-off. He and his men were lying concealed. All choice of return was gone, and the horde was charging the Temple. There was nothing else to do for the moment other than watch and hope to God that they remained unnoticed.

It all looked so surreal. Nobody could quite believe it! The warriors wore black helmets with various designs on them, some made with small pointed spikes on top. What they had in common was their red claw ensign.

One fanatical warrior carried a long flagpole, and was waving it wildly. The flag had a thick black border, a green-brown background splashed with thin yellow zigzags, and it also displayed a blood-red claw ensign.

These black chainmail-clad Devils were sweeping onto the great stone terraces, starting their unstoppable climb. The safe perimeter and Temple was awash with black and green bodies, when suddenly, heavy machine guns began spitting out fire and death into the invaders.

****

The standard of HSALS SLAUGOHTŔ was raised high, waving furiously in the air. It was no coincidence that the same standard was being discussed by two young friends in far off Scotland; right now, the boys were looking at it with scepticism above the village monument. They could not know or guess of its true significance as the horde scaled the at this same moment Temple thousands of miles away.

Its importance was completely unknown, just like that queer old caretaker who watched over the Prophet Monument where the flag was already flying. The old man thought to be eccentric, or at best, weird was shunned by the villagers. The village folk would say he was nothing more than an "old crank", and to stay away from him. So, there it was flying high in semi-darkness that late afternoon, an outlandish standard flapping resolutely and in solitude on top of the Prophet Monument.

As the battle began in South-America, in Mauchline, that tranquil Scottish village—where nothing much happened—would someday soon pay a heavy price for its innocence.

The last time conflict came to the village was hundreds of years before, way back in the Seventeenth Century and in the days of the Reformation, in sixteen eighty-five, where five covenanters were hung from the gibbet, including the poor boy, John Bruning. He said nothing of God's Link to his captor and judge, General William Drummond, commander of the Kings Arms in Scotland. The general had heard of a rumour and talk of a relic—an object with awesome powers. The general wanted it for his King.

In those protester days of the covenanters, known in a grim period of history as the "Killing Times", the boy was put mercilessly to death by the Highland troops. With his death, the secret of the Holy Bond died with him. His silence saved the whereabouts of its keeper, a tall pilgrim who had come to stay at his home. The boy had seen this Holy man's sacred object without his permission and for this indiscretion, the boy swore a bond of silence to the pilgrim until he died.

Today, more plans of conquest were afoot and this time, from a different enemy.

The reason was the same.

To possess the Link to God!

It was late in the afternoon, when after school, the two boys were walking up the road towards the Prophets Monument, stopping to watch an unknown flag blowing wildly on the tower top. Teenagers, Scott and Cammy looked up foolhardily, wondering why it was not the Saltire. But the legend was much older than this mark of Scotland. It was born from a myth, and spanned longer than only three or four centuries. Oh, yes! The myth was much, much older. The world gradually awoke to a new threat and by the end of that year, even here in that remote village, like the Temple of MalisIblis thousands of miles away, Mauchline too would come of age.

****

Meanwhile, back inside the MalisIblis vale, death and desperation was being dealt out in every direction from the Temple stockade. The defenders were again sending rocket-propelled grenades and other high explosives down into the midst of the devilish enemy. Once again, these hideous hordes of HSALS SLAUGOHTŔ were scaling the steps against Humanity. These huge chainmail-clad warriors were climbing fast, establishing a quick foothold on the stone Terraces, with one thing in mind: Death to the Humans! Man's Armageddon had begun.

In reply to the hail of bullets chewing them up, they sent masses of black bolts through the air from archers below. The archers wore their black chainmail and dark green tunics. A yellow crossbow ensign was stamped on their helmets and told of their vital importance.

The crossbows seemed to have an outward sharp concave curve at each end of the crossbar with no strings. The projectile twanged sharply on rapid release.

What a paradox it all seemed to be. The crossbow insignias seen on the shoulder pads of the Swiss guardsmen, with their own brown crossbow badge with its red scribed and gold edging bearing the immortal words "Croce di Luce", pitted against the darkness of HSALS SLAUGOHTŘ's archers.

The forces of light and dark. This old enemy once again battling for supremacy, and so it was that an irresistible onslaught came upon these united Christian and Islamic defenders.

Some soldiers were killed instantly. Their bodies were torn apart by these black energy bolts. This high velocity weaponry was most effective against the defenders.

Earth filled bags surrounded the defenders in their nests and heavy machine guns blasted at the easy targets. There were so many. The barriers held back the energy from the bolts, but bit-by-bit, the soil-filled bags were torn to pieces. Pinned down by the invaders, the human garrison returned fire as best as they could, watching their demise unfolding in horror.

Explosions from hand-grenades fell all around the besieged Temple, the humans burning and maiming these vile creatures as they climbed higher and higher. Their chainmail was not enough protection against high explosives. The noises resonated war and death throughout the rainforest.

Bam, Bam, Bam, Bam!

The gun sounds echoed between blasts.

Bam, Bam, Bam, Bam, Bam, Bam!

The noises of contiguous belt-fed mechanics spewed spent cartridges like a rain in the clattering bursts of heavy machine gun fire. Each second told of death in delivery, firing again and again, strafing left and right, with wide fireballs seen surrounding their lit-up nozzles like clouds of fire.

In the echo of each burst, more of the enemy fell like packs of cards, defending gunners and concentrating their deadly firepower across the central steps. So many kept coming. The warriors' suicidality closing in towards this lethal arsenal. As they desperately leaped up, they were suddenly blown away.

Wild shouts were heard from both sides. Some yells were that of orders from macabre commanders, remaining unheard by the human ears, since their alien vocal cords were set at pitches the men could not hear.

This was unnerving to the soldiers of "light", who could not believe their ears. The men could not hear a word or call of pain. Only the drums and clash of arms. The whole attack was bizarre. Inhuman.

These evil foes were being strategically guided by their Primus and subordinate commanders, each using a natural and unique organic auditory system, channelling their commands like an integral communications device. Always in continual contact with each legionnaire, this instant feed enabled them to act immediately.

It was obvious to all the defenders that there were just too many of the relentless Devils. The colonel stared at them and could see that his combined forces would soon be overpowered. It was an awesome sight to behold, dreadful as it was — a sea of black and green bodies moving everywhere. The commander knew there were only so many bullets and a limited number of grenades. Khosrau watched the crazy scene. Some of the weapons were already beginning to melt and jam.

Allah help us!

"Mashir! Mashir! What can I do?" Harjit was yelling at Nabeel. The girl unexpectedly appeared from inside. Having had one look, she began shouting over the battle, "Tell me!". The girl looked down at the frightening sight, shaking her head watching the maniacal creatures jumping high and scaling the stone steps to get to them.

Harjit took a deep breath and walked calmly over to stand beside the Colonel Nabeel Khosrau, the commander.

"Go back inside, Harjit, Mathieson will need you. Please Harjit, this is no place for you," he said under immense pressure; observing the current gains made against his defence. His voice pressing. Nabeel hoped that at least she would survive a little longer.

"Mathieson." Harjit swallowed hard.

"Yes?" Nabeel took a deep breath in, the colour draining from his face.

"Is dead."

His eyes welled up with tears. More bad news!

Surrounded by the enemy on this stone island, Colonel Nabeel Khosrau looked away from Harjit, shocked. Closing his tear-filled eyes, he called out in pain and despair.

"At what price!" he yelled outwards at the forest and the blackened fog, "AT WHAT PRICE?" his tone was defiant to God. Then, opening his angry eyes to stare upwards, "ALLAH!" his voice echoed in the din of battle, "ALLAH, HEAR US CALLING YOU!" The men looking around to see their commander standing with his hand in the air!

"Is this the price we have to pay?"

Suddenly, Nabeel's brown eyes turned downwards to look with deep vehemence on these accursed things who were rampaging upwards towards them. His knuckles were white with hatred. They would pay heavily.

****

"Harjit, I plead with you, please. You must take two of my men and go inside the Temple. Hide." His tone was rock hard and steady, "My men are loyal, and they will defend you until the end." Our extraction will not reach us in time. "I will stay and hold these apparitions at bay as long as I can."

"They will come." She looked at him. Was he saying goodbye?

"Dear Harj, you see, this way you might stand a chance."

The colonel positioned himself into a fighting stance and immediately began firing his automatic machine gun. His heart hardened upon seeing them this close. His knuckles whitened again as he gripped the weapon.

FRRRRRRRRRAK! FRRRRRRRRRAK! FRRRRRRRRRAK!

His machine gun blasted into the monsters scaling the steps below, as he waited for her reply.

"No," she replied firmly, "There is no way, no way that I'm going back inside that place! I know what lurks inside there. I will never return."

Casting her a fraught look, he could see that her plucky posture was unbreakable, and he smiled. Nabeel was proud that she would want to stand with him, Hindu and Muslim together and united in the eyes of God.

"Then, do this for me." Nabeel requested.

"Yes?"

"Right then, get up to the top of the Temple. I will come with you!" Nabeel turned to the mixed soldiers near him.

"And your men, what of them?" she asked.

"My proud Scimitar guardians and these men too. The men of the valiant Crossbow Regiment." He looked at them. "Soldiers, it has been a great honour and privilege."

"Sarhang, what do you bid?" one of the Scimitar guardians asked, knowing that no less than martyrdom would do.

"Cover us while we get to the top. Allah willing, men of Islam and of Christ, for he is our saviour, that the Helicopter arrives in time. Hold them back and we will lay suppressing fire for you to follow us. So, as soon as we start shooting, get your asses up to me."

"Give me a weapon," Harjit demanded. The girl was quickly handed a machine gun. The men immediately shouted a call of solidarity and respect to him and her, and in ultimate defiance to the black forces.

"Before I go, I have a surprise." Nabeel said, looking directly at corporal Jansher Dilawar, and his Scimitar guardians. Give me a hand with those oil drums."

"Sarhang," Dilawar affirmed in a resolute tone.

Nabeel Khosrau, a meticulous planner as always, was ready with a well thought out strategy. The men with weapons kept their shooting to the minimum, while the others rallied together to help roll out as many wooden drums with what contained a light viscous oil like petroleum, drums from inside the Temple. Oil that had been stockpiled by its previous occupants. They worked hard to move them quickly out from the Temple entrance.

"Cease firing men!" Dilawar called the order to the defenders to let the creatures get closer.

Puncturing the sides, the liquid began pouring out, and each drum was sent reeling down the stone steps. The drums battered down, striking the brutes away. The fluid splashed on down, some of the drums breaking and bursting open and covering the Terraces below in all directions. The stinking liquid was unavoidable, and it coated everything.

The creatures were about thirty feet below them now. The men waited for Nabeel. A single shot was all it took to start the conflagration.

Whoosh!

Immediately, flames were sent leaping over the fuel-filled steps, with much of the top parts of the stone suddenly ablaze.

The drums of flammable liquid continued their way quickly bouncing and cascading downwards. Each one rapidly shot by Khosrau and Dilawar. The drums instantly exploded and ripped through the assailants.

They could see the creatures screaming in silent agony, all caught inside fierce flames and black smoke. The plan was working.

"Now!" Khosrau ordered Dilawar. Corporal Dilawar to send a signal to men in key positions to pull hidden levers inside the Temple opening secret Vat holes in the stone on each side of the Temple. Sticky fluid released moved fast like lava flows that ignited instantly into high flames. Everything caught below would die.

The fluid coming from huge vats of fuel used by previous occupants discovered by Khosrau's troops. The heat forces the garrison to seek shelter feeling an immense heat on their faces. The inferno was right in front of them, yet they still could not believe that they could not hear these creatures suffering as they died.

Retribution smiled at Nabeel, and the soldier were satisfied with his planning, seeing as the assault stopped.

Ah, the smell of oil and burning flesh! Oh, yes, they can feel pain! It is a glorious and awful sight and one befitting Hell itself, thought Khosrau, narrowing his eyes at the barbeque below. He knew it would not last long. *And, that one's for Mathieson!*

"Come on, Harjit, this is our chance. Follow me!" The enemy advance was held in check for the moment. This was their last hope. Harjit and Nabeel set out for the top in a final climb.

****

Dormant in this world for all these years and surrounded in darkness, something horrible suddenly stirred—a deep rooted evil. It pulled itself up and rose slowly, with its huge body creaking, out of the pit from where it had been dwelling for so long. Heading for the world above and emerging out from within the dark fog that had kept it companion. Its sickness pouring out into the rainforest. The fog was the blackest and thickest right here. It started moving slowly and deliberately inside the forest. It was coming, as told in the Legend.

Immense trees that had stood here for countless centuries were slowly pushed over and out the way, felled by this immense thorny bodied creature. The thing, powerful and mighty, stood up, and as it did so, burst through several canopies like an explosion, breaking everything around it.

Its colossal body was now standing fully erect amongst the trees, with a repressed rage in its makeup. Waiting not a moment longer, it hurdled through the forest with a fury of an untamed beast, pulling out smaller trees by the root and breaking them in half as it went in fury, as it smashed a slow and deliberate pathway through the forest. This creature, its form on Earth, a giant being! It began searching once again for *the Link* known as, the "Link to Osleiotect"

****

CHAPTER XVIII

LORD SMITE

"This is Buzzard Two, do you copy, Nest? This is Buzzard Two, to Nest, do you copy? Over." The pilot's calm voice broke through the U/VHF radio reception.

There was smoke everywhere and some fires were still roasting the enemy on the steps below. The conflagration was not enough.

"My God!" the radioman said in disbelief. A fellow soldier was almost falling over, scrambling to continue an insane shooting gallery from the gunner at a renewed assault on the Temple! Once again, the creatures were everywhere.

"This is Eagle, this is Eagle! Come in, this is Eagle, do you copy?" He could only hear the loneliness of static. "This is Eagle, do you copy, Buzzard Two. Over."

"We copy you, Eagle! Glad to hear you. Over!" the pilot replied. The shouting on the Temple was ecstatic as they knew help was on the way. The pilot continued. "On approach to your Nest, E.T.A. five minutes! What is that black smoke coming from your area, Eagle?" The pilot's "IHADSS" equipment was projecting flight sensors onto his helmet display.

In his immediate view, the airman could see the thick black smoke dead ahead, rising from the tops of the trees. The chopper was coming in low and in rapid approach, and the pilot quickly switched to use his forward looking "FLIR" system to see through the smoke. Its infra-red camera instantly allowed him to see better.

Numerous bodies moved quickly all over the Temple slopes and the pilot saw what appeared to be a fire-fight. He immediately checked all his weaponry, as the chopper went in faster.

Skimming close to the treetops, the weird claw like wisps of fog lifted from below the canopy, and began reaching upwards, trying to grab at their fast-moving underbelly. In such a low flight path, the cockpit pilots saw the uncanny fog passing underneath. The pilots stared blankly at each other, holding back their misgivings while maintaining their route. Both men were vaguely aware that the fog was not natural, and evasively lifted the helicopter to a slightly higher elevation.

For miles around, the attentive pilots could see many islands of bunching branches and bits of treetops submerged in places, and surrounded in others by the curious black patchwork, as more and more fog appeared to float up and down from a devilish black soup underneath. The whole spectacle was not what they had expected. The place looked so alien.

"Buzzard Two, this is Eagle! Your bird better be ready to fly faster, Signore! These things are all over us! Hurry for God's sake, hurry!" the soldier shrieked into the radio.

The radioman stared around desperately, then quickly grabbed onto the heavy machine gun's trigger, swivelled the weapon around and fired in blasts.

Bam! Bam! Bam! Bam!

The pneumatic sounds exploded and echoed extreme violence from his weapon, while he and the remaining garrison on top of the first tier began fighting off increasing numbers of these huge warriors.

"What things, Eagle? Over. Eagle, Eagle, do you copy?" The pilot stole a worried look at his co-pilot, "My fuck! Phew!" Knowing men would be dying, the pilot accelerated the chopper faster towards the Temple! Meanwhile, the communication device was still open. The aircrew heard it all.

FRRRRRRRRRAK! FRRRRRRRRRAK! FRRRRRRRRRAK!

Machine guns blasted left and right, again and again.

The machine gun post was completely overrun. The gruesome fighters were running all over the first tier. Fanatical for blood and flesh, they killed as they scaled upwards.

The pilot and co-pilot maintained contact with the dead, listening in with horror, picturing the running mayhem as it happened, and viewing everything in their DVO system.

FRRRRRRRRRAK! FRRRRRRRRRAK!

"They are on us! They are on us!" a Swiss guardsman warned.

The soldier was quickly distracted as he brought around his pistol to meet a huge warrior charging at him.

The brute ran along the terrace wall. The soldier dropped his radio and quickly taking aim, fired his semi-automatic handgun straight at it. The pilots could still hear the killing.

Bang! Bang! Bang! Bang! Bang!

"We are cut off! They are everywhere!" the guardsman screamed to everyone.

"Soldiers, fall back! Get inside the Temple!" The pilot's heard another soldier called out orders and they gathered that a last handful of soldiers were forced to retreat into the Temple. The soldiers quickly left their heavy machine guns behind, nozzles still smoking.

By now in the thousands, the hoards swarmed upwards on all sides! Of the Temple, with hundreds already cramming their way inside the front entrance, and running through the many corridors and system of passageways like bloodhounds after the retreating few soldiers. The majority of HSALS SLAUGOHTŔ swept upwards on all sides, and headed for the top. A last few humans remained. There would be no escape, none.

****

Watching from his hiding place, Christopher could not believe his horrified eyes, as he watched uncountable numbers speeding right past him, heading up towards the Temple. His position with the handful of soldiers seemed masked for the moment, as more and more Bloodhort warriors charged on.

He carefully watched the spectacle through the thicket. He and the other men lay unmoving and as silent witnesses to the surrounding battle.

The depleted garrison, under severe pressure from all directions, were being pushed back up to the top tier, when unexpectedly, they began observing lots of oil drums rolling down into the warriors. The barrels started exploding into flames like mini-volcanos, roasting hundreds of creatures and engulfing most of the South-side.

"This is no coincidence. It is a well organised attack." Trentino stared in grim acknowledgement.

"Come on, let's try to get over. They're distracted." Christopher was about to rise and run for the Temple but Trentino grabbed his arm and pulled him abruptly back down.

"Quiet, signore." The major whispered, putting his finger to his lips. It was hopeless. There was nowhere to run.

"Harjit." Christopher swallowed hard.

The attackers quickly regrouped and waited until some of the flames died away. In minutes, they renewed their frontal attack.

Some had already moved in from the left and right ends to the South side at the top of the first tier of the Temple, outflanking and compromising the defenders. Soon after, distant explosions could be heard coming from inside the tunnel entrance, followed by more sounds of automatic staccato fire.

The attack was back on. Their vile bodies smothered over the terraces as the group helplessly watched the unstoppable surge. Christopher felt nauseated seconds before experiencing an out of body experience.

Echoes of hand grenade explosions could be heard coming from further inside the Temple. The chase was on. After this, too far in and too deep, no further sounds could be heard from there at all—absolutely nothing.

Christopher was caught somewhere in a macabre dreamland, a silent onlooker, when reality cut into his catatonic mind. Panic caught a hold of him, when he realised that these depraved creatures had reached the top.

Oh, my God, Harjit! "Give me your binoculars, soldier, *NOW!*" he demanded, grabbing them snappishly from the man and immediately focusing in. There she was, a small image jumping around! "Harjit! Harjit!" Chris screamed in desperation!

Blind to their own safety, watching the enemy piling over the top, too many to count, their huge numbers overwhelming any remnants of human resistance. Christopher watching, horror struck seeing Harjit and Mashir and a few others avoiding best they could these attackers, calling out warnings in despair! The Temple had fallen.

****

On the Temple top, Colonel Nabeel Khosrau looked desperately all around him, knowing his mission was doomed. He had failed. More bloodthirsty beasts appeared over the rim, so he quickly tossed a grenade into the amassing black helmets. The first warrior completely disintegrated into a mess of tissue and blood, bone and body parts. The defenders were ready for more, as sizzling bits of warrior flesh came raining down with guts and gore.

Other horrid apparitions were coming towards Colonel Khosrau on his right side, but the commander was unaware of two other adversaries charging in at him from his left flank.

Harjit, who was standing close to him, inhaled deeply to get as much air as possible, then locked her jaw at their despairing plight. She felt no mercy towards these filthy creatures.

"Mashir, look out!" Harjit warned, as she moved like lightning and stepped in and with her fast wielding double-edged axe, coming between the creature and Nabeel. With determination and inherent bravery, she swiftly brought her axe down with brutal violence, deflecting one of the thrusting tridents in a quick sweeping arc and deflecting it, and enough to jam it then sparks sent flying, metal on metal! The middle spear point on top of the Battle Axe's head rasping in towards the Warrior! Her weapon's tip blazing in a deep Royal blue easily penetrating the creatures' body and puncturing its green Tunic. Using her shoulder and putting her back into it, she kept on going, breaking through its black Chainmail and instantly bursting its internal organs! Blood shooting everywhere! Harjit no more the girl, transformed into Harjit, the warrior.

Her technique not finished, pulling the axe out, swinging it around in a wide arc over her head and brought it down hard, catching the other assailant. Both creatures were down.

Harjit the warrior smiled at having taken control. Her axe's blade was illuminated wildly with some unexplained white luminosity, its sharp edge gleaming with a thin blue inner band.

"Phew! Damn too close, Harjit!" he said, looking relieved at the girl. Nabeel saw something in her he had not seen before — her spirit. The girl was more alive now than ever before. "You fight bravely. Thank you." Nabeel nodded with respect.

Their religious differences held no barrier, no obstacle and at last they were unified! The Muslim, Hindu, Christian, Islam and Judaism religions, some of the ancient texts with Buddhist punctuations bonding the Prophecy. Now, everyone was brothers in arms, all fighting the same enemy, all united against some nameless tyranny that threatened all life.

****

"Sarhang, Sarhang, signore, we are completely overrun!" a Christian soldier shouted to the garrison commander.

"Get over to the altar, soldier! Everyone! Everyone to the Altar!" Nabeel commanded. "And Harjit, that means you too! Come on, move it, NOW!" Nabeel directed the girl and the remaining survivors.

Insanity was gaining ground on the Temple top. The creatures gathered on top with their malicious tridents, swords and maces—their weapons of choice. The survivors reached the altar and waited, watching on helplessly.

As black smoke continued to billow upwards, they readied themselves. The reek of burning still rose above the Temple. Green tunics appeared everywhere over the rim. Despite their size, the creatures were very agile.

"Where have these foul creatures come from, Mashir?" Harjit still wanted to understand.

"From *Nowhere!*" corporal Jansher Dilawar shouted.

"He might be right about that," Colonel Khosrau guessed, with the Prophecy in mind.

In an instant, a whirlwind of hot air pressurised heavily downwards onto them, hunching their backs. Everyone was caught in a huge vortex of swirling air. Thunderous noises deafened them and flattened their voices. The turbulence forced them to crouch protectively while looking up. It felt as though they were inside a man-made wind-tunnel.

To the surprise of everyone, the impressive noises and power came from twin Rolls-Royce Jewel Engines. They could not believe their eyes as they watched the fast-moving rotor blades of a helicopter move above them. The defenders could not hear themselves shout let alone think inside this rush of hot air, but what luck, "Buzzard Two" had arrived.

****

The pilots of Buzzard Two unperturbed, pirouetted briefly above them, assessing the survivors' status and enemy assault, then pushed forward sweeping smoothly on between the huge stone monoliths at the Temple corners. The chopper then curved steeply and rapidly upwards in a tight circle to the shouts of encouragement. It began rampaging through the air!

The pentagonal observatory building behind the was a five-faced pyramid, with a large-foot base, the observatory was designed with a flattop. It seemed to be an ideal landing platform for a helicopter like this.

The Mangusta, a two-pilot attack helicopter, typically used as an escort or as a scout aircraft for close sorties, had quickly identified this potential landing area.

On the Temple, the sacrificial altar was set between two tall stone-carved pillars. The stones bore macabre drawings of humans being offered to some forgotten God in the sky. A long stone table with squat legs was set solid into position at the centre of the altar. These legs, about waist-height stood on top of tiered square slabs, with each slab being one foot thick.

Here is where the defenders stood, with weapons ready, eyes staring everywhere at the surrounding enemy quickly closing in. This place was their refuge, their last stand.

On top of the final third step of the altar, was the cold sacrificial table on which an evil stone-plate had been made, specifically for extracting a victim's heart. Unless the Mangusta quickly destroyed the enemy, then death by sacrifice might likely be their fate too!

A tall stone monolith towered over the head of the altar. It was an integral part of the overall construction of worship. Near its top, a hole existed in the stone, which was once used to focus the dawn of sunlight. Now, it was replaced by a black hole, which was set permanently inside this stone circle like a dark eye into another world. This hole contained "dark matter", which was unable to absorb, reflect or emit light. This freak of nature was held inside the stone circle, and had become an integral part of the monolith, its purpose unknown to the defenders.

They could see the pilot's head watching them from inside his cockpit. Wearing his helmet, air supply mask and dark visor, the airman sat above the co-pilot. The co-pilot was positioned in the forward seat, in the gunner position. Both pilots observed the defenders desperate plight.

Buzzard Two's shark-like fuselage held a stub weapon carrying A500-030 Medusa - 91mm Rocket Wings and tandem stepped glass-in flat plated cockpits, giving the chopper a gigantic metal hornet appearance.

Now, the gunship was turning tightly and sweeping over the Battlefront.

****

"Open Fire! All flanks!" the pilot ordered sharply to the front gunner. The co-pilot responded immediately, steering and whirling his triple barrel 20mm Cannon turret, which was mounted under the chopper's nose, targeting its hi-tech weaponry onto the enemy and suddenly firing a fury that Hell would be proud of. Instantly, multitudes of devilish creatures began dancing a death of disintegration, limbs flying off, tissue and organs exploding violently like blood-filled balloons around the defenders.

Huge legionnaires kept pouring over the top of the Temple from all sides. So many came, and so many died. The number of gruesome creatures resembled a colony of locusts, climbing and jumping onto the top, like a macabre plague. The Mangusta targeted them head on, releasing its ferocious cannon arsenal. The pilots nodded their heads and watched their gruesome bodies crumbling into mush.

The chopper then stopped and waited, hovering for a few seconds while rotating at low levels above the Temple, shooting non-stop and wheeling around. Some of the creatures attempted to jump high, trying to catch the Mangusta.

The pilots quickly realised their immediate danger, and judging that if enough of these brutes were to attach, it might bring her down. Then, out of nowhere, one jumped onto the front windscreen, baring its teeth, trying to get at the pilots.

The pilot jerked his joystick, lifting and wobbling the aircraft just enough for the creature to slip and fall off, as the gunner blasted it with his barrel machine gun.

A little higher now and revolving in a central pivot position, the gunner quickly readjusted his aim and spat fire in bursts, clinically obliterating all the enemy around the defenders. It was an awful bloody spectacle to watch, cutting them all down, like taking a giant scythe and sweeping them all away.

"It's not big enough! It's not big enough!" Harjit kept calling out in despair, finding it hard to believe.

"It's a scout aircraft, a light attack gunship! A close quarter all-rounder, this is exactly what we need right now, Harj, a fast killing machine!"

Nabeel shouted back over the din, gasping at seeing its lethal handiwork!

"No, it's not! We need to get out of here, and right now!" Harjit was desperate to escape.

"Steady Harj, the larger utility helicopter cannot be far behind!" Colonel Khosrau tried to calm her. However, at this moment, Buzzard Two was heading for LZ Pink Flamenco first to pick up the others.

At close range like this, the helicopter was taking hits, the light armour struck with the high velocity black bolts from on and around the Temple.

The pilot's immediate answer was to swoop around and down, surgically removing all the new targets as he flew. Those that dared, dropped like flies, the Mangusta rapidly accelerating and flying right over the South wall, observing another mass of devil like creatures jumping up onto the Terraces and racing up the steps again.

Strange. To the pilot, it felt like he had been shooting for ages, not seconds. Trying to comprehend the scale of this macabre assault, he was sure that in less than twenty seconds, they had killed hundreds. When suddenly, all Hell broke loose. The captain quickly tapped the helmet of his co-pilot, catching his attention.

"Hey! Look at them!" The captain could not believe his eyes, as a thousand more suddenly emerged from the forest periphery. "It's a full-scale assault, shit!"

"This is fucking it!" said the co-pilot, targeting them with his Medusa missiles, and firing them into the devilish masses!

Great explosions began blasting all over the Terraces, while the defenders on top took cover.

Bewildering for the aircrew, the unearthly stonework remained undamaged, not even a scratch. Yet fire and brimstone dealt quick justice for these ungodly things. Their ignorance of the Temple's hardness was understandable; they knew nothing of its history and less of its construction. The stone type held together by a power bigger than bombs and bullets — a power much greater than anything they could ever imagine.

Immediately, as this repulse was taking place, some of the vile creatures automatically changed shape.

No amount of training could have prepared the Mangusta crew for this. The airmen watched as these bizarre creatures suddenly spun their capes around themselves into a protective sheet and the flexible material somehow formed into a solid cone shape container, like a metal wigwam.

This wrapped cloth had suddenly become each warrior's form of protection, its colour blending into the same shade of red stone exactly like the Terraces, and rapidly became a personal camouflage. Motionless, they were completely hidden and fully protected. Everything happened so fast before the airmen's astonished eyes. The thousands of creatures had suddenly disappeared.

"Die bastardos!" the gunner screamed at nothing, releasing a four round Spike ER Missile pack, then flying to each outer pylon and sending them crashing into the empty terraces below.

He quickly switched to his FLIR system (Forward Looking using Infra-Red Camera). "Where are they, signore?" the confused gunner asked his superior officer. "IR is not showing up anything."

"I don't know. Just keep shooting!" the first officer's frayed voice replied, his logic and training taking a confidence knock. "Give the steps another volley!"

"Affirmative, signore!" He released the rocket and both pilots watched as they smashed into the empty walls, frustrating him even more. The only dead bodies seen were the hundreds already lying there. Their firepower assault was now ineffective.

The airship quickly encircled the Temple. By now, most of the warriors were completely camouflaged. The Mangusta cannons blasted at a vanished enemy, ammunition ricocheting fire in all directions.

"Shall I give them the "hellfire" missiles for good measure, capitano?" The gunner waited calmly for confirmation, skilfully adjusting his weapons systems.

Unknown to the Mangusta crew, the creatures were still there, invisibly adhered like unmovable limpets, as if bonded into the stone. Even with the high explosive detonations, in this formation, they were not for shifting.

Gradually, the warriors would move, suddenly appearing and running, or leaping upwards in the direction of the Temple top. Those, the chopper easily sorted. Unfortunately, the Mangusta could only be in one place at a time. In this way, the enemy was always ascending, slowly but inexorably, moving upwards. Their sole purpose was to clear the Temple of humankind.

Others would randomly appear, releasing a bolt at the circling gunship and hitting the armoured exterior, then would vanish. The bolt an annoyance only because the armoured Mangusta could easily deflect these high velocity projectiles.

Changing tact, the captain moved the cyclic control forward, bringing the nose pitch down, while decreasing the chopper's collective control, dropping the Mangusta's power to lose altitude and thereby, increasing its airspeed.

This manoeuvre suddenly sent the gunship veering downwards, sweeping low and fast, and hugging at ground level next to base camp. Passing quickly between the forest on one side and the Temple on the other, the aircraft easily manoeuvred within the boundaries of the safe perimeter.

At this lower level, the infrared detectors illuminated objects on the ground, and immediately detected a cluster of four figures. The pilot looked down and was astonished at seeing four men.

The soldiers were crouching down in the shaking foliage, less than a stones-throw away. The chopper sped right past them and channelling below the treeline, swept along and blasted at anything that was not human. The captain tapped his co-pilot's helmet.

"There are soldiers hiding on the port-side back there!" the pilot advised, while the unstoppable helicopter continued its current manoeuvre, its flight path reaping more death through the perimeter.

"Affirmative, signore," the gunner concurred. "Signore! Signore, look!" the co-pilot shouted into his communication device. "Those creatures are attacking again! My God, hundreds!"

"Buzzard Two to Buzzard One! Buzzard Two to Buzzard One! Do you copy Buzzard One? Over." The captain of Buzzard Two reached out to forewarn the incoming aircrew. The frequencies, full of static noise, made communication difficult or non-existent. "Buzzard Two to—", the captain was caught mid-sentence, when suddenly, the trees exploded in towards them from the forest.

It was a force so colossal that it sent a wall of broken timber straight at them. This splintering eruption of trees, branches, bushes and dirt came hurdling and crashing into the side of the yawing Mangusta gunship.

Seconds after, a huge clearance abruptly appeared where the forest had been, its uprooting leaving a massive hole and black fog beyond. Then, an insane-looking beast filled the space.

Impossible! Yet they all could see it! A monster! A heinous and horrible thing, coming out and breaking through the perimeter. It was hurdling everything it had at the flying machine. The pilot automatically took evasive action. He pulled his airship away, and the Mangusta reared backwards.

With a fury unknown, the thing screamed at high pitch. This, they could hear. The devilish monster forced everyone in the forest to cover their ears as the sound was too painful. It had come from a place called, *Nowhere.*

The enraged beast powered up, and stretched high, then higher still. It appeared to be larger than a tower block. It was broad, with an awful convoluted wooden head. Its wide shoulders moved and wriggled like writhing snakes.

The creature's undefined form was changeable, it could take the form of a giant humanoid, all covered in un-shapely vine masses and waving branches. A monster with a warped torso, thick and twisted hamstring legs and thick and twisted bulging arms that flailed unpredictably around.

As it screeched and moved, the maniacal beast terrified everything.

As it moved, it pulled more clots of forest floor out of the ground with its rooted feet. Long roots writhed in every direction around its woody limbs. Many thick and thin tentacles with large sharp thorns kept whipping insanely around through the air. They were identical to those thorny vines that were seen climbing from the fissure walls.

An awesome sight indeed! The monster burst out of the forest, throwing its lethal mass of flailing vines in a rage. It seemed it had come out as if it had been watching from inside the forest — watching and waiting for the right moment; its timing set with purpose. With great strides, it quickly moved out after the low flying Mangusta.

****

"Fuck!" the pilot captain gasped, "What in God's name is it?"

The monster quickly swung its big woody arms, smashing violently downwards and narrowly missing them. The creature had been watching and waiting patiently in the trees for the Mangusta to sweep past. It did!

Fortunately, for the crew of the helicopter, their recovery was instant; strafing bullets defensively and yawing starboards. Then, another long, heavy and thorny vine smacked down again. It's heavy wooden tentacle battered down, making a massive trough, with mud going in every direction. The chopper barely escaped.

They couldn't believe what was happening. Yet all their onboard systems told them that it was real enough. The pilots were also acutely aware of the many movements of hostile activities around the Temple too. Recovering from their initial shock, they systematically computed their offensive possibilities once again.

The radar scanner inside his monitor helmet allowed him to see the Temple and terrain in shades of greys. The FLIR remained the same, showing only a few allied combat troops on the Temple top.

Switching onto the Radar ESA Vision Systems, he could clearly see the troops indicated by blue lined triangles and enemy targets indicated by red lined triangles. The mission critical elements could be seen inside a large 360-degree circle in shaded light green.

Suddenly, everything turned into a huge red area made up of multiple triangles, giving the monster a clearly defined 3D image. Danger. Dead ahead.

"Too close!" the pilot shouted. Their attention switched to the huge monster right in front of them, as the captain continued their evasive manoeuvre.

He was a skilful pilot, and the Mangusta was like an extension of his body, with the gunship going in reverse, and retreating while pitching upwards and gaining altitude. The chopper and the immediate forest were all destined for immanent destruction.

He turned off the ESA System to see what it really looked like. However, the monster blended into the environment too well, making it difficult to see.

Its body extended and retracted, and its branched tentacle-like vines wriggled and writhed around like the serpents of a Gorgon. Now, standing fully erect, the monster was blaring at them. Here at last in its true glory.

They saw it for what it was: wicked. A vile hideous monster mass with a horrible head attached to a huge body, with a distinction undefined. It bore what looked like many knotted rings or wrinkles around its wide round lifeless eyes.

It had only appeared seconds ago, but the Mangusta was already squaring up, right in front of this irate apparition. The beast was moving at them, and fast. This thing brought with it an evil that was deep-rooted — a wickedness from somewhere beyond this place, a place not human.

Everything about it was evil. Its hatred glared at them in total malice. Its black eyes staring hypnotically down at them and this, their manmade flying machine.

Opening its foul wooden mouth, it began releasing a wide woody unearthly howl, blowing a cold death towards the two captivated pilots.

"We're too close!" the co-pilot screamed. The A500 Mongoose was already blasting its cannon guns and locking its Medusa Missiles to terminate, but it was too late.

The Airmen looked at its foul bark fast moving past their eyes, as the Mangusta's altitude lifted faster and higher.

"Smite" had arrived! *The Prophecy.*

Peculiar and paradoxical, Smite's beautiful yellow flowers could be seen growing over some lengths of its flailing vine like-limbs, sending its vicious tentacles waving angrily around in the air. Its force easily felled trees in half. Where Smite stood, nothing was left intact. And for the lovely blossoms growing on the trees, these would all soon turn black.

Caught in the wrong position, the helicopter was still precariously too low and too close, its engines roaring to lift and pull away against this wailing beast's flailing limbs.

The Mangusta rose up and up and back down a few seconds more. Smite burst onto them like a tsunami. There was no doubt in their horrified minds that this monster intended to kill them.

With no time to think, let alone react, the thing screamed out another malevolence howl of immorality and death — the noise reverberating through the aircraft's body. Both pilots stared up helplessly in despair, confirming their proximity.

The monstrous creature's impassionate black eyes measured them coldly, while cruelly bringing its thick tearing limbs down hard, dropping the chopper. It's great ripping thorns opened the Mangusta like a tin opener, smashing right through their cockpit, sending the air attack gunship crashing into the ground.

Bellowing mightily at the devastation it had caused and the obliteration of Buzzard Two below it, the wrecked helicopter waited on the ground for Smite.

****

Just before Smite appeared.

This was the moment when the ill-fated Mangusta's flight path continued flying past the men lying concealed in the forest. The bloodthirsty warriors had already sensed their mighty Lord's imminent arrival, changing their tact into an offensive fighting machine, and again, assaulting the Temple. Their numbers too great to count, the legionnaires scaled the Temple walls right away and piled over the Temple top in vast numbers. On the top, the humans saw them coming.

"Things are not going too well, Harjit!" Mashir shouted, staring at them in despair, plainly seeing the marauders appearing from over the rim and from every direction.

"Mashir, those things are everywhere. What are they? What is this place?" she asked, shaking her head.

"We can't hold them." Nabeel knew it.

"I know."

Unexpectedly, from below, a cataclysmic noise erupted. It was the breaking of a mass of trees. This was the moment they first saw it.

From their high vantage point, the humans relegated to being spectators to a dreadfulness that had suddenly appeared—a massive creature exploding out from the forest next to the Mangusta. Timber and foliage was bursting in all directions! It was a nightmare.

Their minds were reeling in disbelief at the size of this thing as it burst through the open perimeter, highly aware of its environment and assimilating the immediate battlefront against humankind. Lord Smite, a super-being and highly intelligent, was engaged in its immediate attack while observing its own servants storm the Temple as it commanded.

Smite was enraged at the stunned flying machine. The Chopper floundered as the pilots locking the Mangusta's deadly payload in front of Smite's thorny arms.

Lord Smite howled triumphantly over humankind.

In the seconds before Smite appeared, something changed in the environment— something quite astonishing. Suddenly, the struggling human forces could hear all the battle cries coming from their aggressors. It was crazy, it was all crazy.

Colonel Khosrau threw his last grenade at the oncoming brutes, the din of the war cries was incredible.

On the West side, a Swiss guardsman picked up an RPG and fired the last rocket into numerous chainmail-clad creatures. It was ineffective as more of them overran his position.

Colonel Khosrau was busily firing his machine-gun from left to right, when from the East side warrior creatures began appearing and leaping up in an insane frenzy!

Khosrau sighed long and hard. He was out of bullets and out of luck. He took a deep breath in and watched as the creatures charged at him.

Harjit saw them coming and quickly stood up on top of the sacrificial altar, with her battle axe gleaming magically.

The ancient weapon emanated a mysterious energy. It was super-charged with an enchanted blue light that radiated from its double-headed blade — the burning blue-white flame waiting for combat. She did not question its magic or its origin. There seemed no point.

Everything looked senseless. She looked at the helicopter as it whirled next to the hideous creature — it was their only hope.

"In the name of Shiva, Mashir, look!" Harjit caught Khosrau's attention and pointed her Axe down at Smite.

"Allah, protect us." Colonel Khosrau picked up a dropped weapon from a dead soldier, then turned around to see creatures yelling at him from behind the observatory.

****

At the Treeline, in those critical moments before Buzzard Two's destruction.

Trentino and his group watched helplessly. The fighting around them was more furious than ever and the deaths were real enough. This reality was theirs. Everyone had to deal with it somehow.

Smite had already smashed a path into the clearing from the dense foliage, howling like a ship's foghorn, blasting out hatred at the aircraft below it. In the blink of an eye, the Mangusta fell like a swatted fly.

Smite bellowed for all to hear and it sounded as though a wicked laugh came from somewhere inside the creature.

"What now?" Barbaro was trembling.

"Oh, God," Christopher gasped as he looked up at the Temple. Like magic, thousands of shapes transformed into large warriors.

The men lay below Smite in disbelief at what was happening. "Ooooooooo!" Smite screamed.

The heavy monster brought its foot down onto the helicopter, crushing it completely. The aircraft burst into flames.

Suddenly, several rockets exploded, echoing the Mangusta's exothermic destruction.

Trees instantly caught on fire around Smite. The conflagration was like Hell on Earth. Everything around Smite was ablaze.

The heat was intense and the soldiers could feel it from their hiding place. But Smite did not feel it. *Oh no, not Smite.*

Standing among the flames and destruction, Smite was unaffected. Lord Smite could not burn.

The stink of death and terror was everywhere and what followed could instantly stop the heart of anything.

Smite waited for a moment as it surveyed its domain. It bellowed a great blood-curdling war cry to the world, then crushed the helicopter into the mud.

"Ooooooooo!"

"What in Khali's name is that thing?" the horror-stricken girl could not bring herself to look into the eyes of the creature, knowing that the devil had burst out from the forest.

Harjit kept her sanity by blocking the creature's face away from her gaze.

"Allah! We pray to you in this *'yawm ad-dī'*, Day of Judgment, and in our *'as-sā`a'*, last hour!" Colonel Khosrau called out for divine help. He questioned his own worth and whether he had failed. *"Is this truly the Prophecy?"*

The creature stood below him in all its glory. Nabeel felt sick and asked, "Allah, is this to be my fate?"

At this exact moment, the Bloodhort suddenly stopped their offensive at the same time. The great lord commanded their complete obedience. They all turned to him and payed homage. The warriors worshipped their great lord with trepidation.

"What are they waiting for?" she asked Mashir.

"For the end," stated Nabeel.

****

"Ooooooooo!" Smite's shriek sent shivers through everyone. Lifting its unearthly great head, it stared arrogantly up with large black eyes. The Temple had fallen.

His Bloodhort Legion was in complete control. Lord Smite displayed no remorse or mercy and wickedly watched the last remnants of humankind in their despair. It knew that humankind would soon be gone for he is a destroyer of worlds!

Nabeel froze from fear. He knew his psyche was being attacked. His own willpower was weakening but he was somehow still able to resist. Nabeel began speaking steadily and answered Harjit's last question by quoting fate and the prophecy.

"Words are power.

"To enter this place is to touch the past.
Those thou art not pure will surely perish.
Be warned Malis and Crossed Sons the sacred words must be spoken. Open is this way now to things that are evil. Be warned Malis and Crossed Sons there is nowhere to hide and they will come from here to claim it.

To enter this place is to touch the present.
Powerful thou are in prayer if not pure thee will surely perish. Be warned Malis and Crossed Sons those before sacrificed their souls to him and were overcome and they were all destroyed.
It is purely evil so do not falter in vain pursuits.

To enter this place is to touch the future. The three ships will sink alone comradeship membership and friendship fine as is the might of arms but will not be enough alone against his hordes. Remember the presence and humble yourself to unity to one god with patient perseverance faith and prayer. All will be tested and so look east north east from MalisIblis for help as Iblis Smite surrounds you with despair.

To enter this place is to go to nowhere and is also to this land. Where time is nothing and time is everything. The lost is found so must be taken as unified it must never be or all is lost for all time and purification illumination and glorification will be never more.

Say the word Nasom and enter to meet your soul or be lost and forever in nowhere."

Nabeel's words of power broke Smite's spell. The great Lord Smite had no sway over everything, *not yet.*

It all looked so clear to them now. While the Bloodhort remained still under their lord's spell, this gave Harjit and Nabeel a moment to piece this part of the prophecy together.

"Listen," he said tightly, "we can still do this thing." His face had a renewed purpose. "Think."

"Open is the way," she repeated, "open is the way now to things that are evil, this Mahavidyas, manifestation! There is nowhere to hide and we are not pure. I have sinned, Mashir, I have sinned so badly." Harjit was sobbing because of her intimate relationship with Christopher. *"My love, Christopher. The darkness has won."* Christopher was a Catholic priest. Being in love with someone from a different religion seemed like sin.

How wrong she was. Their love was true but at this moment, Harjit felt lower than ever, sensing that the end was going to be horrible.

"Listen," Nabeel said, aware that their time was fast running out. "If it comes to that, we are all sinners. God, knows this already! He knows the truth of your love. We have already spoken the magical word 'Nasom'. An anagram and truly it relates directly to Mason."

"Yes, and?"

"There is much more to this tale than we know, do you remember the words spoken inside the cubed chamber before we could enter the inner Temple, a warning or a condition telling us that we all as humanity need to come together in order to win or give us hope for the future. Chris and the Doctor spoke about the three ships that will sink alone, Islam, Hindu and Christianity, refers to us, humanity. We are now united and that can only be for good! This is a greater test than the might of arms alone, against his horde! We soldiers' could not prevail, only help, protect until things happen or until we fall. Harjit, all our faiths are being tested in this place."

"*His horde?*"

"Yes, this devilish army we see before us and that hellish creature down there. It is called 'Smite'." Nabeel paused to consider his own words and enlightenment.

"How can you possibly know this?"

"We have already been told. Recall, these are the magical words spoken before the Temple opened. Remember the codex narrated by Doctor Castiglion before he died? *'All will be tested and so look east north east from MalisIblis for help as Iblis Smite surrounds you with despair'*? This is what we are seeing now, 'IBLIS Smite' and he now surrounds us." As he spoke, the girl remembered Beppi, her mentor. She then recognised the grim truth of their defeat and their despair. The Prophecy was true.

"Great Vishnu, I pray to you for help!" Harjit looked to the sky and called out, "Save our souls!"

"Have hope, Harjit, please. Look to the North East from MalisIblis. We must do what it says in the Prophecy.

"Oh Mashir," she said almost sobbing.

Nabeel took a deep breath and shook his head defiantly, "No, we will not! We will not despair!" Nabeel shouted. "Harjit, stand up. Stand up against his evil!" he said, encouraging her spirit and everyone else's.

"Where have they come from, where have they come from?" Harjit kept repeating.

"Where have they come from?" Nabeel shrugged. "They come from a place we do not know or can never understand. Read the scripture closely and assimilate all the information. This too, has been provided for us. It is a place that we humans will come to know as *'Nowhere'*. Do you not see, Harj?"

"Provided by whom? This is all too unbelievable, it really is," she said, shaking her head.

"I cannot answer your question. Maybe it was that great prince whom Christopher beheld inside the Temple, or maybe, Allah is giving us a chance."

"A chance! You call this, a chance!" Harjit struggled to see the justice.

"Yes, a chance. We have been given a chance to put things right and see the light." Nabeel paused. "To know the truth and to do good while we are here." Nabeel looked over the Temple and sensed something. "That, Harjit, is all we can do."

The attack had stopped for a brief reprieve when suddenly, a different battle cry was called.

A clear commanding voice came from below, and Centurion Kgnash appeared, smelling victory. HSALS SLAUGOHTŔ shouted its allegiance.

Overseen by Lord SMITE, this was the final fight. With no hesitation, his dark legion began springing over the Temple top like a cloud of ravenous Locusts. All driven onwards by the shear horror and vengeance of their master.

"There are greater powers at work in this place than we know, Mashir. Can I call you Nabeel?" She felt awkward. Nabeel returned a warm smile.

"Oh Harj," he said, shaking his head. Her concern for his feelings made him feel a deep friendship for her. Even with the enemy attacking, Harjit did not want to hurt his feelings.

"Watch out, Nabeel, let us rid the world of these vile creatures!" she shouted.

Good against evil, light against darkness, both battling together on the top of MalisIblis.

Maybe it was because of the words spoken by Nabeel, no one could tell, but at that moment, everyone could hear the enemy screaming. Amplified full blast it stunned them.

"What power, what magic this evil have?" he thought. Nabeel and the other survivors fired their machine guns, and with so many combatants charging at them, they could not miss.

The brutes lifted their strange killing arms and quickly shot out their long darts at high speed.

The familiar castanet sounds were heard while numerous darts were sent speeding past them. Unfortunately, others found their mark.

Several lethal points struck Nabeel. Their sudden impact knocked him clean off his feet, puncturing his body and shoulders. The last Christian soldier was hit at the same time, and both lay on the altar steps. Death dealt out by a dart—the preferred choice for a warrior. This made their kills more personal and pleasurable. It was a true mark of a warrior.

Harjit was the only person left standing on top of the altar. She despised these vile creatures. She hated everything about them. Standing alone and looking around at a sea of bodies, she watched as more of them appeared over the rim. The outpost was taken. They stopped.

****

"Allah, martyr me." Nabeel raised his voice weakly as he lay awkwardly on the hard stone steps before the altar. He was barely alive. He moaned in pain.

Nabeel looked upwards to see Harjit standing there on top of the altar. Blood flowed out his holed body as he watched the army approaching.

Night is closing, getting dark, he thought. The wounded man was disengaging from reality, not knowing where he was. He was simply floating in a dream state. He could not hold back the blackness.

Sighing softly, Nabeel released himself from all pain and emotion. Curiously, the dark haze reminded him of that black fog he had once seen encroaching from inside the forest.

I am so very, very tired, he thought. His thoughts drifted to the sands of his country and the friendships made on this expedition. *There is no real difference between us in kind or spirit, we are all the same in the eyes of God, Allah, we are all the same.* Nabeel's heart began beating harder.

"*Harjit,*" his soft voice reached her, as he lifted his bloodied arm. Alarmed, she looked down when Nabeel's eyes touched her heart and said, "I have looked down on the sand, Harjit and I see God in all his glory." His breathing was becoming more shallow. "Harj," he whispered.

Harjit jumped down and cradled his head. She brought him in closer to her chest.

"Yes, Nabeel," she asked softly with tears in her eyes.

"I am sorry that I could not protect you more." His throat was dry as sandpaper. "I have prayed for you, *Harjit*." He then turned to face the sky and became still. Colonel Nabeel Khosrau died.

****

CHAPTER XIX

THE PROPHECY

Harjit wept. She dropped her fiery axe and looked among the surrounding dead, while cradling him back and forth for comfort. Tears stung her eyes.

"We are not so different, Nabeel, *my Mashir,*" she said as though he could hear her. Sensing that the enemy was getting closer, Harjit looked up and saw the creature warriors slowly closing in around her.

They were in no rush because this last survivor was very special to them. The Osleiotectian female had nowhere to run. A vile creature shouted some obscenity at her, making Harjit's blood boil.

"Take the Osleiotectian alive! Take it for sacrifice!" the creature screamed and attacked Harjit from only five metres away.

Dread and despair, changed to courage and valour in an instant. The girl skilfully dodged the creature's grabbing claws! She picked up her fiery axe and cut the creature's leg in half.

The double-headed blade sliced through flesh and bone. As she watched the thing collapse in agony and fall backwards into a heap, another chainmail- clad warrior decided to take her on.

Bad idea. Harjit stuck the spearheaded axe into the warrior's throat.

Light-footed and sure, the Indian girl quickly sprang onto the top of the sacrificial table, with her lethal axe blazing a fiery death at them.

Moving like a gymnast, she balanced on top of the altar while jumping from one side to the next in a grisly dance of death, parrying off one weapon after another. Yet, Harjit the Warrior, kept going. She spun and traversed up and down the length, avoiding the many clutching claws, and sliced left and right. Heads flew off in flames, while stamping on others, trying to evade the creatures gangly grabbing limbs from pulling her down.

This one-sided fight could not last and even though she had killed many, many more gathered around, watching in amusement.

Harjit knew they could kill her easily from a distance at any time. *Why weren't they trying?* Sensing they wanted her for something else, the last thing she wanted now was to be dragged down by the mob. *They want me alive!*

Using its powerful hind legs, one creature leapt up with its outstretched claws and landed solidly on the table, grabbing at her back, but missed her. Harjit moved out of its reach and sliced it in half with her axe.

"Uuugh!" she screamed with the extra effort as the body of the dead creature crumpled on the steps, with bits of its bisected head in flames lying decapitated on the altar with her.

She kicked the bits off unceremoniously, then surveyed her attackers in dismay. Hundreds surrounded her. There were thousands below. They began walking steadily towards her. It was a terrifying sight to behold. Their jaws displayed rows of disgusting black teeth.

Harjit continued hacking at the grabbing limbs all around her, their huge powerful bodies and chainmail was no match to her magical weaponry, with its curved blades blazing death and defiance at them. She suddenly felt as though she regained a new energy from deep within her.

Harjit's unique resourcefulness, courage and skills shone brightly amid the dark mass. The girl was made of the stuff of warriors. She decided that this would be a day these vile creatures would never forget.

As more cruel claws began pulling at her, one bit her on the ankle. Harjit screamed in pain.

"Aaagh!" she instinctively kicked its helmet. It went down. Another grabbed her lower leg and without thinking, Harjit swiftly cleaved its arm off, but the claw still held onto her, cutting into her calf.

"Ich!" Harjit almost fell in excruciating anguish. Suddenly, a terrifying shrill screeched through the air. Smite stood up in the forest in defiance of natural law.

"Oooooooooooooooooooooooo!" Lord Smite howled from below.

She whirled around to see Smite. Its massive limbs were flailing wildly in the air! Smite raised itself up glaring at her from the forest floor, the last Osleiotectian – human. Her life blood froze in fear.

Harjit reached down and grabbed the claw that was sticking into her leg. She pulled it out and screamed in pain.

As she looked at Smite, she recognised defeat. "Great Vishnu," she said, speaking to her God, "What is this new world that I behold?"

They think that I have the talisman! This is why I am not dead. The Link of God, that is it! It must be!

It then seemed odd that in this very moment, she caught sight of something trivial.

What is that? I know I saw the slightest of movement inside the forest, a tiny movement inside the perimeter. But what?

Her leg was torn and bleeding. Harjit was hurt but continued to fight. Soon, they would have their way. She then saw the sign again and for a reason of unknown significance, she remembered the scripture Nabeel had quoted.

"All will be tested and so look East North East from Malisiblis for help, as Iblis smite surrounds you with despair."

"Yes. I see you and your minions, Smite," Harjit scoffed at the enemy. She stopped and stood still for a moment. "So, this will be my fate too," she said to herself between heavy breaths. Resigned to her fate, and knowing that her own God would hear her words, she said, "Great Vishnu, have I done well?" She then realised she was already looking in the direction of East North East, the same direction where she saw something down inside the treeline – *The Prophecy!*

She knew she had to see it again. *I must!* Intuition told her that she would.

Ah, there it is again! Right there! She looked at it and tried to interpret it, as the creatures continued to claw at her. She longed to see Christopher one last time.

A single cognitive thought was all it took, and in that instant, there was no passage of time. She had contact—a pure one to one connection with Christopher.

"*Oh Chris,*" she gently said. Her tear-filled eyes saw a flash of white—a dot of light, then it was gone. *I love,* was her last thought.

****

At the treeline, in those critical moments after Buzzard Two's destruction.

Buzzard Two lay burning and both pilots were dead. Smite watched the fighting triumphantly from inside the flames. Trentino, Christopher and the others watched the chaos around them. The helicopter burned and emitted its pungent odour. They kept their heads down while high explosives began detonating in no fixed pattern, creating even more havoc.

The colossal creature continuously screamed in triumph.

What lunacy possessed it? Its hatred of Mankind knew, no bounds. Fear emanated from this ungodly beast, driving the creature warriors insane. Thousands of them made their way up on each side of the Temple walls after the last survivors. Christopher and the others looked on helplessly.

Machine gun fire and explosions came from the top, and Christopher took a quick breath in, as he witnessed the defenders running around the high altar, fighting for their lives.

"It's Harjit!" Christopher yelled. "Harjit!" He called to her but it was hopeless.

All he could do was watch his love fighting for her life. Christopher swallowed hard as he watched her swing her fiery weapon, striking and moving back and forth and hacking away at the creatures.

He knew the fight was futile. Then, he saw her stop and turn around and look in his direction. *Is she looking at me?* He sensed, it seemed as if she was calling down to him. Somehow, Christopher heard her voice, he was right. He somehow saw her eyes, *yes*, they were looking at him all the same. Her soft voice echoed his name clearly inside his mind. Their spirits were destined to be one.

Contact. Miraculously, their eyes met in the same line of sight, and were fixed on each other

She knows I am here. He understood. His heart banged inside his chest in fear for her life. Both of their minds came together. Their connection more than physical, more than a feeling, so strong and so real that their time together in the past was suddenly all played in that moment. They were bonded by the spirit of light and spirit of life. Bonded by love, inseparable.

A sudden flash of white light startled him. He saw it from the corner of his eye. It jerked his body into shock. He saw the same point of light Harjit did.

She knows. I love.

Hearing the sharp report of a high-powered rifle made his body stiffen in shock. Christopher's face dropped. He could no longer see or feel her. Their invisible thread of life was broken in that instant. His heart faltered and his eyes welled up with tears. Christopher's head felt heavy. He tilted forward in sorrow onto his chest. He knew.

Red on Dead. Trentino steadily lowered his weapon and looked gravely at Christopher.

It was a clean shot through the heart. There was no mistake in it. The gravity of his deed made the youthful major look older. The man would never say what he saw through his telescopic lens in Harjit's final moment amid the enemy.

"NO!" Christopher screamed loudly, dropping to his knees. His anguish was quelled by the bedlam and turmoil of belated explosions and flare-ups from the burning helicopter.

Christopher's darkened eyes sought solace from the man who had killed his only true love.

Fire and chaos, death and despair and, *oh yes!* Smite had come. Lord Smite, the First of the Dark Lords to stamp upon the World of Man. More would come. Again, the Prophecy.

****

"I am so very sorry, Christopher." Trentino swallowed hard, "There was no other way," the man affirmed. He knew that, taken alive, her death would have been a slow and an agonizing one. "We could not leave Harjit to her fate." The major braced the priest's shoulder between his outstretched arms. Christopher wept like a child.

Trentino's thoughts of profound guilt and failure cut deeply. Once again, he had to kill one of his own.

It seemed like a lifetime in the jungle. Yet, it had been less than forty-eight hours from their drop zone "Jesuit", where they entered by Parachute. Last time, he had killed the Swiss guardsman, Lucchese. He painfully recalled how the big man was engulfed by arriadoracid ants. The bullet was the only way out. In the end, it had all come down to this. Guilt gripped his heart. The major felt a great loss of another innocent life. Trentino had witnessed too many dead faces.

The major assimilated the facts. To live they needed to leave immediately!

"She fought like a warrior," said Private Narváez, lowering his binoculars.

"Let's get out of here. Chris, let's go!" Trentino knew they had to escape. There was no more time and somehow, they needed to get the bio-technologist motivated again. "Come on, Chris!"

"She is gone, signore," Private Hernán Narváez spoke to the priest.

"That monster has not seen us yet," Barbaro said. "Come on!" The media man was eager to escape.

Christopher nodded and without saying anything further, they quickly and quietly retreated, and followed tightly behind the major. Right now, the creature and its minions were preoccupied with events at the Temple.

Smite took a deep breath and blasted out a foghorn of evil, screaming its malevolence into the late afternoon sky, when the dark fog gathered and moved in closer to Smite. It came so close it was as though it caressed him. They were one.

It was dark magic indeed. The vines seemed to be never-ending as they continued to multiply from its woody torso, growing and springing out, then dropping down and wriggling along the forest floor.

Its unholy creepers writhed and wriggled up the south-facing stone terraces like wild spaghetti, violently knocking over its own soldiers as it voraciously climbed, seeking the entrance.

Creature warriors leapt out of its pathway in time, as the evil vines searched for any remaining human survivors inside the Temple. It wanted them all.

In the Temple, a numbed group of survivors tried to run from the horror that approached them.

Meanwhile, back inside the rainforest, Trentino led the beleaguered group consisting of Barbaro, Private Hernán Narváez, Christopher and Abdul-Haleem, to their landing zone and Buzzard One.

Smite stood before the Temple, its long woody tentacles stretched through the entranceway and fed into the many stone passageways. Using its thinner twiglet-like finger tips to probe through the many tunnels, it searched and felt for the link.

The fleeing soldiers retreated deeper and deeper inside the complex where they waited in a last stand before the inner Temple. They had used up all their bullets and resorted to vicious hand-to-claw combat.

In the end, there was never a real chance of survival. Even here, Smite's long reach found them. Its limbs wildly flowed through the stone corridor like water in a pipe, rushing to the chamber and like a burst dam, crashed and flooded through from behind its own warriors. Everything was caught in its barbed limbs.

It destroyed humans and Preyweeps—no life mattered to Smite, only power. Smite sought God's Link. All life next to the inner Temple was simply killed off without care or mercy.

It had done the same before, aeons ago. It strangled all life. Its appendages eventually died off when the Temple closed its great doors.

It continued to tear through the Temple, but it did not find the Link. These humans did not have it. By the time Smite understood this lure, the other Osleiotectian's in the forest had escaped and melted away into the darkness as the light went out.

****

"Where to, Maggiore?" Private Narváez needed direction.

"Heading for LZ Pink Flamenco, private," he confirmed, while looking back at the group to make sure they understood too. "Our landing zone." It was another challenge but he replied with a tenacious nod, "Piss easy. Right, everyone, keep your heads down and follow me. Quick!"

Narváez smiled and saluted. The only survivors of the brutal onslaught of the Temple began jogging away, concealed by foliage, with each man continually checking for signs of pursuit and any hidden enemies. There had been much evidence of enemy troop movement by the trampled vegetation to the Temple. The group's narrow escape automatically picking up their pace. Soon they would be picked up and out of danger.

On their way, they only saw one animal. Not far off, and blending seamlessly in with its habitat, they caught a rare glimpse of a lone Jaguar. Upon seeing them, it stopped and waited, and watched thoughtfully for a long moment. This beautiful beast a powerhouse and top of the food chain, exposed its strong teeth and snarled. The powerful cat wanted them to see it.

The great beast had observed them many times before and had now caught their scent again. For the massive cat, its prey had become too abundant to count. All were hunted down and killed. The invaders had become prey. The proud jaguar killed not because it was hungry but for sport. It hated the HSALS SLAUGOHTŔ with a passion.

High above the rainforest, a distant flying creature surveyed the mighty Smite's triumphant conquest! A mutant hybrid between a prehistoric reptile and featherless bird spawned from *Nowhere*. It had grown a patchwork of scaly feathers on the wing and body, as it encircled the invasion force underneath.

Watching the carnage below and smelling meat burning, DEATH had come again to pick and clean the bones of many. War against the Osleiotectian world had begun. Lord Smite looked up and saw DEATH encircling the Temple high and they both screamed in mutual hatred at each other.

> **They will come first and Smite**
> **All will shake in terror**
> **Cold is the land**
> **Nowhere to hide**

The Prophecy!

Smite's purpose to complete Gods Chain, to become a God of Gods and destroyer of worlds!

****

The group slowed down. They were exhausted. Suddenly, they heard growling and saw the jaguar watching them, as though it was acknowledging their passing. Then with a snarl, it suddenly vanished. The men could not stop as they knew that transportation would not wait. Everyone quickened their pace again. With new speed and renewed vigour, their survival was a race against time. If they did not reach the landing zone as scheduled, then the Mangusta would move onto the Temple. What they could not know was everybody was dead.

After a while, they noticed that the wind was becoming stronger. As they carried on, they eventually came across a large clearing. Being at the front, the major stopped abruptly at its edge with gauged dismay. This place was not what he remembered or expected. The large space was filled mostly with black fog. It did not move.

Everybody sensed it was not natural. They were unsure where to go next, feeling a simultaneous cold chill on them. The temperature had suddenly dropped. The climatic change felt totally out of place in a cloud forest at this height. The damp grey moisture was replaced by something that defied nature. Unmoving in the wind, it waited.

The major perceived a great danger within it. He needed no explanations. Instead, his acute sense of survival warned him not to venture through. That would be suicide.

The fog was much blacker than anything he had ever seen before. No light would leave it. This conundrum had enveloped the Iblis vale almost as if it wanted to prevent any escape. *How stupid,* he thought to himself. *Impossible!* He questioned his own logic but his gut instincts told him that this phenomenon was much different to any natural fog, as he observed its uncanny smooth edges. The trees and bushes close by appeared to be bending away from it.

The men could not see the top of the fog lifting to loftier heights or distances beyond their limited gaze. No sound of any animal or insects came from inside that dark place, not even mosquitoes. The wind rushed past their faces in the open space and made no difference to the fog's position in the clearing. The fog remained silent and very, very still, as though it was watching them.

The major thought about Colonel Rossi. *He is too late. Chameleon would have made it if he could and would have saved the Temple.*

Perplexed, Trentino knew Greco Rossi had to be dead. The major stared at the fog's smooth surface and now, he knew there was no way out of the vale either, except by air. This fog confirmed it.

"Stay away from it, major," Christopher whispered softly, not wanting it to hear him speak. "It is pure evil." The priest felt sick being so close to this black mass. A horrible smell pervaded the air around. It was the same rotten stench that exuded from that awful thing that had come out of the forest and destroyed the helicopter.

As they waited, it seemed to suck at them as if it had an evil willpower of its own. Everyone felt the same mixture of vile emotions. Grave fears taking hold, they knew that something was wrong, *very, very wrong!* Its black soul molested their minds, trying to provoke them into some reaction.

The priest spoke in a calm and gentle tone, not wanting to disturb the mouldering black mass.

"It is listening to us," Christopher advised. "There is no sound of animals or insects, listen. Nothing lives here." His vocal cords cringed while the men on edge stood like statues.

The blackness had a wickedness that extended far back into the distant rainforest and away to the Southern and Eastern parts of the vale.

Going ahead would be like walking into a minefield. With no option, the major waved them to slowly retreat. They moved backwards cautiously. At a presumed safe distance, the major stopped and grabbed Christopher roughly by the shirt collar.

"Right, bloody tell me the truth! What is really going on here, signore? What have you and your scientists unleashed from your tiny little test tubes. SPEAK! Be quick!" the major eyes insisted. "Let me see your waistband," he said, suspecting that something was hidden inside.

****

The assault on MalisIblis was over. Victorious, the legion of HSALS SLAUGOHTŔ stood proudly around the Temple base. Tall warriors in thousands lined up in numerous rows of green leather tunics, black chainmail and black helmets with stamped red claw ensigns. On the Temple, they presented themselves as conquerors to their leaders. The officers were organised on each side of the Temple terraces with Primus Centurion Kgnash and his personal guards. The First Bloodhort stood with him, front and centre. They were the elite. Their arrogance was startling.

His legions waited in formations, with their long green brown cloaks, and their thin yellow zigzag patterns blowing in the gathering breeze. The fog moved back from the legion. The main battle force was waiting within the forest.

This highly disciplined battle force had been originally made from the combined forces of Preyweep and Ráevil, both rival species and all controlled by Lord Smite. But the murder of the smaller Ráevil force was down to the Primus himself, and their deaths smelled of brutal politics.

Primus Centurion Kgnash waited at the Temple entrance. He was taller than the subordinates that stood on each side of him. Despite all his might and power, a fear gripped the Primus. He displayed no emotion as he looked downwards at his warriors. He then looked in awe and terror at his lord and master, Smite. Fear gripped him and his Bloodhort, and none dared to speak until now.

"My Lord!" Primus shouted, "The Temple of MalisIblis is yours again!" his tone rasped as he bowed to Smite. The others on the Temple also bowed. "What is your will, my Lord?" Primus feared nothing except his Master Lord Smite. He was wise to do so.

The army was terrified of Smite. Smite impaled death into their every living cell and sinew. Great Smite wailed loudly at its Primus. Its search inside the Temple showed no clues to the whereabouts of the lost link, but it knew it had to be somewhere. Smite bellowed again and this time, bellowed so loud that the legion quaked where it stood as the forest took a deep breath.

****

"Ok major," Christopher stopped, opened his concealed waistband and took out the Link of Osleiotect. "It was put inside without my knowing. I felt its presence the further away I got from the Temple. Honestly! I really do not know what kind of conjuring has done this."

"That's bull." The major was sceptical. He had no concept of magic things and yet, he was Christian, so surely he believed in miracles?

Everyone stared questionably at the silver object. It resembled a large chain link. A link made of a strange silver metal with a golden lustre appearance.

Christopher clenched it with his fingers. It did not look anything much out of the ordinary and yet, it held an untapped power of awesome proportions.

"Liar!" Barbaro sharply replied.

"Eh? Is this it?" the major stared wildly. "Is this what it's all about?" The soldier could not help but look disappointed, "All this death, for this stupid thing?"

The Link was imperfect with a weakness. Even now, in its weakening state, it still held power and strength to hold the Temple doorway shut for an Epoch of time, until this time, the time of the Prophecy. The Link of Osleiotect was flawed.

Every 500 years the rays of the sun would focus its spiritual energy onto the south wall of the observatory forming an image of a golden face disc, but not this year 5125 – on the Mayan calendar. This special year being the ending of the world as predicted. The sun's rise, a misalignment had occurred through the Temple top Obelisk and the rays of "life and light" had already missed the inner curvatures of the stone circle. The darkness now held the Obelisk in its power.

The doorway had been unlocked by the combined events of human sacrifices and with the imperceptible fracture within the Osleiotect link, in time that flaw diminished its power to hold the Temple doors shut. The first lord of darkness had appeared to take the link, other dark lords would come and claim the other hidden links on earth. They all wanted the power of god.

Also, as predicted, at the same time the "Osleiotectian brothers" had appeared, unknown to them their purpose was also to take the link before the darkness could combine the links to form more of gods chain and become omnipotent! The explorers had stood at the inner Temple and used those ancient "words of power" to enter the "Bastion of Nelumakragasian". This place was known to the humans as the "Inner Temple". Its entry allowed Christopher to take the Link of God away first before the darkness took it, a small and powerful piece of God's power that linked God's chain together. There were others, but not here.

Unseen by everyone, including Christopher, there were invisible writings within the link. They were ancient and powerful words that had released the link for the taking.

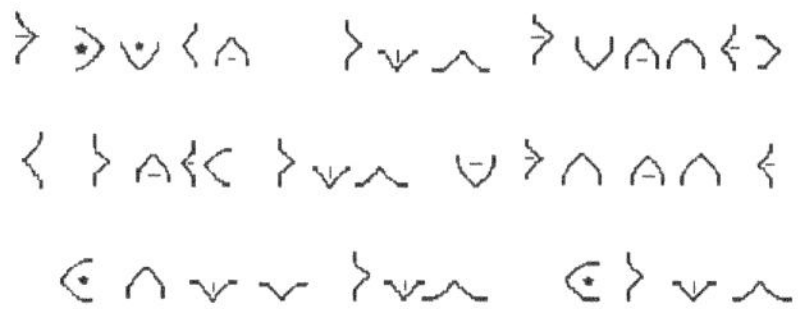

These symbols said.

POWER and PURITY

EARTH and SPIRIT

LINK and LAND

It was about the size of his palm and at this moment, the object of power felt cold to the touch. His knowledge in these matters was small but he knew it had uncanny changing abilities. Christopher could only guess that some unexplained chemical reaction seemed to take place within its atomic structure. Being a scientist, he attempted to use logic and rationality to explain or understand some of the bizarre properties it held, and yet, this thing defied all logic and all understanding.

"This, is nothing!" Barbaro ridiculed Christopher at the insignificance and sight of it.

"Let me show you something. A simple thing." Christopher repositioned the link, and held it lightly in his left hand using his thumb and forefinger. With his other hand, he made a circle with his other thumb and forefinger, each touching inside the metal loop, taking care not to touch the link itself. Then, he let go of it.

They looked at it in disbelief, with widening eyes trying to understand whether this was a joke, yet there it was.

Suspended in the air, it remained between his thumb and forefinger. It did not falter, it did not fall, but stayed there by some invisible force, like a magnet.

Christopher smiled and looked up at the men's faces of incredulity.

"How can this be?" Barbaro was not quite sure of this thing. "What kind of cheap magician's trick is this, priest?"

"It is no trick, paper boy." Christopher was livid. He took his hand away, leaving the link in the air.

There it sat completely static, completely still. "Explain that Arsehole." For a few silent seconds, everyone judged the mystery they beheld.

"So! You did have this object of trickery this entire time. You lied to us. You made us search for it, yet you had it all along. You are a liar! A charlatan!" the Vatican press officer wanted to discredit Christopher.

"Tell me, Christopher, what do you know of this thing?" major Trentino narrowed his eyes suspiciously at the suspended object. He needed to decide what was best to do next.

"Professor Mancini confided in us that a sacred object was held within the tomb of the

Temple. When it was found, he had orders to take it to Italy to be included as part of the Papal treasures. A symbol of Christianity and it's rite over any other ungodly ancient religion."

"I know nothing of this arrangement. The professor would never have trusted you with official Papal Business, not at this level! You stole it!" Barbaro snapped. "You have overstepped your authority and have stolen it! You are not an archaeologist or a scientist but a common thief. Now give it over to me!" Barbaro demanded. "It is not yours!"

Christopher could not believe that the media man was losing his composure like this. It was not Barbaro who discovered it and if anything, Christopher believed it belonged to him.

The object seemed to sense the mood around its environment, as though it was conscious of feelings. Invisibly, it exerted a mysterious influence in every direction that moved through material or mind and with an ability to somehow magnify emotions or increase a person's goodness or badness.

Christopher suddenly gripped it once again from mid-air and it suddenly felt denser and much heavier. There was a shift in its own properties with a new event happening.

A sudden change inside its sub-atomic level surprised Christopher, the "bond bearer". Its density increased exponentially in an instant, and he dropped down onto one knee with a loud grunt.

He struggled to lift it, with his arms began shaking violently like a weight lifter trying to hold up a dead weight. The major quickly took advantage and went to him.

****

Primus bowed long and low for his master, then knelt on one knee in reverence before his Lord Smite. Smite's infinite number of long and sensitive vine fingers touched and felt their way through the expanse of the forest floor. He would never give up the search. He wanted the link for himself and howled in discontentment and rage. The monster's vines wriggled madly, its woody tentacles battering off the ground in fury and frustration. The power was missing, and he needed it. Howling insanely, Smite smashed the legion directly before him knocking them over like dominos in a blind rage. They had failed him.

The rest all cringed, powerless to stop this beast of evil. Then, quite by chance, SMITE touched an echo of the link's power. An imprint of omnipotence remained here, where the Link to God had once lay. It had escaped from here, and the mighty Smite would now follow it. As for the Bloodhort and Primus, he would let them live.

****

"I will take it," major Trentino said, demanding he take the object from Christopher.

Page 598

The soldier raised his rifle a little. There was no mistaking what he meant. The military would take it, and with this, his mission would be complete.

"No," said Christopher. "Major, this is a scientific expedition and any —" His sentence was cut short when Trentino snatched the link.

The major gasped as the thing felt antagonistic in his hand. It was as if two magnets were moving away from each other. Trentino's brow furrowed as he worked hard to keep hold of this slippery object.

The object was strangely conscious that it had been taken without being freely given. Christopher felt a strange attraction to this artefact and knew that the officer had overstepped his authority. The link was sending invisible alarm signals into the surrounding environment.

"It is not yours to take, major. Give it back! It is mine. It was given to me as a gift. You are the thief now!" Christopher shouted. Barbaro sneered at them with a smile at their shared antagonism.

Trentino gripped it harder, imagining that it deliberately wanted to escape from him as if it had a will of its own.

"This is a military operation, priest and your expedition has cost the lives of many of my men." The soldier was becoming more and more unreasonable.

"What about the civilian cost? What about them?" Christopher retorted defiantly. The major began walking away. Christopher and Barbaro followed him. "Don't you understand? Don't you get it, major? Taking this talisman by force will be your own undoing. This war is not only about might of arms." Christopher tried hard to rationalize and reason with the officer.

He could see that somehow, the major had flipped. When quite unexpectedly, the conflict ended when they heard a fearful howling in the forest, echoing their doom.

The horrible ghostly woodwind wail stripped their courage and brought them right back to reality. The evil creature Smite told of its chase. Like a horn for the hounds, the hunt was on.

Picturing the beast, the men sobered up instantly and all arguments were settled. They hunched their shoulders to hide, but there was no hiding place in the vale. Smite would find them and they knew it. What they did not know was that the Link of God blared out their position like a beacon.

"What is this thing that I possess? Speak now or by God, I'll leave both you civvies behind." Trentino had changed. The major changed into a raving lunatic, and his self-control was gone. They were at his mercy but Narváez smiled, *I can take him.*

****

Smite lurched away from the Temple. The colossal brute howled and crashed insanely into the black fog where it had first emerged. The First

Bloodhort knew what to do. They immediately began marching, while the lighter-footed legionnaires ran at full speed on the trail left by the remnants of the expedition.

Major Trentino knew the hunt was on. Somehow, he managed to regain some of his former composure and commanding sensibility. He shook his head in disbelief. He knew he had lost his self-control in a psychotic mood swing that had impaired his judgment. *Inexcusable,* he thought.

The link's power was more than capable of magnifying the holder between its own paradox — good and bad. Who could say which paradox the link would fall under?

He had acquired the link by force as instructed by Apostle and was now in possession of it.

"Come on, follow me, those swine will be on us in no time. Do not fall behind."

Hacking and pulling desperately at the jungle barricade, ill fortune found them going through an area of treacherous thorns. Everyone was slashing at the unforgiving long spikes. Trentino took the front. The major relentlessly kept going, knowing that their lives depended on getting to the LZ on time.

Taking less care, some of the barbs cruelly caught him and ripped his heavy camouflage tunic. Suddenly, a long thorny branch shot down like a whip, ripping off his beret and nicking his forehead.

The major gasped and cursed at the dangerous barbs, while picking up his ripped beret.

"Watch out here!" he warned, while dodging another set of razor-edge barbs flying past him.

Undaunted, the major pressed on, making a safer route until there was a clear pathway through the injurious undergrowth.

Christopher saw tattered cloth left behind by the preoccupied major. Upon closer inspection, his badge of the Phoenix — their unique ensign — was torn from his beret. Christopher studied it and its coveted words, which read: "*Apostle of God*". The Phoenix — the legendary bird — was gold and scarlet in colour. Its eyes were sharp and focused in flight, and its large wings were poised and elevated in steep descent. They were shaped powerfully upwards and looked almost like cupped hands. Its finger-like feathers were stitched on the wing with a delicate fine weave, and were enclosed by a small shield with blue a background. An upturned enflamed dagger with an open parachute sat at the top, and in its fierce talons were the following words:

"Silendo Libertatem Servo Mobil"
Their motto, interpreted.
"Serving Liberty Silently in Motion"

Fine words, thought Christopher as he put the major's badge inside his waistband for safety.

He would return it to the officer at a better time. Meanwhile, it was enough just to survive this ordeal and remarkably, the civilians did very well keeping up with the major. Later, and utterly spent, the shattered band of men dug deeper into their reserves as they went through the dangerous terrain.

Without warning, the field radio that the major carried on his back like a rucksack suddenly burst into life.

"Buzzard One to Phoenix, come in Phoenix! Buzzard One to Phoenix, come in Phoenix! Phoenix, do you copy? Over?" the pilot's calm and polite voice spoke clearly through the airwaves. The group could just about hear a vague hint of rock music in the background when the pilot spoke again. "We are set on approach towards Pink Flamenco, E.T.A. Fifteen minutes. Over." The Buzzard already knew of the loss of Buzzard Two, but not its circumstances.

"Phoenix to Buzzard One, rendezvous with us at LZ, Pink Flamenco. Copy on that," replied the major.

"Copy, Phoenix. Buzzard One to Phoenix, what is your operational status?" His question was implicit. His orders before had been clear: no "Golden Egg", no pickup.

"The nest has been raided, there are no chicks left to fly, repeat there are no chicks left to fly, rendezvous at LZ will be on time. Buzzard Two is down. No survivors. Sorry, capitano," major Trentino said, confirming the bad news. The sound of noisy static echoed through the radio for a second or two as the pilot assimilated the facts.

"How many are ready to fly, Phoenix? Over?" the pilot wanted more information.

"Two Phoenix and three chicks have escaped from the nest. There should be some other birds already waiting for you at LZ, Pink Flamenco. We are heading there to meet them. Over!"

"Copy on that. Any other payload, Phoenix? Over." The pilot waited. This part was of utmost importance to the mission.

"I have the Golden Egg. I repeat, I have the Golden Egg. Do you copy? Over," the major responded with no hesitation, knowing he would have said this in any case just to get picked up.

"Copy on that Phoenix! I will transmit your welcome news to Apostle when normal communication is restored. Well done. There is a lot of unusual interference around this area, the atmosphere is jamming just about everything. Our estimated time of arrival at LZ is fourteen minutes. Over." The captain turned up his music.

"What's the music, capitano?"

"It's the 'Stones', man! It helps me chill out. Take care and I will see you at LZ, this is Buzzard One. Out." The Mangusta captain turned up the volume on *Painted Black*.

"Roger that, Buzzard One. Over and out." The major looked troubled. "Come, we have very little time, about ten minutes to get there. They will wait only for a short time. The landing zone is not far from here, hurry!"

Pushed on by pressure, the five men were quickly making good progress again after their short rest. Everyone was desperately weaving in and out the sporadic foliage. The route was a bit easier as they were running on a previously-chopped down path by the other soldiers — the soldiers who diligently prepared the landing zone where they would be waiting.

Yet, no matter, this place was disturbing and unnatural. Everything around them seemed so wrong. There were no birds singing or monkeys screeching. The forest was dead of all animal life.

"It's too quiet, major," said captain Haleem apprehensively.

"I know."

Nothing wanted to be there. Even the plants were growing away from this unnamed danger.

The forest insects had also vanished. Mosquitoes were non-existent. Soon this life-cycle would be replaced. An unearthly calm settled around them, until the major sensed something more was wrong. Unknown to them, *Death* was flying above them.

"Down!" the major warned, sensing the wicked flying beast.

"What is it?" Abdul-Haleem asked in a low voice.

"I'm not sure," the major replied.

For a moment too long, Death began soaring directly above them, almost as if it knew that humankind was close.

The carrion suddenly flapped its wings and began accelerating its flightpath, and was soon travelling miles away from their location. Its soulful eyes watched the surrounding hills and impossible rock-face confines below, leaving that rotten stench in its wake. Riding on the hot air currents, its malevolence was felt over the valley. It could see everything within its borders. As it screeched its unearthly signature once again, Smite heard its calling.

The men looked at each other for solace, and cringed at the sound of the unearthly wail. With no option, they dared to continue, when unexpectedly, the group heard something different—the chuckle of a nearby river.

They were unaware that enemy trackers were closing in and coming from a Southeast, which was where the black fog was densest. Suddenly, they heard that unholy howling from that monster in the forest again. It sounded closer this time.

Smite was still far off but was traversing fast through the forest alongside them, striding parallel at a greater speed and attempting to outflank their escape. The major decided to change direction. Going to the LZ would be their death.

"This way and keep up. That thing is after us. Come on, move faster!" Trentino urged everyone.

All animals depend on their instincts to survive. Humans had long lost that fine balance or ability of survival with nature. But not the major. He had always been a unique fighter and survivalist. His sharp decision-making was always a key to his success in field missions.

Yet, he felt different this time, sensing the blood hunt. Without seeing, he knew the enemy was tracking them. He could almost see the Preyweep legionnaires bounding strongly through the forest. Trentino felt more in touch with nature at this moment than he ever did in his life. The link's influence was getting stronger.

"Where to, major?" Christopher asked between laboured breaths, staring at a large clearing of trees. A large open area covered with tall grasses about head height stood in front of them. He looked unsure.

"This way, and don't get lost," the soldier snapped. Wasting no time, he quickly swung his machete in the right direction, slashing hard, and making a rough path through the sweeping vegetation.

"Get your backs into it, signores!" Private Narváez encouraged them. The wall of grass fell before them, but was replaced by even more grass. Uncannily, his navigation was perfect, the major knew exactly how to locate the landing zone. Trentino fleetingly turned and looked back at the weary men when something flashed into his mind. He dropped weakly down on his knees.

"Damnation," Trentino swore quietly, confused at what was happening to him. The body blow left him staring blindly into the tall grasses wafting in the strong breeze. He knew this and yet was receiving something very clearly into his mind—the enemy.

He shook his head to clear the stupor inside him. He watched the Bloodhort closing in fast. The images of them appeared so real. They were coming. As he observed the men around him it was as though he was watching two movies simultaneously.

He questioned his sanity. *How can I see all this?* the dazed major thought, looking around and seeing even more images flooding into him.

It was as if a strange switch had been turned on in his mind, like a television. But, this was no illusion because an illusion would not be real.

Unknown to him, his new senses and visions were all being created by the link.

Detached like this, his distant spirit seemed to be dancing like an unseen ghost, moving along with the enemy. The Link had become some sort of enthral transporter, a spiritual channel, and was warning him of their impending fate.

His fraught companions tried to help him up. They needed to know what was wrong. Raising his hand up to stop them, the queer sensation passed when he looked up at them.

He came out of his semi-delirium and stood unaided and simply shrugged. He had accepted what the link had told him, and he adapted his senses without question.

"They are very close," the major said in a commanding tone. "Keep going."

The officer expected them to follow. Their abused bodies stumbled on. They were a band of desperate men engulfed inside the tall grasses, wading through the soft swishing sounds to the coarse noises of trees being cut. The buzzing not too far away now.

Suddenly, another area of trees came into view. They could also hear a shallow stream. It seemed like the men had started cutting down even more trees. The buzzing sounds were within earshot again and directly ahead.

As they moved closer to the stream, it looked much faster and more powerful and it drowned out the sound of the chainsaws.

"My God, are they still cutting those trees?" Barbaro screwed up his face in disbelief.

"Our detachment is behind that area of trees." The major was convinced that the landing zone was located just beyond them. "They must be clearing a wider area for the chopper to land. Ok men, get into the water. It is the fastest way around. We will follow it along the banks, then nip in the backend of the trees."

"It looks too strong," Barbaro cautiously advised.

"Piss easy! Get into the river." The major would have none of it.

"Why?" Barbaro wanted a more direct route.

"Because it flows right past the landing zone." Trentino's tone hardened and without hesitation, he jumped into the ice-cold water. "Follow me," he commanded with no compromise.

Trentino set off. The water rose to just below his knees but even at this depth, the water's treachery made walking a dangerous struggle. The strong currents pushed him forward as he held onto the banks to keep stable.

"They've had ages and the LZ is still not finished by the sounds of it. I bloody hope the chopper can land!" Private Hernán Narváez said as he got into the water.

"It will just have to do," Sarvan Abdul-Haleem added.

They followed the stream around a long bend, and were soon making good headway. The banks were covered in high reeds and provided excellent cover, restricting the activity beyond. They pushed through the stream for more than five minutes, acutely aware that time was running out.

"Ok, men, the streams are getting faster. Get out of the water. Get up through those reeds and onto the embankment. I will go first." The major pulled himself out of the stream using the long reeds to take his weight. The others followed the major's lead. They exited through the high reeds and found themselves standing in a large oval area cleared of trees.

They looked ahead and observed their immediate vicinity. The major could see that this was a clear killing zone for a few hundred-metres. Beyond this was the cover of trees again and where all the current sawing activities seemed loudest.

To their left and right, there was dense forest. Tall trees surrounded the area behind the stream where they had emerged. The stream was connected to a small river at this point, and the water was flowing like a torrent around the clearing ahead of them. It moved in a wide route in front of the noisy treeline. The river flowed on and out of sight, moving down through the vale and eventually escaping into the larger waterways of the greater Amazonian rainforest.

The major sensed that something was badly wrong. How could his men be working in the trees beyond the river? It did not make sense? The LZ already cleared this area.

"Wait, lie down!" commanded Trentino in a hard whisper, using hand signals to wave them down.

"What's wrong, Maggiore? Is this the landing site or not?" Barbaro urged the officer to move on. "Are you not being too cautious? We need to get over there or we will miss the pickup. Come on." Barbaro insisted.

"No," he frowned. "It is a feeling. I cannot say why. I know something is not panning out here."

With the patience of a Watchmaker, Trentino moved the telescopic sites on his rifle very slowly over the large surface area of grassland, searching for anything out of the ordinary and picking up every little detail. He breathed in.

Upon close observation, he saw felled logs and cut branches but they all lay fallen in the wide clearing in disarray. Foliage had been shifted to make room for the helicopter. His detachment had flattened out the central area.

The men had been busy and yet, the sawing noises continued. Beyond more tall trees, the felling there made no sense. Trentino resisted the urge to call out.

What are they doing? The trees are down and the area is clear. Where in the inferno are they cutting now? His patience was tested to the full. Sweat dribbled down from his forehead, adding to his stress levels.

The major continued scanning the foreground patiently. He would not move, not yet!

Barbaro tried to pressure him again, wanting to get moving. Annoyed, the soldier turned and narrowed his eyes in a gesture to be silent. The threat of assault immediately quelled the press officer.

Their lives depended on their stealth and perfect timing. That was what Trentino excelled in. His call sign was not "Mantis" for nothing.

The major payed attention to where the soldiers should have been, acutely aware that at any moment, their rescue might arrive. But he knew not to move. The major's telescopic view had picked up everything in his field of vision and in very fine detail. He had seen everything he needed to.

"Damn," he cursed from under his held breath.

Stone-faced, he re-adjusted his scope to magnify the background, and focused through the darkening trees to where all the buzzing saw sounds were coming from. The black fog was inside. *My God.*

****

CHAPTER XX

NOWHERE TO HIDE

The major breathed out, when a black fog suddenly appeared, moving swiftly out from inside the forest. Its height was about the same as the trees. It looked like a colossal hole in the world, coming away from the treeline. Its silent black mass glided smoothly along the surface of the river. It was there before they even grasped its presence. It emerged unexpectedly, then suddenly stopped moving. The fog seemed to wait there, as if thinking.

A long minute passed, and the inky blackness jerked into movement again. It did not come forward but instead, it began quickly stretching upwards with a menace. The dense fog completely dominated the river and much of the forest closer to them. This peril appeared to be holding steady on top of the water surface, while absorbing the liquid's natural sounds. The fog was unmoving and impenetrable.

Through the major's telescopic rifle, the major could see that the fog was something much more sinister.

The major's new-found senses overwhelmed him with sensory danger. He knew this was something wicked and it had come to meet them.

At first appearance, the black surface was more like a membrane than a diffuse mist or fog. It was a substance with a defined surface and contained an oil-like viscosity on the inside. *Weird,* thought the major.

They wondered why it did not waver in the hot Amazonian breeze. Yet, it was more than just a film, and something was moving inside! It had come from "Nowhere".

The major's mind worked on alternative escape options. There were three ways to go: back the way they came, wait here for their ride or by take a very deep breath and swim under the water and hope for freedom. The latter was the worse-case scenario as the river was strong and they didn't know how extensive the fog was.

"We cannot go any further. This is it. This is the landing zone," Trentino stated calmly. The major was careful not to take his eye away from his telescopic view, as he scanned for his missing men. "The chopper will be here soon. We stay still and wait." His voice commanded obedience.

"Thanks to you, Maggiore, you have got us here!" Barbaro patted the major's arm in full admiration. "We have made it!" Barbaro grinned excitedly.

The Vatican media man was suddenly overcome with emotion. He slobbered as he wiped his emotional tears away from his eyes. Then, he began hugging the major in unwanted appreciation, forcing the major to lower his weapon.

Christopher looked on. *Pathetic,* he thought. Brown nosing like this irritated him. It was obvious the press officer wanted to be rescued first. He could never fathom the paper man's warped mind. In Christopher's eyes, everyone was equal, no matter what. *Pitiful.* He looked at Barbaro pawing at the major. The soldier was distracted from his scan of the forest.

"What the fuck? Get off me!" the major said abruptly. "Sit down quietly." His diplomacy was on the verge of breaking. The major realised that under these conditions, stress affected people in different ways.

Christopher looked at the major. *He's worried.*

Trentino felt suddenly lost, as if he was unsure what to do next. Mixed feelings of dread and deep regret came over him. With the death of each man, it felt as though a member of his family was lost. Surprisingly the major could not sense the encompassing enemy anymore. His instincts were now dulled, and his new-found abilities of awareness were blunted.

Squatting down, they all waited for extraction by air. It would be a long five minutes.

"Is something wrong, major? It's your men." The captain knew the major's men were in danger.

"I still cannot see them." *He lied.*

"Are they not cutting somewhere over there? We can still hear them." Christopher said. "They need to be here too, *don't they?*" Christopher spoke softly, presuming that the loud buzzing noises coming from somewhere beyond the black fog were them. *Who else could it be?*

Sensing fear, Christopher watched the sky even closer, praying under his breath for their rescue to come quicker. Major Trentino did not mention what he had really seen. There would be little point. One of his men was lying partially covered in the undergrowth, dead. The officer knew that all his men must be dead too. He was right about that. His men were somewhere in the middle of the landing zone. It was an ideal place for an ambush.

Suddenly, a renewed hope flooded into their veins. They could hear the muffled sounds of the chopper getting louder by the second. Its low approach disguised both sound and sight.

The reassuring noises of heavy engines lifted their acute anxieties, all except Trentino's. Watching and listening intently to its growing powerful engines and fast rotating blades, the men's hearts quickened in excitement.

"It's the chopper!" captain Abdul-Haleem said, looking skywards.

"It's Buzzard One, Maggiore." Private Hernán Narváez being a psychopath appeared to be bored, knowing the rescue gunship was closing in and that meant he would not be able to kill anything!

The A2012 Mangusta could manage flights over greater distances like these. It was a twin pilot helicopter, where the pilots sat parallel to each other in the same cockpit. The aircraft could open its sides and rear, which allowed for quick troop deployment. This heavy machine could hold a cargo of fifty men and could refuel the Scout A500 Helicopter, the smaller brother aircraft, in mid-flight.

These helicopters were transported from the Italian Peninsula as part of this top-secret sortie. They were stamped, "Classified - Mission Aequinoxium", then re-designated and labelled as "On Manoeuvres" inside the green continent.

The aircraft was operated by the Fifteen Degree Stormo Stefano Cagna Aerial Brigade. It was an ideal machine for search and rescue missions. It was equipped with a light armoury, a single front swivel barrel with 20mm cannon, and kitted with very effective medusa missiles.

"Wait," the major cautioned. "Stay down and wait until the very last moment." The major studied the terrain. "Private Narváez and Sarvan Haleem, take flanking positions and scout ahead. I will cover you both." He raised his weapon for comfort. "It'll be p—"

"Piss easy, eh Maggiore?" Narváez butted in, using Trentino's hallmark expression. The soldier was suddenly not bored because it looked like he might get to kill something again.

Both men displayed no hesitation. Haleem and Narváez began crawling forward, spreading out left and right through waist-high grasses blowing around them. The men were completely hidden.

Narváez smiled to himself. The soldier knew "Mantis" all too well. The major was holding back for the civilian's safety. Narváez also understood that the other men were dead, so the thought of killing the enemy made him much happier.

They are out there, somewhere, Private Narváez thought as he crawled quickly through the shortened undergrowth. Private Narváez was trigger-happy and was prepared to murder the next thing he came across.

"Ok, when the chopper lands," Trentino prepped the civilians, "we need you men over at the central landing area, near those bushes. Narváez and Haleem will be in position by then. They will cover you. The pilots have to see us standing there before they can land. When I tell you to run, run fast and —"

"Here it comes! Here it comes!" Barbaro interrupted the major as he heard the chopper coming in much closer. The chopper was not even in plain sight, yet he was shouting like a crazed lunatic and jumping up and down. "Here it comes!" he shouted again and with complete disregard to the major, Barbaro was suddenly running hard, charging like an Olympic sprinter.

"Hell fire! That fucker broke our cover too soon!" major Trentino yelled.

"You next, Christopher, get going, signore," he ordered, knowing that the advantage of surprise was gone.

"Come with me, major, you too!" Christopher insisted. "Call your men into the middle and we can all get out together." Christopher felt that the soldiers were taking too many risks for them.

"Christopher, listen. We need to provide cover for you and that little rat bag, Lettiere. Be very careful, something is not right over by that black stuff," he stated, pausing to look at it again. "I know you are handy with that sword of yours," he said, looking at Christopher's sword strapped safely to the side of his small backpack. "Here, take my Beretta, your sword may not be enough," he said, handing him his gun. "The safety. is off."

"Thanks, major."

"Be careful, priest."

Christopher hesitated. Something else was bothering him, in fact, a lot. He could not make a dash for safety without insisting on one last thing from the major.

"What about the link? I must take it with me, major," Christopher said, seriously. He was not going to leave without it.

Major Trentino, a pragmatist, judged that the best chance for getting the sacred link out of Amazonia and to Vatican City was for the priest to take it. He must let Christopher secure his mission's success. He could easily take it onboard.

The major went into his pocket to retrieve it, but realised it was gone. He looked at Christopher with shock. The colour in his face drained instantly in disbelief.

The noise from the chopper was getting louder. Its distinctive resonances heralded their imminent departure.

Like a tornado, the camouflaged gunship burst into view. It was a wonderful sight.

In a few seconds, the Mangusta had passed over Trentino and Christopher and the others. It was now hovering above the landing area. Its huge rotor blades were cutting the foliage vigorously, sending it flying in all directions, while the sound of the blades disguised a more sinister noise.

****

On approach to the LZ, from the Mangusta's low height coming in above the trees.

The aircrew could see the distant Temple and a black fog covering vast areas. The cockpit and fuselage filled the airwaves with "Stones" blues — they needed something to take their minds off their growing trepidation. The pilots had never seen anything quite like this ground fog before.

They had observed this strange phenomenon since entering the vale. It had engulfed substantial sections of forest, but in this place, their latest observations measured it to be the darkest right here. They could also see that the men on the ground were cut-off. There was no other way out except by air. Suddenly, they spotted somebody already running into the clearing just ahead of them.

The two pilots were perplexed. The horror and scale struck them just like the previous ill-fated flight crew of "Buzzard Two". Nobody could believe this nightmarish scene.

Captain Bonifacio (Capitano) and his co-pilot Flight Lieutenant Azzurra (Tenente) inspected everything in their approach, when the black cloud protruded and tried to catch onto them.

The captain adjusted his aircraft, elevating it a little higher and out of reach from this unnatural cloud formation. Once again, it seemed the right thing to do. The helicopter utility gunship quickly passed untouched. He had done this manoeuvre before.

The Mangusta was finally in the centre of the clearing. Both pilots scanned for hostiles underneath. With IHADSS projecting flight sensors onto their helmet displays, the aircraft began hovering directly above Pink Flamenco.

"Cargo still in view capitano." The co-pilot was watching Barbaro running and stumbling across the clearing towards them.

"Do you see any hostiles?" the flight captain asked his aircrew sitting inside the main body of the ship. The co-pilot switched over onto his FLIR system and answered.

"We have another running man, capitano." The co-pilot spotted Christopher chasing after Barbaro.

"Affirmative," replied the captain.

"One of our guys is to the Northern perimeter and two others are moving slowly, going wide." The infrared camera picked up all three soldiers, their bodies illuminated to differing degrees. "Five IR images Signore. Strange, two of the images seem, less hot." the co-pilot watched the activity.

"Well, what is strange about that?"

"The soldiers heat images are less bright and getting colder, signore. The barrels of their weapons are red hot. They were used only a few seconds ago." The co-pilot was aghast, when suddenly he could see the intense brightness of a trailing fire. "The soldiers are exchanging fire, signore!" The co-pilot shouted as he saw Trentino fire his weapon on semi-automatic.

"Let's get down there, Tenente," commanded the captain to his Flight Lieutenant, "Captain to flight-crew, we are going down. Our people are in trouble. Stay alert and get them inside ASAP!" The massive utility gunship opened its side door and immediately began its descent.

****

A minute before the Chopper had made its appearance.

Barbaro ran as fast as he could. He was looking straight ahead with no thoughts of the major or anyone else. The noise of the helicopter was enough for him to make the dash.

He could hear that the airship was getting closer. The rough forest floor in front was harder than he imagined, especially when the fallen trees could easily trip him. Plenty of debris was left. It could also catch the helicopter's undercarriage if the pilots were not careful.

Hurry, come on. Keep going. Barbaro thought.

He was breathing heavily and covering thirty metres flat out. But, he was getting tired and began to slow down. He stumbled here and there. Then, the chopper appeared from over the tree tops. *Halleluiah!* he thought, his heart lifting with excitement. His rescue was imminent.

Every sound was drowned by the helicopter's engines. Barbaro felt both pilots watching him. A strange sensation indeed, he had never experienced anything quite like it before. *Insight,* he thought. *It is a gift of knowing. The link has this power.*

Everything blew around him in the gathering winds. The helicopter's propellers sent branches, twigs and greenery flying everywhere. The rushing air whooshed around him. Screwing up his face against the storm, Barbaro looked upwards with anticipation.

"Si! Down here! Down here!" he shouted.

Suddenly, Barbaro was knocked to the ground by the heavy winds from the chopper. But, something else was going on. *Noises. Oh no!* Distracted, he tried to figure out where it was coming from. He heard sawing noises, except this time, they were much louder and much closer. His knew found ability of survival, instantly told him about the noises. *These are not power-saws,* he thought. He was being warned by the link.

He looked over to the tree perimeter, his strange abilities probing inside and beyond.

It was there, inside the fog. *The trees are disappearing. What are those things inside?* Barbaro's mind almost stalling in panic, as more trees began disappearing into the thick black fog.

Something else is inside, but what? Barbaro watched as vague objects moved quickly about inside the fog. *What the hell is going on?*

Within its blackness, numerous images appeared for a fleeting moment at its surface, then strangely vanished. They were vague shapes, and were very difficult to distinguish but his abilities were showing him things.

"I can see," he whispered to himself, his fear growing. "My God, they are real!" Suddenly, the black blanket before him jerked without indication, surging forward like a burst dam, a flood of blackness engulfing much of the foreground and making him step backwards in shock. Then, it stopped.

"Oh!" he shouted. The treeline was simply absorbed inside the blackness, where nothing green lived. Mother Nature could not combat such desecration. The mountainous mass of fog waited again.

The way back was suicide and with no way forward, the media man knew that this was going to be close.

The others could see many vague shapes that were barely perceivable to the human eye. There were outlines of obscure greys and opaque black images. They were coming and going close to the fog's inner surface. They were there for a fleeting instant to see outside and then were gone again. The surface was more akin to a thick membrane than a diffuse cloud, with its skin acting like an unnatural barrier.

This appeared very different to Barbaro. His vision of these devilish images was clearer. As for the link, it was like a curse. It was a Pandora's Box.

Barbaro was horrified. He was unsure whether he was running or simply static, like jogging on the spot. His consciousness moved between dimensions in time and space. He was stuck in a weird hypnosis as he stared at these lurid things; things that devoured their own spawn.

Inside this bog of filth, he could see thousands of dark blobs accelerating, then slowing down. They were moving in a "ping-pong" way from nowhere, in random motion inside their black container. Yet, he felt there was something else. Barbaro dared not look away, yet he had to. Otherwise, he would lose his sanity completely.

There was something much further inside the fog, something unspoken. A deeper and darker terror that he could not see. It moved like a slow thunder as if his distant probing disturbed it.

The unique ability of God's Link made all this possible. Barbaro shivered because he felt its evil. The media man knew that something unspeakable lurked there.

Cold sweat poured from all his pores, each droplet tasting of fear. He saw the tar-black creatures swimming inside this nightmarish oily broth, and it was then that he understood what these ungodly things were, and that they had only one purpose: to escape.

Barbaro could see everything in gory glory, for inside this madness, these things went spinning around in disarray and chaos. He felt something. Something was inside his mind.

My God, what is happening to me? My mind, they're inside my mind!

The man was in anguish. Barbaro could no longer understand anything. His senses had delved into the murkiness, and he was unable to control the power of the link. It took Barbaro too deep. What he saw there were horrible creatures moving with intent.

An infinite numbers of pestilent life-forms bred here, all competing to live and die. They wanted to get closer to the surface and to the light.

The creatures hugged the membrane for a moment, watching the outside world. The vile things crowded around and slithered against the surface for a short second until they were violently knocked away by another.

These ink-like things changed shape at will. One moment, their devilish bodies were soft and buoyant, then changed shape in an instant. The creatures became denser and dropped to ground level where they would squeeze themselves flat into a hard disc, suddenly inflating and bouncing back upwards at some unpredictable angle. In this way, they moved in a grotesque dance of death. The link's macabre enlightenment turned Barbaro's mind into mush.

In this way, these devilish organisms had a very short lifespan inside the iniquitous black soup. When they collided hard on impact, this ensured mutual destruction. Their "maker" had cruelly imprisoned them here and Barbaro knew that all they wanted to do was escape into the light.

In their state, each could instantly-spin at very high speeds. Spinning in this way generated a high-pitched wailing or buzzing sound, like that of the chainsaws heard in the forest.

This uncanny noise was heard at great distances, and such was the perverted existence of these hellish things. The black surface seemed nothing short of complete and utter pandemonium.

Barbaro could see these sickening things and their lurid activities inside his mind. Such was the double-edged ability with the *Link to Osleiotect*, it cared not, its powers magnified good and the ill inside the mind of its bearer.

Barbaro had had enough. He felt psychologically raped at the sight of these creatures, and his psyche was fighting to get away.

Get me out of here, he begged and pleaded with the link. *Let me leave, please let me go!*

It would not.

Like fish in a bowl, these weird creatures swam around him, bouncing on and off his fraying consciousness. But more than this, they sensed a change of substance in their soup from where he watched. They were becoming increasingly more agitated around his mindful presence. They were going berserk. It was almost as if they knew he was there. Barbaro heard their hum. Their bodies buzzing in his mind. He wished he had never taken the link by deceit.

The creatures suddenly changed into disc shapes and spun at him, attacking his mind, then killing each other. Such was the curse instilled by their maker.

"Stop it! Stop it! EAAAH!" Barbaro screamed. "Get out of my mind!", his ears began bleeding. then, the excitable apparitions spun rapidly out of control with their curved razor-sharp edges cutting through anything. Hard blades that projected outwards like sharp teeth, making them formidable Death Discs. "EAAAH!"

****

The link's presence inside this black habitat energised the creatures even more, one more aggressive than the last. With their buzzing teeth spinning at high speeds, they turned into circular saws.

This disc shape also gave them Frisbee-like abilities, they could easily propel themselves in any direction, simply by angling its protruding teeth like aeroplane flaps.

Barbaro was scared. He realised that the membrane could not take any more. It was weakening in parts due to the creatures' attraction to him next to the thin wall holding them inside.

"Oh, my God," Barbaro said from where he stood in the forest. Like a reaction to acid, the skin quickly formed into a blister. He gasped when the membrane burst in a black detonation, releasing the first few creatures.

The creatures propelled outwards at high speed towards the men.

Barbaro was unable to run. Luckily, he had stopped at the pickup point but his nightmare gripped him severely. He squatted, unable to protect himself. He rocked himself back and forth with his hands on his head. His mind was still caught inside that insane place. He screamed and screamed and screamed.

"EAAAH! EAAAH! EAAAH!" The link kept him encased inside the bog with no end to these vile creatures' gruesome slaughter. Barbaro was going mad as he watched the membrane burst.

****

The major watched Barbaro, but was distracted by Christopher's demands. At the same time, the chopper soared downwards from the trees pressing Christopher's escape too. The Scientist did not quite understand the feeling of the bond's weakening proximity.

"I really need that link, major!" He could not comprehend where the precious object had gone to.

The talisman had been inside his breast pocket, but now it was gone.

Christopher was distraught. The link had been gifted to him and no one else. Christopher remembered that when he was inside the Temple, he had heard the lipless voice of the great prince speaking into his mind.

"Two others lay hidden and protected in this world. Be first to find them. Ahead of you lies the footpaths to God's Chain."

"GOD'S CHAIN," Christopher said aloud and understood that two other links lay secret somewhere.

Both men struggled in the buffeting air around them, as the helicopter approached above them.

They watched as it passed overhead, then knocked Barbaro down on his way to the pickup point. The major turned to Christopher.

"I had it! I had it in my pocket! It's gone!" Trentino shouted. Then, something clicked inside the major's mind, making his eyes narrow suspiciously. It was stolen.

"This is critical, what have you done with it?" Christopher asked.

"Look, I don't have it anymore. Now, go! Go! The chopper will not wait!" He urged him to run, when quite unexpectedly, something unusual caught the major's eye. *Bloody Hell, what is it?*

"What do you mean, stolen?" Chris asked while a circular object peeled away from the black surface. The soldiers suddenly began shooting.

"Chris, it's that rat. Barbaro! He must have it! The fucker was right next to me a moment ago, pawing over me like a rash, remember? He nicked it then, he must have!" Trentino said, realising what had happened.

The clattering of automatic machine gun fire began rattling out on both flanks, the shots resonating all around.

FRRRRRRRRAK! FRRRRRRRRAK!

"I have to catch him!" Christopher looked seriously at the major.

"Good luck." Trentino smiled a little in admiration and pride for Christopher's smart intellect. Christopher nodded his friendship. "And, watch out for those buzzers too!"

"Look out for yourself, major!" he said, as he accepted Trentino's handgun. He turned and was off, running at full speed after the Vatican press officer.

Chris could see both Private Narváez and Sarvan Haleem getting up, both soldiers firing in rapid bursts at the nasty saucer-like objects.

He could not make out what they were. It seemed like suicide because he was running right towards them.

The death discs randomly pulled free from their black gluey existences, immediately propelling themselves faster towards any human scent. The things were half-gliding and half-flying, while curving smoothly around the men, angling acutely behind the soldiers closest to them.

FRRRRRRRRAK! FRRRRRRRRRAK! FRRRRRRRRAK! FRRRRRRRRRAK!

Private Narváez blasted four of them out of the air, quickly emptying his magazine. However, his luck was running out as another one of the buzzer's in the cluster sliced off his arm at the shoulder. He screamed and fell into the grass, while another dived into him as he lay on the ground. Blood and guts erupted into the air as the creature buried itself into him.

Sarvan Haleem wiped out a full group of five or six, and dodged just as many. There were too many. Haleem contemplated retreating, but there was nowhere to run. Instead, he chose to stand his ground, firing at them in every direction. Each time one was hit, the creature would burst wide open, splattering its black filth on the ground.

They encircled Haleem in a buzzing frenzy, when suddenly they all came in at once. It could end only one way: they would saw him to pieces.

Christopher could see the brave soldiers being brutally killed; it almost broke his heart and his courage too but his determination and anger for Barbaro kicked in. He ran faster. He could not let Barbaro get away with it. Christopher was enraged.

"It is not yours to take!" Christopher started screaming towards the quaking media man. Chris knew exactly what to do, as the creatures began finishing off the soldiers. His tunnel vision was fixed ahead and on Barbaro, the man had become his touchline.

"Run!" the major kept shouting! "Run! Keep going!" Christopher heard Trentino's voice from behind. He raised his rifle and measured the fast-moving targets streaking towards Christopher.

Strangely, almost fatefully, the major found Barbaro right in his sights. The major positioned his Sig Saur SSG 30000 rifle with expert ease.

Bang! Bang! Bang! Bang! Bang! Bang!

His semi-automatic hit the creatures with deadly accuracy.

Each high velocity bullet passed Christopher with ruthless efficiency and straight through the black and grey leathery bodies of the buzzers. Their spiteful disc shapes made them harder and more difficult to hit. But, this ability was no contest for the skilful major. He was in perfect form.

Remarkably, the major killed three of the depraved creatures in a single shot, but more kept coming.

****

Christopher's mind was only on the finishing line as he honed in on Barbaro. He saw the media man crouching and holding his head and babbling insanities. Christopher began sprinting, closing the gap between them.

Barbaro unexpectedly ducked to live, when a high velocity bullet flew past his head. The link had saved his life and his insanity. The skilful major missed his target, when another went whizzing past Barbaro, and then another.

The high velocity bullets somehow snapped him out of a frozen lunacy. Barbaro cleared his mind from his hypnotic horror. He was livid. He turned around with madness in his eyes sand saw the major. He missed again.

Barbaro's insight warned him of the major. With his opportunity gone, the major decided to give Christopher a better chance, so he turned his aim at the creatures in Christopher's path instead.

Barbaro dismissed the major, knowing he was no longer a threat to him. However, Christopher was getting closer and would be with him in the next few seconds. Trentino shot at the creatures in Christopher's way, making the way possible. Barbaro stared blankly at Christopher.

He knows I have it!

****

Inside the core of the black fog, a hideous place existed known as the Demongoyle Bog. It was a demon's soup, bulging with carnivorous creatures, where death was a cruel incentive for escape from their murky habitat. Once outside, these Buzzers raged for lifeblood, the vile creatures' vision was as bad as a garden mole's. Yet, this did not matter because they were born with accurate auditory ability. Like so many such things that came from "Nowhere", these accursed life-forms could find their prey easily. Each had an unnatural ability to sense only warm-blooded creatures and they craved human blood.

Major Trentino panned the wide black surface with his telescopic sights.

"Damn them!" spat Trentino. "There must be thousands inside that fog. Phew!" the major gasped, while tracking them as they unleashed themselves.

The major studied the whole scale of the black wall's surface area. It was enormous and far too extensive to cover. Once outside their rotten confines, each instantly gliding and able to quickly stop-start their rotating bodies at will to shift through the air. Swivelling their malleable physiques by using their serrated blades sticking out, and by angling them to best fit their flight direction. Spinning faster made them accelerate more, this giving them their signature buzz-saw noises! These beasts were specially born to fly!

When the creatures attempted to burst from the bog, its flexible skin somehow flapped after the escapees, trying to catch after them, and quickly pulled itself back, sealing the breach. The bog's own wicked existence tried to keep these things inside and make them suffer even more.

As he aimed at the creatures, Trentino tried to calculate how long it would take for the chopper to pick up the civilians.

More of the creatures managed to escape with furious fervour.

Barbaro stared blankly at the flying beasts sweeping in towards him. He crouched down and raised his hands up for protection. The chopper was directly above. It did not matter anymore, caught in the long grasses and was buffeted down by the heavy air turbulence, causing the long blades to whip viciously around his body. It was too late for a rescue. He in his madness, would die too.

"AAAAGH!" Barbaro screamed as the buzzing infested his head, hoping for a swift death. Feeling a strange phenomenon come over him, his special insight gauged that these creatures were showing signs of flocking.

****

The helicopter's huge armoured body swiftly lowered in between the two nearest men and the attacking creatures. Its great metal body shielding them, when four or five heavy bangs thudded hard in quick succession into the chopper's side. The sudden impacts killed each of these suicidal death discs, leaving a dripping mess all over the Mangusta's solid carriage. But, more kept coming.

The filtered rock music was still playing inside their helmets. The aircrew felt more thuds on the side of their aircraft, and with each additional impact, they became more terrified as the creatures swarmed around the aircraft.

Hovering near to the forest floor, the Mangusta's rotor blades spun rapidly and minced some of the creatures in the process. Their buzzing swelled to a maddening height. Barbaro and Christopher could not see beyond the massive hovering frame. Living became a lottery. Barbaro knew he had a better chance of survival; the "gift of insight" could not be underestimated.

It seemed longer, but it had only been about ten or fifteen seconds since Christopher started running. The powerful Mangusta became his shield. With a renewed hope, Christopher sprinted even faster towards Barbaro.

A Buzzer flew right over the aircraft, avoiding the chopper's lethal blades. It curved downwards and swivelled in towards the two men. Its flight path angle was too quick and too acute to strike Barbaro. It buzzed right past him, leaving Christopher face to face with the creature. He pulled out his Beretta and kept on running.

****

A few seconds before being faced with the creature's attack, Christopher had jumped over many awkward tufts of grass, dodging the felled trees with the skills of a football player.

As he did so, he saw some of the missing soldiers lying underneath. They were all dead. He was angry. He had to get to Barbaro. *Poor bastards. It's strange, an ambush,* he thought. He instantly realised that another danger was heading their way. Some of the soldiers had darts in their necks. *Shit, those big warriors, they must be here. I'm going to get that swine, Barbaro! I am going to get him.*

The helicopter had finally landed and to a degree, he felt relief. But, it was short-lived. Christopher suddenly winced in agony. He couldn't comprehend what had happened.

He fell down onto his weakened left side where an acute pain burned tightly! "Aagh." *Hamstring!* He thought, but he was wrong. He suddenly noticed something blurry flying quickly past him. He was convinced that the object had come from somewhere behind the major's position, when another quickly followed.

A Dart! He couldn't avoid it and it ripped through his tunic and cut his right flank. He saw Barbaro ahead.

Christopher could not stop his momentum and kept stumbling forward.

It was then that those dreaded sounds of wooden castanets caught up, their warnings echoing an attack from somewhere behind. He knew those vile warrior creatures had been waiting in the vicinity. The chopper gave the group's positions away.

Christopher stumbled on as more darts flew past him. He knew he would have to do something remarkable if he were to survive.

The Helicopter had landed.

This was Mantis' moment of truth. Anticipating the next Buzzer's flight path, major Trentino did not flinch, his sure aim focussed automatically. There it was. *Chris does not have the time to shoot!* Assuming it would strike Christopher in the next second, he fixated on the target, undistracted by a new and present danger behind him.

He hit his target and it exploded in mid-air, leaving the parasite whirling in a floppy mess around Christopher.

Major Trentino sighed in relief after having saved Christopher from the creature, but saw that he had taken a few hits. Dart wounds banged into Chris, knocking him hard. Remarkably, the scientist was still trying his best to keep going, yelling aloud in anguish.

Reassuringly, the Mangusta's engines began roaring louder with enormous power. Christopher was in shock, calling out in agony while watching the helicopter's cannon turret turning into position.

The wind from the chopper made it more difficult for Christopher to make headway.

Chris is not going to make it, shit, thought the major.

His expert eyes measured Chris through his telescopic-sights, both civilians were his responsibility. He reckoned a quick death would be far better than a slow one from the creatures. It would be over in an instant, and at this range, his high velocity bullet would be certain.

Right now, he could see both men in the same line of sight. It was a perfect crosshair shot.

Red on dead. Bang! Bang! Two clean shots.

Two more flying creatures unexpectedly appeared over the roaring Mangusta. All the buzzers were driving right into the major's telescopic view. Trentino fired in very quick succession.

Remarkably, Christopher killed the nearest one to him. The major watched. The scientist was within a stone's throw from the chopper.

Bang! Bang! Two more were blown away, but there was no end to these things.

One of the Aircrew appeared from the side door, jumping out to land firmly on the ground. Barbaro was closest and was paralysed with fear. The airman roughly grabbed him and bundled him into the aircraft, while another provided a shield against the fire with a handgun. Barbaro and the airman were soon inside.

Christopher fell flat in agony and the pilot saw he was down. Very anxious to get going, the chopper began to lift off a little from the forest floor, waiting as it hovered a few feet from the ground.

"Get up, get the fuck up and keep going!" Trentino yelled from a distance. "You can do it, Chris! You can do it!"

Christopher heard Trentino's calls and they helped. Gritting his teeth, he got up unsteadily. His leg and side wounds were seeping blood. He would not be able to go much further. He dropped down again, but then started crawling, crawling for his life.

The Mangusta roared and began slowly lifting off from the forest floor. The pilot watched in horror as numerous flying organisms surrounded them.

Unexpectedly, a rope ladder dropped to the ground.

"Wait!" Christopher lifted his arm as if to hold onto a rung, but the air was all he clenched. Screaming at the pilot again, the airman watched his struggle. "WAIT!" he rasped again. "Wait for me." The airman waved him forward. He would have to be quick. Then, another creature battered hard into the chopper's side. The airman shook his head.

The unsteady helicopter hovered tantalisingly too close to Christopher, whose wounded body lay on the ground. His outstretched arm reaching upwards for a lift.

The buzzing mixed with the Mangusta's engines competed for sound supremacy. The sheer number of creatures flocking away from the gigantic black wall threatened the chopper's existence. It seemed like the buzzing was getting increasingly louder. The helicopter hovered unsteadily at about eight feet above the forest floor.

****

Moments before lift-off, the maniac creatures continued their unyielding barrage as the helicopter sat exposed on the ground. Made of metal, it could withstand only so much of the hammering. The rotor blades were its weak point, its engines another.

The pilot needed to leave or risk everything. He elevated the chopper as he watched the wounded man on the ground. The captain quickly ordered for the rope ladder to be dropped again, while the co-pilot kept waving his hands downwards at Christopher. He signalled for him to keep low, turning his guns above the crawling man.

Chris could not believe his eyes. *A last chance, move!* Struggling against the turbulence of the engines, he pushed but there was no chance. The chopper might as well have been ten miles from him because even at this distance, he was still not going to make it.

Co-pilot Andreas Lieutenant Azzurra could see the man's plight and wasted no time immediately firing a sharp volley above Christopher's head before swivelling a 20mm cannon quickly to the right, blasting at countless numbers of depraved flying discs flocking together. Some of the heavy shells entering the black wall.

Captain Eliyah Bonifacio kept cursing because his shot only released more of those damned creatures. The cannon panned back and forth and up and down, the heavy machine spitting its fire at a fearsome rate.

For each one that it killed, five or more others would take its place.

These suicidal creatures were not intelligent but they sensed the helicopter's weak points by the noise it made. These creatures threatened to bring down the mighty kite.

Onboard, Barbaro twisted a secret smile through the open doorway as he watched Christopher alone on the ground.

However, the scientist's determination and drive to live spurned him to get up. Christopher dug deeper than ever before. Making a last and frantic run, he stretched out his upheld hand to the dangling rope ladder. This time, he got a hold of it.

Barbaro's weasel eyes widened. He was horrified and watched as Christopher pulled.

Fall, please fall, Barbaro hoped. A dark light switched on inside the delirious mind of the Vatican official, and his concern suddenly changed. *He won't make it.* The Vatican press officer foresaw it. Again, it was the Link. Christopher's bloody fingers slipped off the rung and he dropped onto the ground again.

"Come on, signore! Come on, signore, you can still do it!" the two airmen shouted from the open side door.

From inside the aircraft, the aircrew could also see the major in the far distance. He needed help too. Captain Bonifacio ordered the side-gunner to fire from the hatchway. The airman aimed his machine gun and opened his firepower above Christopher's head. He fired rapid rounds in that direction.

Major Trentino had become entrenched and encircled, lying alone on the ground. His aim steady and sure. Even now, he continued dealing out death to those strange life forms flying crazily around Christopher. Professional as always,

Trentino would not stop. He continued, at his own risk, to deliver death and help the priest escape.

"Capitano, we are taking damage!" the worried flight lieutenant said, looking outside at the struggling man.

The pilots could not see the untold damage to the aircraft but could judge that with a few more hits, the rotor blades would come off. Right now, they knew the clogged mechanics produced by the Buzzers would soon force them down to the forest floor and their mission would be over.

"Check that he has the "Egg"! Hurry, Hurry!" the pilot ordered the airman to search Barbaro.

"Have you got it?" the airman demanded from the Vatican official.

"What do you mean?" Barbaro answered, staring blankly at the man as if he knew nothing.

"Let me see it now!" he demanded, unaware of Barbaro's insanity. The airman needed an instant answer.

Barbaro's survival was instinctive. He sensed that the big airman was prepared to pull every garment off him. He knew resistance would be futile.

Barbaro held up the Link between his fingers with a twisted smile. *Odd, it feels very slippery.* He was unaware of the Link's changeable properties. The lieutenant quickly grabbed it from him!

"Capitano! Capitano! The Golden Egg is secure. I have it!" he said.

"God help those poor buggers," said the pilot, guilt hidden behind his visor. The pilot questioned his own conscience, then shook his head sadly. His orders were perfectly clear. Retain the "Egg" at all costs and take no chances.

"Signore! There are still men down there!" the co-pilot shouted, sensing the chopper rising. "We can't leave!"

"If we take any more damage, we'll drop. We have our orders, lieutenant."

"But..." Azzurra protested. When suddenly, the helicopter shook violently.

"Apostle will have his prize." The Capitano sighed, while adjusting the Mangusta's balance.

Capitano Bonifacio stared down at Christopher one last time, watching the man's helplessness. The priest got up and stood in the long grasses wounded, staring upwards disbelieving what was happening. The rope ladder was out of reach!

The "Egg" was in the basket. For the crew of the Mangusta, their job done, and any collateral damage was deemed acceptable by higher authority. Their mission was complete, and they could not wait here any longer.

"Signore, you cannot leave them to die!" the lieutenant protested again.

"Mission orders." The captain felt cold. It was the only way. He lifted the A2012 Mangusta slowly upwards.

Its powerful Rolls Royce engines roasting more of those flying discs in a slow pirouette, its great body swung around, to leave the dead zone.

Capitano Bonifacio fired a salvo of rockets followed by Medusa missiles for good measure into the surrounding black infested wall. He did not smile.

The Medusa missiles entered the blackness. It was a direct hit. The crew waited.

One second, two seconds then three seconds passed, as the aircrew held their breaths. But there was no explosion. They watched in disbelief. The only thing that came out of the black void was more buzzing. It seemed that the missiles had been swallowed up by the darkness. There was no detonation, nothing.

"That was a direct hit. Damage nil," the Capitano said. He sounded disappointed. He had hoped to blow the black fog apart in an act of vengeance.

"It's incredible, signore," the co-pilot concurred.

Barbaro began babbling some nonsense that nobody could understand. The big airmen assumed he was suffering some sort of lunacy. The chopper sustained more hits buffeting the aircraft.

The helicopter continued its vertical ascent to rise above the towering blackness. Barbaro stopped talking, his eyes widening insanely in some malformed enlightenment that the link enabled him to see seconds into the future. He smiled at the big airman.

Next to them, the black mass suddenly exploded outwards, creating a massive hole. Was that the detonation? No! The membrane quickly peeled away and opened a massive black orifice to the bog's abhorrent innards. This hole was not created from a missile or rocket explosion.

Something came out — something much worse. It was a direct response to their pre-emptive attack! None of the pilots saw the massive creature shooting from within. Their IHADSS sensors didn't pick up anything.

A huge beast emerged, striking the helicopter full on.

At first, it resembled a huge spherical shape covered in thick flat bristles. It measured roughly over half the size of the chopper. It had come from "Nowhere".

This explosive impact made the aircraft shake and threw the chopper into a mad spin in the opposite direction. Both pilots struggled to compensate against this sudden and unexpected attack. The hit knocked the big lieutenant forward. Barbaro viciously grabbed the link back!

Every ounce of skill Capitano Bonifacio had, he needed. The alarm systems were blaring warnings everywhere on board and on his visor, too.

The Capitano did everything he could to get control back. He struggled to give the aircraft forward momentum, and then critically overcompensated and sent the aircraft heading towards the black wall.

At the same time, out in the open, this colossal monster was on the hunt, lumbering behind the helicopter like a super-tanker.

Within a few seconds of life on Earth, its transformation was fascinating to watch. It emerged as a massive flying ball, but was now rapidly thinning down into a disc shape, just like the smaller creatures.

Its metamorphosis was design for flight. It stuck out its large blades for flight-control and demolition, increasing its rotation. This generated even more buzzing. It began chasing after the chopper.

Inside the aircraft, everyone could feel the air reverberating throughout the helicopter. The men in the cockpit knew it would be over in the next minute. They focused their attention on trying to regain control and balance of the Mangusta, which was still diving in a mad rotation towards the black wall.

The streamlined monster charged at high speed after them, rotating fast while increasing its acceleration with every second that passed. Its sharp flat teeth, hard as steel edges, were ready to destroy them.

This super-beast was now moving with the agility of a heat-seeking missile.

Inside the helicopter, the men were being tossed around helplessly.

As they listened to the enormous buzzing coming after them, it felt like their execution was certain. If they did not crash first, then that thing would certainly finish them off. The aircrew screamed blind obscenities because there was nothing else they could do.

The beast's thunder reverberated around the landing zone. Both pilots concentrated on their instruments as they dived towards the fog.

Nobody could guess how long they would last inside the oily black fog, with all those creatures flying about. Each second that passed, spelled disaster.

On the forest floor, Christopher and Trentino looked up in awe at what was happening.

Impact was imminent. The men yelled frantically at the Capitano to do something. Yet, in each man's mind something perverse was already at work, something wicked that chilled the very soul. In that last moment of terror, the aircraft twisted upwards.

The Mangusta's Rolls Royce engines protested loudly, forcing it to veer at an incredible angle away from the evil soup that had a second ago, threatened to engulf it.

Inside, the big lieutenant found himself holding on grimly onto a leather holder fixed above the doorway. Hanging for his life in a precarious angle, he stared out the open side door. Below him he could not help but observe the small figures far below, stranded on the forest floor.

The Capitano was still battling for supremacy of control. By taking this unavoidable evasive manoeuvre to outwit the pursuing monster, he put terrible stress on his airship. In that last second, he forced another sharper evasive angle and sent the demon careering straight past them with only a few feet to spare.

Without warning, the big airman suddenly lost his balance and came swinging around and completely out of position. His body was partially thrown outside the aircraft and he hung on only by a strap from the inside.

The ill-fated Lieutenant caught short by the sudden G forces pulling him outside by the Mangusta's sudden twisting manoeuvre. Lunging desperately upwards for Barbaro's helping hand. Bad timing. The poor airman could not have known that Barbaro Lettiere would not save him!

Curious. Barbaro thought tentatively, only now aware of its changeable properties squeezing it harder was like squeezing grease, his fingers and the link moving automatically apart, Barbaro began squeezing it more to getter a better grip. His actions so instant, so quick, squeezing it more causing it to move further away from his own fingers. He needed that Link! All these actions occurring in a split second.

Barbaro with one arm holding on the machine gun mount the other holding out the link. So suddenly the airman reached inside with his other hand to attempt to grasp for what he thought was Barbaro's helping hand, touching him. It held the link.

But the laws of physics could not be undone. He could no longer hold on and fell from the aircraft. Gone! The link too!

"Noooo!" Barbaro screamed outside while holding onto the secured gun mount for support while staring precariously outside as he watched the man fall to the forest floor. Uninjured and with only a few minor scratches, Barbaro was lucky. He slumped down inside the aircraft, utterly exhausted.

The same laws that killed the airman governed the huge monster's momentum. The creature was accelerating faster than the chopper. The super-beast, unable to quickly change its direction, overshot its target and plunged itself straight back into the Demongoyle bog. The bog swallowed it hole with a loud ending slurp. Gone!

The rest of the crew were preoccupied trying to save themselves being jostled and uselessly thrown around the fuselage. In the mayhem, the crew could not properly see what had really happened. The airmen had been thrown unceremoniously around like ragdolls, with no time to belt up before the attack. Blood flowed from their cuts, but their helmets saved them from worse injuries. The chopper began regaining its stability and the crewmen their former composure. With the immediate danger over, then sprang into action to help the miserable Vatican official.

****

CHAPTER XXI

THE VALLEY OF DEATH

On the ground, seconds before the airman's death. Christopher watched as a figure unexpectedly dropped from the aircraft, while at the same time, the giant super-bug vanished straight back into that mountainous black wall.

Christopher could do nothing except watch and listen to the increasing screams.

"My God," he stated in horror, hearing a final heavy thump into the nearby ground. Death put an end to that shriek.

The Capitano had regained control once again and the chopper rose once more above the mighty trees and huge black wall.

The great Mangusta slowly pivoted in the air for a defining moment, safely out of the clutching arms of that grabbing beastly fog. The engines roared confidently once again and with a forward thrust, Buzzard One was gone.

Christopher gulped hard, not quite believing that they had left them behind. He slumped down in the long grass. Perturbed thoughts swirled around in his mind, *everyone has been used.*

For an unexplainable reason, he felt a sudden urge to go see the dead airman. Crawling through the grasses, Christopher's wounds bled his life away. He resigned himself to be in the company of another human being before his end.

When he found the man, he lay down next to him. Christopher could not move any further. The two nasty flesh wounds he knew had come from those warrior beasts. They had to be close.

Lifting his head to look a little above the swimming grasses, he could see Trentino in the distance, fighting off lots of flying creatures buzzing around the area, the sharp-shooter keeping the swarm at bay. *Piss easy,* the Scotsman thought.

Unexpectedly, a peculiar sensation came over him. Feeling very tired, Christopher sank down into the grasses. He lay there peacefully with his small backpack propping him up, as he looked upwards into the warm sky. His mind started drifting lazily, almost uncaring to the world. He was done with it.

Occasionally, one or two eager buzzers would fly over him, the creatures unaware of his presence. He couldn't care less. The buzzing and shots reverberating across the landing zone seemed somehow more distant, more remote and almost unimportant to him.

A weakness washed over him. Turning his head, he found himself staring into the face of the dead airman's closed eyes. His battle for life was over. Christopher asked himself, *Why did you come here, only to leave us behind?*

Another unanswered question. Christopher considered it for a few fleeting moments more. Even this thought soon became of no consequence to him.

The buzzing began to sound more like bees, melting into the calming sounds of long green grasses swaying serenely in the warm breeze. He smiled deliriously. The sounds reminded him of home and a nice summer day, where he would lie in a field full of honey-coloured barley on the hilltop above his village. Sleepily, he understood it was time.

Boy priest and distinguished scientist, Christopher Hrycuik began reciting the Lord's Prayer for both him and the dead airman. It was over.

"Our Father, who art in heaven, hallowed be thy name. Thy Kingdom come, thy will be done, on Earth as it is in Heaven. Give us this day our daily bread. And forgive us our trespasses, as we forgive those who trespass against us. And lead us not into temptation but deliver us from evil."

Sadly, he paused and looked at the man. Chris swallowed as a tear ran down and off his temple, dropping onto the ground. He finished his prayer.

"For thine is the kingdom, the power and the glory forever and ever. Amen."

Christopher lay his head back and looked upwards to a blue patch in the sky. As each precious second ticked away, his breathing was becoming more laboured. Suddenly, his heart started to stop.

"God, help." Chris paused for more air, more life and more words, trying again, "God help all our souls."

He swallowed dry spit and turned for a last look at the airman. Unexpectedly, the dead man's eyes opened wide.

"Aaagh!" Christopher shouted as his heart jolted in shock. A huge electric shock passed straight through his body, kick-starting his life again. It was a miracle.

The airman's lifeless watery eyes were peculiar and reflected like a mirror. It reminded Christopher of the lake's water inside the almost airless mines. Its surface was completely calm, not a ripple or a blemish. Its purity was true. In his dead eyes, he saw something unforeseen.

No! It can't be.

****

In the reflection of the dead airman's eyes, he saw his own staring straight back. This sent a weird feeling rippling through his body. *How?* He wondered.

True enough, they were green with black speckles. They were his own, the airman's reflecting like a mirror. It was as though he and the airman were one. There was something else. *Unbelievable,* he gasped. Something else reflected in the corner of his eye, something precious. He could see it. It was a small metallic object with a polished surface. It was sparkling of silver. It was the link!

His breathing quickened with excitement because this was more than a miracle. It lay partially hidden below a large leaf next to the airman's open hand on the forest floor. In front of his startled eyes and after all that had happened, there it was, the "Link of Osleiotect". This Godly talisman glinting in the last rays of the sunshine.

He could not know how it got there but what he did know was this, it had returned to him by an open hand. It was given back to him. It was *a wonder!* Christopher closed his eyes not wanting to believe this to be true. God had asked too much of him. A secret thought pained him and yet he answered God's call, for God wanted him for a purpose. He was Chosen. Christopher opened his eyes again to confirm it was real, then whispered, "Yes." Shakily, he stretched out his blood-stained hands and said, "Mine again."

****

During the rescue operation with the Helicopter Gunship.

Trentino knew something was not right. Behind him, the major started hearing what sounded like wooden Castanets, seeing more lethal darts showering over his location! The major safe enough disguised in the grasses and lying camouflaged providing covering fire. Trentino's mind set on "Red".

Other Buzzers following his rifle sounds like Sonar, quickly swarming around him again and all with a wild urge to dive at him! Enraged, Trentino blew as many away as possible but more kept coming. *Hells fire, is there no end to these things!*

The major felt betrayed and very disappointed because he knew Christopher had not made it, looking upwards with tightly controlled anger, cursed the crew. When without warning, like an obscene afterbirth from Hell, something big came bursting out from the Bog! In a colossal explosion of filth, a gigantic spherical Superbug came out! The enormous monster striking the Chopper smack on its side sending it reeling!!!

The major quickly turned around, knowing that his pursuers were somewhere behind. They had been caught!

There they stood in the clearing, the Bloodhort of HSALS SLAUGOHTŘ. All kitted out in full black battle gear, flexible Chainmail, heavy green tunics with their capes flowing in the breeze.

Impressive, their red triple clawed ensigns stood out in triumph on each helmet.

The Preyweep Army stood in front of him at the tree line edge, behind him the formidable Demongoyle Bog waited. They were ensnared in the Hunters net! In a lined formation the major measured this elite Bloodhort for weaknesses, however it did not matter because. he was out of ammo!

Bravely standing up like a Lion, undaunted and unclipping his vicious bayonet, the major quickly pulling out the large blade out of its sheath readied it for immediate use. Trentino greeting his enemy with an expressionless blunt face, there was nothing else for it because. there was *"Nowhere to hide"*. The Prophecy! Trentino's mind conditioned and set for close combat, his eyes staring ice-cold stone Emerald green. But the courageous major did not see his real danger.

****

Silent and smooth, a Super-bug came gliding in with the breeze, descending swiftly behind the major. Unseen and unheard with no rotational buzz to warn him of its deadly approach, stealth its weapon.

Not until that very last moment the death disc began buzzing in final acceleration! High speed generated in an instant right behind the major's back, its razor-sharp teeth protruding for the kill. Its position given away, Trentino hearing it too late!

Mantis's body torn apart as the flying creature ripped through him, its deadly flight path continuing and heading directly towards the Preyweep army, leaving the dead major behind.

The vile Superbug driving itself harder into the lightning fast warriors, the Bloodhort Elite instantly hacking the creature into pieces! As for major Trentino the shock instantly killing him. Red on Dead.

The big brutes all laughing at their sport! All laughing together, even more so seeing other flying discs heading their way. The Warriors quite used to these vile creatures, commonly using them for target practice! The Demonoid Superbugs easily shot out of the air, until eventually the mad flurry stopped. The Fog held like a bad breath.

****

Christopher's small rucksack was supporting him like a back rest, and his sword was firmly secured to it by straps. Wounded and weakened as he was, he felt an urge to finish his journal, to warn anyone who might find his remains. It was still inside his backpack. He barely had the energy to write. The journal would have to remain an obituary.

"I Akyaron" Prince and Lord of a race called the Nelumakragasian. Christopher sighed and

questioned himself, the Expedition, and the dead. *All this for nothing.*

It was beyond his "ken", when impossibly, Mashir began speaking behind him.

"All is as God wills it, my friend, even unto death," he said softly.

Recognising Mashir's voice and words of wisdom, Christopher froze.

"Mashy, is that you?" Christopher asked loudly. He knew the surveyor's voice so well. "Mashir are you there?" There was no reply, but it unmistakably had been Mashir's voice.

Christopher swallowed hard, resigned himself with a slow sigh of disappointment and *delirium*. His mind sail on an ebbing tide and he wondered again at the prince's undoing. *Is this what it was like for him, for Akyaron, before his end? "Nowhere" to hide and "Nowhere" to go! Where is "Nowhere"?* Closing his eyes he said, "God protect all our souls."

Christopher heard something strange, something different that seemed to be getting closer to him.

The bio-technologist's heart began drumming harder and harder. His chest began to heave explosively. *Is this really it, God?* He was in shock and anticipated the worst.

What is that strange sound? What is it? Suddenly he knew!

"It's music. MUSIC!" he said to himself.

Melodies floated through his mind and calmed his racing heart.

The young man lay there, immobile in the long grass, caring only to listen to the soft tunes coming closer and closer, while staring sleepily up to the sky. The sun would be gone in a minute. He sensed the darkness of night encroaching over the Amazonian rainforest to the sound of... bag pipes!

Bag pipes. Music from his childhood that transcended time all the way from the West Coast of Scotland.

My home. He felt a tear dribble down his cheek, Christopher's eyes blurred and his heart jolted! And jolted again!

He was dying in the memory of his life, his home, and his mother. Christopher began sobbing, realising that he would never see his younger brother again. *Scott, my responsibility, my brother. Who will look after him, Lord, if it can't be me? Who then?*

"God, what will become of them?" he called out in despair.

The bog continued to hold its dreadful contents together, when suddenly, it released another creature. Out from its shady confines exploded a furry bristling ball. The thing streamlined itself and started spinning in the air. The death disc whirled around, sensing him by sound and smell. It set off buzzing.

The music came once again through the airwaves. His heart jolted again. Strangely, its slow lament changed into something lovely, something that moved his spirit. Listening to its lively South American melody of bamboo flutes he could not help but smile at its sweetness and bubbliness, as it became louder and livelier by the second. The music was soon resounding everywhere, calming his tortured mind, his synapses dancing in a symphony of sounds. Highly harmonic, the young man's soul began to lift.

"Oh, God, I am ready."

No sooner were his soft words spoken, Christopher began seeing things he could not understand or comprehend. When the huge wall of death suddenly opened to reveal a tunnel of brilliant light, the evil black membrane scorched outwards by this mysterious and dazzling white-blue light.

The light channelling his body and mind through an enchanted passageway. Cocooned in a veil of Godly light he transcended through the black bog. Captured in a dreamlike state, Chris could not tell if it was real or not.

Is this my passageway to Heaven, oh, Lord? he asked inside a brilliance so colossal it awestruck its beholder. Its great luminosity pushed back the blackness and evil things around him. Travelling smoothly inside the oily gaseous medium, the blackness was held in check. The luminous energy revealed the way to him, another perilous escape created by some act of God. A miracle. *The link!*

The bouncing creatures tried to get to him, but as they got closer to the light, they were struck, like an electric shock. Each vile creature was instantly rejected by the tunnel's blue edges of energy, sent spinning off and out of control, whirling madly in some crazed disarray back into "Nowhere" whence they came.

Christopher continued his journey, while listening to the cheerful music. *Oh, how it moved his soul!*

My gift. His heart cherished this last moment. With this knowledge, the boy priest slowly opened his eyes towards the luminous blue pathway before him and his soul followed the direction of the bag pipes. *Let me go home, Lord. Please, let me go home.* And so, Doctor Christopher Hrycuik's life, passed on.

With a last visualization, there came a blinding ethereal blue light. Christopher's tired eyes closed, submerged in complete contentment. He no longer feared anything, not even the evil within the Vale of MalisIblis. At twenty-three years of age, his young mind began floating peacefully through the Valley of Death.

****

Far ahead of them was base and civilisation, as the Mangusta gunship sped out of the area, skimming the treetops quickly as it reached the edge of the Iblis vale. Capitano Eliyah Bonifacio stared back in fear at the huge flying thing following behind him. It was still there.

DEATH on the wing, the great creature opening its wide mouth of malcontent was seeing them off. Screeching wildly, this great carrion sent a defiant message to any that would enter its realm. Without warning, it began gliding swiftly off on another hot air eddy, swooping in a wide arc back into MalisIblis.

Ahead of the Mangusta, lay an ambient orange twilight, the early evening stretching beautifully across the full length of the horizon. A heavy silence lingered inside the chopper, where a relieved aircrew sat watching God's paradise quickly changing before them. The world transcending from its warm orange tones and dazzling blood reds, these melting into a deep dark blue expanse before becoming the blackness of space. Night had come.

Tonight, the moon was distant and lonely. Beyond, the heavens above were awash with a myriad of suns. Celestial wonders were twinkling in numerous star dances beyond our "ken", reminding everyone that somewhere out there, a Great Geometrician looked on.

****

**DESTROYER OF WORLDS
will be continued in the fourth book in
GOD'S CHAIN.**